I0825190

MAGIC
AND
BULLETS

ALSO BY LARRY CORREIA

Monster Hunters International

Monster Hunters International
Monster Hunter Vendetta
Monster Hunter Alpha
Monster Hunter Legion
Monster Hunter Nemesis
Monster Hunter Siege
Monster Hunter Guardian
Monster Hunter Bloodlines

Saga of the Forgotten Warrior

Son of the Black Sword
House of Assassins
Destroyer of Worlds
Tower of Silence
Graveyard of Demons
Heart of the Mountain

The Grimnoir Chronicles

Hard Magic
Spellbound
Warbound

ACADEMY OF OUTCASTS BOOK 2

MAGIC AND BULLETS

LARRY CORREIA

MAGIC AND BULLETS
Published by Vault
In association with Aethon Books

ISBN 978-1-63849-381-5 (paperback)

First AETHON: Vault Edition: Summer 2026

Printed in the United States of America.
1st Printing.

Aethon Books
www.aethonbooks.com

Vault Storyworks
www.vaultstoryworks.com

Cover art by Matt Sellers. Cover typography by Steve Beaulieu.
Print formatting by Kevin G. Summers, Adam Cahoon, and Rikki Midnight.

MAGIC
AND
BULLETS

1

The newly formed Academy of Outcasts was the talk of the Under Slump.

Sure, we had no money, barely any magical element to work with, and no clue what we were doing, but we were an officially sanctioned school of wizardry now, and that made us special. Most of the other magical academies in the Core were located in the prestigious Collegium District. While it took a great deal of natural aptitude—or a lot of bribe money—to get admitted into one of those fancy schools, we'd accept anybody!

Word had gotten out among the city's aspiring mages that our academy wasn't very good, *but*… we were open for business, and that was something.

Our founder was the legendary wizard, Gaul "the Mutilator" Haddar. Only, he'd left the Core City and returned to the Elemental Plane of Fire to hunt pirates. Leaving me—a lowly rank-one nobody—in charge in his absence, which would take who knew how long.

So, deprived of actual knowledgeable experienced leadership, I'd spent the last few months getting things running and trying to keep our new students from blowing themselves up or unleashing curses which might kill us all.

I'd been successful… Mostly.

"Carnavon! Come quick."

I looked up from my latest spell-crafting experiment to see what all the commotion was about. Diverting my attention took a bit of finesse, because I was experimenting with Red, the volatile magical element from my home plane, which got real excitable once you started enchanting it. Azarin Garzade was standing in the entrance to the fire practice room, gesturing for me to follow her.

"What is it?"

"Trouble in the earth room."

Though she was a little flustered from running across our tower to get here, I found her pretty as ever. Tall, graceful, and blonde, she was the opposite of the hardy Fogo girls I'd grown up around. It turned out I had a thing for air-realm girls. Though, to be fair, I'd only met one air-realm girl so far, but I'd already fallen for her reckless and impulsive ways.

"I thought you were getting better at earth magic."

"I am. I've been practicing my ass off," she said with quite a bit of pride. "But this one's not my fault. Sifuso is being attacked by a dirt slug."

"Again?" I carefully moved the small pieces of lead away from the activated Red powder so as to not accidentally melt a hole in the metal workbench. Since this was the room we'd set aside for experimenting with fire magic, the only flammable things allowed in here was us. "That's the second time this week."

"He's really bad at that spell, Oz."

Sifuso was a nearly seven-foot-tall lizard man, who looked like he'd stepped out of a swampy nightmare, who tested as a natural rank two, one whole rank above me and Azarin, which meant he should have been far more capable at magic than either of us… Except, running this place had rapidly taught me that natural talent and brains weren't synonyms.

"Sifuso really should be able to handle one little Elemental spirit without the rest of us holding his claws."

"You'd think that, but—" Azarin was interrupted by an extremely loud bang from down the hall. "I think this slug might be a bit of a mutant."

As one of the five founding members of our academy, Azarin and I were part of our *Student Council.* Those appointments were based on who I'd trusted to not rob the place or accidentally kill us. We were supposed to be the responsible ones. With Azarin being the most reckless and headstrong of us five, if she'd swallowed her pride enough to come ask for my help, the situation was actually bad.

Someone began screaming. That noise was followed by the crashing of furniture and the breaking of glass.

"You're going to want to bring your gun and fire magic."

I sighed, fairly certain this was *not* how the proper magical academies functioned. I brushed all the Red I'd been working with back into its protective pouch and shoved that in my pocket. After we left the fire room, I grabbed my gun belt from where I'd left it hanging on a peg in the hall, far enough away that the cartridges in the loops wouldn't cook off if my spell went wrong.

"I swear, Azarin, if Sifuso keeps screwing up, we might need to kick him out."

"He's far from our dumbest student; that's clearly Rufus! And Sifuso's one of the few who actually had the coin to pay his tuition. That lacertian is the reason we bought food this month."

"Good point." It turned out there was a valid reason all the proper academies turned away so many applicants. Frankly, it was because most aspiring wizards were trash at magic and not rich enough to make up for the inconvenience they caused by learning. "Let's go slap a bandage on the latest self-inflicted wound."

The Academy of Outcasts was situated in one of the unshattered sections of the fallen Tower of Primopolus, which had once been the tallest structure in all the realms. The nice thing about living in the ruins of an ancient mage tower was that we had a large, sturdy structure all to ourselves. The main downside was that everything was sideways, because that was how this section landed fifty years ago when the spell holding the whole unnatural thing up had failed.

The tower had toppled over and flattened whole neighborhoods beneath. What had once been The Tower was now known as The Tube. Many internal walls were shattered, and floors had buckled. Our stairs and doorways were difficult to navigate, and many of the surfaces we walked around on were concave because they'd been part of the outer walls of the once mile-tall structure.

The worst part, though? The place was also obnoxiously haunted. A mad wizard's prideful experiment squishing thousands of innocent bystanders all at once tends to create a lot of restless dead who refuse to move on, but our ghosts had been quiet so far today. If Sifuso's latest mistake riled them up and they started moaning and throwing things again, I was going to be extra annoyed.

Due to the sideways architecture, it took Azarin and me a minute to get to the earth room. Fifty years ago, when this edge of the toppling tower had struck the buildings below, this part of the outer wall had been pulverized and driven deep into the ground. The result was a dirt floor in this section, which was perfect for practicing earth spells.

As we got closer, I could hear Sifuso calling out, "Can someone help? The ground's trying to eat me."

The noise had attracted some curious students, and they were clustered around the entrance, peering through the earth room's sideways doorway. "Don't worry. Carnavon is here," one of them shouted.

They were relieved I'd arrived. If rank ten Gaul Haddar had left me in charge, surely that meant I was somewhat competent.

Boy, I had them fooled!

The other students got out of the way, revealing that, across the room, our lacertian student had climbed up the wall to escape the three-foot-tall, four-foot-wide blob of awakened earth magic that was rolling about beneath him. The thing appeared to be a pile of dirt and small rocks, but it was moving about like it was disturbingly alive.

Azarin had been so nonchalant when she'd fetched me, I'd been expecting a little creature like last time. Not this massive thing.

"You could have warned me it was nearly the size of a wagon."

"It's grown. It was only about as big as a bucket when I left to get you." Azarin, who came from a people known for their adventurous storm-chasing, giant eagle-riding ways was by nature an over confident sort, yet she took one look at the menacing thing and grimaced. "Want me to evacuate the place?"

"Maybe? How should I know?" Then I shouted at Sifuso, who was about fifteen yards away, "What the hell did you unleash this time?"

"I don't know, Carnavon. It was an accident. I was attempting *Shape Earth.*"

That was a spell I'd had no success with myself. So far, I'd learned some fire, air, and a bit of death, but earth, water, and life eluded me. *Shape Earth* was supposed to be a simpler spell, directing minor Elemental spirits to move dirt into different useful forms, but this was certainly not that.

I'd not known lacertians could climb so well, and poor Sifuso was doing everything he could to remain stuck to the wall. In their home kingdoms, lacertians were known as vicious hunters—honestly, I found him a little frightening to look at, not that I would ever admit such a thing—but there wasn't much his claws or fangs were going to accomplish against this thing.

The blob was currently occupied eating a wooden bench we'd salvaged from the dump. It had formed a hole for a mouth and was gnawing on the boards with rows of teeth made of gravel. Another mouth formed on the opposite side, and it began eating a shelf. I didn't know much about the beings of the Elemental Plane of Earth, but something about this thing reminded me of the gurglers of my home realm, a dumb—but hungry—bit of the plane come to life.

If this was anything like a gurgler, we were all in terrible danger.

"If you survive, you're banned from doing that spell in the Tube again. Got it?"

"Never again. I swear!" Sifuso's yellow eyes were wide with fear as the earth monster effortlessly snapped big planks in half beneath him. "What do we do?"

That was a really good question. Lacertians had thick, scaly skin, that could supposedly even stop a knife thrust, but this thing was contentedly grinding boards into splinters, so I doubted that natural armor would make much difference if it got hold of him. I looked back toward the students clustered around the door. "Who's got some offensive spells handy?"

A couple hands reluctantly went up.

"Great. You two get in here. If it tries to eat Sifuso, we'll blast it. Morton, go fetch Krachma. He'll know what to do."

Krachma was a lob from the Elemental Plane of Earth. He was by far the strongest among us at this type of magic, and also the source of this particular spell. Unfortunately, Krachma was also a lousy teacher who barely spoke any of the trade language everyone else spoke in the Core, and none of us were fluent in Lobbish. I suspected if Krachma was better at explaining how earth spells worked, then our gang of morons probably wouldn't keep unleashing monsters to eat our basement.

"On it, Mr. Carnavon, sir," Morton the gnome shouted as he sped off on his short little legs. I probably should've sent somebody faster, but it was already too late.

I yelled after him, "And send Trax Bloodtrail if you see him!"

"Trax is a monk, not a wizard. What's Trax going to do to a living dirt pile?" Azarin asked. "Punch it?"

"I don't know. He's handy, though."

"True," Azarin agreed. Because say what you will about our Squalo friend, the toothy fellow was comforting to have at your side in a fight. Though he was a lot more useful when the enemy was something edible.

Instead of the lethally efficient Trax, we'd have to make do with two of our newer students: Rufus the dwarf from Bergwald, and Danny, a local human. Neither had exactly impressed me with their magical aptitude so far, even though both had papers from a tester declaring they'd been born more gifted than I'd been.

Danny was so scared, he looked like he was about to piss his pants. Rufus' mood was inscrutable, but I'd found that to be true with most of the dwarves I'd met so far. It was probably because their beards covered up so much of their faces. He caught me eyeballing him and puffed up his chest. "Never fear, hotlander. This pathetic brute is nothing to a mighty war mage of Clan Rudnik."

Rufus' tester papers marked him as a rank two, but *war mage* sounded like it should be a lot more impressive an office than a mere two. Rank ten Gaul Haddar didn't even have a title like that, and I'd seen him shrug off getting hit by buildings.

"That's great."

"Aye. I am great," Rufus said.

Rufus was also something of an idiot, with a history of spectacularly failing at most of the spells he'd attempted, so I spoke real slow in the hopes he'd get it. "Don't use any magic until I say so."

"Right, Mr. Carnavon," Danny said as he readied a wand. Except his hand was shaking so much, I thought he was going to drop it.

"It's going to eat me!" Sifuso wailed.

"Nobody's getting eaten. Everybody stay calm." I wasn't particularly calm myself, but I did a pretty good job of hiding it, I think. "We'll take this nice and easy. This is a low-level spell. Hopefully, it'll fizzle out on its own."

The blog wasn't growing any more that I could tell, but it finished eating the bench with its one mouth, and the shelf with its other, then, once deprived of furniture, it began slowly rumbling its way up the wall toward our lacertian. It didn't have any apparent eyes or a nose, but it still seemed to know where there was something else edible.

"The spell's not fizzling," Azarin warned.

It didn't look like Krachma was going to make it in time. "Alright, if it's a fight this thing wants, it's a fight it'll get. We'll take turns hitting it with spells so we don't get in each other's way. Azarin first, get its attention."

"Oh, here we go!" Being an air-realmer, who were a violent yet flashy people, Azarin had a certain dramatic flair as she threw back her cape to reveal the pouch full of copper rods on her belt. She drew one, cocked back her arm, and shouted, "*Jolt!*" as she threw it.

The rod flashed blue as it spun through the air. It hit the dirt blob, sparking and popping for several seconds. I knew from experience when those rods stuck to flesh, it hurt like the dickens and made all your muscles twitch uncontrollably for a few seconds.

Except the blob didn't seem to notice the minor electrocution. Then it absorbed the copper rod and went back to trying to eat Sifuso.

"Well, that's a bit of a letdown now, isn't it?"

I patted her on the shoulder. "It was a good effort." I looked to our next would-be mage. "What've you got, kid?"

It was probably unfair to call Danny a kid, since he was only a year or two younger than me, but those were the perks of leadership. He held up the stick he'd enchanted. "I've been practicing my ice magic spell."

I'd found out that particular water spell was a relatively common enchantment in the Slumps, popular among criminals because they could hit people with a blast of cold to subdue them for an easy robbery. A rather potent version of that spell had once been used by a local gang to ice over a drainage ditch Trax was sleeping in to immobilize him. I made no comment on how Danny had learned that particular spell, because it wasn't like I had a perfectly clean record, spotless from any criminal acts, myself.

"Give it a go, then."

"Right." Danny pointed the wand and scrunched up his pimply face in concentration, trying to awaken the Blue he'd embedded in the stick. There was a shimmer between us and the blob. A cold breeze washed by, causing me to instinctively flinch. I'm from Fogo, on the Realm of Fire. I *hate* cold magic. This whole city is perpetually chilled far too much for my standards as it is. And this was legitimately cold enough that even being close to the beam made me pull my cloak tight in a desperate attempt to remain warm. Unfortunately, Danny's aim was trogshit.

Sparkling ice crystals formed across the top of the dirt blob, but also on the wall, and then all over poor Sifuso.

"What're you doing, stupid?" the lacertian hissed.

"Sorry!"

Our lizard man could cling to regular stones, but apparently not when they became iced over. As his limbs lost strength, he began to slip. Clawing desperately, Sifuso slid down toward the hungry blob.

He needed a distraction, fast. As I rushed to get in range, I pulled out a pinch of Red dust. I flicked it toward the monster, then concentrated on awakening the energy embedded in the magical element. There was a flash as the Red ignited. The outer edge of the blob was scorched and blackened. The sudden warmth was a nice bonus.

I don't know if my *Shroud of Fire* actually hurt the thing, or if it merely sensed something else fleshy to eat was now in reach, but either way, it started lumbering in my direction. I backed up quickly, and as it followed me, that gave Sifuso room to drop to the safety of normal—not-alive—ground.

"While it's watching me, go around," I told Sifuso as I kept retreating. Some of the bits of wood the monster had absorbed caught fire, but that didn't seem to bother it in the least as it gradually avalanched my way. "Anybody got any ideas?"

"I've got this," Rufus announced as he stepped forward with his battle axe. He lifted it high, then brought the shaft down hard against the hard-packed dirt. "*Crush!*"

Too late, I realized which spell Rufus was using... He'd just launched an earth spell at an out-of-control Elemental spirit from the same plane.

The blob began to shake. Pebbles rolled down its sides as it absorbed more of our floor.

I looked at Rufus, incredulous, and had time to say, "You absolute moron," before the blob rose up, *twice as big as before*, and crashed in our direction. "Run!"

2

Everyone fled the practice room and the living mud slide followed. I was the last one out.

"Get out! Monster on the loose!" I shouted as I dove through the sideways door. Luckily, everybody who'd been coming to see what the commotion was about heard me and ran for their lives. The monster was far too vast to fit through the door now, but it crashed through anyway, pulverizing a big section of wall into dust and bricks.

The earth blob landed in the hall and lay there, trembling like an isolated earthquake. I almost got my hopes up that the spell's duration was running down and it would just expire on its own. Surely the tiny bit of element Sifuso used had been consumed by now. Then the monster slowly rotated most of its bulk directly toward the lacertian that had accidentally summoned it, and another row of gravel teeth popped and began to hungrily grind.

"It was an accident, I swear!" Sifuso apologized as he fled.

The dirt pile rumbled after our lizard. Azarin and I were between the blob and its target, so for us, it was run after Sifuso or get flattened.

Students fled in every direction. Danny grabbed hold of a rope ladder and climbed toward the upper rooms. Even though he was the one who'd made everything far worse, Rufus went in the opposite direction as fast as his stubby dwarf legs could carry him. The out-of-control elemental curse was fixated on Sifuso, so it didn't divert to grab any of the other nearby students to grind them into paste.

The great Tower of Primopolus had a spiral staircase which once ran through its center. Now that this section was set on its side, that shaft was our main hall through the Tube. Over the last couple of months, all of us students had chipped in, piling up rubble and building platforms and ladders so we could reach more rooms. It'd taken lots of work and sweat. The earth monster smashed all our efforts to pieces in seconds. Boards snapped, ropes broke, and hundreds of hours of our labor came crashing down.

"Lead it outside!"

Thankfully, Sifuso listened to me, because he turned toward the nearest exit. Normally, lacertians are shockingly fast—they're a predatory species after all—but he was still suffering from Danny's poorly aimed cold spell, so was sluggishly limping along.

You wouldn't think a few tons of living dirt would be that fast, but it was gaining on us. Its movement shook the floor so much that we were in danger of getting knocked off our feet.

Azarin looked toward one of the windows high above. "Running is stupid."

"Wait, what—"

Except she'd already lifted one gloved hand. "*Ascend.*" And was promptly dragged straight up by air magic. As she rose with a graceful swiftness, she yelled after me, "Don't worry. I'm not abandoning you. I'll flank it."

I cursed myself for not having my own air-enchanted glove on me, but I'd been working with fire magic at the time and hadn't wanted to cause an unexpected reaction between the two elements. I was jealous of her, because levitating away sure beat the foolishness I was currently engaged in.

Sifuso and I pushed open the scrap wood that covered what had once been a window in the side of the mighty tower, which now served as our front door, and rushed out into the daylight. Daylight, of course, was a bit of a misnomer in the Under Slump, as this district existed in the perpetual shade cast by the Slump, which was the neighborhood floating directly over our heads, but it was still brighter out here than our handful of light charms kept throughout the interior of the Tube.

The cold smacked me in the face. The endless chill was the worst thing about this city, and this was the time of year they called *winter.* The others didn't seem to mind it so much, but they came from realms that had things like seasons, whereas I came from a land where even our rain was made of fire, so I hated it.

I shoved the scrap wood door closed in the monster's nonexistent face, but that didn't slow it down at all. When the blob slammed into the gap, only a portion of it squeezed through. That was enough to send our door flying and me sliding away. Cracks appeared in the Tube's walls as it pushed, but because the exterior walls were a lot sturdier than the interior, the creature was momentarily stuck. The gravel teeth kept chomping and mud slobber flew out.

"What do we do, Carnavon?"

"It only seems to want to eat you. Maybe I should let it."

"You wouldn't!"

Sadly, Sifuso was right. Gaul Haddar had left me in charge. Honor demanded I do my best to keep his dumb apprentices alive. I drew my pistol, thumbed back the hammer, and fired. I didn't even need to aim much, it was such a big target. The bullet, unfortunately, did nothing except raise a puff of dust and make my ears ring.

The blast of the gunshot made nearby residents of the Under Slump look our way, because normally when there was random gunfire in this condemned district, it meant there'd been a murder or a gang fight was breaking out. Such activities were proper, normal, respectable things here. Instead, they saw a pile of angry earth crashing about, so the residents calmly began gathering their children and valuables to leave the area. Having dealt with our neighbors a lot over recent weeks, I could even imagine what they were muttering. *This used to be a nice street until those damnable wizards moved in and ruined the place.*

Telepathic Squalo language images formed in my head. The question was posed in Trax Bloodtrail's usual enthusiastic and oblivious way: "*Hello, my friend. Why is this mound of dirt so upset with you?*"

I turned to see the big grey and white fellow had walked up behind me. Squalo were thick, powerfully built, aquatic carnivores from the Elemental Plane of Water, but that didn't keep him from being very quick and quiet on land. "I don't know, Trax. Sifuso tried a simple earth spell and it turned into this."

Trax turned his triangular snout toward the lacertian and stared at Sifuso with his little black eyes. I knew next to nothing about the many kingdoms of the water realm, but it was said Trax's people were a magical hybrid of man and something called a shark. Trax's mouth opened just a bit, revealing rows of razor-sharp teeth, as he politely thought at me, "*I warned you that lizard folk are troublesome and that you should just let me eat him before he eats one of you.*"

Like most people, Sifuso couldn't understand Squalo mind picture speech, and Squalos can't speak aloud. I was an oddity in that I'd picked up their undersea thought language rather easily. Trax said it was because my mind was less squishy than that of most land creatures, which was quite the compliment. Everybody else just got weird nonsensical images flashing in their head when Trax tried to communicate with them.

"What did he say?" Sifuso asked.

"Trax said you should be thankful we're helping clean up your mess."

"*That is a terrible translation and not at all what I meant.*"

The wall bulged as the blob threw itself against it again. This unplanned renovation was giving us a front door big enough to drive a carriage through.

"Do you know what this monster is?"

"*I do not.*" Trax came from a distant empire on an entirely different plane of existence, and he was a monk, not a mage. Him knowing what we were dealing with had been a long shot.

With every would-be wizard we'd gathered being self-taught and low level, our knowledge of spell craft was extremely limited. I imagined that, at a regular academy, this was the sort of cursed thing one of the instructors or high-level students would simply dispel without a second thought. Except we didn't have any instructors, and our highest-ranking members were rank twos. Hell, we didn't even have the books to look up what this thing was. The barge I'd grown up on had possessed a better library.

Azarin stuck her head over the edge of the roof above and shouted down at us, "Is it dead yet?"

"No. It's stuck in the front door and chewing a bigger hole in the wall. I think it still wants to kill Sifuso for waking it up."

"*The earth monster makes a reasonable point there, Carnavon.*"

"Not now, Trax." But that gave me an idea, and I turned toward our lacertian. "Get out of here and hide. Maybe if you're out of sight, it'll calm down."

"This is wise." I didn't know if he actually believed it was wise, or he was just happy to be long gone by the time it broke free and killed the rest of us. Either way, he scurried off.

A moment later, we were joined by the last two members of our less than illustrious student council, as Rade and Krachma appeared. They must have been out on some business in the Under Slump, and were puzzled as Sifuso ran past them. When they turned our way and saw that our front door was filled with furious dirt, Rade shouted, "I go out for one morning and they destroy my house!"

Rade had been living in these ruins first—House Tartaros in Exile, as he called it—and after we helped him out, he'd invited the rest of us to practice magic here, seeing as we'd had nowhere else to go. Like all deadlanders, Rade was white as a blood-drained corpse, and had solid black eyes. Despite the eerie appearance and the reputation his people had for being glum, he was a remarkably cheerful individual. He was from the Elemental Plane of Death, a dreary land where the living were constantly harried by ghosts and undead, so he probably knew about as much about this breed of earth creature as Trax did.

Krachma, on the other hand, was from the Elemental Plane of Earth, same as our problem beast, and he was a rank two, which allegedly meant he was better at magic in general than Azarin or me. Hopefully, he'd know what to do.

"This is a *Shape Earth* spell gone wrong. Can you stop it?"

Krachma was a lob—a warrior race supposedly created by powerful wizards long ago by infusing hobgoblins with earth magic. The gigantic orange fellow was nearly seven feet tall, muscled like a draft animal, and his many scars took on the appearance of black rock. He didn't talk much. It was assumed that was because he didn't know much of the trade language that everyone else used in the Core, but I figured even if he'd been fluent, Krachma would remain the strong, silent type.

He scowled at our mess. "Krachma has seen this before. It is bad."

"You don't say?" I asked as the blob knocked more heavy stones out of our wall. "Do you know how to make it go away?"

Krachma slowly shook his large head in the negative. "Wild spirit snared in spell, tries to grow into real Elemental. Krachma does not know the spell to cleanse."

We certainly couldn't allow that here, because true Elementals were incredibly dangerous. I'd made my living trapping Fire Elementals, and if an Earth Elemental was even half as mean as those, letting one loose around innocent bystanders would be a travesty.

"If we can't banish it back to where it came from, we're going to have to do this the hard way, then." I pulled out my bag of Red and prepared to use up the rest of my precious element. "Just don't hit it with any earth spells. That just makes it bigger."

"Obviously. That's just basic magical logic," Rade said. "Which brainless imbecile tried that?"

"Rufus," Azarin shouted from above.

"Of course it was. As I so ardently stated the last time we argued about this, Carnavon, we shouldn't let in every fool who dreams of becoming a wizard. Yet you continue to take in every stray regardless of their ability, whether it be magical ability or in their ability to pay us, so now we're impoverished *and* drowning in a sea of imbecility."

The blob knocked out another stone. One of its mouths found the sheet we'd painted the words *Outcast Academy* on and hung next to our door as our banner, sucked it in like a noddle, and began chewing.

"Can we postpone this debate until later, Rade?"

He drew his dueling saber. "Very well." Then he looked at his sword and contemplated what exactly he was supposed to accomplish with that against a murderous hill. "We really do need to add some more destructive spells to our repertoire."

Rade wasn't wrong about that. The one requirement we put on our applicants was that they had to be willing to share a spell with the rest of us to learn. This had gotten us to a grand total of two dozen spells between us all, of which I currently held the record at being able to cast the most. But the Outcast's spells were homebrew experiments, and only a few were really potent. Meanwhile, the real academies had shelves full of spellbooks and magic that could shake the worlds at their fingertips.

"Right now, we'll make do." I reloaded my pistol. "Let's kill this thing."

"*Descend.*" Azarin stepped off the roof and floated down to land gently next to me. She was a lot better at that spell than I was.

Trax pulled out his weirdly twisted coral sword. Krachma had left his mace home, but he went to one of the nearby shacks and wrenched a big board off the side of one. He seemed satisfied there were nails sticking out the end of it. At least the residents of that shack had already left, so no one yelled at him.

Sending Sifuso away hadn't calmed the beast. On the contrary, it seemed even more agitated now that its chosen prey escaped. It got even more quivery and bitey when I hit it with a second *Shroud of Fire*, engulfing our now broken door with flames. Azarin struck it with another lightning *Jolt*, as did Rade, as he'd recently learned that spell from her. Once the fire and sparks died down, Krachma—who knew only earth magic—and Trax—who knew no spells at all—took turns hitting the part that was sticking through the doorway.

All that accomplished was using up more of our valuable magical element and knocking some bits off of it. The blob pushed a whole section of the wall over, and we all scrambled to get out of the way. Now it was free.

Most of our school's spells weren't that destructive, but I did have one enchantment that I'd discovered years ago by accident which had proven to be especially dangerous. I pulled out the iron snail shell I always kept on my person for special occasions, and held it up so my friends could see it. "Take cover."

"Snail grenade!" Azarin shouted as she dove behind our neighbor's chicken coop.

The first time I'd put this formula together, I'd blown a big hole in my family's barge and several smaller holes in myself. Iron snails were one of the native animals of Fogo, and it turns out when you enchant their shells with Red, they get extremely explosive. When one of these goes off, high velocity fragments spray everywhere. I didn't like the idea of using this spell with innocent bystanders around, but this situation was getting dire.

"*Try getting it in its mouth. If it blows up on the inside, we are less likely to be injured.*"

"Great idea, Trax." It was still chewing our flag, so that gave me a target. I focused on the magical element embedded in the shell until I felt the Red awaken. As soon the shell began to glow orange, I hurled it with all my might. As a Trapper on the lava wastes, I'd spent a lot of time throwing rocks at various pests, so my aim was rather good.

The snail grenade landed right in the monster's big, weird mouth. By the time it disappeared into the churning dirt, the shell was bright as a light charm.

"Get down!" Then I took my own advice, threw myself face first onto the ground, and covered my head with my arms.

Normally, a snail grenade went off with a *boom*. Covered in dirt, this one was more of a *fwompf.*

It raised quite a cloud of dust, but we didn't get pelted with shrapnel. As the dust settled, the monster was still.

Rade lifted his head from where he was hiding behind a fence and shouted, "We're victorious. Well done!"

Then the blob opened its mouth, let out a bunch of white smoke and a noise that sounded suspiciously like a belch, and went back to chewing our now burning flag.

"Oh, come on!" That had been the most destructive spell in our entire academy. I'd wounded a pirate barge with that one once! We had no one to call for help. The Core City Watch wouldn't even come into the Under Slump. What were we supposed to do now? Just let it eat the place?

"*Banish.*"

That command word came somewhere behind me. The blob immediately froze, the life went right out of it, and it crumbled back into ordinary dead dirt.

There was a contingent of men walking purposefully our way. The locals seemed a lot more scared of them than they had the blob monster and hurried to get out of their way. As soon as I saw they were all wearing the same black arm band, I understood why they were afraid.

These were Latrocinium, the brutal gang who all the other gangs of the Under Slump paid their respects to. There were six in total, each geared up, and appeared eager for a fight. A couple of them must have been wizards, since they were armed with wands and staffs, and at least one was skilled enough to have just demolished an earth monster we could barely scratch.

All that suggested they'd probably best us easily.

"*Predators approach,*" Trax sent.

The silent warning was appreciated, but unnecessary, because the men who wore the black band were legendary in this district. Since the Upper and Lower Aventine had been abandoned by the city to decay into the Slump and Under Slump, the Latrocinium were basically the government here, and the mysterious figure, Carcalla, was their rarely seen, but often heard of, king.

The gangsters looked us over, before the one who was obviously in charge asked, "Which one of you speaks for this sad bunch?"

"I do," Rade and I responded simultaneously. When I scowled at him, he told me, "I'm nobility, and I was here first."

"Nobility, my ass. Gaul Haddar left me in charge."

"Neither of you is *in charge* of shit," the gang leader said. "Carcalla alone is in charge of everything in the Slumps and slits the throats of anyone dumb enough to believe otherwise. I am his appointed representative. As such, I inquired which bum among this gaggle of bums speaks on behalf of the rest of the bums?"

Rade nodded thoughtfully at those words, especially the throat-slitting part. "Perhaps you should handle this one then, Carnavon."

The gangster caught my name. "You're the hotlander, Ozwald Carnavon?"

I stood up and brushed myself off, so I'd look at least half dignified before answering, "That's me."

"Excellent. I am Joran Vanderhelst. Master Carcalla has sent me to collect your rent."

3

We remained in a bit of an awkward standoff, lowly wizard student council on one side, incredibly lethal gang which was likely to beat and murder us on the other, until I asked real slowly, "What rent might that be?"

Their leader, Joran, was a short but fit fellow, wearing a black fur cape carved off some big animal, with short-cropped sandy hair and a scruff of beard. He was probably around forty, so about double my age. He grew puzzled by my question.

"Your rent for living in this here lovely section of tower, obviously."

Maybe this really should have been Rade's business to handle, as he'd been squatting in these ruins for months before our academy had formed. "These ruins have been abandoned for fifty years. Nobody wanted to live in it before us because it's so haunted."

"It really is lousy with ghosts," Azarin chimed in. "They shriek constantly and like to throw things. They've got a nasty temperament."

The ghosts were why Rade—who'd been kicked out of his home realm for annoying the nobles he claimed to be related to—ended up living here while trying to make his way as a gladiator duelist in the Slumps' arenas. Deadlanders are so used to ghosts, they don't mind them. For the rest of us, ghosts are a pain in the ass. The part that galled me the most about them was when they appeared, they'd suck all the warmth out of a room, and this whole damn city was too cold for me already.

"The reasons the property was unoccupied before are irrelevant. It's occupied now. Carcalla is the landlord of this entire neighborhood. It's true, Carcalla cared nothing about the Tube before—seeing as the dead can't pay rent—but it's undeniably got itself a fancy magical academy residing in it now." Joran gestured at our half-burned flag, the name on which could still clearly be seen. "Said academy's rent is past due."

We'd set up here because we couldn't afford to live anywhere else in the Core. If any of us had money, we'd have bribed our way into a real academy like the rest of the aspiring wizards did. All those prestigious institutions in the Collegium were run by rank-ten master mages. We had one of those too, but our founder was off on a mission of vengeance, didn't seem to care if we lived or died, and I suspected he'd allowed the founding of a school in his name simply because it amused him. It really should've been the fearsome and respected Gaul Haddar having this discussion, not me.

"First I'm hearing about this rent," I told him. "How much are we talking about?"

"Upon careful appraisal, Master Carcalla has deemed a hundred Obols a month to be fair for such a spacious habitation."

That was a significant amount of money for the likes of us.

"Absurd!" Azarin exclaimed. "That's robbery even without the ghost infestation."

"Miss, the Latrocinium does not fear ghosts. We *make* ghosts. And it being the thirteenth and final month of our saints' blessed year, and according to the proclamation which you yourselves have until recently had nailed upon your front door..." Joran nodded toward the wood fire which was still crackling, "your academy was founded during the tenth month. Which puts you on the hook for four hundred Obols."

My mouth fell open. "That's outrageous."

Joran spread his hands in mock apology. "Such is the market for housing nowadays."

That was more money than we'd managed to scrounge up between all of us in the whole time we'd been here, including all our winnings in the local arenas. We barely had enough coin to buy magical element to train with as it was.

"That's quite the sum. We'll have to settle up later, I'm afraid, as unfortunately, our instructor is away on important high-ranking wizard business."

"Yeah, unfortunate. Mad Dog Gaul the Mutilator Haddar being distracted pursuing pirates across the Plane of Fire don't absolve you of your debts. This is a topic you should know about, Mr. Carnavon. I heard you skipped out on your contract to the Argents, but unlike your shit realm noblemen, Carcalla always gets paid."

Joran was well informed.

"And if he doesn't get paid?" Azarin asked.

"Azarin Garzade, I presume?" Joran waited for her to nod. "I figured correctly. I was told you would be the lovely one of the bunch. I see I was told the truth, albeit you're a bit too skinny for my tastes... Anyways, you don't want to go down that path, miss. I know defiance is the Stormwolk way, as your home is full of warring clans constantly squabbling, so you might think there's room for such behavior here. That used to be common in the Slumps after the city abandoned us to our fate. Battles between gangs and hostage takings and whatnot, but Carcalla brought order to the Slumps by slaying every fool who stood against him. We're downright civilized here now. But Carcalla's not forgotten the old bloody ways and remains fond of them. He seldom gets to do things the old-fashioned way, and rejoices at the opportunity to spill some blood when it presents itself."

"Is that a threat? What're you trying to say?"

"I'm saying that pretty things like you are fragile but bring a lot of coin in the black markets of the under city."

Honor insulted, Azarin moved one hand toward the copper rods on her belt. "Those are big words backed by so few bodies."

In response, several Latros opened their coats to display pistols and daggers on their belts. Rade was a braggart, and possibly delusional, but he was no coward, as he immediately moved to Azarin's side and readied his sword.

"And the black-eyed, corpse-looking swordsman must be Mr. Tartaros."

"That's Lord Tartaros to you."

"You mistake the Slumps for a place where birth titles mean something. The only titles that matter here are the ones we earn." Joran chuckled. "I've seen one of your gladiator bouts. You're an entertaining amateur at best, giving them a bit of a show. But in that field, I'm what's known as a professional."

"I recognize you now." Normally, Rade was a cocky bastard, but his voice broke just a little bit. That squeak told me a lot about the manner of man we were dealing with, because I'd seen Rade rather fight a Death Elemental than lose face. "You're Cutter Joran."

"That's right. Now, *Cutter*, that's a title that means something in these parts."

"I heard you retired from the arena."

"Expanded my career horizons is more like it. I fought for twenty years a gladiator before Master Carcalla retained my services. Now the whole of the Slumps is my arena." Joran spread his hands wide, and when he did so, his fur coat opened enough to reveal a nasty cleaver of a sword at his side. "And this my adoring crowd."

There wasn't much of a crowd, since the locals had all gone into hiding to keep from catching a stray bullet or spell. Krachma probably didn't understand most of what was being said here, but our lob seemed ready to beat someone with his stolen board anyway. He looked to Rade, confused, but our usually confident duelist shook his head in the negative.

"Alas, I didn't come searching for conflict today. What you see before you is but a small welcoming committee. Carcalla has an army the likes of which makes the City Watch sweat. What're all of you, rank ones? Perhaps a two?" He pointed at one of his wizards. "Rank three." Then he pointed at another. "Rank four. And I've got fifty more just like them and better to call upon to seed these haunted grounds with even more ghosts, should it be required."

"There's no need for hostility," I said.

"I doubt that," Azarin whispered.

"Easy." It was troubling me that Joran knew so much about us. This wasn't some ordinary shakedown. This was something worse.

Azarin didn't understand the criminal mindset. Her people were contentious as could be, but they had a certain integrity about how they conducted their many wars. I assumed the Latrocinium were more like the gangs I'd known in Fort Silver, just bigger, more organized, and deadlier.

Knowing this was some kind of trap, I addressed Joran as politely as I could. "You're proper businessmen. We're peaceful students trying to learn the ways of magic. I'm sure we can come to an equitable arrangement."

"A common plea when one is behind on his rent. I'd suggest correcting that forthwith, because the Latrocinium's eviction process being what it is, I cannot guarantee all your body parts will remain attached during it." Joran raised his voice so the students who remained inside could hear him too. "That applies to all who reside here, for Carcalla is a fair landlord, but he is not a patient one."

Even from down here, I could hear the nervous whispers of the other students watching from the windows. "I'm afraid we're a bit short of coin right now."

The satisfied look on Joran's face told me I'd told him exactly what he'd been waiting to hear. "Ah, this inability to pay means we need to consider an alternative manner for you to work off this crushing debt you lot have acquired."

The gangsters eyed us. From who they were most fixated on, apparently, our Squalo's reputation for casually biting people's limbs had gotten back to the Latrocinium. Trax must have picked up that thought of mine, because he projected to me, "*I only bite humans when they are rude to me. I cannot abide rudeness. Do you feel these are being rude? Should I eat them?*"

Surprisingly, Joran must have been another rarity among us land folk who could understand the undersea thought speech. "You'd try, but you'd go hungry today, Squalo. Your kind don't even understand housing or commerce. You'd best stay out of this dispute."

"*Remarkable. This human just sent me an image of me being sliced into pieces and thrown into the canal. That is not very nice.*"

Even more of our students had appeared in the windows above, so the Latros were watching them as well, and now that the gang was outnumbered, hands were beginning to stray toward wands and guns. They weren't nearly as confident as their boss. Our Outcasts might not have been very good wizards, but there were a dozen of us, and quantity had a quality all its own.

Trying to prevent a blood bath, I said, "My apologies, Mr. Vanderhelst. I'd love to invite you gentlemen in to discuss this matter further, but it appears our front door is currently blocked by several tons of dirt."

"That's fine. We were just leaving… and you're coming with us." When Joran smiled with his regular human teeth, it was almost as frightening as Trax's mouth full of razors. "Carcalla has summoned you in particular, Mr. Carnavon, to a meeting at his fortress. It would be wise not keep him waiting."

4

I walked with the Latros across the Under Slump to the nearest bridge, and we began our long, spiraling climb up to the Slump. I went unarmed, a feeling I very much disliked, but I'd been told to leave my weapons and magic behind, to avoid any *misunderstandings.* It had not been a suggestion.

The constant shade kept it dim and damp in the Under Slump. Out here, the sun was shining, but it remained freezing cold due to the bitter wind. It was even snowing a bit. As a native of Fogo, I'd been astounded the first time I'd seen snow. The idea of frozen fluffy water bits falling from the sky had been incredible to me. It was like an ash storm that wouldn't burn your skin off. That first snow storm of mine was a fun experience, and I'd run into it with Azarin, who'd thought me a silly fool as I'd slid about, but she had still been entertained by my antics. I'd even stuck my tongue out and eaten some of the falling snowflakes. They tasted like water. You sure couldn't do that in an ash storm!

Little had I realized that winter meant it would keep snowing and snowing, over and over, for months, until I got sick of the miserable, slick white shit piling up everywhere. The two *seasons* I'd experienced thus far in the Core had been awful. The next one was called spring, which everyone assured me was much nicer. I'd believe that when I saw it. For now, I kept my cloak wrapped tight around me and my hood up to protect my ears from frostbite—which was not a medical condition I'd been familiar with before coming here.

Even though the magic which had kept the Slump suspended in the air for thousands of years was slowly dying, and the whole neighborhood was gradually sinking and threatening to crush the Under Slump beneath it to death, on the bright side, having an entire district as a roof kept most of the snow off our heads. Out here, that wasn't the case, and with a lot more ice collected on the bridges, several times, I slipped on the nasty stuff.

That caused the Latros surrounding me to laugh at my misfortune. "Stupid hotlander," said one. "How can you walk across lava but not on a little dusting of snow?"

"We wait for the lava to cool enough to form a solid crust first. Failure to do so, we call that the old pegleg surprise."

They laughed at that. I might be slipping and sliding to my demise, but it couldn't hurt to try and stay on friendly terms with the resident gang. Despite basically being a captive, I was in relatively good spirits. Realistically, if Carcalla wanted me dead, the deed would already be done, and he wouldn't have had his men put on this show of force for our benefit. Oh, I was certain I wasn't being dragged to his lair for any good reasons, as I was surely about to be extorted and threatened, but my murder was unlikely, provided I didn't piss him off.

Joran was far ahead at the front of the black-banded group. Everyone else using this narrow high road was quick to get out of our way. Even wagons and carts pulled aside for us and waited respectfully when they saw that Carcalla's men were out. The Latrocinium weren't overtly threatening. They didn't need to be. By reputation alone, they controlled these streets.

"So why do they call him the Cutter?" I asked the same Latro.

"On account of how many people Joran cut up in the arena, I suppose."

That wasn't an unexpected revelation, but I'd been hoping that maybe there'd been a more innocuous reason for the title. Like he enjoyed cutting delicious cakes to serve to his guests.

"What rank is he?"

"Joran ain't no mage, hotlander. He hunts mages for sport."

"What do you mean?"

"I thought by now everybody in the Slumps knew of Cutter Joran's trick," said the Latro wizard walking behind me. "Magic don't work on him."

That made no sense. Even from here, I could see he was wearing several enchanted charms, and because of my affinity to the element, I could even tell a few were imbued with Red. "He's got magic on him right now."

"Sure. Protections that turn on automatic against incoming bullet or blade, but he can't use magic himself, and magic can't affect him. It makes him right deadly against our kind."

Nulls were a rare thing indeed. Overwhelmingly, most intelligent beings tested as zeros. Which meant they couldn't work magic themselves, but spells worked on them for good or ill, and they could use enchanted items if they were simple enough. Through practice and exercise, zeros could grow their magical abilities. For example, the first time I'd been tested, I'd been a zero, and after a few years of illicit practice with stolen element, I'd tested again as a rank one. I'd been trying ever since to master more spells in the hopes of reaching rank two. Individuals blessed by the saints were born possessing more natural magical abilities, and might test as high as three or four, even without any training.

But Nulls were something else entirely. I'd read about them in the encyclopedia. They went the opposite direction of everyone else, born less than a zero, in that magic simply wouldn't touch them at all. It was a double-edged sword; they could never learn magic, but they were also immune to its effects. They couldn't be strengthened or healed by the Green or Blue, but they also couldn't be burned by Red, hurled by Clear, or slain by Black.

In a city ruled by wizards, I could see how a Null would be so valuable. I made a note that if I ever had to fight Cutter Joran to just shoot him… Except, apparently, defensive charms could still place their shields around a Null. I'd have to ponder on how best to kill him, and in the meantime hope I wouldn't need to.

But he'd also sort of threatened to sell my girlfriend into slavery, so I really wanted to.

5

Coming from a humble realm, it was odd to me that a criminal organization should have their own estate, bigger than the fort belonging to the noble family who owned my family. Then again, Fogo was poor, and the Core City was so wealthy that even the gang which ruled its lowest parts could lord it over our nobles. The Latrocinium's holdings were nice enough; they would've fit in better in the Collegium than here. With most residents of the Slumps living in wretched poverty, it was clear to whose pocket most of the coins in these two districts flowed.

As befitted its position floating in the sky, the Slump was nicer than the Under Slump beneath it, and the Latrocinium's blocks were the nicest part of the Slump. These were real homes, not shacks. There were craftsmen and markets. We passed pubs and brothels. The ladies upon the balconies blew kisses and hiked up their tiny skirts to expose even more thigh. The thugs escorting me loved the attention. I was just amazed that Core dwellers could wear so little clothing in this chilly place without perishing. None of those girls were from Fogo, that was for sure!

The huge structure in the middle of the district must have been some kind of important government building before the Upper Aventine had begun sinking its way into Slumphood. Now it served as a casino. Bands were playing. People were singing. There was a huge crowd gathered for the many entertainments. Those wearing masks to hide their identity were surely respectable types from the other, more law-abiding parts of the city, come here to engage in a bit of debauchery.

As fun as this place seemed, there were reminders as to the nature of who ran this establishment. I watched as one crying man was dragged past, screaming and begging for mercy, because some Latros were going to toss him over the edge of the district for failing to pay his gambling debts.

On one end of the casino's plaza was a mansion the likes of which I'd never seen before. The building was covered in beautiful pillars and arches, yet the more I looked, the more I realized it was as much fortress as a home. The towers and walls weren't just decorative, but defensive. This was the only place I'd been in the Slumps where the ancient statues hadn't been torn down and carried off. There were even fountains that spit water. Upon the mansion's central peak flew a black flag with a yellow sign, marking this as the headquarters of the infamous Carcalla.

There were guards everywhere, and despite being criminals, they seemed more squared away than the Argent enforcers had back home. They were probably quite a bit tougher too, because the Latrocinium had far more opportunities to fight. From what I'd been told, there wasn't a crooked endeavor in this great city that the Latros weren't involved in.

We went up the steps, past the statues of naked women whose bottom halves were fish.

"Why don't they have legs?"

"They're supposed to be mermaids," Joran said.

Seeing as how the fish tails probably meant they came from the water realm, I'd have to ask Trax if mermaids were real. That whole arrangement seemed rather impractical.

I got checked at the door for weapons and then checked again on the other side by a mage with some kind of device designed to spot hidden magic. Once he was sure I didn't have any extra dimensional pockets or illusions upon me, most of my escort left. It was just Joran and the two Latro wizards now.

"Take your boots off and leave them in the entry hall," Joran ordered as he took his own off.

"Why?"

"Because we're fucking civilized here."

It was hard for me to comprehend, but the inside of this place was even richer than the exterior. This house was as big as the barge I'd been raised on, and the front room was as wide as our cargo bay had been.

I'd heard of paintings, but I'd never seen any until arriving in the Core. Now I was walking past dozens of them. From the many wildly different styles, I assumed they'd been collected from across many different realms and kingdoms. I knew some of the portraits must have been of various saints, because the artists liked to put glowing halos around their heads. The wildly different items in their hands must have been symbolic and helped identified which saint was which, but I'd not gone to enough church to identify most of these. None of these saints were posed in a land of fire and carrying mining tools, so my patron, Ketekunan, Saint of Persistence, wasn't represented.

Of the many landscapes, I recognized the Great Machine towering over the market, but what lands the others showed were mysteries to me. There were flat green plains of endless grass. There were cities on clouds with herds of giant floating animals between and no ground beneath. There was a village inside an enormous cave, lit by glowing crystals on the walls, where the odd-looking residents lived in giant hollowed-out mushrooms.

Sadly, Joran never slowed so I could get a better look at any of them.

It seemed odd to shove so much beauty into a place it clearly didn't belong. As if Carcalla was trying to create his own personal fake Collegium here, but all the riches were piled up in such a way it was gaudy to me.

From my staring, Joran must have assumed I was overcome by the opulence. "You a connoisseur of art, Carnavon?"

"Nope. Canvas catches on fire where I'm from. My barge cadre had a set of the Encyclopedia Ettymus which was illustrated, but half of the volumes had been lost or burned by the time I was old enough to read them. I don't know a thing about this stuff."

"Me neither."

"I do like all the pretty colors, though."

"I couldn't care less about that shit."

At the end of the hall was a huge door. On either side was a matching black stone statue, sculpted to be some kind of spikey, armored creature, roughly humanoid, but with bug-like features, and each had an extra set of arms. Two ended in hands, while the other ended in swords.

"Those are a lot uglier than the mermaids. What're they based on? Because I'll avoid whatever kingdom that race is from if possible!"

"Those aren't artwork, dummy. Those are some of Master Carcalla's security."

One of the statues tilted its elongated face to the side to study me with its blank stone eyes. I knew very little about the golems, beyond creating them required several different elements and a very skilled enchanter, and that they could be very dangerous.

"I'll remain on my best behavior," I assured it.

"They don't talk. I wish I could say the same for you. Have a seat and shut up. Carcalla should be here in a minute."

The room reminded me a bit of Bargemaster Gax's office on Barge 519, in that this was clearly a place for a commander to ponder important issues and then hand down orders, except it was bigger and nicer in every way. Which was appropriate, since Carcalla was managing a far larger operation than one little Red mining cadre.

When we walked in, it was *soft* beneath my socks, and when I looked down, I was surprised to see the entirety of the floor was covered in short brown fur.

"It's called carpet," Joran answered before I could even ask. "Saints alive, you are a fucking bumpkin."

There was a gigantic round table in the center of the room, and detailed maps of all the Core City's many districts on the walls. There were books everywhere. Hundreds of them. More books than I'd ever seen anywhere, except maybe in all the market's booksellers booths I'd ever passed by combined. If these weren't just a display of wealth, and Carcalla had actually read all of them, he must be a very smart man.

There was a desk at the end of the room, with a couple of leather chairs in front. Behind the desk was a big picture window, from which could be seen some of the city's magnificent palaces and bridges magically suspended high above us, golden, and currently capped in snow.

Unlike this slowly sinking neighborhood, those splendid floating districts were still safely anchored in place by air magic. They were governed by the watch. We got gangsters. I was a bit jealous.

I sat on one chair. Joran had to pull the sheathed cleaver sword off his belt to fit between the armrests of the other. Having his sword already resting on his lap would also make it easier for him to swiftly strike me down should his master say so. I doubted that would happen, because this marvelous carpet thing was far too luxurious to risk soaking all my blood into it. The two wizards remained standing by the table behind us.

A moment later, I realized it wasn't a window behind the desk at all, because the image shifted, and we were no longer looking at the Core City, but at some strange realm, where the sky was made of furious clouds and dancing lightning, with incredibly tall but thin mountains stretching upward. I could see the distant lights of civilization clinging precariously to those rocky walls.

"You like the window?"

It was incredible. "Is it some kind of far seer?"

"Don't be a rube. There's no seeing into other realms except for when that realm is aligned through the Nexus upon the Great Machine. Today's the 18th. That's the third Landay of the month, which means today the gate's open to Tarklinberg on the Plane of Earth. While that image there is of Beskrajan, upon the Plane of Air."

"You've been there?"

"Yes, to both." Joran was well travelled for a gangster's lackey.

"So, it's an image recorded from sometime before, placed as an illusion upon this glass." There were even droplets of rain collecting on the window. It vibrated in its frame along with the thunder. It really felt as if there was a violent storm right outside. "That's an impressive enchantment."

"And a not too uncommon one among those wealthy enough to afford one. How is it a man who's got no magic himself knows more about magic than an ostensible wizard who's supposedly running a magical academy? Seems a bit suspect to me."

I didn't take his bait. I'd only been in the Core for a few months, and before that, every spell I'd learned had been self-taught. There was no shame to be taken from my lack of learning, because I'd done the best I could with what was available and created my own opportunity along the way. "I never claimed to be that skilled. I'm just a lowly student who is temporarily watching over Gaul Haddar's academy until he returns."

"Seeing as how Haddar's been gone the whole time your academy has existed, it seems more your endeavor than his."

The Outcast Academy had been my idea. I'd been the one who had saved Haddar's life and helped get his promotion to rank-ten master wizard. In return, his last act before leaving through the gate had been to order the formation of an academy in his name, as was the right of all rank tens. But I wasn't going to explain all that to this mouthy thug.

"The Nexus Council saw fit to make us an official academy, so we must be doing something right."

Joran snorted. "It sure don't look like it to me."

"You should file a complaint with the Council."

The two of us remained quiet for a long time, as the window changed again, now showing some kingdom covered in more plants and wildlife than I'd ever imagined. There were vast trees hundreds of feet tall, and a multitude of animals, colorful birds, and weird little furry things leaping between the branches. I didn't know what any of them were because we had hardly any animals on Fogo, and the only animals I'd seen so far in the Core had been for labor or eating.

The door by the golems opened. Carcalla had arrived.

Joran leaned over and whispered, "By the way, you overconfident bastard, that dirt monster rampaging when we arrived? That's the result of a minor Elemental spirit lingering from a previous spell getting bound to a new one, which twists up the formula. You've got to purge the area periodically to avoid contamination. You'd know that if you had a fucking clue what you're doing."

That surprise information was just enough to leave me off-balance for when the gang lord master of the Slumps and my new landlord walked past us on the way to his desk. Cutter Joran had surely timed that on purpose.

Carcalla was tall and thin, dressed in the kind of dark silk suit that was fashionable in the Collegium. There was no hair atop his head, but he had a pointy white beard on his chin. A scar ran from forehead to cheek, crossing one eye. At first, I thought he was young, but his manner suggested he was old, and then I saw those damnable pointy ears and knew he was both at the same time.

I should've known Carcalla would be a fucking elf.

It was said elves lived so long, they had a tendency to end up in charge of things and then stay that way forever. I'd had bad luck with elves. Well, I'd only met two so far. One was a pirate who'd killed half my family and shot down our barge. The other had been a standoffish academy instructor who'd turned out to be mildly helpful. I suppose my luck was more like fifty-fifty. I guess when it comes to me and elves, flip a coin.

"This is the hotlander?" Carcalla asked.

"Delivered as requested," Joran replied.

"Then why does he not rise and pay me the respect I am due?"

"You know what they say about hotlanders, boss. They've got strong backs and feeble minds."

I promptly stood up and bowed my head, as I'd been taught as a child to do whenever a nobleman was around. For all practical purposes, Carcalla and the Argents were the same thing to me—powerful bullies with the clout to ruin or end my life on a whim.

"Apologies, sir. I'm from a humble realm. I don't know the protocols around… landlords." I'd almost said *gangsters* but caught myself in time.

"Barely sufficient." Carcalla went around the desk and sat in the plush chair on the other side. Behind him, the window changed to a land of unforgiving glaciers and endless ice. He scowled as he looked me over. "Sit."

I did as I was told.

The elf leaned back and steepled his fingers. There was a magic ring on every single one. "I will begin by saying that I'm amazed you had the audacity to think you could get away with running a scam in my territory… and *not* pay me for the privilege?"

Threatened or not, that was an insult. "The Outcast Academy is no scam."

"I do not mind you fleecing desperate fools deluded enough to think they could someday become respectable wizards, but to do so while not giving me my rightful percentage is unforgivable." Carcalla had an odd manner of speaking, regal yet disinterested, but there were terrible consequences implicit in every word he said. "You've got some stones on you, boy. I ought to have Cutter remove them."

It appeared this elven coin flip was going to be tails.

"With all due respect, sir, you've been given a mistaken impression of us. Our students do intend to become respectable wizards. We've all tested too low and lack the means to get into the usual traditional academies, but we're no frauds."

"These students of yours are paying you *tuition*, are they not?"

"I wish. That's the idea to cover our costs and eventually pay some teachers and a tester, as the regular academies do, but most of our students show up as broke as I was when I came through the gate. We've not actually collected much in the way of tuition yet." I didn't want to tell him how pathetic we really were, but if it hadn't been for Morton and Sifuso getting a bit of money from their families, we'd be catching and eating ratlets to survive by now.

"And you take these paupers in anyway?" Carcalla asked, suspicious. He might have a portrait of Saint Charity in the room below, but she did not live in his heart. "Why?"

"That's a good question. They're all rejects, same as I was. The reasoning is if they've got a spell to share, that's one more for the rest of us to learn, and each spell makes us a bit better. The more spells we learn, the more we train, the more experience we get, the more our magical ability grows, the better we'll test, and the higher we'll rank. Higher ranks grant better opportunities. Eventually, or so our theory goes, given enough time and magic, we'll become proper mages, same as those trained in the Collegium above."

"Fascinating." Except Carcalla said that so deadpan that I couldn't tell if he was being sarcastic or not. "And how many of these lost sheep have you gathered to your flock?"

We didn't have sheep on Fogo, but I knew those were the wooly ones. They must have had a problem with wandering off and getting lost. "About a dozen."

"That part's true, and among their number are dangerous sorts like a great white Squalo and a good-sized lobgoblin," Joran said. "I saw for myself he's assembled a decent-sized gang."

"We're not a gang," I protested. "We are what we say we are. Students of magic. That's all… My first week here, a wise man told me that wizards run this city, so they're real particular who they let into their club. If you want in, you've either got to be too talented to ignore, they like you for some reason, or you're paying them enough to like you. We're not that good, they don't like us, and we're too poor to afford the bribes… So, we're just circumventing a system designed to keep our kind out."

Joran scoffed. "You're supposedly running a magical academy, not a soup kitchen for the poor."

"I guess you could consider us the community gruel pot of wizardry, then."

Joran looked toward his boss. "He's lying or he's the most gullible fool to cross the Nexus in a long time."

"And this city eats fools." Carcalla stared through me, cold as the glaciers on the window behind him. It was then that I realized one of his eyes was fake and made out of some kind of glass that looked almost but not quite natural. Whatever had given him that scar had taken his real eye as well.

I didn't flinch away from that judgmental gaze. There's a certain power that comes from having a bit of integrity.

After an uncomfortable amount of time, Carcalla announced, "I do not believe he's a fool."

"I'm no liar either."

"That remains to be determined," Carcalla stated flatly.

"They have magical charms that can test that."

He ignored my helpful suggestion. "Enchantments can be wrong. My instincts never are. What is your ultimate goal, Mr. Carnavon? I speak not about your idealistic organization, but you personally. What is your purpose here?"

I'd made no secret of that the entire time I'd been in the Core. "I intend to become a high-ranking wizard."

"Why?"

This was getting personal, but I might as well put it out there. "The rest of the Carnavon family lives in indentured servitude. Generations of us have been worked to death mining the Red. It'll take a lot of coin to buy out all their contracts from the Argents. Powerful wizards command wealth. I'm going to free my family someday."

Carcalla continued with that piercing gaze. It was downright unnerving. "There's more."

Maybe he was better than a truth charm after all. "There is also a matter of revenge."

"Against who?"

"An elf pirate who's been attacking barges across the Plane of Fire for the last few years."

Carcalla was unmoved that I wanted to kill one of his kind. "Revenge is not that complicated. Why does this elf in particular require potent magic?"

"Because he's an extremely powerful mage himself, and nobody else, even the mighty Gaul Haddar, has been able to find, or even identify him. From the skills he's demonstrated, Haddar thinks he's equal in might to a Councilman, something crazy like a rank fifteen or higher. Do you happen to know of this pirate?"

"It is rare for one of the most blessed of all races to turn to a life of crime, but unfortunately, those of us who have done so are not all acquainted." Carcalla replied so cooly that he might have been lying right to my face, but who could tell with an elf? "Who did this pirate kill of yours?"

"My mom and dad, among a great many others, when he shelled our barge and left it to burn."

Carcalla pondered my words, then stated, "Power and revenge are two motives which I both understand… and respect… Leave us, Joran."

The subordinate nodded and departed without another word, taking the two wizards with him. Whatever Carcalla's magical defenses were, he certainly wasn't worried about unarmed, elementless me presenting any danger to him.

Once the door was closed, the gang lord went over to a cabinet full of liquor bottles. "Care for a drink, Mr. Carnavon?"

I figured there were easier ways to kill me than by poisoning. "Sure."

He got out two glasses, poured some dark brown liquid into each, then handed me one.

"Thanks." Though I wasn't sure why he'd shown me the kindness of offering me anything. His manner remained as icy as before. I took a sip, which burned and made my eyes water so bad, that for a second, I thought he had poisoned me after all.

I loved a good stiff drink as much as the next guy, but this was downright painful. I was used to the beer the Argents imported for our barges because it was basically wet bread to help feed the miners and keep us content enough not to strike. This stuff made the strongest drink in Fort Silver taste like water straight from the globe.

"Gwynfar Dragon Rum, distilled upon a lonely peak where the Elemental Plane of Life collides with Death and Fire." Carcalla downed the whole glass in one gulp. "Ah. Refreshing."

Sign of weakness or not, I had to cough.

Carcalla wandered to one of the maps on his wall. While he did so, the magic window changed to a land of sand and dull red plateaus. A distant caravan was crossing the horizon. Even with his back turned, he somehow knew what the window showed, because he explained, "That view is of Ashen Harran, the Blood Drenched Sands of the Elemental Plane of Earth."

"That's where Gaul Haddar is from."

"A harsh man, from a harsh kingdom. It might even be as inhospitable as the one you hail from."

By my standards, the image looked rather pleasant. None of the mountains were squirting lava and the sky wasn't covered in smoke. "I don't know. It doesn't look so bad."

Carcalla was so effortlessly intimidating, he even managed to make studying a map seem like a threatening gesture. "Both of those kingdoms are unforgiving in their own way. Yours by environment, his by the nature of the people who reside there. Ashen Harran has been consumed by endless war for hundreds of years. The various tribes live for war. Conflict runs in their veins. Of the thousand kingdoms, they are among the most capable. Orcs rage, lobs hold grudges, but you humans are relentless, and the Ashen Harran are the most so of all of you. To the Ashen Harran, war simply is. Your master is a product of this land."

From what I knew of Haddar, that seemed accurate. "He is rather intense in person."

"Haddar may not worship Saint Violence or Saint Murder, but he's been blessed by the gods just the same. The man has a gift for inflicting harm. His time studying magic here made him something of a legend in this city. Which is why the idea that upon finally reaching the tenth rank, so long denied to him by the spineless weaklings of the Council, the fearsome Gaul Haddar would decide to become a *teacher* amused me so."

"Maybe he's becoming more gentle as he's aged?"

Carcalla turned to scowl at me. "You claimed you were not a liar."

"Just throwing out a possibility."

"An unlikely one." The gang lord went back to his map. "I don't understand Haddar's reasoning in granting you this responsibility, but I have decided that you are not a fraud."

"I appreciate that, sir."

"You should. If I thought you were trying to rob me, I'd have you horribly disfigured and sent back to live as an example to all what happens when I am crossed."

Having seen the occasional Slumper missing their ears, nose, or lips for just that reason, I was extra thankful. I took another sip of the loathsome liquor to calm my nerves and managed to not choke that time.

"Except I do not think what you are running is an academy either."

"What are we then?"

"You're the living manifestation of Gaul Haddar's disdain for the Nexus Council."

That description probably wasn't too far off the truth. "Well… we're *trying* to be an academy."

"Indeed. Yet with your founder away, you have no resources. You lack knowledge. The only way to advance in rank is through increased aptitude, which requires spells. Real spells, not just the pathetic home-brewed experiments of rank-one amateurs. Learning new spells requires the formula and the magical elements to fuel them. You have neither, nor the money sufficient to purchase any. And there still remains the matter of the rent."

"Yeah, about that—"

"By now, you have surely realized your academy has nowhere else to go. Tradition demands the Council respect a rank-ten master's right to take on apprentices, but that is all they will grant you. They will stymie you in every other way possible for the simple fact Haddar's promotion offends them, as does your very existence. If the Council's disdain alone did not render your academy politically toxic, the fact magical experimentation can be dangerous to the property and bystanders would. Even if you could afford to live elsewhere, there would be no home for your rejects in any other district of this great city."

I could see exactly where this was heading. "Except for somewhere the Council's already forsaken and ignores."

"Correct. I am the ruler of your only option. And while you may choose to be kind to those who cannot pay… I do not. Such weakness would set a terrible precedent for my business."

I'd been a trapper, so I knew a trap when I stepped in it. "You've recognized yourself we lack the money to even buy enough element to practice with. We sure as hell can't swing another hundred Obols a month to keep you from siccing Cutter Joran on us." I gestured at the image of Ashen Harran. "For how dangerous you say Gaul Haddar is, your man sure don't hesitate to threaten harm against Haddar's students."

"Joran is a valuable servant, because he loves a challenge more than he fears death. I suspect he would enjoy fighting Haddar to the death. He's defeated rank sevens and eights, but I don't think he's ever had the opportunity to fight a nine or ten. I suspect a ten might even be beyond Joran's considerable abilities to kill. I'd prefer not to lose such a valuable and loyal servant, though. Thus, when your master returns, I will gladly renegotiate a new deal with him. Haddar demands respect. You do not. Therefore, you get the lesser deal. For now, be thankful you receive any courtesy at all."

Carcalla had me there, because Haddar might not ever return. He'd told me that the elf pirate was incredibly dangerous, so even if Haddar did finally manage to track him down, he might not survive the confrontation. And in the off chance he did, he still might not come back to the Core City ever again, simply because he despised this place and the Council who ran it. For all I knew, he'd already forgotten he'd ever founded an academy at all.

"What do you have in mind, Mr. Carcalla?"

"If you cannot pay your debt with coin, I will allow you and your students to work it off instead. Your options are one hundred Obols, or providing a service of corresponding value, per month."

"That doesn't sound like much of a choice."

"There is always eviction and painful dismemberment." Carcalla must have threatened so many people over the years that he managed to sound bored as he told me that.

"I believe I speak on behalf of all of our students when I say we enjoy keeping all our limbs attached. What manner of service?"

He seemed amused by my concern. "Simple tasks. Nothing too complicated."

I really didn't like what that implied. "There's other ways we might be able to earn that much money."

"Indeed. You and a few of your fellow Outcasts have earned a tidy sum fighting in the Slump arenas. It would be dangerous, but if you won enough matches every month, that would more than cover it. However, you forget who those goblin bookies work for. It would be a shame if every Outcast was suddenly and permanently banned from those establishments."

Seeing as how fighting in the arenas was how we were barely scraping by at all, getting cut off meant being starved of food and element, and then getting evicted anyway. "That would be a shame."

"Indeed. Come and look at this."

I grudgingly got up and joined him at the map. I'd been dreading this part. Carcalla was surely going to ask us to do something nefarious and illegal on his behalf. "We're not crooks. We're not thieves or leg breakers."

"Don't flatter yourself, Mr. Carnavon. I have plenty of those already." He pointed at a small island on the Core City's southern bay labeled Korthican's Warning. It had words written around it like *danger, cursed,* and *here be monsters.* "I am in need of *adventurers.*"

I swallowed the rest of the dragon murder rum or whatever it was called in one gulp. Unfortunately, it didn't put me out of my misery.

6

While most of the Elemental Plane of Fire is constantly shifting and churning, and solid ground comes and goes, there remain some permanent places. Those stable areas were created through powerful spells utilizing chronomancy long ago. My people weren't the first to settle Fogo, not by a long shot, and there are quite a few ancient ruins scattered across those enduring islands atop our plane of fire.

Us locals knew better than to fuck with those places.

But not the adventurers. Oh no.

Ancient ruins mean treasure, treasure brings adventurers, and adventurers have got to be the dumbest bastards there are. What kind of lunacy must possess a man to make him want to delve into the darkness, searching for lost magic, when everyone knows that old magic draws unnatural creatures to it? Sometimes old magic even *spawns* monsters. Not to mention the ancient wizards very much seemed to be of the *if I can't have it, no one can* philosophy when it came to their property, so they tended to leave all manner of brutal boobytraps around their homes for unwitting trespassers, which remained effective long after the wizards were dead and gone.

Yet, along comes these blithering idiot adventurers, full of swagger and bravado, thinking they could stroll through the Fogo gate and strike it rich quick. All they had to do was go into one of our selections of ancient ruins, defeat the traps and whatever horrific beasties had accumulated therein, and carry their loot back to the Core to sell in the grand market, so they could retire and live the rest of their life in luxury. Easy.

As a trapper, I actually knew how to navigate the fiery wastes, so on a few occasions, I'd been hired by adventuring companies from other realms to be their guide. This was a profitable side job for those in my profession, but we all understood to always get paid up front. Because it was all too common for one of us to guide a party of adventurers to their location, and then return to Port Silver alone after none of them came back out.

I always tried to warn these fools about how dangerous it was, but they never listened to me. What did I know? I was just a local who'd grown up in this godforsaken realm who knew it like the back of my hand. They were mighty *adventurers.* They had enchantments. They had weapons and skills! They fought monsters and found treasure for a living! I'd just smile and nod, take their coin, wish them good fortune on their noble endeavor, and wave as they descended into the dark, before setting up camp outside for the agreed upon amount of time to await their return.

Then after a few days, I'd return to Fort Silver alone. Occasionally, I'd be tempted to go in after them to loot their bodies, thinking I could sell their fine weapons and armor in town, but I wasn't ever greedy or stupid enough for that.

Now, adventurers didn't *always* perish. Other trappers had told me of parties they'd guided who'd actually made it out alive. Well, some of them at least. And most of those hadn't come out with armloads of treasure either. It was more like a handful of trinkets that were hardly worth dying over.

I suppose once in a great while, some party must have found something incredibly valuable, because their triumphant return to the Core was enough to inspire the next batch of morons who weren't very good at calculating odds or probability to come die horribly in my back yard.

Needless to say, I thought that being an adventurer was the stupidest career possible.

Only now, apparently, I was one, because a crime boss said so.

"I hereby call this meeting of the Outcast Academy student council to order." Since he didn't have a gavel, Rade banged his fist on the table.

Since our door was still covered in tons of dirt, which our students were having to dig out with shovels because we were afraid to try another *Shape Earth* spell to move it, our council had convened at a seedy tavern down the street. There were enough bitter drunks in the Slumps that the place was always busy. I liked to imagine the proprietor had promptly given us our own table because we were the respected new wizards in the neighborhood, but more than likely, it was because we had Trax with us, and everyone around here was terrified our Squalo might get upset and start eating people again.

"*I bit a few humans upon my arrival here—in self-defense, mind you—and I never hear the end of it.*"

"It's a cruel world, buddy."

"*Humans are very judgmental.*"

"Ahem. Chair has the floor." Rade, being a fake nobleman, enjoyed having a bit of decorum in our meetings. "Our first order of business is, of course, discussing Carnavon's volunteering us to work for the deadliest criminal organization in the Slumps."

"The word 'volunteering' makes it sound so... *voluntary*," Azarin said in my defense. "I doubt that was the case. Was it, Oz?"

On the walk here, I'd already told them how my meeting with Carcalla had gone. "What was I supposed to do? Tell Carcalla no?" Just my saying that name caused a dozen other patrons to glance our way nervously, and I hadn't even been talking loud. I leaned in a bit closer and lowered my voice. "Believe me when I say he's not the sort of fellow one haggles with. When Gaul Haddar gets back—"

"If," Azarin corrected.

"When, if, whatever, then Haddar will demand more respect than I got. With him back, we can renegotiate terms from a position of strength. In the meantime, it's just us and our merry band of rejects."

"Useless." Krachma rarely spoke during these meetings.

"Me or the students?"

Krachma nodded. *Yes.*

"I beat you in the arena, didn't I?"

The gigantic lob folded his massive arms, as he was still salty about that defeat. "War is not arena."

Our big guy might have been ready to fight to the death rather than bend the knee, but I knew our students wouldn't be nearly so keen on dying pointlessly. "If we threw down against the Latrocinium, it wouldn't be a war. I know the trade tongue isn't your strength, but the word *war* implies there being a fight. This would be more like us getting massacred a hundred to one, and our survivors—in the unlikely event there are any—getting run out of town."

Krachma shrugged. His peculiar sense of honor was probably fine with that kind of futile noble gesture.

"The other option is to leave," Rade suggested. "We pack our things and vanish into the night."

"You could. That's probably the smart thing to do. We're getting sent on a dangerous task by a very dangerous man. I wouldn't blame anybody for having the sense to get out while they can. But I vowed to become a mage, and after getting rejected by every prick in the Collegium, by some miracle, we found a way to make it on our own. I've got my whole family counting on me to buy their freedom, and I've worked too hard to turn back now. I'm staying."

Azarin nodded along as I said that. She'd left her realm because she'd angered her family and was too proud to go back as a failure. "I'm with Oz. I'll stick around. Weathering storms is what my people do best."

"Isn't your patron saint the one who watches over fools who make terrible decisions?" Rade asked rhetorically.

"That is among Naanwalla's duties to the gods, only I don't need the gods to tell me it's wrong to abandon my friends. I've put in too much work to hang it up now."

Me and Azarin had an odd relationship. She could be unpredictable as the wind. I liked her. I think she really liked me. She'd saved my life once, I'd repaid the favor. We'd even messed around a bit. But I was under no delusion she was sticking around just for me. Flighty as Azarin could be at times, she was adamant about becoming a real wizard, and wasn't going to return to her beloved Stormwolk until she could do so with pride, showing up everybody who'd ever doubted her.

Rade shrugged. "Let the record show that the follower of the saint of *bad choices* sees no problem with this plan."

"It's not so much a plan as an ultimatum," I said. "Carcalla's given us five days to clean the place out and bring him whatever treasure we find. We split that evenly, except for one thing. There's rumors of a particular item hidden there that he's interested in. He told me it would look like a lamp."

Azarin perked up at that. "Like the kind you rub and a genie comes out and grants you wishes?"

"Naw, more like a really big light charm."

"Well, that's boring… Why risk our lives for something that mundane? And how does he know it's still there? It could've been looted long ago."

Those were good questions, but it turned out that vicious crime lords weren't exactly forthcoming about their intelligence. "Carcalla said if we made it all the way to the lowest chamber, there'd be a secret door that's hard to spot, but he gave me what's supposed to be the magic password to open it. The good stuff should be undisturbed in there."

The relatively pretty serving girls brought our drinks out. They were usually happy to flirt with Rade, who loved putting on airs as the dashing duelist, but since Trax was present, they just dropped the mugs on the table and retreated as fast as possible. Well, *we* got mugs. Trax got a bucket of whatever raw viscera was left over in the kitchen. We didn't get charged for that bucket either. Trax's dinner was always on the house, because the locals believed a Squalo with a full belly would remain mellow, while a hungry Squalo was nothing but trouble.

"Thank you, ladies." Rade seemed sad to see the girls go. "Ah, as stalwart a companion as Trax may be, his savage demeanor tends to frighten off the local girls."

"*You are welcome,*" Trax sent obliviously as he sniffed his bloody dinner. "*Females will steal your food.*"

"Enjoy the drinks, because this is the last of our budget. After this, it's back to scrounging." It wasn't like we had official positions in this half-assed outfit, but I was nominally our treasurer, and that purse was empty. "So where do we all stand on our latest crisis?"

"I believe that's two for working with Carcalla." Rade waved one corpse-pale hand toward me and Azarin. Then at Krachma. "One vote for provoking an unwinnable war, I think."

"Krachma cares not," Krachma muttered. "Present Krachma enemy to kill. It will die."

"Splendid." I honestly believed Krachma to be a decent sort, but from what I'd heard, his people mostly survived by getting hired out as mercenaries, and since none of us knew where Krachma's many rocky scars had come from, he'd probably seen some shit.

"What do you think, Mr. Bloodtrail?" Rade asked.

Trax was busy pouring the contents of the slop bucket into his maw and chomping noisily. Bits were flying everywhere. It was scaring the other customers. "*Apologies, Carnavon. This gelatinous pig snout is delicious. What were you discussing?*"

Since nobody else could understand him, I simplified things. "Trax says he's voting with me and Azarin."

"*I do not know what is happening, but this sounds acceptable to me.*"

"The Squalo always agrees with you. Very well. It is decided. Though my vote is now meaningless, let the record show that Rade Tartaros, sword of the underworld, rightful heir of House Tartaros in exile, fears neither gangs nor cursed isles, and he shall fight for the honor of his academy, whether it be by gang war or adventuring."

"If we had a secretary writing things down, then that would surely be recorded in the minutes."

"Excellent." Rade seemed rather pleased with that. "I know you've got a sour outlook on the concept of adventuring, my friend, but I for one am not opposed to it. Adventuring is a fine opportunity to gain wealth and glory."

I should have known he would feel that way, because our deadlander was just as brash as the fools I'd guided to their doom. "Then let that same official record show that I think this is a terrible idea, except we're stuck, and if we're going to save the academy, I see no other choice. My recognizing this shitty reality doesn't mean I like our predicament one bit… If we're going to keep putting things on the record, I suppose we should elect a secretary to keep notes and make it official."

"Not it," Azarin said quickly.

"Krachma does not *write.*"

"Alas, my swordsmanship is better than my penmanship. How about you, Carnavon?"

"I'm already treasurer." Not that we ever had enough money for that office to matter. I looked to Trax. "Congratulations. You've been elected secretary of the Academy of Outcast's student council."

"*I have never held a title among humans before.*"

"Trax says he'll be honored to serve."

He stopped crunching a rotten ham hock long enough to look at me with his beady black eyes. "*Secretary? What does that word mean? Do I get to eat anyone?*"

His mission among the land creatures was to study our ways, and every night, he recorded his observations onto a magical crystal sphere which served the same purpose to him as a notebook would to us, since undersea creatures didn't have paper. "Just remember what we say in these meetings and put it on your thought globe thing."

"*I shall remember this extra hard.*"

"So as much as our situation stinks, and we're bound to get screwed somehow, we're in agreement about working with the Latros, then."

"I'm sure it will be fine, Carnavon," Rade assured me. "Remember our little jaunt to my homeland? A few hours of work netted us a tidy amount of Black—it would've been a fortune if my damnable relatives hadn't come along—and it was that very element which later saved your life from a corrupt inspector of the watch."

"I recall on that *little jaunt* a Death Elemental wanting to hollow one of us out to wear our corpse as a suit."

"That was but a small setback on our road to glory!"

Somedays I wished I'd just stayed a miner on a barge. "Alright, we're committed to this foolishness. Now, how do we get the students onboard after Joran scared the piss out of them?"

"I don't know if we can," Azarin said. "Two of them packed their things and walked out before you even got back from Carcalla's. The idea of being on the Latrocinium's bad side was enough to unnerve them."

I'd not known about the desertions. "Which ones left?"

"Nils and Luwan."

That was disappointing, as both of them had been halfway talented, and they hadn't done anything too annoying since we'd taken them in. The only thing keeping them from a spot in the real academies was that neither had come from money. "It's not a good sign that our smartest students were the ones to get out while they could. At least they shared their spells first. Too bad it wasn't some of the dumber ones abandoning us."

Rade laughed at our misfortune. "You're the one who keeps letting in every mangy stray. I know the Collegium's exclusionary nature insulted you, but there's a reason those schools are picky… Let me motivate the rest. I'll give a speech that'll put a fire in their bellies. Those who are cowards may leave. We're better off without them. Then we'll take all the brave souls who remain, and lay waste to the monsters on this island of whatever it's called."

"Korthican's Warning."

"Yes. We'll go there, slay our foes, retrieve Carcalla's treasure, and the reputation of our academy will grow across the city. Better recruits will flock to our door, bringing their superior spells and purses heavy with Obols!" Rade grinned at his grand vision. "That's settled. Now on to our second order of business."

"Let me guess," I said. "We're almost out of element, money, food, and every other resource needed to run a functioning school? And we really need some higher-ranking teachers to keep our morons from unleashing curses, but we can't afford to hire anyone, and only a sucker would volunteer to help the likes of us?"

Rade laughed. "That goes without saying, my friend! But this is *new* business."

The black-eyed, white-haired, corpse-looking people of the Elemental Plane of Death were supposed to be dour, but Rade was just so obnoxiously chipper that it was impossible to dislike the man.

"What now?"

"We must add to that list that we require the services of a tester as soon as possible. This issue can no longer be delayed."

"Rade's right," Azarin said. "Nobody worth a shit is going to join up unless there's a chance for them to advance. Achieving higher ranks opens more doors, and we're studying our butts off trying to get better. Except, even if we do manage to increase in skill, that means nothing until a tester makes it official."

The Testers' Guild was who determined just how capable a mage really was. They were a select group, paid by the various kingdoms to travel the realms, checking to see who was worth spending effort and element on to develop their magical skill. The only way to get promoted through the lower ranks of wizardry was by a tester's say so. With rank came respect and opportunities for more lucrative work.

"They're not cheap." It cost me a few ounces of prime element to bribe my way into a second test. "Anybody here friends with a tester?" I waited, but of course they weren't. Testers were rare, high-class specialists. We were us.

"Alas, I've never known anyone from that respected order."

"Wait… You've at least been tested, right?" Azarin gave Rade a suspicious look. "You told us you were a rank two."

"Forgive me. I misspoke." Rade easily laughed that off. "I met that one, obviously."

Come to think of it, Rade had produced about as much evidence of his magical prowess as he had his claimed noble lineage. He only knew a few spells and hadn't yet mastered any of the ones we'd shared with him.

"You must at least have your papers showing you're a two from when you got tested, right?"

"Tragically, I lost my papers in a boating mishap."

Of course he had. "Well, I did have a nice conversation with a tester in Fogo not too long ago. Tester Pivorotto seemed like a decent fellow. I don't know if he's returned to the Core yet, but I can check."

"Splendid. Secretary Trax, please note that Carnavon has promised to find a tester for us."

With congealed pig blood dripping down his face, Trax looked at me and sent, "*I will be the best secretary ever.*"

"Don't worry, my friends. We're likely to find so much treasure on this abandoned isle, that hiring this tester of yours will be easy. We'll sell our loot in the market—after our crime lord gets his cut, of course—and then we'll fill our coffers with element. We won't need to search out teachers, because they'll come to us. This is an exciting day for our merry band." Rade might be delusional, but I couldn't fault the man his enthusiasm. "I believe that concludes our new business. Anyone else? No? Then let us adjourn."

"Seconded," I said, because I had a whole lot of work to do.

Rade banged his fist on the table again, then lifted his mug high. "To adventuring!"

Caught up in the excitement, Azarin returned the toast. "To adventuring!"

Krachma didn't appear to understand what we were doing and frowned as Azarin banged her mug into his hard enough to spill a bit. Trax went back to slurping rotten pork bits. I resentfully, sullenly, lifted my mug and muttered, "Hooray, adventure."

7

This was the year 4581 AN, which stood for After Nexus. Our years had begun counting the day the Great Machine was activated, connecting the seven realms to the central Core. For over four and a half millennia, the mountain-sized Great Machine steadily turned. Each dawn, the Nexus gradually opened one of the gates around its base, connecting the Core City to another realm, until the gate slowly closed at sundown, and the Core was cut off for the night. The next morning, the process began again.

There were seven gates upon the Great Machine, one for each day of the week, and four corresponding gates inside each realm, scattered across various distant kingdoms. That meant the Nexus connected to twenty-eight different locations a month, thirteen months a year. I'd seen a grand total of two of those realms, Fogo for nineteen years, and Acheron for a few hours.

Around the Great Machine had been built a grand market where all the realms could trade their vital supplies. A thousand kingdoms' worth of merchants, coming and going, selling the products of their kingdoms, then taking home goods which came from whole other worlds.

Each realm produced one distinct magical element. By themselves, each of the seven were potent. Combined together, they could create miracles.

The Core City around the Great Machine had grown ever larger over those centuries. They'd filled the available land, terraced the mountains, and even built out over the sea. They erected great towers and castles so vast, they were like entire towns housed in a single building. As spell craft advanced, powerful wizards began building artificial islands suspended in the sky. There were dozens of these feats of magical engineering levitating above us today, housing tens of thousands, or maybe even hundreds of thousands. I wasn't sure how crowded they were. I'd never been to any of those because the City Watch wouldn't let someone of my impoverished nature past the checkpoints on those golden bridges.

Regardless, everyone knew the Core was the biggest, most populated, and most impressive city there'd ever been. Without the flow of trade through the market, many kingdoms—like my home of Fogo—would perish, because they simply couldn't survive on what they produced on their own. Trade was the only thing keeping those kingdoms alive. The city's majesty was reflective of its importance.

Sadly, after losing access to one of those seven realms—Time—and its corresponding element—Permeance—five hundred years ago, all that growth had slowed, and a creeping decay had set in. That was why the floating Upper Aventine was incrementally losing altitude—and accordingly been renamed the Slump—and was now threatening to flatten the Lower Aventine beneath—which was why that once prosperous district was now called the Under Slump. This was likely also what caused the mile-tall, gravity-defying, Tower of Primopolus to suddenly fall over one day, crushing whole neighborhoods beneath... Where I now lived in a section of that sideways ruin and had to pay the rent.

That pressing debt was why, that afternoon, I'd travelled to the Core City's southern bay. The long walk through several districts, past all that stately and historic architecture, was what brought to mind this history lesson. Nothing drove home just how large and old this city was quite like walking through part of it.

Once I reached the rocky cliffs overlooking the water, I got my first view of Korthican's Warning. I'd been told the island was a small tan lump of sand, only a few acres in total, with some crumbling structures and handful of trees atop it, about half a mile out... and that description was accurate.

The Core had been around for over four thousand five hundred and some odd years—I had no idea how long it took them to actually build the massive Great Machine before they turned it on—but those twenty-eight mighty wizards built this place upon a civilization that had already been old when they'd gotten here. According to Carcalla, this island was once home to a lighthouse even back then. And like most of those structures, it was ruins now.

I'd been in part of that ancient undercity once, though only briefly. I'd been trying my best to not get murdered by Linus Adderlane and a bunch of Tempus cultists the entire time, so I'd not been able to do much sightseeing. But, whoever built those structures had been advanced, capable of making things just as nice as the upper-class districts I'd strolled through. The dungeons beneath Korthican's Warning had been dug by that same mysterious civilization.

They were also cursed as fuck, which was why most sensible people left the place alone.

I'd come here to gather information about an island, but paused at the overlook to marvel for a while, because I had never actually seen an ocean before.

That was a *lot* of water.

Coming from the Elemental Plane of Fire, the vista before me was downright inconceivable. When a body of water formed in Fogo, it would boil away in no time. I'd nearly drowned in one of the city's canals, the water proving swift and overwhelming, and from here, five of those canals were visible, dumping into this bay. They were but a trickle compared to the big blue mass that seemed to go on forever.

The big crashy white parts must be waves. I'd never imagined water could be so *loud.* When the waves hit the rocks below, it threw salty mist into the air. Everything felt damp, and then I suddenly felt a whole lot colder, as the ocean breeze cut right through me.

It was too bad those old wizards hadn't decided to place the Nexus someplace warmer, but it seemed to be only those of us from the Elemental Plane of Fire who really struggled here. Everybody else got by fine. I was wearing a coat, cloak, scarf, and gloves, and was still freezing, but at least it'd stopped snowing.

There were many ships in the bay. Most had masts and rigging. The ones that didn't probably utilized magical means of propulsion. The concept of ocean-going ships wasn't too strange to me. They weren't that different in principle from the barges I'd grown up on, except these sat on top of water instead of levitating over lava. Seeing all these docked here reminded me of where the barges landed in Fort Silver.

My attention was irresistibly dragged back toward the ocean, because it was just so damned endless. And to think Trax came from an entire realm of this material, and his people lived far beneath its surface. I would have brought Trax with me, and he likely would've enjoyed having a nice swim, but people tended to get real nervous around Squalos, and I was here hoping to make friends.

"From the gawking, that's a man who just came through the gate and never seen the sea before."

I looked over to see a few men trudging up from the beach, carrying baskets of fish. The baskets were really full, which probably explained their good mood.

"You'd be correct, sir. I'm from Fogo."

"Ah, a hotlander. We don't get many of those 'round here."

"I had a great uncle was from Vuur," said another of the fishermen.

"We've all heard that story, Ted." Because fish are heavy, they kept walking, and I walked with them. The first one turned his attention back to me. "If you're looking for work, you're in luck. It's common knowledge you hotlanders love to get in fights once you're in port, but put one of you on a crew and he'll do the labor of any two regular men by himself."

It was nice to hear my people be complimented for once. Most Core dwellers focused on our reputation for fiery tempers and left out the dignified, stubborn, hard-working parts. "It's because when you grow up mining the Red, everything else seems downright safe and restful in comparison."

"If it's dock labor you're interested in, you'll need to talk to the foreman. For working the boats, best to catch the captains when they're in the pub and ask."

"Thank you kindly, but I'm already employed." Saying this next part made me want to gag. "I'm an adventurer. I'm putting together an expedition to Korthican's Warning."

They all had a good laugh at that, not too different a reaction from the one me and my trapper friends would've had in Fort Silver when someone asked us about travelling to our deadly, adventurer-consuming ruins.

"Don't do it. Everybody around here knows to stay away from that place!"

"I'd avoid that isle if I were you, son." That fisherman was the oldest of the lot. "Brave fools used to take a run at it ever so often, thinking there might still be riches within, but it got picked clean centuries ago, so they all got chewed up and spit out for no reason. It's been a few years since anyone's gone back."

"What do you mean by chewed and spit?"

"Well, gnawed-upon parts of them wash up on shore, so they didn't get swallowed!"

I couldn't say I was surprised the place was still infested with some manner of monster. "That's unfortunate to hear."

"You sure you don't want an honest job, lad?" their chief asked. "We're short-handed."

That was sorely tempting right now. "Thanks, fellas, but I've made a commitment. You got any idea what manner of critters were doing that gnawing?"

"Something with ripping claws. At least I'm guessing claws. Hard to tell when you only get a leg or a torso stuck in your nets. I'll tell you, it's a bit of a surprise, thinking you're hauling up a fish, and instead it's an adventurer's boot with his foot still in it."

It was a good thing they were so forthcoming with the stories, because I didn't even have enough coin left to buy them a round of drinks. "Being that you're short-handed, I'll help you unload your catch, if while we do so you keep telling me what you know about that place."

"We're not gonna turn down an extra pair of hands, and maybe once you hear what we have to say, we can talk you out of committing suicide."

8

After getting a few hours' sleep behind a barn, followed by a busy morning of prying stories out of folks who lived near the bay, I returned to the Under Slump armed with a bit of knowledge and a lot of trepidation.

The dead dirt monster had been shoveled out of the way and placed next to the tower's edge. Should we ever find a student with any knowledge of life magic, we'd be able to plant a garden there. It would surely take magic, because it wasn't like anything would grow naturally in this endless shade. I looked up toward the sky of pipes and foundations, and already missed the star-filled sky I'd slept beneath next to the bay. The Slump only descended a few inches a year, and was barely crunching the tops of our tallest buildings, but still, that oppressive weight somehow felt a bit heavier than when I'd left.

It was hard to believe I was embarking on such a dangerous endeavor for this place, but such is life.

Inside the Tube, I was greeted by one nervous student and an angry poltergeist, which threw a rock at me. I've got good reflexes, so I caught it, and hurled it back through the shimmering mist floating in the corner. "Fuck off, ghost."

Thankfully, it vanished, which made the room feel about ten degrees warmer.

"It's good that you have returned, Mr. Carnavon!" Morton Smorp was our gnome. He was a tiny fellow who only came up a bit over my knee. At forty, he was about twice my age, which meant he was still young by gnomish standards, but the oldest person here. Having tested as a rank two, Morton was supposedly more magically gifted than myself. Except he only knew two spells: a basic light spell—which wasn't particularly useful since light charms were so common and cheap—and a simple warding that chased off fleas and ticks, which admittedly wasn't going to win any arena fights, but was incredibly useful when you lived in a shit hole.

"I'm glad to be back."

Since Gaul Haddar had left me in charge, and gnomes were big on orderly protocol, Morton was constantly sucking up to me. Today would be no different. "We need your wise leadership. There is rebellion afoot!"

"What now?"

"Mr. Tartaros gave a very rousing speech last night. So moved by his call to action, I even shed a single tear. However, not all of the students agree about this adventuring business. Since you weren't here, some of them claimed that after Cutter Joran's threats, you'd fled in fear, abandoning the rest of us to our fate."

"Well, that's stupid." As a follower of Saint Persistence, the idea I'd be such a cowardly quitter was downright insulting. I'd have warned my friends first, *then* run.

"Indeed. I told all who would listen that Mr. Carnavon would never forsake this academy which he has strived so hard to organize. You should have them flogged for their impudence. I have kept a list of names—"

I stopped Morton before he could get the folded note out of his vest. "Nobody's getting flogged. We're being extorted by a crime lord. It's natural to grouse about that. Where's Azarin?"

"Last I saw, your lady was in the main chamber for the day's practice."

"Great. But don't call her my lady in front of her, or she's likely to hit you with a jolt stick."

"But I thought—"

"It's complicated, Morton."

"Forgive me. Human courtship remains a mystery to me."

"Yeah, me too."

"Among gnomes, the courting families simply enter into a period of prolonged contractual negotiations, debating the pros and cons of the arrangement for both family businesses until the two sides reach a mutually beneficial—"

"Now's not the time." He was nearly as bad as Trax telling me all I needed to do was kill some whales to impress Azarin. "Gather everybody else and send them to the main chamber. I've got to tell the whole school what we're up against."

"I believe they're already there, sir, but I shall check for stragglers."

I headed for the largest room in the Tube. The central stairwell that we used as our hall had loose dirt and gravel everywhere from the monster barreling down it, and most of the wooden platforms and ladders we'd cobbled together hadn't been repaired yet. Broken bits dangled everywhere. Seeing that destruction was profoundly depressing after having put in so much work.

There were enough windows and light charms floating above that our big space was kept bright. I discovered that most of our students were already there, though rather than practicing their spell craft, they were sparring. Which was surprising, because many of them weren't particularly skilled at violence. Today, it was mostly sticks wrapped in rags playing at sword fighting, and what looked to be some boxing and wrestling.

I was rather decent at the brawling, as Fogo folk have an instinctual love of beating the snot out of each other over petty grievances or rivalries, or just for fun, but I knew nothing about all that slashy, flashy sword business. Rade was our only trained swordsman.

All mages needed some way of defending themselves when their magic wasn't handy, and having been a trapper, I preferred the pragmatic application of bullets. There were a handful of firearms among us, but we lacked the money for practice ammunition. I had twenty rounds in the loops of my belt, and a few dismantled shells in the fire room I'd been experimenting with recently, and that was all.

Azarin quit her playing at combat and strolled over, happy to see me. "Good to have you back. How went the reconnaissance?"

"The locals were more helpful than I'd hoped. Turns out fishermen and stevedores are a talkative bunch. Only, the stories they told aren't exactly confidence inspiring. I'll give the rundown to the whole group. Why the fighting?"

"Practice for our adventuring. We figured we'd best save what element we've got left for our expedition rather than use any more up in practice."

"Smart." I watched the awkward flailing of some of our students. There were a few who could handle themselves. The rest, not so much. Our ten remaining students came from a wide variety of backgrounds, some of which apparently hadn't offered many opportunities to learn proper stabbing or head smashing. "They look ridiculous."

"That's what Krachma's been saying all morning."

"He's talking to them?"

"He's not really expounding; more like he paces around them as they spar, grunting out words like *awful* or *pathetic* over and over. I do think he's actually trying to teach them, though."

Krachma was probably our most experienced combatant, and other than his single loss to me, he had the best record in the arena of any of us. I'd only bested him by trickery. In a straight-up battle where I couldn't fake him out with magic, he'd probably have ripped my arm off and beaten me with it, as he'd done to one poor bastard while rescuing Azarin from Adderlane's hired goons.

As I watched, the lob stopped two stick fighters. He shook his head angrily, took Bognar's stick away, and showed him the correct way to thrust it like a short sword. When he handed it back, that student promptly stuck Danny hard in the gut with it. The injured student fell to his knees, gasping, and I think for just a moment, Krachma might have smiled a little at his suffering.

"By the saints, I think Krachma's enjoying himself."

She grinned. "I think we might've finally found something the big fellow is good at here."

Trax was probably more dangerous than Krachma, but what was Trax going to teach these people to improve themselves? Simply move with inhuman speed and bite the enemy with your rows of razor teeth while letting their daggers bounce uselessly off your resilient aquatic hide? I'm sure such tactics would work out splendidly for our soft land dwellers.

Krachma picked out another student, adjusted his grip, then showed him how to block an overhand blow, turn into it, and slice his opponent across the neck. He actually nodded approvingly when the student did it correctly by himself. *Krachma satisfied?* That was a first.

It wasn't magic, but they were learning something useful, and sweating builds character. It pained me to have to interrupt the fun, but it was time to make my speech. By dumb luck, these people were my responsibility, so I wasn't about to send them on a fool's errand, blind.

"Alright, listen up!" I walked to the center of the room. "Here's the plan."

I'm a pretty good talker, by Fogo standards at least. I tried to remember how my father used to call the shots on Barge 519, because though he hadn't been our bargemaster, he'd been our real leader. Men had trusted him with their lives. There could be lava shooting up over the sides, and he'd keep them calm, focused on the work, and even make them laugh to break the tension. I was no Myles Carnavon, but I was his son, so I'd try to make him proud.

"Contrary to rumors some of you circulated, Ozwald Carnavon is no quitter." From the way Bognar and Rufus looked at their feet as I said that, I knew who'd been muttering behind my back; Morton hadn't even needed to make his list. "However, I hold no resentment toward any among you who grumbled, because I'm not overjoyed about our predicament either. The Latrocinium has got us over a barrel. I don't know what Rade told you about our deal last night, but it was either take this job or disband the academy."

I'd not noticed Rade sitting at the back of the room, wiping the sweat from his brow with a rag. "It was a rather moving speech, if I do say so."

"I'm sure it was stupendous. Anyways, if any of you have got no stomach for this sordid alliance with the Latrocinium, it's best for you to leave now, and there'll be no hard feelings. Because we're going to have to pay a hundred Obols or do something of this dangerous nature for the Latrocinium every month from now on, or face eviction."

There was a whole lot of swearing at that, because apparently, Rade's call to adventure speech left out some minor pesky details. Like, how we were on the hook forever. It was ironic, as I was playing at being a leader like unto my dad, who'd had to handle the difficult day-to-day challenges aboard our barge, he'd had Bargemaster Gax who concerned himself more with the *big picture*, just how I had Rade. Such was life.

"However, I have negotiated that this first expedition erases our previous months' back rent—trogshit that may be—and wipes our debt clean. I've also negotiated that other than one specific item that Master Carcalla believes might be present which he in particular wants, any other treasure we find will be split evenly between the Latros and the Outcasts. Our half will be split in even shares among every one of us."

Oh, they liked that part. Too bad I was about to ruin it for some of them.

"And by *us*, I mean those who go and participate in the dangerous bits. Henceforth, we're having to change a few things around here. We can afford to give no more free rides. If you're part of this academy, you're earning your keep. Everybody chips in somehow or you're out. If you're not willing to delve beneath a haunted island, find another way to bring us a bunch of coins to make up for it. Sharing the formula to a spell got you in here, but it won't pay for your element, our time, resources, or especially now, your rent. Got it?"

They seemed to. We might lose those who were inclined to laziness or cowardice, which I was fine with. I'd been put to work crawling lava tubes looking for Red dust when I was a little boy. I had no patience for shirkers.

"This isn't the Collegium, land of silk and comfort. We took you in when no other school would, so by the sweat of your brow, you shall earn your keep. And if your only spells aren't that strong and you're physically weak…" I couldn't help that my eyes drifted toward tiny Morton as I said that. "Come and talk to the student council and we'll figure out something useful for you to do."

Rufus the dwarf raised his hand. "When does Gaul Haddar get back?"

"Same answer as last time you asked me that. I don't know. If you're tired of waiting for the mighty rank ten to come and teach you correctly, feel free to leave. Thc front door is currently unblocked by the corpse of the monster you embiggened yesterday. And this isn't an interview. Shut your trap and listen."

Rufus slowly put his hand down.

"Good. We've got four days to clear out the dungeon beneath Korthican's Warning and loot it of valuables. Carcalla told me a bit about it, but being the untrusting sort, last night, I went to the bay to hear what the locals have to say about the place. Sadly for us, their tales match. The city's condemned that isle, same as our beloved Under Slump, so the watch leaves it be. But while our home is infested with robbers and ratlets, that island's got some kind of deadly carnivorous amphibious creatures living upon it."

"You say that like it is a bad thing," Sifuso exclaimed, offended on behalf of his kind.

"Apologies." I nodded toward our lacertian's hurt feelings. "Not all carnivorous amphibians are bad, obviously. My best friend is a carnivorous amphibian."

If Trax had been present, he wouldn't have been offended. Whether they ate plants or meat, walked or swam, Squalo considered most other intelligent races to be food. Call a Squalo a deadly carnivore and they'd take it as a compliment.

"These monsters are unidentified. They hide in the tunnels or underwater during the day, and on rare occasion swim out to menace the locals at night. They sometimes kill livestock and have got no problem ripping up a full-grown pig or goat, but they don't attack the people very often. At least not enough to for the watch to care about exterminating them."

"That doesn't sound too unmanageable." Of course, Azarin had an upbeat outlook. She came from a realm where griffons constantly swooped down to pluck travelers from the mountainside to drop down steep cliffs. To her, danger was a relative thing.

"*Unless* people set foot on the island. Then the creatures immediately swarm and rip them apart."

She sighed. "I should've known to adjust my expectations."

"The bay folk who've seen them say the monsters are about four to five feet tall, but they walk hunched over and shuffling. They're slimy, and dark blue or green in color. They've got big bulby eyes that poke out the sides of their heads, beaks like birds, and long floppy arms with claws on the end. They make a kind of a *scritch* noise when they're sneaking up on you… Anybody know what those are?"

All I got was a bunch of head shakes. Our students came from six different realms and the Core, so I'd hoped to get lucky and someone would know. From the description, I figured the monsters had come from the Elemental Plane of Water originally, so Trax might know. Sadly, he was off doing his own thing, most likely observing humanity from the safety of one of the city's many canals.

"Besides the unknown creatures who've moved in, after that, there's the matter of any traps or curses the ancients may have left behind. The locals couldn't help me there. Do any of you have any experience with that sort of thing?"

They shared awkward glances—of course nobody did. That was a rather select skillset, and if they were good enough to get paid for that, they certainly wouldn't be slumming it here.

"Then we'll figure that out once we get down here." I tried to sound more confident than I was. "We've got four days to prepare. If you've got any bright ideas, come and talk to me, because Waterday morning, we're earning the rent."

9

When you ask a gaggle of would-be mages if they've got any bright ideas to solve a problem, be forewarned, you are about to receive a deluge of the dumbest concepts imaginable. Those inclined toward wizardry as a profession are not, as a rule, stupid, but rather they're so smart that their intellect becomes uncoupled from the pesky facts of reality.

I don't know how many times that day I had to tell someone, no, we can't afford that sort of enchantment, or no, we have insufficient element to accomplish that, or no, none of us know a spell that can pick the whole island up and fly it to shore... And each time when I was done, the look of defeat on their once hopeful face made me feel like I'd just shot their pet unicorn.

Rufus Rudnik, self-proclaimed *war mage*, may have been dumber than a bag of rocks, but he'd at least come up with a respectable suggestion. We needed money for supplies. Some of our students thought they were capable of earning money as gladiators, but had never worked up the courage to risk it. Let's go fight and hopefully get paid. Which was what brought a group of us to the market side of the Under Slump that night.

This was Skerret family territory, and after my unfortunate encounters with my rat bastard countrymen, I wouldn't go to this side of the Under Slump without a bunch of friends. The Skerret family had gotten banished from Fogo for being crooks, and now they were one of the many smaller gangs infesting the Slumps who paid taxes to Carcalla. Hopefully, the Skerrets had gotten word that us Outcasts had come to terms with the Latrocinium, so in the off chance I did run into one of them, they'd overlook their resentment against me long enough to not do anything foolishly violent enough to anger our local crime boss.

But you know what they say about us hotlanders!

I kept my scarf over my face and my hood over my head as we walked, in the hopes of not being recognized. And if I was picked out of the crowd by a wrathful member of the Skerret gang, I had Krachma, Rade, Rufus, Danny, Bognar, and Sifuso with me. The Skerrets had quite a few men, but my group consisted of seven gladiators—well, three with a few fights under our belts and four rookies, but we've all got to start somewhere.

There were several fighting arenas around the Slumps. The Livnight mage fights were held just off the ramp down from the grand market. That put us only a few blocks from the notorious Crumpled House, home of the Skerret gang, but as Rufus had so helpfully pointed out, if we were going adventuring, we needed to buy more element, and fast. Other than robbery—and I put my foot down against that sort of behavior—there was no faster way to make some coin in the Slumps than fighting in the arena. So, as it stood, us three with a bit of experience, and the new guys who'd been eager to try their hand at mage fighting, found ourselves at this particular arena.

We had to use up our own magic in the arena, but even if you lost, you got five percent off the house. Even losers usually broke even on the element use, unless of course you wasted too much magic, or put on a bad show that the crowd didn't bet much. But if you won, it was twenty percent. The better the match, the more people would bet, which equaled more coins in your pocket at the end of the night. Slump fight crowds were pretty bloodthirsty and even upper-class citizens from the finer districts would come down here to watch us low-ranking fighters injure each other. Our magic wasn't nearly as potent or refined down here, but everyone loved to watch a good vicious beating.

The biggest danger in a mage fight—especially in these shoddy conditions—was that if the protective charm the goblins issued you fizzled and failed to stop a blow, you'd get crippled or die. But that didn't happen *too* often. Deaths were bad for business, as it scared off competitors. From what I'd learned about Carcalla's nature, he didn't tolerate failure. If a goblin enchanter screwed up too many times, he'd end up in the canal chained to the corpse of the last gladiator he'd let down, along with some concrete to make sure neither of them would float.

Because the Great Machine had been aligned with the Elemental Plane of Life all day, the air actually smelled nice, as opposed to the usual stink of garbage and piss common to this trash-strewn section of the Under Slump.

"What is that lovely fragrance?" Rade asked.

"That there's the scent of wildflowers upon the wind," Rufus said. "I'm from the Realm of Life, so I know it well. Today, the gate's pointed at our sister city, Hutan upon the Gunang. It's a thousand miles south of my home, but it's a place that's ever green."

"Mine is ever on fire," I said.

"My homeland is also always green. Same as lacertian skin," Sifuso hissed. "Better to hide in ambush waiting to strike."

"Acheron is cloaked in an endless fog," Rade said, not to be outdone. "And teeming with the restless dead."

"Krachma had only dirt."

Young Danny shrugged. "I was born like twelve blocks that way. I'm not exotic like you guys."

"Core City, me self." Big Bognar pointed up toward the Slump. "You can probably see me mum's basement from here."

Rufus couldn't let us get the wrong impression that he'd led a sheltered life. "Don't let the name of my realm fool you. Our element makes things grow, fast and concentrated, so the place is teeming with life, but for one thing to live, something else must die to feed it. It's a savage, wild land, with deadly predators lurking behind every tree, and Bergwald's got a great many trees!"

I caught sight of a few ruffians watching us at the mouth of the next alley. "We've got no trees in the Under Slump, but we've still got predators a plenty."

They were clearly searching for a victim to shank and roll, but when they saw the size of our group, and that one was a rock-scarred lob and the other a tall lizard beast, they took their hunt in the opposite direction.

It annoyed me that bandits could be so brazen here, but the Slumps were a lawless place. We'd surely have more students if we weren't in such a bad part of town. The watch wouldn't ever come down these ramps because, officially, this neighborhood didn't exist anymore, so it was all poor folks with nowhere else to go, getting picked on by violent scum.

"It shouldn't be like this. Someday, when the Outcast Academy has grown strong, we're going to clean this place up."

"That's what I like about you, Mr. Carnavon, sir. You dream big," Danny said.

We reached the arena. I'd not fought at this particular venue yet, but Krachma and Rade both had. Every mage fighting arena was set up a bit differently. This one was a big pit that had once been a quarry. There were a bunch of stone blocks haphazardly scattered around the bottom to provide cover and give some variety to the terrain. The contestants had to climb the scaffolding along the sides to get up and down. A rambunctious crowd stood around the top, cheering for their favorite or booing their enemy, as goblins moved between them taking bets.

The line for aspiring fighters was short tonight, so the goblins were excited to see so many of us show up at once. From their reaction, Carcalla hadn't preemptively cut us off from fighting. I knew if I hadn't agreed to his demand for adventurers, the bouncers would be tossing us out of here.

The goblin bookie waddled over to examine us. Like most goblins, he was short and hideous, with huge ears, and limbs that should be too long and spindly to support his ponderous gut.

"Ah, I know this ponderous lob. Krachma the Killer, a fan favorite. What're you now, six-and-one?"

"Seven."

Then he squinted up at me. "And you're the upstart who beat him, the mysterious Put Down Tom."

It was a dumb name, used by accident, but not wanting to lose my record, I'd kept it. "I'm three-and-oh."

"Nice to see you two made friends." Then he scowled at Rade. "I remember you, knife of the dark below or something."

"You know damned well it's *Sword of the Underworld.* I've fought here before, Clotz."

"You deadlanders all look the same to me: bloodless, pale, demon-eyed freaks. What's your record now?"

"An undefeated four."

"No it's not. I watched you lose to Veroy Durrel back in tenth month."

"That one doesn't count. Veroy cheated or your shitty goblin magic failed." Rade pulled open the neck of his black shirt to display a big scar. "I had to pay the Olgaites for a healing. If this happens again, I'm blaming you."

Goblins had a malicious giggle. "He he he. Splat, right in the throat!"

I cut in before Rade got mad enough to duel a bookie. I wasn't too worried about fighting one goblin, but rather his hundred nearby friends. "We've brought some fresh faces for you tonight."

The goblin scowled at Bognar and Danny, neither of whom looked like they'd put up a good fight, but then he grinned a mouth full of crooked yellow teeth when he sized up Sifuso. "A lacertian? The crowd loves the lizards. Make sure to do that hissing thing your kind does and show them the fangs!" Then he snarled at Rufus. "This crowd is bored of dwarves. It's always dwarves, dwarves, dwarves. I'm stocked up on short, fat dummies with beards tonight. Come back next week."

"How dare—"

I stepped in front of Rufus to keep him from strangling the goblin. "Oh, you're going to want this one, Clotz. This is no ordinary dwarf. This here's a Clan Rudnik *war mage.*"

"What's that?"

I honestly had no idea, other than Rufus was bafflingly proud in claiming to be one. "Only the baddest of the bad, axe-swinging maniacs from a realm full of monsters lurking behind every rock and tree."

"Hmmm..." The bookie scratched his booger-colored chin with his cracked dirty fingernails. "The announcer can work with that." Then he turned and shrieked at one of his assistants, "Bounce that other dwarf off the roster and put this uglier one in his place."

"Which is which?" that goblin asked. "They're all ugly."

"This one. The fatter one," Clotz pointed at Rufus. "He's hideous."

I should have warned the new guys that arena goblins were notoriously mean little shits. It was a good thing Trax had never accompanied me to a mage fight, because with his tolerance for rudeness, he'd end up eating these obnoxious bastards like they were popped corn. I'd thought about bringing my Squalo friend, because there probably wasn't a fighter the goblins could scrape up from the Slumps who could best him in a fight, but Trax, being Trax, would probably end up biting his opponent's head off or something equally lethal, which would get the locals even more spun up about him, and our lives were complicated enough already.

"Your group benefits me, Put Down Tom. It was looking to be a slow night, but Krachma is main event worthy, and the rest of you have filled my undercard."

I'd watched my dad barter with enough merchants for barge supplies to recognize an opportunity when I saw it. "I expect a bonus for the finder's fee at the end of the night."

"For bringing me two stupid boring humans? Look at them! They don't even have any extra arms! Can they even do magic? And another damned dwarf?"

"Don't forget the lizard. He's terrifying. Bonus percent or all seven of us walk and you're back to searching the gutter for passed-out drunks to throw in the pit."

"I don't need your army of scrubs!"

Rufus tugged on the back of my cloak and whispered, "Carnavon, what are you doing?"

I smacked Rufus' hand away. "I'm not playing around, Clotz."

The goblin growled at me as he considered my ultimatum. "So these fools have got themselves a manager. Fine. You'll get an additional percent on every match of these seven fighters." He spit a gob of phlegm on his hand and held it out.

"Deal." I pulled my glove off, spit on my palm, and we shook on it. As soon as the nasty little thing let go of me, I wiped my hand on my pants.

10

Danny was our first to fight. He fought about as well as a pimple-faced, gangly, teenage rank one could be expected to... As in, he lost in under a minute.

For tonight's earlier fights, which didn't have as much crowd interest, the goblins were using protective charms that had only two charges. When the user got hit with a blow sufficient to pass his own magical defenses and still maim or kill, the goblin enchantment kicked in, enveloping them in a magical shield. Of course, for the enjoyment of the crowd, those charms had the extra bonus of making it so the user still felt all the pain of the injury, even if they didn't receive any of the actual damage.

I was just proud that poor young Danny didn't wet his pants in public when he got nailed with a minor lightning spell. It was a snap and pop and then he'd gone flying back into a big white stone so hard that the goblin charm activated to keep him from breaking his spine. He'd tried to come back from that by hitting his opponent with his icy slow spell, but once again, his aim was off, and an empty patch of ground was frosted instead. Then he'd gotten clobbered over the head with a sword that bounced off the goblin charm's second activation. That ended the match, but not Danny's life.

Rade was sitting next to me on the scaffolding. "You know, I've never thought to check the lad's eyesight. Danny might actually be part blind."

Having just felt a terrible shock of electricity and a blow to the noggin that would've spilled out his brains had it been real, four goblins were having to carry the incoherent Outcast from the arena.

I shouted, "Hey, Danny! How many fingers am I holding up?"

He looked up at me, blinking rapidly, as if he might cry. "I can't rightly tell, Mr. Carnavon."

The correct answer had been three. "You might be onto something, Rade." Then I shouted at Danny again, "Good try. Excellent show."

We awaited our turn with the rest of the night's fighters staged on the platforms, while our opponents waited on the other side of the pit across from us. On the bookie's chalkboard, I'd seen that I was up against someone named Dathka Shadow Walker, which was an ostentatious name belonging to a fighter I'd never heard of. That was most certainly a fake name like many of us amateur gladiators used in the arenas. Though he had one more win than I did, the current odds favored me slightly, which made me suspicious.

"Do you know Dathka Shadow Walker?"

"I don't, which is odd, as there's not that many of us deadlanders foolhardy enough to do this. A ring name like that has got to be from my realm." Rade's people had a lot of spells based on manipulating darkness and causing fear, and they really liked to lean into that. "He's got you both as rank ones on the board, but I wouldn't be surprised if Clotz intends to give you some payback for squeezing him. He might be serving you up to some professional killer who's really a three or four."

Because I'd finagled an extra percent out of Bookie Clotz, bringing in a ringer to teach me a lesson sounded like something he'd do. "Vindictive little bastards, goblins."

"You know, if you're destined for defeat, we could take advantage of this treachery, Carnavon."

"You going to go bet against me, Rade?" That might be the savvy thing to do, but I had too much pride for that. In any fight, I'd do my honest best and take my honest loss. I wouldn't sully it with even a suggestion that I'd thrown it. I was the only Carnavon in the Core, and my family were in an entirely different plane of existence. Despite that, if I did such a thing, they'd surely hear about it somehow and I'd never live down the indignity. Among my people, it was more respectable to be a thieving murderer than to take a fall in a brawl.

"I was just thinking through the mathematical possibilities."

"Don't you fucking dare."

Rade feigned offense. "It was merely an idea. I would *never* do such a thing."

"Good. I'd hate for my victory to be the reason you go broke again."

Several different-colored light charms drifted to the center of the arena to place extra eye-catching illumination upon the announcer, who was using some kind of enchantment to magnify his voice so the entire crowd above could hear him.

"Ladies and gentlemen, our next combatant is homegrown from the Slump above, joining us in his debut appearance, a rank-one conjurer, knowing potent spells of earth and water, I give you, *Big Bognar*!"

The announcer was so good at his job, he even made Bognar sound like a real contender. In reality, Bognar was a bit of a schlump. He lived up to his nickname by being big, but it was that awkward, chunky, tripping-over-his-own-feet sort of bigness. To be fair, Bognar was strong, as he'd been a carpenter's assistant before deciding to follow his dreams of becoming a wizard. He knew a grand total of two spells, neither very well, so if he pulled this match out, it would be through beating the other fellow with his mace. And he'd even had to borrow the mace from Krachma.

The crowd clapped a bit for him, probably out of pity.

"What're the odds on this match?" I asked Rade.

"Five to one against Bognar."

"You didn't bet on him, did you?"

"Oh, saints no. I wouldn't bet on Bognar tying his shoes correctly."

"And upon the south scaffold, coming all the way from the wild Sajetti of the Elemental Plane of Air, a rank-one transmuter, with a Slump fight record of two wins and zero losses, follower of the Saint of Storms, *Garshab 'Griffon Slayer' Falamazarian*!"

That name was a mouthful, and the spectators reacted with only mild enthusiasm. Except then the airlander dove from the *top* of the scaffold, plummeted headfirst toward the ground, to stop in midair only a few feet from impact, do a flip, and land on his feet, which caused the crowd to go wild.

"Bognar's about to die," Rade stated.

"You never know. This other guy might be all flash, no meat to him."

The airlander got a running start, leapt ten feet into the air, and threw a weirdly shaped knife that smacked Bognar right in the face.

"Or, maybe not."

Twenty seconds later, Bognar was getting used as a pin cushion by some spell that turned the air into a cloud of stabbing needles. It looked like a remarkably painful way to end the match.

"There's no way that's a low-level spell," I muttered. "Rank one, my ass."

"To be fair, my friend, you yourself know a disturbing number of exceedingly destructive spells for a rank one."

Rade had me there, and the way this night was looking, I might be busting out a snail grenade before it was over, but I was still suspicious. "When we get a tester, I bet I'll make it to two now. But how come none of our recruits show up with talent like that guy?"

"Give it time. Soon, our academy will be famous throughout all the realms, and the best of the best will come, hat in hand, eager to train with us."

Up next was a dwarf against a gnome. As soon as the announcer said *fight,* the gnome immediately pulled a small handgun and shot at the dwarf.

When I'd first heard about mage fights, I'd been surprised that firearms were allowed, but the rules said any regular weapons or spells were useable. With magical enchantments that protected against bullets being relatively common and popular in the Core, anybody who was serious about making it in the arena invested in one, so guns weren't as big of an advantage as you'd think.

Which the dwarf demonstrated, as the bullet fragmented off the shield created by one of his enchanted items. It didn't even get close enough to his skin to activate the goblin charm. Then the dwarf conjured a water spout out of thin air that spun the gnome until he nearly drowned, before cutting it and slamming the poor little fellow against the ground. The dwarf didn't even use magic to finish the fight. He simply walked over while the gnome was coughing up water, picked him up by the ankles and started slamming him back and forth between two stone blocks, like he was beating the dust out of a rug.

Sifuso's match was next. And it was… underwhelming.

Lacertians have a reputation for being vicious ambush killers, taking down prey with fangs and claws, and they are really scary to look at, all scaley and reptilian, with their weird hungry eyes. I didn't know if that mystique was a lie and if it was all lacertians who were cowardly, or just ours.

When Sifuso walked into the arena, with so many eyes upon him, his knees started to shake. It was clear he had already lost his nerve. His yellow eyes were darting about wildly, like he was overwhelmed by the crowd watching him. Normally, our lacertian stood tall, but he was currently crouched, like he wanted to hide.

"Oh, that's not looking good," Rade said.

Sifuso had drawn a young man from the Cantor District, which was somewhere on the other side of the market. The announcer said he was an *unleashed descendent*, which was some kind of disciple of Saint Violence, but I wasn't really a church-going sort, and didn't know much about the various sects. It turned out this kid had picked the appropriate saint to follow, because he was so mean that he spent the next ten minutes chasing our lacertian all over the quarry.

It was a terrible match. It opened with Sifuso lunging in for a quick stab, getting slapped for his efforts, and that must have scared him into timidity. Sifuso was quick, but all that speed was good for was to scurry out of the way or clamber up the stone blocks to try and hide on top. At one point, he even climbed our side's scaffolding and clung there, thirty feet up as the kid shouted at him to come down and fight. The angry audience threw trash and bottles at Sifuso. Eventually, two goblins came down the ladders and poked at Sifuso with poles until he was forced back down into the quarry. When he finally got caught, the human threw him down and beat him mercilessly until both charges activated, and then the goblins had to come out and break them up, because the kid wanted to beat him some more, just out of frustration.

The crowd seemed relieved it was over.

"Well, that was embarrassing." Rade was barely audible over the booing. "Maybe lizard men are only bold when they can strike unseen."

"I don't know, but at oh-and-three… I'm sensing a disturbing trend developing with our students' matches tonight." It wasn't looking like my new career of fight manager was going to work out.

There were a couple more fights before our next Outcast was up, so I studied the gladiators on the other side of the pit, trying to guess which one was Dathka Shadow Walker. The name suggested a deadlander, but I didn't see anyone that pale over there. Except there were a few who—like me—hid their weapons under cloaks and their faces beneath hoods. Better to keep the fighters mysterious, I suppose. Though for me, the attempt at disguise was more about dodging vengeful Skerrets.

Then it was Rufus' turn.

"Well, let's see how our *war mage* does."

"Don't get too hopeful," Rade pointed out. "His opponent's favored four-to-one."

Our dwarf was up against a muscular orc, who had a winning record, and carried a gigantic polearm with a nasty hook on the end. When they met in the center, Rufus only came up to the big green guy's chest.

"I can see why."

The announcer got out of the way. The challengers went to their respective scaffolds. The match started. And then Rufus surprised the hell out of me.

"*FOR RUDNIK!*"

Rufus ran across the arena floor, straight for the orc, who invoked a beam of fire. Like me, the orc must have had an affinity for fire magic. Rufus' beard got singed as he rolled out of the way. He popped right back up, launching his own spell. A cloud of stinging sand flew into the orc's face, causing his next fire spell to go wild, slashing across the scaffolding and setting nearby ropes on fire.

Rade yelped as we got hit by sparks. I smiled, because that just felt like home.

As Rufus slammed the end of his axe against the ground, he shouted, "*Crush!*"

A wave of dirt rose up and slammed into the orc's legs, sending him stumbling. That spell worked a lot better on bipeds than Elemental Earth Spirits! That distraction was all it took for Rufus to be on him, swinging like he was chopping wood. There was a flash as the orc's own enchantment stopped a hit, followed by another, and then Rufus had hacked through the orc's protective spells, and the goblin's charm stopped the last blow.

The crowd all stood up at what would've been a disemboweling axe wound to the guts.

Rufus seemed stunned by the cheering, and from the look on his face, I realized this might be the first time in his life he'd heard anything like that. He lifted one fist and pumped it in the air. "*FOR RUDNIK!*"

Then the two of them went at it again, and it was a great match. They circled, continuously striking and blocking. Fire lanced and rocks flew. They went for five straight minutes like that, dripping sweat and burning element. I'd underestimated our dwarf, that was for sure.

"Go Rufus!"

The orc managed to hook one of Rufus' legs with his polearm and yanked him off his feet. Rufus landed on his back, and the orc slashed him hard across the chest. Unlike the orc, Rufus had no extra protective enchantments—that wasn't one of the spells any of us Outcasts knew yet—and the hit went straight to the goblin charm.

It was now down to the last good blow, and both fighters were hurting. The crowd was loving it. So, I figured, why not? And started chanting, "Rudnik! Rudnik!" Rade joined in, and it caught on with the fans above. Quickly, the chant filled the quarry.

Rufus blinded the orc with more sand, slammed him sideways with a surge of dirt, then ran up a boulder to jump and put axe to neck so hard that if the goblin's enchanter hadn't done his job right, the orc's head would've flown across the arena.

The mighty orc fell, and a star was born.

"*Rudnik! Rudnik! Rudnik!*" Crowds loved getting surprised by an underdog.

"That ought to be a nice payout." When Rufus looked our way, I gave him the most respectful up-nod I could, brawler to brawler. There was no way he could hear me over the noise of the crowd chanting the name of his clan, so I said, "Well, now I feel bad for thinking he was a blustering dummy."

"He's still a dummy. You were just wrong on the blustering part. That boy can *fight.*"

A goblin swung his head over the scaffolding from above. They were even uglier upside down. "Put Down Tom, you're on deck. Time to kit up."

"Good luck, Carnavon. I promise to not place any bets against you in your absence."

11

When you grow up in a barge cadre, you fight your brothers and all the other kids aboard; all in good fun, of course. And whenever your cadre lands, and the work is done, you fight all the boys from the other barges too. That's just how it is. Then, as adults, we keep doing the same thing, just the work gets harder and the brawls turn bloodier, depending on how much drink everybody's got in them, at least. We do back-breaking labor, then we fight at the slightest provocation, then we go back to work. That's just the Fogo way, and probably one of the reasons my people have got the bad reputation we do here in the Core.

Except in my experience so far, the Core was actually the meaner of the two places. By that, I mean the nature of the people who lived there, not the realms themselves. Fogo's unforgiving, and will kill you the instant you get careless, and sometimes kill you even if you're not, but most of the people who lived there were decent. You could be tough without being cruel. We'd knock a guy senseless over a dumb argument, but the next day, we have to go back to work with him on the same crew, and our lives depended on each other doing our jobs, so no hard feelings. Murder was rare among the cadres, and when we had somebody who did real evil, we'd toss them over the side into the lava for everyone's benefit. If a whole family turned rotten—like the Skerrets and Roches had—we'd banish the lot of them. Our nobles were pricks and we had crooks like Smiling Jemmy, same as everywhere else, but most cadre folk were like one big rough family.

Here in the Core, though, where the population came from a thousand kingdoms and three dozen species, most didn't like each other much before they got here, and cramming them in tight next to each other didn't improve those feelings any. Generally, people here struck me as more spiteful and petty. Bloodshed and treachery were common. There was a vindictiveness to this place. It might not all be that way, but the poor parts I'd spent time in were, and even the glorious Collegium was dismissive and unkind.

I suspected that, long ago, the mage fights had become a thing here so the different group's champions could fight each other rather than the masses having at it. Instead of real battles, which tended to get messy and upset trade, the Nexus Council encouraged magical duels that kept the death toll at a minimum and the destruction confined to one controlled space. Mage fights weren't just a Slump thing. These were unofficial bouts run by gangsters for the lowest of the low, but they also did this sort of thing in the fancier districts, except those were held in great golden arenas, featuring far more powerful wizards who could put on a real show for the much more respectable audience.

One of these days, I'd be up there too, but tonight, I was fighting for the pocket change of the Under Slump dregs.

Watching the other bouts had been a good distraction. As the ring goblin was checking my protective charms, I began feeling the nerves. I'd fought my whole life, but stopping fists and knees with my face was a lot less frightening than getting pierced with bullets, steel, and spells, which would theoretically be blocked only by the tarnished necklace placed around my neck by a cross-eyed goblin who I was fairly certain was drunk.

I was primarily an enchanter, which meant I had to cast my spells beforehand, binding them to objects to be activated later. I did a quick inventory of my equipment to make sure everything was where it was supposed to be, and I'd not gotten pickpocketed while awaiting my turn.

On my hip, I had the ceremonial handgun given to me by my old bargemaster, Davis Gax, before I fled to the Core. The ornate thing had 519 carved on the side, a reminder of where I'd come from. It held one of my precious cartridges in its chamber, and the rest were in loops on my belt.

Beneath my cloak I wore a vest that I'd purchased from the market, because it had a great number of pockets and pouches. I kept a small bag of Red on each side for the one invoked spell I knew. I had four different pockets' worth of enchanted screws ready to scoop and throw, as well as some *Obscura* balls—which was a simple shadow spell I'd gotten from Rade—and I'd brought a single snail grenade, just in case. That last one I would most likely *not* be using tonight because one of the few rules of the arena was no killing of the audience. Carcalla was displeased by the death of paying customers, and my snail grenades would be an extremely dangerous spell to unleash in public.

Sheathed opposite my gun was the same trapper's knife I'd been using to carve up the corpses of dead Fire Elementals for the last few years, and next to it were two small copper rods, enchanted with a spell recently taught to me by Azarin. I'd not quite mastered *Jolt* yet, so hoped I wouldn't need to test it tonight.

Then I checked my charms. The most valuable one—besides the one on temporary loan from the goblins—was the protective bracelet I'd taken off an unfortunate Frunza Tarlev student. It would activate automatically to stop a bullet, then required a moment to recharge before it could stop another. I also had the charms leftover from my crawler and trapper days, which would help protect me from poisonous air and extreme heat.

And that cursory pat down was performed by my hands, which were covered with leather gloves that had both been enchanted with another air spell, also of Azarin's invention. We thought of *Ascend* and *Descend* as two different spells, though technically, I think it was just two different effects from the same spell, as supposedly, you can't really start putting multiple enchantments on a single object until around rank six. Recently, I'd been experimenting with the gloves to see if I could use them for quick movement besides up or down, and so far, all I had to show for the effort was bruises from magically flinging myself into the ground, but the idea held promise.

My corner goblin and I were under the scaffolding, separated from the current bout by a small wooden fence. I couldn't make out much of what was going on between the cracks, but from the noise, falling dust, and the way everything was shaking, one of the gladiators was using some kind of wind spell and the other was hurling earth. One of these days, this clattery old quarry structure would finally receive enough punishment and fall, crushing dozens of gladiators and a large number of goblins to death in the process. Hopefully, I'd have gained enough ranks to be fighting in the Collegium by then and miss that inevitable spectacle.

The goblin pressed one of his boggle eyes to a gap between the boards. "Ha ha! That one got stabbed in the dick!" The wind died, the trembling stopped, and somebody started screaming for a healer. "Match's over. You're next."

Ignoring the pained wailing outside, I bowed my head and said a silent prayer to Ketekunan, asking that Saint Persistence would grant me the tenacity to win, because we had an adventure to go on and the academy really could use the money. Also, it would help if I could win without using up too much magic, because elements are expensive. *Amen.* A few minutes later, they opened the gate and I walked out into the quarry to see that two goblins were dumping buckets of sawdust to soak up a large puddle of blood.

"Looks like someone's charm didn't work."

"Don't fret, human. That was stupid Blork's spell. Blork does shoddy work. You have good charm from Bruxt. They're brothers, but Bruxt's the smart one." The goblin closed the gate behind me. "Wait. Maybe I mix those two up? Eh. You're good."

I should have asked Ketekunan to keep me from getting hit at all, because goblins suck, and I was an idiot for trusting them. But I wasn't going to turn back now. My patron saint despised that kind of quitter attitude!

My opponent hadn't come out yet. Despite the magically augmented voice, I barely even heard the announcer say my introduction, because I was too busy watching that opposite gate, curious to see what I was going to be up against.

When he got to the drawn out *Put Down Tom,* I raised one hand in salute toward the audience above. There were some isolated cheers from the handful who'd seen my previous fights. I was no Rufus, but you've got to give the people what they want. The ones who were calling over goblins to put coin on me winning had probably been there when I'd beaten Krachma.

The gate opened and another cloaked figure walked out, hood down, limbs hidden, face averted. I was going to laugh if it turned out I'd been worried Clotz had brought in a ringer, but instead, he'd picked my opponent because we were dressed the same.

This time, I paid attention to the announcer. "And fighting from the south scaffold, with her first appearance in the Under Slump—"

Her? Surely the announcer misspoke.

"All the way from the skull fields of Surnod Lin upon the Plane of Death, an enchanter of the first rank, I give you *Dathka Shadow Walker!*"

He made that last word last for a long time, and the instant the announcer was done, my opponent threw back the hood, revealing that I was in fact fighting a deadlander, because the eerily colorless skin and solid black eyes were unmistakable features of that haunted realm, but this one was actually a female.

And a rather striking one at that.

"I can't hit a girl."

"Not with that attitude you won't," my goblin shouted through the gate. "Don't just stand there. Do the face-off! That's when the hesitating gamblers get off their ass and decide who to bet on. Walk to the middle and greet your enemy, stupid human!"

I did so, seething the whole way, because what kind of nasty goblin trick was Clotz pulling here? Different kingdoms had different customs, like Azarin's people were fine with girls riding giant eagles and dangerous storm-chasing business I didn't entirely understand, but the arena was for brutish men to beat the ever-living shit out of each other, and while death and serious permanent injury was rare, it wasn't uncommon, as demonstrated by Rade's neck scar or the fact these goblins were so proficient at cleaning up blood spills.

I'd never seen a female deadlander before. Azarin was pretty. This girl was downright stunning. I'd thought everyone from her realm had stark white hair, because that was what I'd seen in Acheron, but her hair was as pitch-black as her eyes and her skin was the color of the snow clouds you could see once you got out from under the Slump. Eerie beauty aside, I was also several inches taller, and though I was lean from going hungry so often over the last few months, I still probably outweighed her by fifty pounds or more of Red miner muscle. There was no way I could in good conscience hit her, let alone shoot her or set her on fire.

We stopped fifteen feet apart with the announcer between us. Unlike his boss, the announcer was human, and from the eye patch and general disfigurement, was himself a veteran of the arena. "You know the rules. Normal weapons are fine. Normal spells are fine. You're both rank ones, so you can't do much anyway. You quit after two protective charges go off or your opponent yields. No endangering the audience or I'll shoot you myself. Now you'll return to your corners, I'll get out of the way, and upon my command, you shall proceed to harm each other to the best of your abilities. Any questions?"

"Yeah." I gestured toward the girl. "What's this?"

"It's your demise," she answered before the announcer could. "That feeling you're experiencing is the sense of impending doom."

"Clotz's arena, mate. Clotz's rules," the old timer told me as he backed up. "Good luck."

"Maybe goblins beat their women, but we don't do that where I'm from."

"Don't worry, hotlander. You'll be out long before you get close enough to lay a hand on me." She spun around with a dramatic cloak flip and walked back toward her gate.

"Shit..." What was I supposed to do now? My saint rewarded stubborn determination, but I suspected Ketekunan—being as he was from Fogo before being promoted by the gods—would frown upon me striking a woman.

As I walked to my start position, I saw Rade sitting above, and shouted at him, "You didn't tell me Dathka is a girl's name."

"How would I know? I've never been to Surnod Lin. It's on the other side of the plane. I hear they're odd there."

So the fake noble from a town built on top of an ancient tomb city found someone *odd*? "I can't hit a lady, Rade."

"If she wanted to be ladylike, she wouldn't be here, Carnavon. Get your head right."

The announcer had his own little bunker carved into the wall to duck into during the fight. He looked toward Dathka—who was ready—then toward me—who clearly was not—and shouted "*Fight!*" anyway.

She drew a pistol, lightning fast, and plugged me square in the chest.

12

The impact staggered me. Through the cloud of hanging smoke, I spotted Dathka coming up with a *second* pistol in her off hand, and instinctively threw myself to the side, landing behind a stone block.

My Frunza charm had stopped the bullet, but it still felt like I'd gotten a chipping hammer embedded in my lungs. As I crawled toward better cover, half my chest filled with wheezing, throbbing fire.

I could barely hear Rade's shout over the booing crowd. "I tried to warn you!"

I lay there in the block's shadow, hurting. All my naïve thoughts about honorable fairness and the traditional rules about not hitting women went straight out the window, because that deadland bitch *just shot me.* I drew Gax's pistol.

Oh, we're doing this now.

Risking a peek around the side of the block, Dathka was moving my way, pistol still raised. She fired the instant she spotted my head, and stone chipped in front of me. With an empty gun in each hand, now it was her turn to take cover as I leaned farther out to take a shot at her. By the time I got the sights aligned, she was behind another block.

I jumped up and started running for a better position. Instinct told me as soon as she was reloaded, she'd be doing the same, trying to get an angle on me. Only, I intended to get there first.

Except then, somehow, she was right *behind me.* Which I didn't realize until she shot me right between the shoulder blades.

The Frunza protection hadn't had time to recharge, but thankfully, Bruxt—or maybe it was Blork—had done his job, and the goblin enchantment stopped the bullet. I landed on my face, skidding across the stone, and it felt like I'd had my spine shattered. A goblin charm will save you, but those little bastards make it hurt extra bad on purpose.

Temporarily losing all the strength in my limbs as if paralyzed had also caused me to drop my gun. It went sliding across the stones to stop a few feet from my clumsy, nerve-deadened fingers.

"One down!" the announcer shouted with his artificially loudened voice. "One to go."

How had she gotten all the way over here? When I rolled over, Dathka was standing in the shadow of the block I'd taken cover behind, calmly breaking open her pistol. She dumped the smoking brass case and pulled a fresh cartridge from her belt. "I told you you'd never even get close."

I'd practiced going for my enchantments so many times that I could use them even with tingling hands. I tugged an *Obscura* ball from my vest, concentrated on the simple spell embedded in the clay, and let it roll away. When it hit the ground, it burst into a black shadow cloud.

Dathka fired blind through the magical smoke, but I was already moving. The bullet whizzed past my head. Remembering where Gax's pistol had fallen, I ran my hand along the stone until I hit something metal and scooped it up, then kept running.

"You dare use a shadow spell on *me*?"

"I've got more where that came from." The artificial spine shot pain had faded enough that I'd gotten a bit of dexterity back, so I grabbed a handful of screws. A second of concentration activated the Red bound to the steel, then I tossed them under hand through the smoke. "I call this one *Screws of Chaos.*"

This was one of first formula I'd come up with myself, and it was still one of the nastiest. The Red heated the metal molten hot, super quick, and when the screws hit the ground and scattered, they began their out-of-control dance, bouncing, shrieking, popping, and sticking to anything that might burn.

From Dathka's enraged shout, one of them must have caught her.

The *Obscura* cloud only lasted about seven or eight seconds, just enough time for me to blindly stumble my way to a better position.

And somehow Dathka was now *ahead* of me.

It was a surprise when she appeared around the side of the white stone block I was heading toward. She was limping, and the bottom of her cloak was on fire from the screws, but she was already swinging her pistol my way.

Rather than freeze and marvel how she was getting around so impossibly fast, I dove headfirst into a trench.

It was about a seven-foot drop into the perfectly rectangular hole. I didn't even have time to activate a *Descend*; that landing really hurt. Joints popped, but thankfully, it wasn't enough damage to activate the goblin charge, because that would be a sad way to end the match!

Over the roaring of the crowd, I could barely hear her boots crunching across the gravel as she rushed me, hoping for a final shot. I threw a pinch of Red dust up out of the hole.

She walked straight into a *Shroud of Fire.*

That was the only invoked spell I knew, and creating a magical effect directly from an element with no other ingredients could be rather potent. The size and intensity of the fire this spell created was proportional to the amount of Red I used, and I'd not had time to grab much.

Though, in this case, it was still enough to set her hair aflame.

She was distracted, probably blinded by the flashing fire, and vulnerable, but I didn't have a shot because of the edge of the pit. With cocked pistol in my right, I raised my left hand and made a fist. "*Ascend!*"

The air solidified and curled around my arm, hoisting me violently upward. I flew out of the hole, pointed the gun at Dathka as I passed ground level, and yanked the trigger. There'd been no time to aim. It was purely by instinct, like pointing a finger. Yet by some miracle, I actually hit her.

There was a magical flash as my bullet knocked her off her feet.

The crowd *loved* that.

As I continued my rapid rise, first I realized that the flash had been the wrong color to be a goblin charm. She also had her own protective enchantments. Second, I needed to pick a destination before she recovered and shot me out of the sky. I looked toward the scaffolding, opened my hand—breaking the *Ascent*—and dropped the last few feet to collide with the wooden poles. I managed to grab on to the side and hang on.

Rade was sitting one level below me. "Excellent shot, my friend!"

"From up here, can you see how she's moving around so fast?"

"She's wearing some kind of high-level enchantment."

I'd heard talk about that kind of spell in the Collegium, but there was no way a Slump fighter had such a potent thing. I knew Clotz was going to screw me somehow. "Rank ones can't teleport. That's like an eighth-level spell!"

"It's more as if she steps into one shadow and appears out another. Ah… so that explains her ring name." Then Rade flinched as Dathka's next bullet punched a hole in the planks between us. "Hey! No killing the audience!"

Staying in one place for more than a few seconds against her would get me killed. I let go of the scaffold. Dropping this far normally would break bones or worse, but I'd been practicing my *Descent* a lot and activated it as I fell, aiming my open glove at the ground and imagining I was pushing back against gravity. Those same invisible ropes of air that had pulled me upward were now wrapped around me, drastically slowing my body before impact.

I landed about as soft as jumping down the last three or four steps on a staircase, which stung, though far preferable to breaking both ankles. My opponent was out of sight. While scanning the nearby shadows, I reloaded my gun. As I moved, I looked up toward the crowd. Since they had a bird's eye view, that would tell me where my sneaky opponent was hiding.

It must have been because she had two goblin charges left to my one, because her next move was extremely bold.

A small object came sailing over the blocks. As I saw it falling, my first thought was that it was some kind of offensive enchantment, like my snail grenade, so I ducked down and covered my head. Except when it hit, it didn't spread fiery fragments, but rather concealing smoke. She knew *Obscura* too.

Only she could use the shadows that spell created to travel through.

I was engulfed in darkness. It was only by the instincts developed by years of working in pitch-black tunnels that I sensed her appear next to me. I spun just as she shoved the muzzle of her pistol at the back of my head. It discharged where my skull had just been, and I was already pushing her way. We collided. Her other gun crashed uselessly against my wrist and the reflexive tightening of her grip caused her to launch a bullet uselessly into the ground.

I could imagine the audience was screaming about how they couldn't see. They could only hear the gunshots. *What's happening? What's going on down there?* And they got their answer when I kicked Dathka in the stomach so hard that she flew out of the smoke and bounced her head off a block.

Now, rules of civility about striking women aside, forgive me, Ketekunan, but that had been profoundly satisfying.

I followed her out of the smoke. She was struggling to her hands and knees, and from the shimmer lingering around her, that hit cost her a charge on her goblin charm. Sadly, she was lying in the shade of the block, and before I could shoot her and put an end to the second charge, she fell through the shadow and vanished.

There was no way a rank one had come up with that enchantment on their own!

I glanced toward the scaffolding, to see that Rade was desperately pointing at the far side of the arena. I couldn't see her myself, but that told me approximately where she'd reappeared.

She was surely shaking off the magically induced feeling of a fractured skull—I found that goblin-reinforced pain lasted about ten or twenty seconds—and then she'd be reloading her pistols or readying her next spell. I had an idea.

"*Ascend.*" I didn't fly nearly as high this time, going just to the top of the nearest block before cutting the spell and landing atop it. I still didn't have a line of sight, so I began leaping from block to block. There were only a few feet between them here, the tops were flat, and they were roughly the same size. Moving across the blocks was nothing to someone surefooted enough to be a trapper on the lava wastes.

I caught Dathka reloading. She looked up just as I blocked the light charm above her, and she might have even escaped me using my own shadow, if I'd not been ready for that trick.

The Red dust I hurled wasn't directly at her, but above her. It ignited in a sweeping arc of fire which obliterated all the available shadows she could've dropped into.

It only took a bit of concentration to get my *Shroud of Fire* to linger for a second… Just long enough to line up the pistol's sights on my target and squeeze the trigger. Just in case the goblin charm failed, I aimed low. Regardless of her attempting to put bullets in my lung, spine, and brain… I remained a gentleman and merely shot her in the leg.

Sure, such a wound could still be lethal if she bled out, or it could explode the bone and require an amputation, but you know what they say: It's the thought that counts.

There was a flash as my bullet flattened against the goblin charm. One knee twisted out from beneath her, and she flopped into the dust, crying out in pain. As the sparks from my spell drifted down around her, she shouted, "I yield! I'm done."

I stood atop the block and took a long, deep breath. There was no feeling quite like triumphing in the arena. It was better than bringing in a great haul of Red. I was confused why the audience wasn't roaring. They usually loved high mobility fights, but then I realized they were all on their feet cheering or booing—depending on how they'd bet—they just sounded muted because of the ringing in my ears from all the gunshots. I swear, when I got better at magical formula, I was going to figure out how to make gunpowder explode quietly.

The announcer came out of his bunker to proclaim Put Down Tom the victor. Goblins ran out and directed me back toward my gate. I really wanted to ask Dathka where she'd gotten that powerful shadow magic from, but she was holding her knee and glaring at me with murderous wrath. If that enchantment had come from Clotz, I was going to shoot that snot-faced bastard.

Goblins, being greedy as could be, didn't even let the gladiators stay on the scaffolding after our fights were over. They expected us to buy a ticket if we were going to spectate, so I wouldn't get to watch Rade or Krachma fight. I was on my way to collect my percentage of the earnings when I saw a familiar face standing near the bookie's board. It was Carcalla's menacing right hand, Cutter Joran, and it was obvious he was waiting there for me.

13

The outer arena was packed, and everyone, gladiator and spectator both, was deferential to Joran. That respect was earned by years of winning here, and by his more recent promotion to the leadership of the dreaded Latrocinium.

"Well, well, well. If it isn't Oz Carnavon."

I didn't like that he was using my real name here, but even if there were Skerret gang about, surely none of them would be suicidal enough to provoke a confrontation in Joran's presence. "Good evening to you, Mr. Vanderhelst."

He was sitting on Clotz's table, and the usually sneering and snarling bookie was awfully quiet for once. I'd never seen a goblin be respectful before. For that alone, I didn't hate Joran's presence, but I also couldn't collect my winnings as long as he was sitting there, and Clotz was too cowed to move.

"That was a good match. Lots of shooting and ranging about, both on the horizontal and vertical. The audience finds that sort of fight entertaining. That was never really my style. I was more of a stand there and slug it out sort of fighter, myself."

"Like Rufus and the orc earlier."

"I missed that one. I was outside buying myself a pudding. But from what my friends who watched told me, it was of a similar combative mindset to mine, though in my prime, I could have beaten both of them at the same time easily. Isn't that so, Clotz?"

"Yes, Cutter," the goblin sniveled. "You're the best gladiator either Slump has ever seen."

The post-rush lethargy had set in. My back hurt. My chest hurt. And I'd thrown myself face first into a hole. It was possible that my normal smooth-talking diplomacy might have failed me a bit right then. "You don't need to remind me how dangerous you are. That message's been received. We're already doing as your boss has asked of us. The rent will get paid."

"Can't a man reminisce about his glory days in the arena? I know we've secured the cooperation of your academy. A wise choice on your part, that. But in all truthfulness, I was merely a spectator tonight, come to watch one of the Latrocinium's new associates fight, and it is by pure happenstance that I saw your alias upon the betting board." Joran jerked one thumb toward the chalkboard behind him. "And seeing that reminded me of something I should've cleared up after our first encounter."

There were a lot of people milling about us, coming and going to their seats, buying food and drink from the vendors, and a few adoring fools who were surely waiting to ask Joran for his autograph. "Is this the place to talk about it?"

"It'll do, good as any. We won't discuss the specifics of where you're going or what you're doing for us, yet the issue is that my master gives out tasks. After doing so, he needs not worry himself about the pesky details of how those tasks get done. That's what he's got me for. The detail which concerns me currently, should you not die by monster or get speared upon some ancient's trap, is that you may actually find a bit of loot. However, with no impartial witnesses present, you might lie about your haul, and present to Carcalla an uneven split."

"I wouldn't do that." I wasn't lying either. That just wasn't the sort of thing I'd be inclined to do.

"So you say, but greed makes men dumb. I would hate for you to be led into temptation… Especially with this being but the first adventure of *many* that Master Carcalla has planned for your crew… Monthly… Forever…"

I longed for the day Gaul Haddar returned, not just so we could finally have a proper teacher, but so that he could renegotiate by putting a sword in this bully's guts. Joran was a Null, though I suspected someone as notoriously violent as Haddar would know a way around that, and I'd love to watch him rip Joran's throat out.

Except I just smiled as if I wasn't imagining his horrific demise. "That's our current arrangement."

"Which is nice for us. Master Carcalla's been contemplating dispatching adventurers on these endeavors for him for a long time, but he's been too busy focusing on his paying businesses to waste the Latrocinium's resources on frivolous treasure hunts. Until your gang of expendable wizards came along, that is. The problem with adventuring is often there's no payoff at all, and lots of men die for no good reason. But sometimes, you hit the jackpot."

"And on the off chance we do, since you've deemed my word about what we find to be insufficient, I'm betting you've already got a remedy in mind."

"He's *betting.*" Joran chuckled. "Let's ask the betting expert. Hey, Clotz. What would you place the odds upon this board of yours that Cutter Joran already had a plan in mind for the Outcasts?"

"A hundred to one in your favor, sire, obviously."

I think I liked the goblins more when they were being pricks than groveling ass-kissers. "Sounds like a sure thing, then."

"A sure thing is what I thought I had when I bet against you tonight, but life is full of surprises. Like your opponent tonight. She's mean as a manticore, sneaky as a kobold, and shows real promise as an assassin, but tonight taught her a valuable lesson about underestimating her victims." He nodded at someone approaching behind me. "And there's my associate now. Dathka Walker, meet Oz Carnavon. I was just telling the lad how my faith in you cost me twenty Obols tonight."

"She works for Carcalla too?" That at least explained why she was armed with an enchantment far beyond her rank to create.

"I've given my blood oath to serve the Latrocinium." She sneered at me. "From what Joran's said about you, that means nothing to you, oath breaker."

She must be referring to me skipping out on my contract of indentured servitude. "That's not the same. You picked yours. The Argents held my family's contract long before I was ever born. I just took back what's mine."

"It's amusing you think your life belongs to you."

"Who owns it, then?"

"Every life belongs to whoever is strong enough to take it." Covered in dirt, scratches, and with a cloak that was now charred to ash on the edges, she glared at me, then turned her scorn upon Clotz. "I've come for my winnings, goblin."

"Me as well," I added quickly.

Clotz looked to Joran for permission, and only after the gangster nodded did the goblin open the safe and begin counting coins.

Joran seemed amused by my meager stack of coins. He'd lost ten times more betting on my fight than I'd made fighting it. "Ah, I remember fondly those days, starting out, scraping by, beating rank ones to a pulp to buy my bread… But returning to the original subject. How do I ensure the Latrocinium gets a proper, honest accounting of any treasure found in those ruins? My solution is to send someone I trust to watch you."

"Marvelous," I muttered.

The instant Clotz finished counting out her coins, Dathka snatched them off the table. She tossed a single coin to Joran—who caught it—then she hurried and hid the rest in her pocket. I didn't know what that payment was for, but she was clearly eager to get it over with.

"But who shall I send…" Joran mused as he studied the single Tetar in his hand, though from his tone, it was clear he already knew exactly what he was about to say. Clotz's hundred to one odds that Joran had a plan for everything was sickeningly obsequious, but also probably accurate.

"I'd suggest someone who can defend themselves, because I hear that place is crawling with monsters, and me and my people will take no responsibility for the safety of yours."

"On the contrary, Carnavon. Should my witness perish, a reasonable man would assume it was because you stabbed them in the back to disguise your treachery." Joran's eyes lingered on his new enforcer. "Dathka's loss brought shame to the Latros tonight.

She can make it up to me by accompanying you Outcasts on your adventure."

Dathka froze, body stiff as a board, expression unreadable, before slowly bowing her head. "As you wish, Cutter."

Joran stood up and slapped me hard on my aching shoulder. "Take good care of my assassin."

After he'd walked away, I told the irritated deadlander, "Welcome aboard, I guess."

14

After Rade's and Krachma's victories, we walked back through the Under Slump. The enthusiasm over our four wins out of seven was tempered by the fact our small group had gained an eighth—and hopefully temporary—member.

"She's a bit of a sour puss, ain't she?" Rufus whispered to me.

"I can hear you, imbecilic dwarf," Dathka said.

"That's no way for a loser to address a winner," Rufus responded.

"You really want to pick a fight with me while we're strolling through the *dark*?"

Light charms were few and far between on these poor streets, especially this late at night. There were a few lit windows, and the occasional burn barrel with bums huddled about it to stay warm, but the Under Slump was a very dim place at night. There was no moonlight beneath the Slump, so we navigated entirely by my light charm, which floated in the air above me, providing just enough illumination to keep from tripping over something or stepping in a hole. Fighting a shadow walker here would be rather unpleasant.

"T'was but a statement of fact, m'lady."

"Give it a rest," I said. "She's got a job. We've got a job. Neither side has to like it, but we both have to do it. Bickering's not going to make the time pass any faster."

Rade was his usual charming self, "Well, I for one am glad to have such a lovely addition to our ranks. It is good to finally see for myself that the legendary beauty of the women of Surnod Lin has not been exaggerated."

"She is purty," Big Bognar agreed.

Dathka stopped, turned, and poked Bognar with one finger.

"Me eye!" Normally, a small woman hitting a large man wouldn't do much, but Dathka had fast hands and excellent aim, and must have stuck a finger right in the jelly. Bognar mashed his hands against his face. "Saints! I didn't mean nothing by it!"

"Was that necessary?" I asked.

"I'm not some harlot that your fat goon can ogle my ass. I'm Latrocinium. Don't you forget it."

"Why didn't you hit him, then?" Bognar whined, gesturing toward Rade. "He was staring too."

"Being from the same realm earned him *one* pass. That's used up now."

Rade flashed a smile and tipped his broad-brimmed hat toward her. "Of course, madam."

I kept walking. I'd dealt with enough trogshit for one day and just wanted to go to bed.

Krachma apparently agreed. "Shut up, humans. Krachma is weary. Krachma has won many coins. Krachma will buy food and element tomorrow. Now Krachma wants only sleep."

"You heard the champ," I said.

Even this late, the Under Slump was a busy place, because many of the races which inhabited it were nocturnal anyway. It was a very different feeling than during the day. At night, this place got *strange.* The Under Slump was a dumping ground for refugees from the various war-torn kingdoms, and every other group that was too poor to have anywhere else to go. The tunnels of the undercity beneath us were even worse and weirder. There were shadowed figures scurrying past us, and I could only tell that we were being watched from rooftops and windows because some of the creatures' eyes reflected my lonely light charm.

A few blocks passed before Krachma's demand for silence was forgotten. Danny and Sifuso were bringing up the rear of our group, and since both were despondent about their humiliating loss, they'd begun grumbling.

"I'm such a failure," Danny moaned. "I had a cousin who was a real tough mercenary. He would've laughed at how bad I did. I'm never gonna make it as a wizard. At least your match lasted a while. I got knocked out so fast."

"Mine only lasted because I fled." Sifuso hung his long head-neck in shame. "I am a disgrace to lacertians."

"What happened there anyway?" Danny asked. "'Cause no offense, you're real scary-looking, but then you turned into a chicken."

"I do not know. I have fought many times. I was ready to fight again. Then so many eyes were upon me, and I suddenly felt weak, like I was small again and had just cracked open my egg and had to hide beneath a lily pad to not be eaten by birds."

Such loser talk was bad for morale, so I chimed in, "That's just nerves. Everybody gets those."

"I don't!" Rufus exclaimed, in a completely unhelpful manner.

"That's because you go through life blessedly oblivious to the world around you," Rade said. "What our large lizard experienced is called stage fright by the thespians."

"Thespians is those little mole people from the Plane of Earth, right?"

"No, Rufus, those are Turgunian halflings. Thespians are actors." Rade sighed. "Stage fright is what they call the fear they experience while performing before a crowd."

"Good thing I don't get that, because I got five whole Obols in my pocket!"

I noticed that Rufus' loud boast caused several sets of reflective eyes to turn our direction. "Quiet down."

"Be proud, Carnavon. You cleaned up yourself! And Krachma made more than the rest of us. I bet between us we've got over twenty Obols! Maybe close to thirty even! Our purses clank, heavy with coin tonight!"

I smacked him upside the head. "Shut up."

It was too late, as he'd already advertised that we were a fat, juicy target for robbery, while we were still half a mile from the safety of the Tube.

"What?" Rufus asked, offended.

"Just keep walking."

Except something large and hairy leapt off a roof and landed smoothly on the lane ahead of us. Its voice was a strange wheeze. "*You have many coin?*"

Two more of the hairy things landed behind Danny and Sifuso, and a few more stirred up out of the trash piles of the nearby alleys. We were surrounded in an instant.

"*You give to us this coin.*" The first hairy beast reached behind its back and pulled out a thick dagger. "*Or else.*"

Rufus looked at all the strange things who'd come out of the woodwork, and it slowly dawned on him what he'd done wrong. "Oh... I get it now."

"It's a good thing you can fight, because you've got rocks for brains," Rade told him.

I glanced back at my friends, saw that most were having a similar reaction to this attempted banditry as I was, which was basically an offended *fuck these assholes.* Danny and Bognar were clearly terrified, but the rest of us looked angry or bemused by the threat.

"Listen, whatever you are, you've picked the wrong band to rob. We're mages from the Academy of Outcasts. Those coins were earned in the arena. Fighting is what we do for fun and profit. You'd best scurry along before you get hurt."

"*Arena is fake.*" The thing waved its blade back and forth. "*Steel is real.*"

"Yeah, we saw your little knife the first time, shaggy," Dathka said. "I'm Latrocinium. You nightbolg trash know we're off limits."

The hairy shapes shifted nervously at her words, but their leader calmed them down. "*It does not wear the black band.*"

"I didn't wear Carcalla's mark to the arena because I didn't want to scare whoever I was up against into immediate surrender. So you can fuck right off, or the landlord will send an army down here to burn out your entire hive."

"*It lies. It is not of the black band. It does not want to give up its coin.*"

I despised robbers. Taking the fruit of a man's labor was the same as stealing that part of his life. Having had enough of this foolishness, I reached into my pocket. "Here you go." But rather than an Obol, I tossed a generous pinch of Red.

I invoked the *Shroud of Fire*, and all that greasy hair must have been really flammable, because the creature was immediately engulfed.

Rade drew his sword with lightning quickness, slashing at the creatures to the side. Spiders made of darkness flew from the blade, landed on the monsters, and started biting. Krachma saved his magic and simply punched one in the ribs, which sent it flying into the dark. Dathka appeared behind the pair of creatures blocking the rear, extended her two guns, and simultaneously shot both of them in the back of the head.

Brains splattered poor Danny, but not Sifuso, because surprisingly, our lacertian had reacted with incredible speed and leapt onto another monster, knocked it down, and was rapidly stabbing it in the chest and neck.

The rest of the monsters—sensibly—ran away.

The leader, every inch of him on fire, managed to run only a few feet before flopping over and curling into a crispy ball. I'd not intended to cook him entirely, but how was I supposed to know he'd be that flammable? I'd tried to warn him.

Blood-splattered Sifuso got off the dead whatever it was he'd just stabbed forty times. "See? See, humans? I can kill just fine if no one is watching me!"

"Good for you, lizard," Rade told him, before turning to Rufus. "And you should not speak in public anymore."

"But—"

"Shush."

I couldn't really tell on the crispy one, but the other dead monsters were about orc-sized humanoids with gigantic eyes—probably for hunting in the dark—and were covered in matted ink-black fur. Even by the dim light of my charm, I swear I could see the lice moving about, they were so thick. Morton would probably have to use his spell to delouse us when we got back.

"Anybody know what these are?"

"They're nightbolgs," Danny said, wiping the nasty bits from his face with a handkerchief. "We had a pet cat once, you know, for the mice, but a nightbolg came up out of the sewer and ate it."

"A tribe of them got chased out of their realm a couple years ago and moved into a cavern in the undercity," Dathka explained as she reloaded her pistols. "Roaming up here violates their agreement. We may have to evict them."

"These things pay rent to Carcalla too?"

"Of course. You're not special." She shoved her guns back in the holsters. "Everybody owes someone for something."

15

On Deathday, the Nexus was aligned with the realm of the dead. A chilling fog drifted out the gate and gradually flooded the city. Fog collects downhill, and we were lower than the market, so the already dreary Under Slump always felt a bit dimmer and colder than usual on Deathdays. That temporary connection to the plane, which all spirits must pass through on their way to their eternal reward or punishment, also agitated the Tube's resident ghosts, which made them extra uppity.

Every Deathday morning since I'd been living in these ruins, I'd gotten to wake up cold, to the shrieking antics of people who'd died by getting squished by a toppling tower over fifty years ago, letting us all know they were still rather cross about that.

"*Doom! Doom!*"

My bed was a few old blankets atop a pile of straw. My pillow was a cloth bag stuffed with rags. Putting it over my head wasn't enough to block the noise. Eventually, I rolled over to see a glowing phantasm in the corner, wailing its misery.

"*Dooom!*"

"Yeah, doom. I got it the first time." I'd volunteered to take one of the windowless rooms of the Tube for myself, not out of kindness to the others, but in a desperate attempt to stay warm. Not that I was complaining, because having grown up on a barge, this was the first time in my life I'd actually experienced privacy. But even without being able to see outside, I always knew the precise moment the sun rose and the gate began opening on Deathday, because the stupid ghosts would begin wailing. They were worse than the neighbor's rooster.

"*Doom.*"

"Could you guys give me a break for once? Yeah, you died. That sucks. Move on. I had a late night."

"*Doooooom!*"

I picked up one of my boots and hurled it through the vaguely human-shaped ghost. The boot bounced off the wall, and sadly, the ghost remained. It paused its piteous noise, just long enough for me to get my hopes up, only to go back to yelling at me.

There'd be no sleeping in today. Besides, I had a lot of work to do anyway, so I got up and got dressed.

Due to the sideways nature of our home, my door was a hatch in the floor. I kept it locked at night to keep from sleep walking to my death. When I pulled it open, Azarin was already waiting for me below. She was one of those happy morning people and was usually awake long before the ghosts.

"Oz, why is there a Latrocinium assassin in the female dormitory?"

I tossed out the knotted rope I'd anchored to a protruding stud in the wall and began to climb down from my room. I could've cast *Descend*, but wanted to save the magic for later. "So you met our guest."

"She's so white, at first, I thought she was another ghost. Then she introduced herself, said why she was here. I'd have preferred a ghost, frankly."

"Joran didn't leave me much choice." I landed next to Azarin. "Good thing you didn't throw a shoe at her. She'd likely have shot you. And what do you mean female dormitory? You're our only girl. I put her in a room away from everyone else. It's not my fault you claimed an entire section of the tower for yourself."

"I'm simply planning ahead for the inevitable time when we have a hundred students rather than a handful."

Even though I was the one who'd tricked a rank-ten wizard into blowing his own hand off and scammed my way into having an official academy, bringing together unwanted mages and sharing our homebrewed spells had been Azarin's idea. Her talking about it in the Collegium's pubs was how we'd gotten our first students. It'd worked out far better than expected, and most of us had increased in ability over the last few months, so she'd certainly earned her own space away from Morton's snoring and Sifuso's reptile smells. All the student council got our own rooms, except for Trax, who didn't really understand the concept of *housing*, and slept submerged in the nearby canal anyway.

"We'll get that many students eventually. You're a good recruiter."

"Nobody from Stormwolk would've expected me to make it this far. If only I could see the looks of disappointment on their faces every month the gate opens and I'm not there, tear-stained and begging to be taken back." She gave me a playful smile. "I heard you had an eventful night."

"Between the gladiatorial victories and attempted robbery, you could say that. I need to hit the market and buy more element. Then it's off to see if I can't bribe the same tester I bribed before."

"In the meantime, what am I supposed to do with the Latrocinium's spying bitch?"

"You can begin by not calling me a bitch, air-realm hag."

"Fuck!" Azarin jumped, as she'd not heard Dathka appear in the shadows directly behind her. "Where'd she come from?"

"She does that. Hence her being the *Shadow Walker.*"

"The family name's Walker." Dathka's tone was cold and aloof. "The goblins tacked on the shadow part for the added gravitas. Before you ask the obvious, the nature and source of the item that allows me to do that spell is none of your concern. And no, I will not share any of my own spells with your gaggle of rejects."

"Sharing a spell is our one prerequisite for membership in this academy." Azarin might have been startled by Dathka's sudden appearance, but she was far too willful to be intimidated by anyone. "Pay up or get out."

"Azarin, is it?"

She nodded.

"There's been a bit of a misunderstanding as to the nature of our relationship, Azarin. I've got a home already." Dathka put two fingers to the black and yellow band she was now wearing proudly around her bicep "I'm here to make sure you don't rip off the boss of my existing gang, not join a pathetic new one."

"For the tenth time—"

Azarin cut me off before I could say we weren't a gang. "No spell, no tuition, no bed. You need to accompany us on our adventure, fine. We don't owe you free room and board in the meantime. Perhaps you can check and see if Trax has a watery spot of pond you can share. Maybe a mud puddle would be more to your liking?"

Dathka's lip curled back in disgust. "Are you foolish enough to insult the Latrocinium?"

"Of course not. I'm only insulting *you.*"

Oh boy. I kept watching Dathka, waiting for her to tense up, as I was prepared to stick my body between Azarin's mouth and the assassin's hands, because that seemed to be the proper thing for a boyfriend to do.

"Carcalla will hear of this disrespect."

"Are you going to tattle on me? He's my landlord, not my clan chief. I had one of those once, and I didn't particularly care to put up with his nonsense either."

It was time to head this off before it turned stupid. If Dathka tried to kill Azarin, I'd have to kill Dathka, and then Cutter Joran would kill us all. "Ladies, ladies. You've just gotten off on the wrong foot."

Azarin looked toward Dathka's feet, which were hidden by her cloak. "I bet she's got a big gangly club foot too."

"You skag!"

"And it's all hairy on top, like a halfling's."

"Alrighty then." Now I inserted my body between them. It was either that or a wall of fire. I gently steered Azarin away. "How about you run those errands I was going to do, while I give our guest a tour of our academy? I'll be right back, Ms. Walker."

"Nice to meet you, Azarin," Dathka called after us. "I look forward to continuing our conversation later."

"Oh, absolutely," Azarin said over her shoulder.

"Would you please quit antagonizing the professional killer for a second?" I got Azarin down the hall a ways and shoved the bag of Obols we'd won last night into her hands. "You can go get us some element. Take somebody with you to watch your back while crossing the Slumps and get out of the Tube for a while."

Azarin sniffed at that. "That's not a bad idea. The merchants like me better than you anyway. When they weigh their element, their scales are a bit more generous when the customer has a nice smile."

"Yes, you're much prettier than me. No doubt of that."

She looked back to make sure Dathka was still down the hall and probably out of earshot. "But not prettier than her. Naanwaala have mercy, she's gorgeous. Like someone painted a bit of makeup on one of those marble statues in the Collegium. The gang lord sent her to seduce you, I know it."

"What? No—"

She put her finger on my lip to stop me. "Trust me on this one, Oz. You don't come from a place with warring clans. I do. One clan sending a beautiful emissary to befuddle another clan's male leaders is a classic move where I'm from."

"I shall refrain from befuddlement. You have my word."

"Good. Because unlike the other boys I've known who'd swear that, you actually mean it." Then she gripped a handful of my hair, jerked my head down, and kissed me in a very passionate and theatrically exaggerated manner. I understood logically this move was not for my benefit, but a show for our watcher. Either way, I was fine with it.

"Grab my butt," she whispered.

"What?"

"Just do it."

I did. It was nice. Then she kissed me a bit more, before saying, "Good. She saw that. You can let go now."

Reluctantly, I did so. "You make this clan war business sound not all bad."

"It's actually pretty fun, until the murders begin." Azarin turned her head to let her long flowing golden hair flip about, probably because that was something else Dathka couldn't do. "Well then, I'm off to the market!"

When I returned, Dathka's arms were folded, and she scowled. "Are you done with that absurd and pointless territorial display?"

I'd love to get back to it later, but that went unsaid. "I believe so. Allow me to give you a tour of our facility."

"Why do you want so badly to show off your sad excuse for an academy?"

Spending time with this sanctimonious deadlander sounded about as fun as splashing lava in my eye, but I remained cordial. "I'm proud of what we're doing. Plus, it won't hurt for you to be able to report back to your boss that we're really trying to become a legitimate school for all the mages who've had their hopes crushed by the Collegium. And once he understands that, he'll know there's no way we'd ever risk throwing that away in some attempt at shorting him a bit of treasure."

"You actually believe your own nonsense, don't you?"

"I do, yeah."

"No wonder Joran believed you to be running a scam, because no one could possibly be stupid enough to think such an asinine plan would work… Very well, Carnavon. You may show me your kingdom of delusion."

16

As we walked through the center of the Tube, Dathka said, "It's a big place, to be home to so few people."

"Maybe you could tell your master how wrecked the place is, so he'll adjust the rent accordingly," I suggested. "And I'm assuming by now you've seen it really is haunted."

She scoffed. "I come from the plain of decaying bones which exists beneath an eternal hellish maelstrom. Surnod Lin is the last stop in the physical realms before those destined for eternal torment are dragged into oblivion. They cling there, desperate, bargaining for one last chance. Their pleading amuses us. The spirits of the damned have always been my companions. Their wails were my lullaby."

"That sounds pleasant."

I think Rade's optimism had given me a skewed perspective of deadlanders. He was all charming smiles, big sweeping gestures, and grandiose stories. Dathka was mean-spirited and had a strange economy of motion about her, where there was no flash, and every movement was measured, pragmatic, or stately… Kind of like her life was an endless funeral. I felt safe now assuming Dathka was more representative of her realm than my delusional friend.

"As you can see, the sideways architecture's forced us to make some adaptations. Using whatever scraps we can come up with, we've been able to slowly build up stairs and platforms, allowing us to access more rooms. Bognar was a carpenter's apprentice, so he's been a great help at this."

"That's the corpulent gutter swine I poked in the eye? He should remain a tradesman. I watched his fight. He was awful."

"Everyone's got to start somewhere…" I pointed to the opening above us. "Because that section broke open to the sky when the tower fell, that's our air practice room." It was currently unoccupied, since Azarin was the only one who'd be up this early to use it and she was on her way to the market. "To the left is our water practice room, because the outer wall in that part got broken, and it's lying directly across one of the city canals. It's just like having our own river."

"The mighty Hubur flows past my home. Thousands of ghosts huddle upon the shore, waiting to pay the ferrymen to cross its vastness. That squalid ditch is nothing like having your own river."

"It's flowing fast enough that drinking it doesn't make us sick too often, though we still filter it through a box of sand and charcoal, then boil it to be sure. I've got a spell that's perfect for boiling water, so we've always got a kettle going in the kitchen."

"Sad."

I was rather proud of what we'd built here, so her shitting all over it was starting to grate on my nerves. "Our river has a Squalo in it. Did yours?"

"Only the spirts of the dead Squalos swimming their way to hell, I assume. You're lucky you have such a deadly ally. If it hadn't been for you having a Squalo in your gang, the local Latrocinium would have crushed you the day you disrespectfully pinned that notice upon your door without asking our permission first. By the time we'd gathered enough men to defeat a Squalo, Joran had heard of your endeavor and ordered us to wait and observe instead… Speak of the devil. There's your shark man now."

Trax wandered in, six and a half feet of sleek grey and white muscle, crunching happily on a large but very human-looking femur that he held as if it were a lollipop. "*Good morning, Carnavon. I was delighted to discover that someone threw several corpses into the canal last night. This was an unexpected treat.*"

"Were they about this tall?" I held my hand out a bit over my head. "And covered in black hair?"

"*Yes. They were meaty and very hairy. I cannot digest so much hair and will have to cough up a considerable hairball later. Despite that, they were quite edible. I see from your mind picture that you are responsible for this feast. Thank you for the roasted one. He had a smokey flavor.*"

Dathka's starkly pale face rarely displayed any emotion, but it was clear from the subtle shaking of her hands that Trax scared her. As he should. Only a fool wouldn't be nervous around a Squalo. Despite his massive bulk, Trax padded over in complete silence, staring at her with his tiny black eyes.

"*This one wears the black band. Is she a threat? Should I eat her?*"

"Hold off on that. I'll let you know."

She cringed a bit as her mind was bombarded by Trax's peculiar method of communication. "What's he saying?"

"He says that his name is Tracks the Blood Trail Regardless of Extreme Temperatures or Crushing Pressures, but you can call him Trax or Mr. Bloodtrail. Trax, this is Dathka Walker, of the Latrocinium."

She actually took a knee and gave him a bow of deep respect. "It is an honor to make your acquaintance, Mr. Bloodtrail."

I was a bit surprised. "That's the first time I've seen you address anyone halfway decently."

"My family's patron is Brotbeck, Saint of Murder. That is our legacy." She stood up. "Yet even the heirs of Brotbeck must pay respect to the legendary Hunter Killers of the Squalo Empire."

"*I am flattered by this abnormally pale human's words, Carnavon, but she is mistaken. I am not a member of that elite order. The Hunter Killers are the Empire's finest. You should inform her that I am but a humble monk, come to study the ways of you land creatures.*"

Considering Trax's mere presence had kept the Latros from reflexively stomping on us, I thought back, *We'll keep that part our little secret for now. The Latros thinking you're all that is a deterrent.*

"*I am dangerous, but I am not Squalo elite Hunter Killer dangerous… Ah. This must be the human concept known as* subterfuge. *Fascinating.*"

"Let's continue." I gestured for Dathka to keep walking. Conveniently for me, Trax followed along behind us. His presence might actually keep her humble. "Next to the water room's the kitchen and mess. Over there is the earth room, on account of that tower wall shattering upon impact, so the floor's now made of soil."

"Why's that door boarded up and chained shut?"

"We've put a temporary hiatus on practicing earth spells. There's a rogue Elemental spirit lost here and it keeps sticking itself to earth spells. We have to purge the area before continuing." I said that as if I'd known that all along, and hadn't just picked it up from her boss recently.

"Why don't you just purge it, then?"

"Regrettably, that's not a spell any of us know yet."

"I do."

"Really?" It would be really nice to get our earth room back. "Would you care to demonstrate?"

"What's in it for me?"

A valid question. "It would certainly end any disputes over you taking up space and eating our food until our adventure's done, and Azarin wouldn't suggest you go live in the canal instead."

"*It is a fine canal,*" Trax added helpfully, not that Dathka could understand him. "*There are some fish to eat and occasionally larger corpses float by.*"

"I'll consider it," she said.

"*Does she mean she will consider living in the canal or casting this spell?*"

She means the spell, Trax. It was a good thing I'd learned to silently think letters and pictures to the oblivious Trax, because if some of our conversations were overheard in public, it would surely remove a lot of our Squalo's dangerous mystique.

Harassed from their beds by ghosts, our students had begun going about their day. Last night's winnings had been enough for those of us who'd fought to pay our agreed upon tuition. That ensured we'd be able to buy enough element that we could get back to practicing our spells.

"That room over there is set aside for life magic, but we don't yet have someone who knows any of those. We've got one dwarf from that realm, but all his magic is offensive earth spells."

"Life magic is my deficiency." Dathka wasn't so much admitting a weakness, as insulting an entire branch of magic. "Healers are weak. Inflicting wounds is a far more valuable skill than repairing them."

It was an immutable law of magic that every mage had an affinity to one element, that they could instinctively cast at a much higher level, and that affinity usually corresponded to the realm of their heritage. But we also had a corresponding deficiency in something else, where no matter how hard we tried, we'd only be able to cast spells of that element at a much lower level.

For example, Azarin was brilliant with air magic, but was so talentless at fire, it took a pile of Red for her to barely make sparks. Meanwhile, fire came naturally to me, and those spells were stronger and took less effort to cast. I didn't know what my deficiency was, as I'd not had a chance to play with all of the elements yet, but from my struggles to accomplish anything with earth, I suspected that was it.

"Up there is the male dormitory. I'd avoid that if I were you."

"*It smells of reptiles.*"

"Thank you, Trax. This big area ahead is for combat training." There were a few students there already working, probably in anticipation of our adventure. That made me happy, because I was trying to impress this woman with our professionalism. But, of course, when we walked by, Danny had dropped a war hammer on his toe, and was hopping about on one foot, while Rufus laughed and Krachma called him names in Lobbish.

"Over there's the death practice room. We do have a bit of that."

"Yes, I noticed you used an *Obscura* against me."

"We got that from Rade."

"It is a common enough parlor trick in our realm."

"It worked great on you..." It made me happy to see her frown at that. "And up there at the far end is the fire room, which is something of my specialty."

"Oh really. Then show me what you're working on that's so special."

"I'd rather not."

"Why? Are you afraid your academy's best isn't that impressive?"

She was trying to provoke me into showing off, probably so she could know the rest of my tricks should we fight again in the future. "Sorry. That's proprietary information. Outcasts only."

"What kind of hotlander's afraid of playing with fire? I dare you."

That was insulting my pride, but I wasn't played that easily. "How about a trade? You show me yours, I'll show you mine."

"You pig."

"Don't flatter yourself, deadlander. I'll show you the new fire spell I'm working on—no formula, just a demonstration—if you purge the rogue Elemental spirt from the earth room."

She mulled that over. "You have a deal."

I pointed at Trax. "He's our witness that you promised."

As usual, Trax clearly didn't understand what was going on. "*Should I record this as part of my secretary duties?*"

"That noise in your head was him saying he'll hold you to it."

"I'll happily spit on your grave, Carnavon, and even put you in it, but I would never disrespect such a lethal emissary of the Squalo Empire. Demonstrate your spell and, in return, I'll show you how to cast a simple *Purge.*"

If you can't trust a gang assassin to keep her word, then who can you trust? I sent my light charm ahead into the fire room to hover over the metal workbench. The bullets I'd been working on before leaving for the arena were still there, because every student here knew better than to screw with my stuff. Normally, we didn't leave anything flammable in here, but the paper cases, gun powder, and target were necessary for this experiment.

"A few months ago, I got to watch a really impressive duel between two very powerful wizards. Haddar versus Adderlane, two deadly titans locked in a battle to the death. Adderlane was an enchanter, like me, and you too, I believe, if the arena announcer was accurate."

"He was," Dathka grudgingly admitted, not liking to even give up that much information which might later be used against her.

"So us enchanters do the best by attaching our spells to some kind of object. This enchanter attached a variety of offensive spells to bullets. I like guns and I like magic, so I asked myself why can't I use guns as a delivery system for spells myself?"

"Because that's wasteful foolishness. Then any common defensive charm would stop not just the projectile, but also your attached spell."

"This was a rank ten, so his spells hit so powerful, it didn't matter. He'd just blast through any protections anyway. I can't do that yet. But it did give me an idea. What you say is true. Anybody with some money can go to the market and buy a charm that'll stop a few bullets. I've got one myself."

"I found that out when I shot you the first time last night."

"I'm still sore from the impact. How's the leg?"

She scowled but had no response to that.

I pulled back my sleeve and showed her the magic bracelet I'd taken off a Frunza Tarlev student who'd been dumb enough to try and fight me and Trax.

"*I have one of those as well,*" Trax sent, because if Squalos weren't already terrifying enough, a Squalo who was temporarily bulletproof was even scarier.

"A protective spell activates automatically when something fast comes at it." I took the bracelet off and went over to the big log I set in the corner and set the bracelet on top of it. "How long the shield lasts, how much it stops, and how fast it recharges will depend on the power of the enchanter and the amount and quality of the elements used. But these are so simple that a piece of wood can activate them."

I went back to the workbench and picked up one of the experimental cartridges. I'd already infused these lead bullets with Red dust, using a formula and focus that was somewhere between my warming bowl and a snail grenade. The soft grey metal emitted just a bit of red light, which was barely visible here. In comparison, Adderlane's bullets had been infused with so much magic, they'd glowed like beacons, but I was nowhere near his level.

I kept a few cotton balls in my vest for just such an occasion and squished them into my ear holes. Drawing my gun, I broke it open, unloaded the normal wax paper cartridge, and inserted the magical one.

"It's just going to flatten itself against the shield," Dathka said. "This is why I carry a matched pair of pistols. The first shot sets off the enchantment, then I shoot them with the second while it recharges. Simple."

I suppose that was simpler, but I couldn't afford to buy another pistol yet. Gnomish craftmanship was expensive. "Unless they've got more than one protection on them, or I'd rather not waste an extra bullet. Plug your ears."

I concentrated until I could clearly sense the Red coating the bullet, and once I was sure I'd willed it to life, I hurried and fired it at the target. The last thing I wanted was for that spell to cook off inside my gun.

The sharp crack of the bargemaster's handgun reverberated against the bricks. Through the spreading cloud of smoke could be seen a lingering shimmer from where the shield had activated to stop the bullet. Not so much as a bit of bark had flown off it.

Dathka took her fingers out of her ears and snorted at my obvious and amusing failure.

Except the bullet that had smashed itself flat against the shield and remained there, glowing orange, and that grew brighter and brighter, until it was a molten bit of slag. The protective shield went down, as all magical shields must do, and that bit of slag promptly fused itself to the log. The wood began to char and blacken. Smoke hissed out. Then it burst into a small circle of flames.

"Wood is dense. It should be a lot more impressive on skin and flammable clothing. As a man who's been hit by droplets of lava, believe me, that's going to hurt more than you can imagine." As much as I wanted to brag about my latest creation to this snobbish Latro, I stopped myself from elaborating further. This spell had several useful applications. It wasn't as mean as the *Screws of Chaos*, and nowhere near as destructive as a snail grenade, but I could shoot a bullet a lot farther than I could throw something.

"What happens if your victim's not wearing a shield?"

"I've not tested that yet, but I suspect the bullet would punch a hole like usual and then turn molten while lodged inside their body." The bullet's glow was slowly fading as it began to cool, but it had burned a divot into the log. "Which… yeah… Ouch."

"Something that hot lodged within them, their insides would cook. Their blood would boil around it. The pain would be incomprehensible. How much?"

"How much what?" I asked as I picked up a staged bucket of water to douse the log.

"How much to enchant these molten bullets for me? Would you give me a discount if I purchased a hundred?"

"Saints, woman, how many people do you plan to shoot?"

"The list is long."

"Well, I don't know. I'm still experimenting on this batch. I'm not ready to try them out in real life yet. But in the future, I'll happily take a Latro's money to pay the Latro's rent."

Dathka let out a long sigh. "Alas, I'm low on funds for now. We'll revisit this discussion in the future. A deal's a deal. Let me show you how to purge an Elemental spirit, which I'm amazed none of you know, as it is a spell so simple, even an idiot child should know it."

She ducked out the door and left me there to put out the fire.

"*That female seems pleasant.*"

"She's kind of the opposite of that, Trax."

"*I was guessing. It is hard to tell with you humans sometimes.*"

17

That foggy Deathday afternoon, I walked to the Department of Magical Aptitude and Assessment to see if I could scrounge up a tester for my merry band of Outcasts. The home of the testers was a complex consisting of several large buildings on its own plateau a bit off the Collegium, on the road to the Pallentine, which was an even more illustrious district for statesmen and nobles. I'd not yet dared to visit.

The testers' compound struck me as a lot more humble and businesslike than the ostentatious display of wealth and importance of its neighbors. The Collegium was one massive academy after another, each one in a wildly different architectural style from its founder's homeland, all trying to outdo each other. The place was all looming towers and beautiful palaces, and they even had one great big hollowed-out tree that was practically its own town.

Meanwhile, the testers got a bunch of grey concrete blocks with some windows and a warning sign that if you weren't here on Nexus Council matters, you were trespassing.

There were a couple members of the Core City Watch manning a guard shack at the entrance. I'd worn my best clothes, so they didn't immediately chase me away as a beggar. I had no appointment, but did have a piece of paper signed—grudgingly—by a nobleman which declared I represented a magical academy, so they let me through. Considering how often I'd been snubbed in the Collegium, that victory made me feel smug.

The interior was as boring and utilitarian as the exterior. I didn't know a lot about their organization, but that seemed fitting. Testers didn't need flash to show off their clout. Their power came from giving accurate results, not lightning bolts.

A female gnome sat on a high chair behind a desk overlooking the reception area. The rosy-cheeked, tiny woman flashed me a brilliant smile. "Good day, sir! Welcome to the Department of Magical Aptitude and Assessment. How may I assist you today?"

"I was hoping to speak to Tester Pivorotto. Has he returned from the Plane of Fire yet?"

"He has, just recently, in fact, but he's currently on another assignment." She seemed saddened to disappoint me, but added, "Could another tester help you?"

I'd been hoping for Pivorotto because he'd struck me as a genuinely kind man, giving of his time, and most importantly, willing to take a bribe, but within reasonable limits of bribery. A generous amount of Red had bought me some time on his busy schedule, but nothing would get him to lie about my results. That seemed to me the perfect balance of what the Outcast Academy needed in a tester.

"Sure. I'll see another tester."

"Of course, sir! I shall see who is available."

The gnome was so eager to help, I'd nearly forgotten not everyone from this organization was so nice. "It's not Tester Ewing, is it?"

"No. She's currently on assignment in the Water Realm."

"Oh good." I didn't add that I hoped she drowned or got eaten by a Squalo while there. It was one thing to crush a young boy's dreams of being a wizard, but she hadn't needed to be such a malicious bitch about it. "Anyone else will be fine."

"May I ask who you are and which academy you're from?"

"I'm Ozwald Carnavon of Fogo, representing Gaul Haddar, master of the newly formed Academy of Outcasts." I stated that with pride, because it was nice to feel like a bigshot for once.

"Oh…" The gnome's smile died. Her manner changed so fast, I thought I'd unwittingly wronged her somehow.

"What?"

"You're one of *those people.* Wait here..." She climbed off her chair. "And don't be tempted to steal anything or deface the premises while I'm away. If you do, I'll know it was you!"

I looked around the waiting room. "I'm the only one here."

She pointed one stubby little finger at me menacingly as she left. "Exactly!"

Haddar didn't like this city, and many of the high-ranking mages who ran it felt the same way about him. I didn't know what all the history was there, but his unplanned promotion had surely upset a lot of very important people. Backbiting and rumormongering were popular hobbies among the Core's upper crust, so these people knowing about us wasn't too surprising. I only felt bad because I'd temporarily gotten my hopes up for once.

Five minutes later, the gnome returned, and this time, she had a human with her. He was grey-haired, distinguished, and wearing the insignia of the testers on his robes. While the gnome climbed back up her chair, she said, "This is Mr. Carnavon of the aforementioned academy."

His manner was coldly polite. "Hello. I am Tester Ritter." He handed me a sheet of paper. "This is the price list for our services."

I'd not even said why I was here, but took the paper and looked it over, only to realize they were trying to rip us off worse than Carcalla had. "I intend no offense toward your fine and respected organization, but these amounts quoted seem rather steep."

"Are you questioning my *accuracy*?"

That had to be a major insult among testers, so I quickly said, "No, I'm sure they're right, they're just a bit more than I'd budgeted for."

"I assure you these are the current rates. This humble amount should be but a pittance to a prestigious magical academy. We are the only organization accredited by the Nexus Council to provide an accurate assessment of an individual's magical aptitude. Our services are in great demand."

Of course they were. The only way to gain respect and access as a mage was by increasing your rank, and the only path through the lower ranks was by a tester's say so. "Surely this can't be what you charge a nobleman to test each of his subjects?"

"My organization has existing arrangements with every kingdom, principality, and academy in the realms. Yours is new, and therefore not among those."

"So every time we want to see if one of our students has gained a rank, we have to pay you *this*?" I gestured at the outlandish sum.

"And there are no refunds if they are not advanced. Also note, there is an additional fee each time one of our testers has to travel to a different location."

That had to be the hundreds of Obols for *travel to or through a dangerous realm* clause. They were acting like they'd have to cross lava flows to reach us. "We're still in the city. It's a leisurely hour's carriage ride from here."

"Correction. The Under Slump is *not* part of this fine city, sir." The gnome sniffed after correcting me, like *how dare you insinuate that trash is related to us?* "It's a tumor that has grown upon this city's flank, and frankly, I'm surprised the Council hasn't excised it entirely."

"We can come up here. Surely, I could work out a lower rate than this if we were to make an appointment at your convenience and only bring one student at a time who we're certain is ready to advance in rank. We'd hate to waste anyone's time."

Tester Ritter shook his head. "That's not how things are done around here, Mr. Carnavon. We have a system. That system has rules. Without those rules, there would be pandemonium."

"Bereft of tradition, we'd be no different than the lawless Slumps," the gnome added.

I was asking them to test a handful of students, not to police marauding gangs of nightbolgs. "This seems more a racket than a system."

They both gasped at that, like *how rude, such tone.*

Tester Ritter grew rather annoyed by my plain-speaking ways. "It is unfortunate that your Master Haddar has loudly voiced a similar slanderous opinion in public about this department several times in the past. He has been rather vocal in his criticism of how the Nexus Council chooses to manage things."

So that was the real issue. It was as if every day I got to learn about someone else Gaul Haddar once mortally offended in this city. It was just my luck that the only rank ten who'd adopt us was seen as a barbaric pariah. "Could we discuss—"

Ritter interrupted me. "Look at the time. I'm afraid I have another appointment I must attend to now, Mr. Carnavon. The watchmen will show you out. Good day."

Once outside, I fumed for a bit, but standing around angry wasn't going to accomplish anything. My visit to the testers had proved fruitless, but since I'd come all this way, I decided to stop by a certain location within the Collegium. A saying here in the Core that I liked was *kill two birds with one stone.* That wasn't something we said in Fogo, as we didn't have flesh and blood birds there, since their feathers would promptly catch on fire should they land, but the saying made sense in principle.

Each academy had its own library, full of secret tomes they guarded zealously. I'd been told that there was also a library in the Collegium maintained by the Council, which was open to representatives of all the academies for research purposes. There were no spellbooks there, but rather, this was the place where the city collected all its official documents and records pertaining to magical affairs.

There was no way they'd have let the likes of me in there before, but I was now armed with a fancy letter bearing the stamp of Ambassador Dardick Argent declaring me the official interim representative of a real honest-to-goodness magical academy. It was worth a try.

After asking a passerby, I was told the Collegium's Hall of Public Records was on the far side of the district, backed up against the mountain. When I got there, I found that it was more built into the mountain than on it, as they'd carved a giant vault straight into the stone. From how everything about it appeared squat and brutal, surely the place had been built by dwarves.

It was much busier than expected, with many people coming and going. By some miracle, my letter actually got me past the watchmen and inside. However, it appeared my luck would end there.

The stern old lady at the counter looked me over and could tell I was no scholar. "What do you want, boy?"

"I'm seeking any documentation you've got about a little island in the bay named Korthican's Warning."

"Korthican's Warning, is it?" She laughed in my face. "Are you daft?"

"Not particularly." The sullen testers I could understand, but I wasn't sure what I'd done to give offense here already. I hadn't even shown her my letter, so the government lady wasn't among Gaul Haddar's admiring legions. "What's so funny about my request?"

"You think you're the first dumb-ass adventurer to come here trying to do research, thinking he's going to take a run at that place? So, to get in here, did you bribe some sucker from an academy to vouch for you? Or did you just forge the papers?"

I glanced around, but it was just a bunch of other little old ladies on one side of a counter, separated by thick glass and a small window from the patrons who'd been waiting in line to get help. Once the requests were put in, the ladies would comb through their shelves until they found the right documents and bring them back. I must've gotten in the wrong line.

"Excuse me, ma'am?"

"Don't look to any of them to save you, and don't waste my time acting like your delicate feelings are hurt, kid. I've worked here twice as long as you've been alive. Everyone here can recognize an adventurer looking for an angle a mile away. We're supposed to throw patrons out once we figure out they're illegitimate, *but*… we can be convinced to look away."

"This isn't fake." I took out the letter and handed it through the window. "I'm from a real academy."

"*Sure* you are." She took one brief glance at the Argent's seal, winked at me, then passed it back. "Because public records are only to be used for proper research duties, you're a right proper wizard doing right proper and respectable wizardly research on some notorious ruins, and not some ruffian adventurer looking for information on how to better plunder the city's ancient bits. We've *never* seen that before here, no sir!"

Her manner of speaking reminded me of home. "Are you from Fogo?"

"Close. Born on Ohen, but I've lived in the Core for a real long time. You barge cadre, boy?"

"Yes, ma'am. Barge 519."

"I knew it! You've been here just long enough to get a bit of sun, but I could still smell the smoke on you."

I realized she was the only one of the old lady employees wearing a giant wooly sweater, even though all the Core's vast government buildings had Red-fueled furnaces. "Does this place ever get any warmer or does it always feel like this?"

"Eh, you get used to it after a while. About ten years in, the perpetual shivering stops. Not that any of us hotlanders would ever traipse around this city half naked like those from other lesser realms do, all undignified like. Now, back to business. Don't try to shovel anymore trogshit at me, boy. I know a scam when I see it. The only folks who ask about old places like Korthican are on treasure hunts."

I laughed, as it was nice to finally have an honest exchange in this part of town. "I assure you I am a right proper wizard, from a real academy… *However*, I'm also looking to do some plundering on the side."

"Keep your voice down there, stating the obvious. Most of these Collegium twerps will rat you out to the watch in an instant. The watch frowns on such behavior."

"Yes, ma'am."

Now it was her turn to look around to see if anyone was listening in, but the other white-haired ladies were occupied with their papers. "Here's how it's gonna work. You want the good stuff, the real scoop, you gotta pay a little extra, know what I mean?"

"If I had a little extra, I wouldn't be reduced to looting tombs."

"I suppose that's true... But knowledge is power, young adventurer."

I still hated that title. "I was a trapper back home. We learn the hard way, it's plan and prepare or die."

"I had an uncle who was a trapper. May the saints see to it he rests in peace. Way to prey upon an old woman's nostalgia, boy! I suppose trappers are like adventurers. The smart ones know to do their research before hanging their nuts over the lava to see if it's still hot. Alright, you caught me feeling generous today. On account of me not wanting to see a neighboring countryman get killed stupidly, this time, I'll aid you for free. The next favor will cost you."

"That's more than fair." It would be nice to have a friend here, especially considering Carcalla had us on the hook to do this sort of thing again. "Provided I don't die, who should I ask for next time?"

"I'm Wilma. Now let me get all the records on why you'd have to be a moron to set foot on that evil place!"

18

I spent hours reading old reports from the Core City Watch and complaints from the neighbors from back when it was called Korthican's Landing, before things went horribly wrong there and it'd been renamed Korthican's Warning. Between those papers and the more recent stories I'd gotten from the locals, I felt like I was starting to understand why Carcalla was so interested in the place.

They finally threw me out of the library that night so they could close, and I returned to the Under Slump. I made it home late without getting accosted or having to set anyone on fire and went straight to bed.

In the morning, I got the student council together so I could share my findings.

"The chair hereby calls this meeting to order." Rade thumped his fist against the table that Bognar had built for us out of some planks. "And I shall begin by noting my disappointment that we're meeting in our kitchen rather than our usual establishment, which has decent beer and good-looking serving wenches."

"There's a very good reason for that, which I will explain."

"Come now, Carnavon. I know Azarin spent most of our winnings on element and supplies in the market yesterday—"

Azarin interrupted him to say, "Let the record show that I got us some excellent deals."

"I'm certain you did, but surely there was enough left for us to buy a round of drinks or two."

"*As secretary, am I supposed to remember all this talking or just the part where you humans say* let the record show?"

I lifted one hand, indicating the need for silence. "Responding in order… Rade, this discussion needs to be in private away from prying ears, we probably should have never mentioned in public where we're going to begin with, and I'll explain why. Azarin, thank you for taking care of that. And, Trax, don't worry about that right now, because we've got a bigger problem."

"Bigger problems than our pending dangerous adventure, our murderous landlord, or being saddled with his Latrocinium spy?" Azarin laughed at the absurdity of our situation. "Worse than that?"

"Yeah, it is. Possibly much worse."

My somber response dampened their good moods. Even Krachma looked up from his bowl of oatmeal to see what was so serious.

"I found out that Korthican, who that island is named after, was a very powerful wizard. He was one of the many Councilmen who died five hundred years ago, stopping the surprise invasion that came through the time gate."

It was ironic for me to be telling them about this now, as it was Eternaday, or the Quiet Day as most called it now, since it was the one day of the week the Nexus wasn't open to another realm. The Great Machine was currently rotating past a gate that was forever sealed, protecting us from the evil that had taken over the Elemental Plane of Time.

"Every child knows that story." Rade waved one hand dismissively. "One morning, the gate opened as it always does, only instead of travelers and traders waiting, it was an unspeakable evil which promptly began slaughtering its way across the Core. Heroes fought back. We won. We locked that gate, and there's been no access to the Realm of Time ever since. So on and so forth. What's that ancient history got to do with us?"

"Resources?"

Rade scowled, confused. "You've lost me."

"A high-ranking elf wizard once told me that stopping the invasion wasn't the victory most of us think it is. It was really the beginning of the end for the Core."

Rade snorted. "Five hundred years is a long time for an ending!"

"When that gate got sealed, we lost access to ever getting any more of one of the seven elements. *Permanence*. The stuff that makes spells last longer or forever. What was already here was here, there will never be another resupply, and that's what makes it so valuable."

"Yeah, you can't even buy it in the market," Azarin said. "I've asked. Any Permanence that turns up gets seized by the Council. They say they need it to keep the Great Machine turning."

It was hard to even imagine that mountain-sized device linking all the realms together for over forty-five hundred years could ever stop, but if it did, it would ruin everything. Realms like mine would starve to death in a month. The others might survive, but they'd lose access to every other form of magic except for the one element native to their own.

"Elves call this time *Yavus Olum*. This means *Slow Death*." Krachma speaking up at all was rare. Him knowing anything in Elvish was an even bigger surprise. "Krachma prefers regular death."

"That missing ingredient is why even really powerful wizards like the Council can't do what the ancients did. They can't build floating cities anymore. It's why things are breaking down. That's why the Slump started slumping," I said.

"Indeed, this all sounds very terrible, and this hypothetical death is so slow that I'm sure my great-great grandchildren will surely regret when it all grinds to a halt... What's any of this got to do with us today?" Rade asked impatiently.

"Korthican made his home on that isle, but it had already been settled by the ancient civilization that predates the Core. They'd built a lighthouse there, but it hadn't been used for a long time. Until Korthican enchanted a light so bright it could be seen by ships many miles away to stick on top of the old tower. It was supposed to be symbolic of hope or the greatness of the Core or something. All I know for sure is that other wizards who lived by the bay complained to the Council about the brightness keeping them up at night. I think that light is the lamp Carcalla thinks is still hidden in the secret room beneath where the lighthouse used to stand."

"And?"

"It's said that Korthican enchanted that lamp to *never go out.*"

Rade didn't get it immediately, but Azarin did. "Naanwalla's tits! That thing's got Permanence in it?"

"Most likely. After the sealing of the time gate, the Council sent the watch to round up all the items enchanted with chronomancy, but the lamp was never found. They assumed it was lost in the battle when the lighthouse got blasted to pieces. But if it got hidden beneath the ruins all along, that would explain why the island's infested now. Powerful artifacts are supposed to attract monsters."

"That's true. Like a moth to flame." Rade used an expression I'd never really understood until I'd moved here, as back home, we had flames everywhere, but it was too hot for bugs. Here, I'd watched the dumb little things fly right into a torch and pop themselves into dusty sparks.

"Anything with time magic in it's got to be worth a fortune, but adventurers have looked before and found nothing," Azarin said. "And then somehow Carcalla gets a tip about a secret door and even got the password for it."

"It can't be that reliable of a tip, or surely he would've sent some professionals when he first heard about it, rather than putting it off however long and then sending the likes of us. I'm guessing it's just a small possibility it's still there, but even a hint that there might be some Permanence is enough to get people curious."

"So it's likely been gone for centuries, but this great and splendorous artifact *might* be there, so really nothing's changed for us, except adding a small chance that we might make an obscene profit." Azarin grinned. "And here you were getting me all worried for nothing!"

"Only we've all been running our mouths in public about what we're doing and where we're going for the last few days, and there are many who'd slit our throats for a shot at a bit of Permanence.

We've said who we're working for. Surely someone else knows the old legends about the island, and they'll reason out that's why Carcalla's interested in the place. I nearly got killed by Tempus Metum cultists just a few months ago, and they're obsessed with anything connected to the time realm."

"You think they'd want to protect the lamp or steal it?"

"They were hideous underground mutants trying to murder me, Azarin. I didn't pause to quiz them on their club's purpose in life."

"Oh, you're just being paranoid now, Oz. We've not talked *that* much." Azarin laughed, but then she noticed Rade place his face into his palms. "What?"

"I... may have complicated that."

"*Braden Prescott.* What did you do?"

We all knew it was bad when Rade didn't react poorly to her using his actual given name, as opposed to the fake noble one he'd assigned himself. "I felt some guilt for saying cruel things to Rufus, so I took him out for a drink. We went to a pub last night, where we may have boasted at great length about our pending adventure."

"That's not so bad." Azarin waved one hand dismissively.

"To the whole place... loudly..."

"Why would you do that?" I asked, bewildered.

"To extol our bravery, while a great many people bought us drinks. It turns out that once inebriated, Rufus has a lovely singing voice. He'd have made a fine bard."

"Rufus is an eagle-brained idiot," Azarin said. "You didn't mention anything to anyone about there being a secret hidden chamber no other adventurers have ever known about before, did you?"

"Me? No. Of course not. Rufus, however... That may have been one of the verses in his song. And unfortunately, this particular pub is in the Slump, is rather popular, and caters to clients from mercenary and adventuring companies."

"Trax."

"*Yes, Carnavon?*"

"Let the record show that if we get robbed, it's Rade's fault."

"*I will be sure that goes on the sphere.*"

"Apologies, my friends. I thought we'd only drawn the attention of one wrathful criminal entity, not several... My inadvertent storytelling in pursuit of free drinks and the attention of attractive young ladies aside, it is possible that if someone were to take word of our expedition as a sign that there's still treasure on the island, that they might leave quickly in order to reach it before we do."

I'd not even thought of that. I'd been thinking more like a trapper than an adventurer, because if I was evil and wanted to steal some time magical item, I'd let other fools bleed to get it for me, and then jump them on the way out.

"You let Rufus play song bird last night. If other adventurers left as soon as they heard, they could already be there. Carcalla gave us until Waterday to hit the island, but if he finds out there was time magic there all along, and we were sitting here with our thumbs stuck up our asses while it got hauled off by someone else first, we're getting evicted for sure... and by evicted, I mean evicted from *life*. We've got to go *now*."

"I shall rally the troops!" Rade ran toward the door, then thought better of it and returned to bang his fist on the table again. "Meeting is adjourned."

Krachma sullenly finished his bowl of oatmeal and stood up. "Krachma will fetch his mace."

As everyone left to gather their things, I had an idea. "Hey, Trax. We've got to walk to the bay and then find a boat to take us across. Could you swim down the canal fast and keep an eye on the island until we get there? Then you can let us know if anyone else showed up first."

"*That is a splendid idea. If there are other adventurers present, would you like me to eat them?*"

"Hold off on the eating people until I arrive, alright? And be careful. Don't get too close. I don't want you to get hurt. The island's got those unidentified monsters living around it."

"*Can I eat the dangerous monsters?*"

"Use your best judgment on that."

And it wasn't until after Trax was gone that I realized how incredibly dangerous it might be to tell a hungry Squalo to *use his best judgment* on whether he should devour something or not.

19

Morton the gnome had to run to keep up with my fast walk. "Don't you think at least one of us should stay here to watch over the academy, Mr. Carnavon?"

"No, Morton. Everyone needs to pitch in on this one."

"But, but, what if thieves come and plunder the Tube while we're out?"

"What're they going to steal? Bognar's homemade furniture?"

Not that leaving behind our gnome would scare off any serious thieves anyway. He was tiny, couldn't fight, and had no offensive magic to speak of. Hell, our ghosts were more of a deterrent against thieves than Morton.

"We're not taking everything of value with us."

"We're taking most of our element. I've already hidden my remaining components. If you're worried about your personal belongings, pull up the rope ladder to the barracks, and someone can get back up there with an *Ascend* when we return."

"I really don't know if this is a good idea, sir. My family are merchants specializing in the auctioning of exotic animals and we *never* left the compound unguarded. To do so was practically inviting disaster! Vandals could unlock the cages and let the livestock free!"

"We don't have *livestock.*" The poor little fellow was just trying to shirk the dangerous parts, but I hadn't been joking when I'd said everyone needed to start pulling their weight around here, and he didn't even weigh that much. "Morton, the very survival of the academy is at stake. You know some spells. You can pull a trigger. You'll be fine."

"But what if I'm slain by monsters? Or speared upon some horrible trap?"

"Then you wouldn't be fine, so don't do that." We were almost to the front door. "In the meantime, go help Azarin organize the supplies."

"Mother warned me adventurers always come to a bad end," Morton muttered as he hurried away.

I couldn't even disagree with the tiny fellow there, because my mom had told me the same thing.

The Outcasts were assembling in front of the tower. We were a motley bunch, ten strong—if we counted Trax, who was already ranging ahead—armed with a variety of spells—all low-level home brews—and weapons—most of which were cheap or improvised. We were all rank one or two, though I suspected several of us were due a promotion from having learned so many new spells over the last few months. I myself had picked up a few from the others, so I now knew a grand total of eight well enough to cast them on demand. Which I understood to be a very impressive number for a wizard of the lowly first rank. I just needed to find a tester willing to slum it long enough to prove I was worthy of the second.

There was no sign of our Latrocinium watcher. "Where's Dathka?"

It was Danny who answered, "She went out this morning, said she needed to speak with some of her gang. She wasn't here when you surprise-ordered us to leave early."

Well, that absence was bloody inconvenient. The last thing I needed was Dathka thinking we were trying to give her the slip, but we couldn't wait around for her to get back either. Carcalla would surely be angrier at getting no treasure at all than worried we'd shorted him some.

"I'll leave a note for her. She can catch up."

Bognar trotted over to me, wearing a cooking pot for a helmet. "Hey, Carnavon. We've got some visitors. They say they're seeking to join the academy."

Danny was there stuffing gear into a pack. "You should have them come with us, Mr. Carnavon. We really could use all the help we can get." He laughed nervously. "There's strength in numbers, right?"

Aspiring wizards who'd been turned away by the real academies would hear about us and sometimes come to check us out. Most of those didn't stick around after seeing the nature of our arrangement or the quality of our living conditions. It took a special kind of desperation to join an academy without teachers, traditions, or resources, with the added bonus of getting to live in the dirtiest and most dangerous part of the city. Normally, potential new recruits would be good news, as that meant new knowledge and spells, but their timing was shit.

"Tell them to come back tomorrow."

"Uh..." Bognar hesitated. "I'd rather not. They're kinda scary. How about you be the one to tell them?"

"Scary?" That got me was curious. "Where?"

Bognar pointed toward the corner of the Tube, so I walked over to find a few strangers lounging around our neighbor's chicken coop. From how these three looked, they would've made me suspicious on a normal day, but considering our peculiar circumstances, I knew right away this had to be some kind of trick.

It was two humans and an orc. That alone wasn't odd. Humans were the most common race in the Core, and since there was an enclave of them from just about every kingdom in the Core, I'd seen plenty of orcs too. It was everything else about them that told me they were trouble.

Most of our recruits were young. Both of the humans were several years older than me. I couldn't tell orc ages, since they were green and wrinkly anyway, but this one had nearly as many scars as Krachma, and was almost as physically intimidating. Our recruits were all relatively inexperienced, because why else would someone come train with the likes of us? Except these three carried themselves like seasoned veterans who knew their way around a battlefield.

These three were giving me enough of a bad feeling that I sneakily pinched a bit of Red between my fingers as I approached.

It was the orc who must've been in charge, as he stepped in front of the others to address me. "I was told to look for the one in the cloak and hood. You Carnavon?"

"Yeah, that's me. What can I do for you, gentlemen?"

"I am Gerzog. This is Hans." The one who nodded was a squat muscular fellow with a shaved head. "And Aziz." Who was tall and skinny with strange tattoos on his face. "We were told you're taking in students to learn more magic. We all know some magic. We want to join up and become official wizards too."

I had to crane my neck back to look Gerzog in the eyes. There was something about this orc that warned me I was dealing with a hardened killer.

"I'm afraid we're not interviewing any applicants today." Just in case they weren't thieving scum trying to attach themselves to our outfit to steal our treasure because they'd been tipped off by stupid Rufus, I added, "You can come back next week, and I'll be happy to show you around."

"Why wait? We join now."

All of our other recruits were poor and meager of resource. These three had well-worn rugged clothing, but of quality, and their gear was squared away. They all wore swords, daggers, and pistols of obviously decent quality, and I spotted at least one wand. Cheap wands weren't that rare, but nice ones were. Even Danny had made a wand, but his enchantment was weak, and it had been placed on a stick. The one named Aziz had a fancy bronze wand stuck through his belt, set up for a quick draw like I had my pistol. The end of his wand was in the shape of a grasping hand.

"Nice back scratcher."

Aziz sneered at me. "It's more of a neck breaker."

"It's a strong spell," Gerzog growled. "I heard the cost to join up is but a spell. We got spells like that to share. Good ones."

"I bet. You look pretty experienced to want to become students."

"I'm rank three," Gerzog spoke with confidence. "These two were born twos. It's hard to climb much past that on your own."

He was right about that, but I didn't for a second think pursuing education was what had brought them here today. I'd been a good trapper. All trappers knew when to listen to our paranoia. "We'll have to discuss it later. We've got something important going on today, fellas."

"What're you doing today that's so important?" Hans asked. "Most things is closed on the Quiet Day."

"I'm afraid our affairs are private academy business."

"Don't be pushy to new friends, Hans." When orcs smile, there's a lot of big, intimidating teeth involved. "We also heard the Outcasts were going adventuring soon. From the look of those over there, you must be leaving soon. We can go with you and help. We've all done some adventuring."

From the scars and confident demeanor, that was probably the most truthful thing Gerzog had told me so far, as these three surely had a lot of experience with fighting and pillaging. "I bet you do."

"We go with you. We help. We keep you safe. We ask for nothing in return."

Of course they wouldn't *ask*. They'd just stab us in the back after we found the treasure and keep the lamp for themselves. "Naw. I think we're good."

That big, fake, tusky smile slowly died, and Gerzog's red eyes narrowed. "We tried to be friendly."

"We can be friends next week. Goodbye, gentlemen." I kept the Red on my glove ready as I walked away. If I heard a sudden movement, like a gun or blade clearing leather, I'd toss an arc of fire their way.

But they refrained, and by the time I got back to the others, the three of them were leaving.

"What was that about, Oz?" Azarin asked.

"They said they wanted to join."

"Oh? They looked rather capable."

"Yeah, capable of murdering us."

20

We'd hurried from the Under Slump and then stuck to the edges of the more reputable districts rather than passing directly through them. Taking the wide avenues would've been faster, but we were a large, armed band, obviously up to no good, and the Core City Watch had no patience for fuckery in the peaceful parts of town. Even if what we were doing wasn't—strictly speaking—illegal, it was questionable, and we couldn't afford to be detained while some watchmen figured that out.

The morning was cold. The sky was filled with heavy grey clouds. Snowflakes kept sticking to my face. I really couldn't understand how people lived through this gods awful *winter* nonsense, as they called it, but my fellow hotlander turned longtime Core resident, Wilma, had assured me I'd get used to it *eventually*. Despite hood, cloak, scarf, gloves, and coat, I remained freezing. It was so cold that air-realmer Azarin had even put on a sweater. It felt like the only thing keeping me alive was the warmth generated by the briskness of our pace.

We'd have run the whole way if that wouldn't have drawn a watchman's attention. Well, that and I doubted the short-legged Morton or Rufus could keep up, and Bognar was rather fat and easily winded. Yet we set a brisk pace, because the appearance of Gerzog and his boys was surely a warning of things to come. Even rumors that there might be time magic treasure involved would bring all sorts of unscrupulous sorts down upon us.

I wished Carcalla would have warned me what we were dealing with, but frankly, I doubted he cared what happened to us. If we were murdered, and the lamp was real, he'd simply buy it off our killers. If the lamp wasn't real, this expedition had cost him nothing and his curiosity would be satisfied.

Once we reached the docks district, I went straight to the tavern where I'd listened to the local fishermen tell their stories after I'd helped them unload their catch. I left the rest of the Outcasts outside to be harassed by the squawking white ocean birds. Being so early in the morning in an honest hard-working part of town, there were very few people inside, but I picked out the least drunk among them to see about hiring a boat.

Ten minutes and a bit of haggling later, I'd rented us two row boats. Unfortunately, since the owner demanded to know where we were taking them, and I'd admitted we were going to the notorious Korthican's Warning, I'd been forced to leave a significant deposit, because he doubted we'd survive to return his boats.

I intended to get my deposit back.

As we walked down the dock to where our small wooden boats were tied, I asked, "Any sign of Dathka yet?"

Azarin shook her head *no*. "That Latro skag is going to be furious."

"It's not her anger I'm worried about. It's her boss."

"It's not your fault she was derelict in the duties Cutter Joran assigned her. Some spy she turned out to be! Ooh, maybe he'll be so disappointed in her failure to keep an eye on us that he'll have her murdered." Azarin giggled. "So tragic."

"Tragic will describe our fate if Carcalla decides we ditched her so we could rip him off. My note said where I'd try to find us a ride. Maybe we should wait here a bit."

"There's miles of docks and hundreds of boats around this bay. Every second we delay, an unknown competitor might be catching their own ride, assuming they didn't leave last night and are already there stealing what should be ours."

Azarin was right, but angering the Latros was a deadly gamble. "Then we're screwed either way."

"Ahem." From out of nowhere, Morton appeared at my side. Gnomes were unnerving like that. "If I may be so bold as to offer a suggestion, Mr. Carnavon and Lady Garzade, what if I were to stay here to greet Ms. Walker upon her arrival? However long that may take. Then I will promptly explain the entirety of the circumstances which forced our hasty departure, and then we shall procure transportation and follow after you."

"Oh, come now, Morton!" Rade exclaimed. "There's no opportunity for glory waiting on a dock!"

"It's not about glory, Lord Tartaros. It is about diplomacy and the mitigation of risk. Leaving a representative of our academy is more respectful than some mere note, and surely this show of courtesy will assuage any irritation Ms. Walker might have at being left behind. With luck, you will arrive before our challengers, and we will arrive by the time you've finished slaying all the monsters and defeating all the traps. As long as you wait for Ms. Walker to be present to observe the opening of the secret chamber, then no harm will have been done to our relationship with the Latrocinium."

I knew this was just a ploy to keep his own skin out of danger, but Morton's plan wasn't half bad. "I'm fine with that."

Rade and Azarin both shrugged. It wasn't like leaving the little guy behind was going to cost us much fighting ability on the shore.

"It's settled. Morton stays, everybody else aboard."

The gnome breathed a sigh of relief.

"I don't know what you're happy about," Bognar said. "I'd be more scared of the Latro's murderess than the monsters."

"Yes," Sifuso hissed. "Leave Bognar instead of the gnome so she can poke out his other eye."

"Don't laugh at me. It still hurts."

With four in each boat, we set out. I was cold and uncomfortable. I'd ridden in a water boat once before, but that had been on a lazy deadland's river. The bay was more of an angry, bouncing, crashing mass that kept soaking my clothing with freezing droplets of saltwater. Rade and Rufus both came from places with bodies of water big enough to require boats, so they were our captains, each trying to teach the rest of us how to use the oars to row. I'd tried to hire a crew to ferry us, but no one in the tavern was foolish enough to risk landing on the island.

Don't worry, they'd told me. *You'll be fine. It's not far at all.*

That proved to be a lie. This was not *fine.* Rowing turned out to be a terribly inconvenient way to travel. The island was in sight of the shore, but when you had a bunch of people with no idea what they were doing, on a violently churning sea, where the waves kept pushing us in the wrong direction, our meager progress was taking an agonizing long time. Every time we rode up a big wave, coming down the other side made it feel as if our tiny boat might flip. If it did, we'd surely drown.

The shore was shrinking in the distance and Korthican's Warning was growing, but at this rate, by the time we got there, our arms would be too tired to fight.

"Anybody got a spell that could speed this up?" Bognar shouted as Danny vomited over the side.

"I'm afraid not. This is a fine example why we have to keep studying," Azarin called back cheerfully. Despite being from a realm of absurdly tall mountains and endless skies, Azarin didn't seem in the least bit seasick. It must have been from all that riding about on giant birds.

Danny was sitting next to me, and the poor kid looked so grey, it likely wasn't just the nausea killing him. Suspecting he was overcome with nerves, I leaned over and told him, "It's alright to be scared."

"It's not that..." He looked like he really wanted to tell me something, but then he looked away, ashamed. "No matter what happens, I appreciate you guys giving me a chance."

"You're not going to die, Danny. Being scared when you're doing something scary is normal. The only person here who's not at least a little afraid is Rufus." I nodded toward the other boat, where our dwarf captain had taken up a bawdy rowing song. "And I think that's because he doesn't know any better."

"It's not that... It's just... Never mind."

"It's going to be alright. Cheer up."

"I will, Mr. Carnavon." Danny just gave me a determined nod, like he got it, though I suspected he was faking that temporary courage. He didn't say anything else for the rest of the trip.

There'd been no sign of Trax yet, then at one point, a grey fin popped out of the water and passed swiftly between our boats. "Oh, there he is." Except the fin was far too big, and it'd kept going.

"That's an actual shark." Then Rade added for my hotlander benefit, "It's shaped a bit like our dear Mr. Bloodtrail—facially at least—but a shark is merely a big dumb fish, bereft of hands, feet, or decorum."

"Does it eat things like Trax does?"

"Oh, very much, yes. They're voracious toothy bastards."

Now I really didn't want this stupid boat to flip.

Luckily, a short while later, another fin appeared, and this was accompanied by a mental greeting in the Squalo picture language.

"*Hello, Carnavon. I have been observing as instructed. Now I am observing that human water transportation is cumbersome and inefficient. You should learn to swim.*"

"That's a great idea, buddy."

"*The humans who have settled the upper parts of my realm to harvest the element you know as Blue use spells to propel themselves at great speeds through the water and to breathe beneath it.*" He even helpfully sent me an image of wizards far more powerful than any of us performing those great feats. "*You should get better at magic and do that.*"

I got the whole thing; everybody else got weird pictures, flashing letters, or a bit of a headache.

"What did Mr. Bloodtrail say?" Bognar asked.

"He said you're bad at rowing... Hey, Trax, any chance we could toss you a rope and you could pull us there faster?"

"*I shall do so. Watching you flounder about so pathetically is depressing.*"

After we got a pair of ropes secured to the boats, we tossed them to Trax, and in short order, he got us moving quicker than the rest of us put together could row. That really was kind of sad.

"Did anybody else get to the island ahead of us?"

"*Yes. A small group of humans arrived a few hours before I did.*"

"Dammit." I shouted toward the other boat where Rufus sat, "Your big mouth has brought us more trouble."

"*Do not worry, Carnavon. The invaders were promptly eaten.*"

"By you, or the monsters?"

"*By the monsters. You asked me not to eat any people until you arrived. I am good at following instructions.*"

"What about the monsters?"

"*They are chewy.*"

To be fair, that was on me for telling a Squalo to use his best judgment. "How many of them did you kill?"

"*Only the ones who swam out to challenge me.*"

"Trax..."

"*I slew four. I only ate one, though. The other bodies sank before I could, and I would not abandon my post in pursuit of flesh. I am very responsible. I could not identify the creatures from your earlier description, as these are not native to my plane. However, I believe these are mutants. A combination of human, mollusk, and other unknown species. They are likely a leftover experiment from a prior age.*"

"Can we communicate with them?"

"*You would waste your words. They are very noisy but do not speak. From their mind pictures, they are of minimal intelligence. Perhaps a bit dumber than ratlets even.*"

Trax mostly thought of ratlets as convenient snacks. "How tough are they?"

"*Their meat is rubbery and tastes similar to squid.*"

"I don't mean to chew. How physically tough are they? Can we kill them?"

"*Yes. They seem vulnerable to normal wounds.*"

Finally, some good news.

Trax must have read my thoughts, because he immediately brought me back down, "*I smell approximately fifty more of them.*"

I sighed, then raised my voice so both boats could hear me over the waves. "Trax says they're some kind of mutant, probably an old wizard's experiment, but our weapons should work on them just fine. Issue is, there's a bunch of them."

"*Approximately fifty,*" Trax sent just in case I'd not gotten the number the first time.

"You've got to dole out bad news slowly, so you don't overwhelm people."

"*Fascinating. Then when I have bad news for a human, I should deliver it gradually. This is good to know. There... are... too... many... monsters.*"

I shouted, "Trax says we're badly outnumbered. There's at least fifty of them."

Most of the Outcasts grimaced in fear at that, except for Rade, who got excited at the opportunity for heroic swordplay, and Rufus, who counted on his fingers, before saying, "Aye, each of us only has to slay three of them! That's an easy battle."

I exchanged an uncomfortable glance with Azarin, because Rufus was appallingly bad at math. "It's a good thing he's handy with an axe."

"Just be sure once you get your three to keep swinging to make up for the slower students, Rufus," she shouted at him, before muttering to me, "He's got molasses for brains, but you can't fault his enthusiasm."

With Trax's aid, we were rapidly approaching Korthican's Warning. It wasn't much to look at, just a lump of rocks encircled by sand, with the remains of the lighthouse in the middle, which was nothing but scattered brick piles and a few crumbling walls. A hundred yards away, another boat had been pulled up onto the sand, and mangled bodies of other would-be treasure hunters were turning the surf around them red.

A weirdly shaped figure was crouched on top of the tallest boulder on the island, obviously on look-out. It turned its strangely shaped head our direction, stared at us with its huge eyes that stuck way too far out the side of its head, before opening its black beak to let out a terribly loud hooting noise.

"They know we're here now."

As I said that, a dozen more creatures rose from among the rocks.

Let the adventure begin.

21

A small army of slimy mutants were running across the sand toward us and we weren't even close to the shore yet. If they caught us still in the water, we were doomed. They'd swamp our boats, and we couldn't fight and tread water at the same time. Trax was strong, but he was just one Squalo trying to pull two boats.

"Everybody, row like your life depends on it!"

They did, but I don't know if that extra effort made much difference. We were still a good thirty yards out. At this rate, by the time we reached solid ground, we'd be entirely surrounded, trying to fight aquatic monsters while struggling in who knows-how-deep freezing cold water.

"I'm going to jump ahead and slow them down."

"By yourself?" Azarin grabbed my sleeve. "You'll be killed!"

"It's better than rowing." I gently removed her hand, then lifted one glove and made a fist. "*Ascend.*"

The air solidified around my arm and yanked me violently up and away from the boat. As the wind cut right through my damp clothing, I had a terrible thought. Neither Trax nor the locals mentioned the creatures having anything like arrows or spears they could throw, and I was currently presenting a wonderful target if they did. Luckily, I didn't get knocked out of the air, so that must have been a *no* on them having any missile weapons.

Rather than going straight up, I ascended at an angle. Azarin had taught me to keep my eyes on my destination, so I concentrated on a spot above the beach. When I looked down, the boats were behind me, the shore was still ahead of me, but from here, my arc would let me fall on the beach if I did everything right. I aimed my other glove at the solid ground, released the *Ascent* spell, and began falling.

"*Descend!*"

As I focused on the sand, air magic curled about me and tugged back against gravity. I was still dropping fast, but at a velocity where landing would merely hurt, not break bones. Thankfully, my hasty calculation worked, and I fell toward the island instead of plummeting directly into the water. I even managed to stick the landing—mostly—as my boots hit first, and I took a few running steps before tumbling. My heroic effort got me a face full of grit, and then a wave of saltwater crashed into me, soaking my clothes anyway—I'd landed too close to the edge. That shock of cold made me yelp and jump to my feet.

The monsters were shuffling this way fast. They were of various sizes, between gnome to dwarf height, except they were lumpy, bipedal, and *squishy*. Their awkward gait created a weird, moist *squelch* noise. It was difficult to tell their true shape through the clothing they wore, made from slimy leaves and vines. That had to be what the fishermen called seaweed. Their arms were too long, and flopping about behind them as they waddled, like their bones were too soft. Their gigantic eyes were fixed on me, and their black beaks snapped hungrily.

Trax had been right about one thing. They sure didn't look like they wanted to talk it out.

Azarin landed gracefully beside me. "What're you waiting for? Blow them up!"

I'd not been expecting her to join me, but I was way ahead of her on the blowing them up part, as I'd already pulled a snail grenade from my vest. I concentrated on the Red embedded in the iron, and the instant the magic awoke, I hurled it as far as I could. And I had a good throwing arm!

As the snail grenade sailed through the air, it began to shine. It hit the ground in front of the herd of mutants and bounced. By the time it rolled in front of their stomping feet, it was glowing bright orange.

BOOM!

Iron snail fragments zipped through the monsters. They stumbled through the dust and spreading smoke. A couple of them fell over. A few blundered to the side dazed.

Azarin had not only landed smoothly—she'd not even gotten her shoes wet—but she'd done so with a wand at the ready. This particular wand had been among the magical items I'd taken off the Frunza Tarlev students. There'd been another wand too, but Trax had accidentally eaten that one along with the user's hand.

With Azarin's affinity being air magic, this wand worked a lot better for her than the rest of us, so she'd kept it. She didn't have the skill to replicate the enchantment yet, but Azarin knew enough to set it off.

"*Daggers of Air!*"

It helped me to think of the Clear like it was a sort of heavy air that could solidify temporarily, just like the invisible ropes that helped slow my falls. Only for this spell, the Clear hardened little bits of atmosphere into vicious little knives which sped into mutant flesh.

They were barely visible whipping through the salty mist. The monster Azarin was pointing at began leaking purple blood from the tiny puncture wounds that appeared in its chest. The one behind it must have caught a stray air dagger right in the eye, because that big protruding globe suddenly burst, squirting jelly.

Our attacks surprised them, but they weren't even close to being defeated. Despite injuring several of the creatures, the rest of the weird horde were still approaching, only more cautiously now. They spread out across the sand dunes. Some were still coming right at us, but more started flanking to the sides. Trax's assurances aside, that seemed a lot more cunning than ratlets!

Azarin and I only needed to break the monsters' charge long enough for everyone else to get on solid ground. I threw my second snail grenade at a knot of mutants, but this time, they understood the danger, and threw themselves beak first into the sand. From the angry hooting, some got hit by fragments, but that explosion wasn't nearly as effective as the first one.

"They're surrounding us," Azarin warned as she jabbed another monster with fast pointy air. When that one took the punctures and kept charging, she hurled a copper shock rod at it. "*Jolt!*"

Her aim was off, only hitting it in the foot, but the rod fused to its skin, flashing and crackling with sparks and pops. While the monster's muscles twitched helplessly, I swiftly drew the bargemaster's handgun, aimed, and shot it right through the beak. Purple brains flew out the back side of its pointy skull.

The recoil stung my palm, and grey smoke billowed, but the creatures didn't seem any more frightened of firearms than they had been by our spells.

I glanced back to see that Trax's upper body was out of the water, and he was struggling up the beach, with a pair of taut ropes over his shoulder. As soon as the bottoms of the boats started scraping the unseen bottom, the braver Outcasts jumped over the side to wade the rest of the way. In his enthusiasm, Rufus forgot how short he was, sank beneath the waves, and promptly began flailing and drowning. Krachma hoisted him up by the collar and carried him until the dwarf's kicking feet could touch ground.

We'd bought a bit of time, but not quite enough. Azarin and I were mostly encircled by mutants now. I tossed a pocketful of screws to one side in the hopes of stalling the charge. The little bits of steel went molten hot and began careening about, shrieking at a higher pitch than the creatures. When the screws hit water, they went out in a puff of steam, but when they hit rubbery flesh, they stuck and burned. Purple blood hissed and monsters squealed.

Then the others were on us!

A squishy man-mollusk tried to grab Azarin, and my *Shroud of Fire* covered its face. Its skin was so moist and slimy, it didn't catch, but the flash and heat caused it to flinch and cover its eyes with lids that were so thick, they made a *slap* noise when they closed. Azarin yanked out the tiny double-barreled handgun Neves had left her and plugged that monster in the chest. Azarin was notoriously inaccurate with guns, but they were so close now, even she couldn't miss.

I barely managed to duck a long arm that swung my way. We learned then that their limbs had several extra joints, because it suddenly changed direction, allowing claws to hook the edge of my cloak. It yanked me off-balance, sending me stumbling across the wet sand. Another monster tackled me from behind.

It was on my back. One ropey arm wrapped around my head. Its black beak snapped at my neck. My skin got sliced open by an edge designed to pry open clam shells.

I was about to die.

And then we were both getting the ever-living hell shocked out of us by one of Azarin's *Jolt* sticks. She'd hit the monster with it, but since we were both covered in salt water, the spell jumped bodies and I got zapped too. Having been hit by this spell in training, I knew my muscles would seize up uselessly for several seconds, then I'd be able to act. Which I did, faster than the surprised monster, as I broke away from its arm, spun about on my back across the sand, and kicked it square in the eyeball.

The heel of my boot left a dent. It let out a horrible wail, then began crawling after me, clawing at my legs.

Trax appeared and sliced its entire head off with his coral sword.

"*There is an injury upon your neck, Carnavon.*"

"Not as bad as his," I said as the monster's head rolled past me. I got back up and mashed my glove against my wound. It stung, but nothing was squirting, so it was just a scratch. Back to the fight.

The rest of the Outcasts joined the battle, but so did a bunch more squishy monstrosities. Some were popping out of where they'd been hidden beneath the sand dunes. There were tons of them.

"Oh shit!" I threw a flame shroud onto a sand-coated beast that was wriggling out of the ground only a few feet away. "They're everywhere!"

"Apologies. I could not smell the buried ones. My earlier assessment as to the quantity of mutants may have been optimistic."

Rade swept past me and slashed the monster I'd stunned. Purple blood flew high as the deadlander's sword cut deep. Then he swept the enchanted blade in an arc, and the monsters just beyond his reach were pelted with black bits of shadow that materialized out of thin air. Those congealed into spiders which went to biting. That particular shadow spell was more of a distraction than a weapon, but a distraction was good enough, as Rufus hacked one's legs out from beneath it with his axe, and Krachma brained the other with his mace.

It was utter chaos. Spells were going off everywhere. Monsters were dying and more were replacing them.

The biggest of the mutants were just over five feet tall, and most were far smaller, but their reach was disproportionately long, and their claws were sharp. I got cut again on the arm. Bognar cried out as his helmet pot got swatted off. Danny was run over, then Krachma hit that monster so hard, it flew back and splashed into the sea.

Sifuso might have been a coward when there was an arena full of people watching him, but here he went into a vicious frenzy, stabbing wildly with a pair of daggers, like he'd gone too crazy to remember any spells. Lacertians must have a really strong fight or flight reflex, and there was no chance for flight here! A monster clawed Sifuso across the chest, leaving three deep red lines. Our lizard man hissed angrily and slashed it right back, once, twice, three times, splitting seaweed until a big pile of purple guts sloshed out.

Poor Bognar got clobbered again, and by some miracle, Danny actually landed a spell and froze the monster's arm before it could end our carpenter's life. Slime turned to ice, slowing it long enough for Rade's sword to cut that arm off at its second elbow.

Rufus was going to town chopping mollusk beasts with his battle axe. I remembered he had a spell called *Stinging Sand*, and we were standing on a beach fighting things with gigantic bulging eyeballs. "Rufus, use *Stinging Sand*!"

"Why didn't I think of that? Good idea, Carnavon!" He lifted his axe to slam the haft against the ground.

I shouted, "Everybody, close your eyes!"

The spell went off, and in his excitement, Rufus must have used far too much earth element, because it was like the entire beach rose up to blast us. Sand went everywhere.

When the sand cloud fell, I was glad to see the Outcasts listened to my warning, and the monsters, thankfully, had not. Most of those near us stumbled about, their big rubbery lids crunched shut. All they could do was swing reflexively, and a few even clawed each other. We made fast work of everything around us while they were blind, and many monsters fell to steel, lead, or coral.

"There's a new bunch on the right," Azarin shouted.

I looked over to see at least a dozen fresh mutants lumbering our way, but they were still far enough out that I could use a snail grenade without the risk of hitting my friends.

Krachma's mace dripped purple as he pointed it at the nearest pile of broken bricks. "*Debris.*" When he swept that mace toward the approaching monsters, the bricks shook, then flew up and followed the mace's arc right into the mutants. The bricks hit hard enough to bruise meat and even break bones. As they flailed under the impacts, my glowing snail grenade landed between the injured beasts, and two seconds after that, the explosion sent purple bits flying.

One of the monsters that had been hanging back opened its beak and let out a long *screeeeee.* That must have been their signal to retreat. Every one of them, fresh and wounded alike, waddled down the shore as fast as they could and dove into the ocean.

We all stood there, breathing hard, covered in sand, purple blood, and the sticky mud created when those two things met. There were dismembered monster corpses everywhere. I looked around to make sure none of us were among the dead, and by some miracle, we weren't. Already, the big white sea birds were circling, hoping to feast on the bodies.

The Outcasts were triumphant.

"*I got sand in my gills. That is very irritating. Should I pursue the food?*"

"Naw, Trax, we're not here for them. Let's find the treasure so we can get the hell off this rock."

22

The cold had been forgotten during the excitement of the fight, but after things calmed down, that returned with a vengeance. Our clothes had been soaked, and that created such an extra chilling effect that even the Core dwellers shivered. Sifuso was getting sluggish. My teeth were chattering so hard, it was hard to talk. I got my Red enchanted bowl out of my pack, activated the magic hot enough to simmer a stew, and clutched that against my chest in a desperate attempt to dry out my gloves and warm my fingers enough to feel them. The bowl helped a lot.

We'd received a few minor injuries. The gash on my neck hurt, but it was shallow enough a simple bandage stopped the bleeding. The cut on my arm throbbed, but it wasn't too bad either. Sifuso had gotten the worst injury of anyone with the deep cuts on his scaly chest, but lacertians had really thick skin, so hardly any blood came out. I think being a lizard, the cold might have actually slowed his blood down even more. Bognar and Danny had both gotten roughed up a little, but overall, I think everyone was feeling too triumphant to worry about their aches and pains. The Outcasts had been tested and won!

With me being too cold to think straight, let alone talk, Rade took over the role of the sensible one. Which, frankly, was a rather frightening prospect, but he seemed to have everything in hand. I'm sure his usual bluster would be saved for when our survival wasn't at stake, and he had more of an audience.

"Get those boats pulled all the way up and tied to the rocks. I'd prefer to not have the high tide carry off our ride home." Rade made a good call there. Without our boats, our options were to wait for Morton to come rescue us, which was unlikely, or to send Trax for help, and him successfully communicating what was happening to some random fisherman was even less likely than our gnome suddenly turning courageous. "Krachma, would you kindly do the same with those less fortunate adventurers' boat so we have a spare?"

"And I shall check their bodies for valuables." Azarin had never been the squeamish type. "I'm not expecting much, but you never know. Maybe one of them was an enchanter."

"Danny, climb up top there and keep watch. If you see the monsters coming back, holler. And be careful, there could be more of those things hibernating in the sand."

"What about him?" Bognar asked, nodding toward me. "Carnavon's gone white as a deadlander."

"Indeed," Rade agreed. "That complexion is more suited to my people than someone from the land of perpetual fire. You should get out of this wind."

"I'll be fine," I managed to say between the chattering teeth. "When's this summer thing you keep telling me going to start again?"

"About six months from now."

"Fuck." I hid behind a boulder with my bowl to get out of the wind.

It was ironic that the very first spell I'd learned was still one of my most useful. This humble bowl had saved my hotlander ass from the horrible state that Trax referred to as *hypothermia* a few times now. It was like huddling around my own personal campfire worth of warmth. Holding the fully activated piece of metal in my bare hands was a great way to get burned, but currently, it was just steaming away salt water.

After a few minutes, I even got enough feeling back in my hands to reload my gun. Thankfully, it appeared that only one of the wax paper cartridges on my belt had gotten ruined by moisture. I tried my best to get the rest dried off before their powder got soaked too. I looked forward to the day I could afford nicer ammunition with cases made of brass, which was supposed to be far more reliable.

As I sat there, gradually warming up, I noticed there was an odd pattern to the nearby sand. It was too lumpy, and there seemed to be a pattern. I crawled over, brushed some of the sand aside, and swore to myself when I saw the speckled white color beneath. We didn't have birds where I was from, but I'd seen things like this more recently from our neighbors' chickens, only this was far bigger than what came out of a chicken! I brushed off another two of the lumps and found they also contained half buried eggs. Then I looked gradually outward and realized there were dozens more of the things stashed here.

Azarin stuck her head over the top of the boulder. "I looted the dead adventurers and found three Tetars, a rusty longsword, one silver pinky ring, two useable daggers, and a gold tooth."

I didn't want to ask how she'd gotten the tooth out. "Imagine rowing to your death because you got greedy after hearing Rufus sing a song."

"A sad way to go." Then Azarin saw all the eggs. "Oh, wow."

"Yeah. This must be why those squishy beasts were so dedicated to keeping us away."

"That's a lot of baby monsters waiting to hatch… Well, shit. You know, I really shouldn't feel pity for something that just tried to kill me, but now I do."

I knew what she meant. I'd come here looking for treasure to keep a crime boss off our backs, not to terrorize some strange tribe of mutants. The saint I followed was pragmatic, not cruel.

"We should leave them alone."

"Agreed, Oz, and good. The sooner we're gone, the better. Which is why I came to get you. We've found the entrance to the lower levels."

The narrow stairwell stretched so far down, we couldn't see the bottom. This had to be the entrance to Korthican's lair.

I took out my old crawler light charm and set it floating in the air above my head. A few of the others had light charms as well, which was good, seeing as we didn't have anything to make torches out of unless we busted parts off one of the boats.

There was a significant amount of sand on the steps, but it hadn't been disturbed recently with tracks. It appeared the monsters didn't go down there very often. Probably because they'd learned the hard way that what looked like a perfectly good cave was too dangerous. Powerful wizards loved them some traps.

The Outcasts had turned out to be fairly decent at fighting unarmed mutants, but this was the part I'd really been dreading.

"Well, let's get to getting, then." Rufus began walking down the stairs, but Azarin snagged him by the arm. "What?"

"Hold your eagles. This is an old wizard's laboratory. There's bound to be fifty curses down there waiting to kill us."

"She's right. Korthican was on the Council. Mages like that are always jealous of their secrets. One wrong step…" Rade clapped his hands together. "Dead! There will surely be many traps, both magical and mundane mechanical."

"Not to mention they like to leave behind things like golems or guardian spirits," Danny added. "And those can linger for centuries! Only activating when some foolish adventurer does something that draws its wrath." When we all looked at him, a bit surprised that our young Under Slumper knew about such things, he shrugged. "I had a cousin who was in a mercenary adventuring company and he used to tell us stories, until he got his face ripped off by a tomb wraith."

Brave Rufus Rudnik wasn't about to have the potential removal of his face dissuade him from glory. "No need to worry. We've got Carnavon. He was a trapper. Naturally, he must be an expert about all things trap-related."

"There's got to be a vast difference between what I did to catch Fire Elementals, and whatever fifteenth-level mages leave behind to deter thieves."

But even as I said that, I reasoned the basic principles were probably the same. Traps were all about deception and temptation.

Fire Elementals were angry and hungry and liked to roast living things, so we'd use ourselves as bait to lure them in. Thieves were lured in by the promise of treasure. We were the dumb Fire Elementals.

"If you see something you want to touch, don't. If it looks valuable, it's probably there to tempt you. I'll take the lead. Be sure to only step where I've stepped. We're going to take it real slow. Don't clump up. That'll just cause more casualties if a trap gets tripped."

"Yeah… How about I stay up here and guard the door?" Bognar asked. "You know, in case the monsters come back? Or Morton and the scary girl shows up?"

"That's a good idea." Bognar was a big oaf and constantly bumping into things in places where everything wasn't designed to kill us. Rufus wasn't nearly as clumsy, but he was a bit of a dimwit, and I didn't want him curiously poking at any shiny things. "How about you keep him company, Rufus?"

"What? Do you doubt the courage of House Rudnik?" he sputtered, offended. "How *dare* you?"

"Fine. You can come too, but do exactly as I say and no touching *anything.*"

"I'll stand watch with Bognar," Danny volunteered. "I'm happy with my face remaining attached to the skull bones beneath. Unlike Cousin Fredrick."

I wasn't sad to see Danny stay where it was safer. He struck me as fairly clever, and would surely be safer around the rest of us than our idiot dwarf, but he was such an earnest kid, if he died while under my responsibility, I'd feel terrible about it.

On that note, I looked toward my girlfriend.

"Don't you even fucking dare ask me to stay where it's safe, Ozwald Carnavon. I've got a far lighter step than you do."

Rade laughed at that. "I'll go as well. This isn't my first foray into the dark."

"Were any of those mausoleums you've robbed strewn with traps?"

Rade shrugged. "If they were, I was lucky enough to not step on any of them!"

Azarin was incredibly graceful, and though Rade lied constantly, the one thing he was honest about was being a good swordsman, and he had the footwork to match. That left me with three more rather large, heavy specimens to worry about. Trax was thick, but he also had that unnerving Squalo dexterity, so he was probably good at avoiding danger. I was mostly worried about him eating things he shouldn't. But Krachma was a hulking, ponderous brute, and Sifuso was skinny and really tall. He was normally quick, but the cold was seriously slowing him down a bit.

Having already offended our dwarf, I kept my suggestion gentle. "It might be tight quarters down there."

Sifuso flicked his forked tongue at me, before hunching over to make himself a little shorter. "There."

"Krachma can *Impervious.*" That was the name of our lob's potent protective spell that temporarily turned his skin impenetrable as a rock. "Can you *Impervious?*"

"You know, I've not been able to figure out any of your earth magic yet."

"I have," Azarin said proudly. "Kind of. Sometimes."

Krachma looked smug at my admitting failure.

"Don't rub it in... Fine. If things go sideways and start exploding, you two can just turn to stone. Everybody else, be ready to duck. Let's go."

23

It was nerve-wracking, expecting to set off a magical death trap with every step, but at least it was a lot warmer and drier down here. The shivering from the cold ceased and now my muscles were shaking from the tension.

The stairs went down for a surprisingly long way before we entered a large chamber, which must have stretched beneath the ocean's surface. The room was a long rectangle, so big, my light charm barely illuminated the ceiling or far wall. This was the sort of thing wizards of advanced rank could carve out of solid rock on a whim. As a mere rank one, the construction of such things was far beyond my understanding, but going five hundred years without springing a leak was quite the testament to the skill of the builder.

"You guys stay on the stairs while I range ahead a bit."

"Aww, come on, Carnavon," Rufus whined. "It already took us an hour just to go down this far!"

It had been less than half that, and it had taken that long because I'd used the rusty sword Azarin found to carefully push against each of the steps before placing my own weight on them. Every few steps I'd paused and tossed handfuls of dust to see if the particles would hit anything invisible or hard to see. Then I'd thrown rocks down to see if they set anything off when they hit the floor. After those tests, I'd wait a minute before proceeding, just in case any of the traps had a built-in delay.

"Patience, Rufus. This is hard enough as it is without you barking at me."

"I am no dog!"

Oh so carefully, I started making my way across the room. I was counting on my old crawler's charms to protect me against extreme heat and caustic air, which were two of the more common hazards on Fogo, and from what I heard, popular wizards' traps. If I was really lucky, any surprises left by Korthican would be in the form of fire or poison gas. If I was unlucky, they'd be anything else. There were so many different ways to kill someone with magic, the possibilities were endless, and it would take an incredibly powerful wizard to have defenses prepared against them all.

Trax sent me a thought. "*It is difficult to smell, but a great deal of blood has been spilled here. It is all dried out now, but the scent permeates the stone. I would urge caution.*"

"Duly noted, Trax."

There was still a lot of furniture in the room, but it was covered in five centuries of dust and spiderwebs. All the shelves were empty. That wasn't unexpected. The fishermen warned me that so many other adventurers had hit this place over the years that anything of value that could be easily carried off, had been.

I wasn't the only one to notice the empty shelves and broken open chests. "Hey, Carnavon?"

"What now, Rufus?"

"If this place has already been looted, shouldn't all the traps have been sprung?"

It was Rade who corrected him. "You'd think that, but if a mage is sufficiently powerful, and the original casting involved even a tiny bit of Permanence, a spell can be discharged, then recharged to go off again later. Lesser enchantments, like Azarin's wand or my sword, only have a finite number of uses, but if a wizard uses up a little time magic in the formula, enchantments can last nearly forever."

I turned back to point the rusty long sword at Rufus. "Which is why you keep your grubby mitts in your pockets. Got it?"

"Fine..." Our dwarf was getting huffy. "I just didn't know this part of adventuring would be so *tedious.*"

That was easy for him to say from the safety of the rear. Out here in front, the pressure was killing me. "I've heard rumor there's spells that can detect traps. You should learn one that does that and save us all a lot of time on our next job."

"Oh, I'll do that for sure, mark my words, soon as I find one."

The floor was a tiled mosaic, though it was hard to tell in what image beneath so much dust. I poked each tile before stepping on it. I extended the sword to knock down spiderwebs that might be concealing trip wires. I couldn't see anything threatening above or to the sides either. Once I'd cleared a ten-foot square, I signaled for the next Outcasts in line that it was safe to come down.

On the other side of a desk, I found a skeleton. He'd been wearing some mismatched armor, but the steel cuirass hadn't been tough enough to stop whatever had poked a jagged hole through one side and out the other. It had hit him so hard that bits of rib had gotten blasted out and were lying several feet away. A hit of such violence had probably stuck some of his lungs on the wall, but all the soft bits had long since rotted away or been eaten by bugs.

I picked up one of the rocks I'd thrown down earlier and tossed it at the desk the dead adventurer had probably been searching through. The rock hit a drawer and *BANG!*

A yellow streak flew from one wall to smack into the other. At the point of impact, the dust had been blown off in a big circle, leaving a smoking crater in the middle of the bare stone.

"See?"

Rufus quickly shoved his hands in his pockets.

From that point on, there was a lot less whining.

I found another skeleton. From the diminutive size, I hoped this had been a halfling or one of the equivalent-size races, because I really hoped nobody had let their children play down here. The bones were partially crumbled to ash, which suggested fire, acid, or some kind of disintegration spell. I studied where he'd fallen, what furniture was around, and where it looked likely that something impressive or valuable must have once sat. There was a little podium that had probably once held a treasure, which was probably the lure. I went back, picked up an ancient rotting boot from the last dead fellow, and threw it at the podium. A hungry black mist engulfed the whole thing for a moment, and the half-charred sole fell out the other side.

"I think there's traps all along the sides where things were displayed, but we don't have to mess with those. Carcalla said the secret door would be at the end of the room." I scowled at the distance, as there was a great deal of possibly lethal furniture between me and the far wall, while the last fifty or so feet were wide open and bare.

"I don't like that final empty bit," Azarian said.

"Yeah... me neither. The rest of this place is cluttered. Why's Korthican got a dance floor?"

"You know about dancing? I didn't know you had dances in Fogo. The way you talk, it's all work, work, work."

"You'd be surprised. Work hard, play hard. The cargo bay of a barge is wide and flat, and once you drop off the Red and it's empty, that's the time to celebrate. We've always got a few folks who can play an instrument or hum a tune. Cadre girls love to dance. I'm not too shabby at it myself."

"You'll have to show me later."

Even with the tension, a pretty girl saying such nice things made me smile. "Providing we don't die horribly here, I will."

"I'm holding you to that, Oz."

I set as direct a path as I could for the end of the room. Twenty minutes later, I was a third of the way across. I was surely missing a slew of traps along the way, but as long as nobody strayed off the narrow lane I'd scouted, we should be fine.

Eventually, my compulsive floor-poking paid off, as a bit of pressure with the tip of the sword caused one of the tiles ahead of me to sink. It was right next to a small table that must have once displayed something of value. There was a *click*, and I leapt back as a ghostly arrow shot across the room, about chest high. Luckily, by me being careful, the only thing that got pierced was the cobwebs.

"Everybody remember to avoid that spot," I said.

"You're getting good at this." Azarin shouted that encouragement from a safe distance behind me. "I can't lie, this display of competence is making you rather attractive."

"I suppose it isn't that different than trapping Elementals. Just in reverse."

Rade coughed politely. "As much as I appreciate the necessity of impressing a lady, please do focus on the task at hand, Carnavon."

"Feel free to trade places with me at any time."

Rade tipped his hat respectfully, and I went back to searching.

Where the furniture ended was where it got complicated. The tiles here were unlike the rest. They were in a chaotic pattern, each one shaped differently, but all of them were just big enough to place both your feet. I wasn't very good at sensing magic that wasn't Red-based, but the energy collected here was strong enough that even I could tell this whole section of floor was enchanted. It was like being back home standing before rock that appeared cooled and solid enough to walk on, but which was actually a thin crust over liquid doom, where one wrong step meant burning your foot off. This felt like that, only death and dismemberment would come by magic instead of lava.

The previous traps had all been next to something that had almost certainly once held an item of value. If the secret door was on the other end, this whole section was designed to keep thieves away from it. Maybe I was close enough the password would work? It was worth a shot. I really didn't want to try and cross the part that was practically screaming danger for nothing.

I recalled the exact words Carcalla had made me repeat until memorized, cleared my throat, and loudly announced, "*At the center of the matter cloud, across all realms entwined, shines forth the beacon. Pray to the gods and saints while the enemies of the Council despair.*"

Nothing happened.

"That's a long password." Sifuso let out an angry hiss. "Humans talk too much."

"Did you say it right?" Rade asked.

"I think so. Give it a second. It's been shut for five hundred years."

Sure enough, there was a loud grinding noise, and forty feet away, a seam appeared in the rock. It was perfectly visible because of the trickle of white light shining through the new crack. The door appeared to be stuck, but there was certainly something there.

"Hot damn. It's real."

"What's the hold-up?" Rufus demanded. "Go get our treasure."

"Calm your tits, dwarf. This last part I think is like a puzzle. It's step on the tiles in the right order, or else." Carcalla had somehow gotten ahold of the password, but he'd said nothing about this bit. It looked like the tiles might have been color-coded once or had symbols on them, but it was impossible to tell now with so much dust, and there was no way to sweep them off without touching them. "Anybody got a spell that can make a gust of wind?"

All eyes turned toward our lone air-realmer. "Sorry," Azarin said sheepishly. "Useful as that sounds right about now, that's not one that I've picked up."

"Just poke them with the sword and see what happens," Rufus said. "It can't be that complicated."

I doubted that very much, but didn't see any other choice. There were a dozen different stones I could step onto. Twice that many with a bit of a jump. So, I picked a tile, extended the sword as far as I could, and gently tapped the point upon it.

FWOOSH!

I was engulfed in a terrible pillar of fire.

24

It would've been ironic to survive the Elemental Plane of Fire for nineteen years, only to get burned to death in the Core after a few months.

But three things saved me.

My old crawler charm—which was designed to protect Red miners from extreme heat—activated.

The enchanted band I'd taken off a dead pirate, bearing the mark of Aarhobad, created by the vile elf who'd shelled my barge and murdered half my family, also triggered its protective magic.

And most of all, I'd gotten really fucking lucky.

Everyone is born with a bit of natural resistance to the magical element native to their home realm. As powerful as this spell was, if it had been based on any of the other elements, I would've died instantly. If it had been any of my companions who'd trigger this fire spell, they would've been immolated and burned to a crisp. Since it was me, it just really, really hurt.

It happened fast, but when the heat hit, I'd flung myself backward hard as I could. It was instinct from years of working around spitting lava and fiery plumes. This burned just as hot as one of those, but thankfully only for a few seconds; otherwise, it would've cooked everyone in the room.

I landed on my back, skidded a bit, and promptly had to tear off my burning cloak and fling it aside. Core clothing wasn't nearly as fire resistant as what we wore back home!

The other Outcasts had been far enough back to not get scorched, but it still rocked them. Krachma had temporarily turned his skin to stone with *Impervious*. Azarin was shielding her eyes, and called out, "Oz!"

Swift Trax rushed to my side, coral sword at the ready, which was very brave of him because fire magic was notoriously unforgiving against creatures from the Plane of Water. As he stood over me, the cobwebs above us burned away into sparks. Then all the dust that had been blasted began to rain down in a choking cloud.

"Hold your position!" Rade shouted. "If anyone runs, you'll just set off another trap. Carnavon, are you alive?"

"I'm alright." I stood up and began stamping the fire from my burning cloak before it got ruined entirely. "Fuck, that was hot!"

"Is anyone else injured?"

From the responses to Rade's question, I'd been the only one struck, and magic and natural immunity left me with nothing more than a reddened face and some of my beard and eyebrows charred off. When I checked my protections, the metal of my old crawler charm broke apart and crumbled to pieces. This hadn't been the first time it saved my life, but it would be the last. *Farewell, old friend.*

"*My condolences on the loss of your bracelet,*" Trax sent solemnly.

That trap had been a lot flashier than the previous ones, and easily been ten times nastier than the biggest *Shroud of Fire* I'd ever managed to cast. Even a few seconds of burning had raised the temperature in the gigantic room dramatically. The other humans had surely begun sweating, but for me, it was a taste of home.

At least I wasn't cold anymore!

Luckily, my light charm survived, and it revealed that the blast had struck the dust from the oddly shaped tiles. They were in various colors, and upon each was carved a different symbol. There were *a lot* of symbols.

"Well, that's just lovely. It's even more complicated than I thought. There's got to be a pattern to this."

"That one didn't work, so just poke a different one," Rufus shouted helpfully from where he was safely away from Korthican's incredibly destructive magic. "You've got this."

"Picking wrong once cost me a charm and nearly ended my life. There's surely a bunch more spells ready just as dangerous or worse waiting, and I'd only need to guess about a dozen more right in a row to make it across safely, assuming that's even possible at all. How about we think this through instead?"

"But that'll take all day," Rufus whined.

"Poking things until I die is a fine idea, but oh, look at that, the end of the sword got melted off." And being at the center of the blast, that wasn't even an exaggeration to shut him up. The tip was gone entirely, and the rest of the blade still glowed orange. "Sadly, we'll just have to use our brains."

"Huh… I suppose I'll stay over here, then."

"Why don't you go check on Danny and Bognar?"

Rufus left after that, and the other—less stupid—Outcasts carefully retraced my steps so they could get close enough to see the puzzling tiles for themselves. There were dozens of highly stylized symbols, used repeatedly, across different color tiles. The one I'd touched was red, and carved on it was some lines with a sun on top. I recognized many of the symbols from the *Encyclopedia Ettymus*, while others were a mystery, and it all seemed too random to make any sense to me.

"Anybody good at puzzles?" I asked.

"Krachma hates puzzles."

That wasn't a surprise. "Thanks, big fella. Anyone else?"

"*The Squalo do not understand the concept of* puzzles. *It appears to be a complicated ritual designed to burn oneself to death.*"

"A puzzle is more like a game, Trax. It's a problem you've got to persist at until you figure it out and get a reward. They're supposed to be fun."

"*Land dwellers are very confusing.*"

"I didn't say they were all fun."

Rade was coming at it from a different angle. "Perhaps you could use your *Ascend* and jump across?"

I'd considered that myself. "There's still the matter of picking which tile to land on by the door."

Sifuso was looking at the ceiling, which was now more visible with the cobwebs burned off. "I could climb. Stick to walls. Reach the door and slip inside. All without touching the floor."

"You're welcome to try, but you really think Korthican took the time to fortify this place this much, to hide his greatest enchantment, and he didn't think of that?"

"Before Carnavon jumps or Sifuso climbs to blow themselves to bits, give me a second on the puzzle." Azarin squatted at the edge and studied the tiles. "There's seven colors. Red, blue, white, brown, green, black, and gold. Same as the elements."

"Korthican was on the Council. They love their sevens. Seven gates, seven realms, seven days of the week."

"Assuming they're in the usual order, red should be first. Only you touched red and got roasted for it." Azarin scowled as she looked over the first row of tiles. "There's four red ones in reach, but each of those tiles has got a different sign on it. Circle. Mountain. Hands pushed together. And the one you pushed already, tower with a ball on top of it."

"That's a lighthouse," Rade said. "Probably this one, I'd assume."

"And the hands are palm-to-palm..." I noted. "Praying, maybe?"

"Interesting." Azarin got so dangerously close to one of the tiles that she had to hold her hair with one hand to keep it from falling and touching the dangerous floor. "That's not a plain mountain. It's the Great Machine. The Nexus is the *center* of all the realms..." She squinted toward the next line. "From there is there a blue tile with a cloud on it? And yes, there is, assuming that's what the swirly thing is supposed to be... I think I've got it." She rose and took a deep breath. "Everybody, stand back."

Azarin was alarmingly impulsive, but this was a really bad idea, even by her standards. Her saint blessed those who acted without hesitation, but that was ridiculous. "What're you doing?"

She demonstrated she had a good memory, by repeating back the password exactly. "*At the center of the matter cloud, across all realms entwined, shines forth the beacon. Pray to the gods and saints while the enemies of the council despair.* There's a symbol for each part of that. We just need to match the next symbol in the password to the colors in order."

"Let's consider it a bit more, and then I should be the one to—"

Except she did it anyway.

We all winced as she hopped onto the red tile with the mountain, but she didn't immediately explode.

"Oh, thank Naanwalla, I was only half sure that was going to work! But see? It's the password. It's not just to unlock the door, it's the key to make it across the floor too."

"What're you doing?" My heart was pounding. "You could get killed!"

"Sure, but it's not fair for you to take all the risk. We're in this together. But we've got it now. It's all in the password. *At the center.* What's the center of everything? The Nexus within the Great Machine. *Of the matter cloud,* which is all that everything of all the realms rolled together, and there happens to be a cloud, on a blue tile, and water is next after fire." She lifted one foot.

"Wait, wait, wait! You don't know if you're actually right, or if the fire trap just hasn't recharged yet."

"Then logically, if I'm wrong, when I step on this next one, I'll be promptly killed by some manner of water spell. Welp… I'm sort of committed now."

"*I am resistant to that form of magic. May I?*"

"Hang on! Trax says he'll do it. If you're wrong, water spells won't hurt him as much."

"An excellent point." Azarin put her foot back down on the red tile and breathed a sigh of relief. "After you, Master Bloodtrail."

Trax jumped smoothly onto the indicated blue tile. He landed without incident.

"*Please inform your female that I am happy to take it from here, because if something goes wrong, my reflexes are far superior to hers. I do not intend offense, but humans are rather sluggish when compared to Squalos.*"

"Trax says he'll do the rest. He's fast enough to dodge a trap."

"But air is after water, and—"

"Azarin... *please.* You've shared enough risk already."

She must have heard the fear in my voice, because she relented—which was rare—and stepped back onto solid ground. "Alright, Trax, what do you see?"

He bombarded our brains with all the choices. The white tile with seven strings wrapping around each other had to be next. And when Trax moved to that one without incident, we knew we were on the right track. Then there was a brown tile with the sun on it, and Trax stepped to it without getting crushed or smashed.

Azarin went through the next set of images. "Green tile with a lighthouse. That's got to be the beacon mentioned."

Worrying about my friends in danger was a lot worse than being in danger myself. "Step careful, Trax. Green tile. Lighthouse."

Trax stepped onto that one, muscles tensed, ready to leap for safety. Squalo's had no expression to read, but he seemed to be having a fine time. "*You were correct, Carnavon. Puzzles can be fun.*"

Black tile, hands in prayer. Trax made it safely. Then there was a gold tile with the crown and throne for the assembly of gods. Appropriate that, combining the religious with the element representing the eternal. Then we got into a debate over the next one, as the eighth time was in theory back to Red, and there were a couple of those to choose from which both made sense in context.

"If the password lumps gods and saints together, then the monster-looking thing is the enemies," I argued.

"But why separate out the two in the password?" Rade pointed out. "The circle on the other red tile is surely a halo. In the paintings, saints always have halos."

"Or it could just be a circle."

"*This is very exciting,*" Trax sent.

"If we choose wrong, you could die."

"*Correct. That is why it is exciting. I have decided that I like puzzles. But please, do not chose incorrectly because dying would be most unfortunate. I have a lot of things to do.*"

"We're trying our best... There's nothing on the tile he's standing on now for saints, just the gods. And if he goes to the circle one, from it, there's a logical path for the next few to get him to the end." Rade and Azarin were probably right, but the uncertainty gnawed at me. Fire was the element Trax was most vulnerable to, and if he got hit by the same intensity of spell I had, he'd surely die. "You guys are probably right... Ready, Trax?"

"*Yes. If I am burned to death, I want you to know that I have enjoyed my time among the land creatures and you have been the best friend I have ever had who is a mammal.*"

"Thanks, Trax. And you're the best fish man thing I've ever known. I really mean that. Now go to the red tile with a circle."

Trax stepped onto it, and nothing happened. I breathed a sigh of relief. It turned out even Krachma had been holding his breath.

Someone called down from the top of the stairs. I could barely hear them, but it sounded like Bognar. He was probably trying to tell us that Morton and Dathka had finally arrived. Now that it seemed we were past the truly dangerous bits, Morton's timing was perfect.

There was only one blue tile that could possibly represent enemies. The Council had their own well-known symbol, which hadn't changed over the last five hundred years, and then, of the four tiles which touched the secret door, only one was the right color, and had tears beneath an eye, symbolizing despair. Which seemed an appropriate last step, since Korthican had hidden his shining beacon during an invasion when all seemed lost.

We all cheered when Trax reached the door without dying.

"*Splendid. We should do puzzles more often.*"

The door swung gently inward, and an extremely bright light spilled out. Trax slipped inside.

"*There are a few things in here. What would you like for me to retrieve first?*"

"Do you see the lamp?"

I heard a commotion behind us. Someone was running down the stairs, yelling, but I couldn't understand what they were saying.

Trax sent me a mind picture of a rusting metal container, which contained a light charm so bright that even what slipped between the gaps in the seams was blinding. "*Is this it?*"

The noise was getting louder. It was Rufus, and he was really upset about something.

"Yes, Trax, grab it."

"*I have obtained the device.*"

An ominous rumble surrounded us. Dust and bits of rock rained down from the ceiling.

With its prize given up, the chamber no longer had a need to exist, and the magic which had been keeping out the relentless barrage of the sea for five centuries *cracked.*

Seawater began squirting from the walls.

25

This end of the chamber was coming apart. Water was spraying everywhere. Cracks were spreading. We ran for it.

"Be careful of the traps!" I shouted as loudly as possible, but it was doubtful any of them heard me over the roar of rushing water. "You've still got to retrace your steps!"

Trax came out of the secret door carrying a metal chest that was casting brilliant beams of light as the lamp rolled about inside. On the wrong side of the deadly puzzle tiles, Trax had by far the most complicated path to freedom.

"*I do not think it is wise for me to rush through the puzzle in reverse. Based upon our current situation, I could wait and then swim out when the chamber is fully flooded.*"

That might work for Trax, but the rest of us were going to drown if we stuck around. One nice thing about Squalo thought-speech was that Trax didn't need to hear me speak; I just needed to think hard and I knew he'd get it. *Do what you need to do, but don't lose the lamp.*

"*It might not survive being submerged. Here.*" Trax tossed the box to me.

I watched the possibly fragile treasure fly across the room and just managed to catch it. "Oof!" Weighing about twenty pounds and being hurled with Squalo might, the box bruised my arms and damned near knocked me over. Trax had a tendency to forget his strength.

The ground shuddered, and all of us stumbled. Krachma turned *Impervious* again, just as some rocks fell from the ceiling and bounced off his temporarily indestructible head.

Rufus Rudnik came running down the stairs, shouting unintelligibly. He reached the bottom and splashed our way. Heedless of danger, this was a dwarf on a mission, so focused that he didn't even notice the chamber was falling down and flooding. With axe in hand and a wild look in his eye, he was yelling furiously, but for the life of me, I couldn't understand what he was saying over all the noise. He was running fast and heedless of danger… right down the middle of the room.

"Rufus, wait!"

He didn't hear my warning, but I finally understood what he was saying over and dover. "Treachery! We've been betray—"

THUNK!

The ghostly arrow trap that had been about chest high on me, was head high on poor Rufus.

He stopped, blinked, looked at all of us with dimwitted surprise, and then slowly put his hand to his temple, where the fletching of a glowing arrow was sticking out. Then he dropped his axe and touched his other hand to the arrowhead… which was poking out the other side of his head.

"Huh…" Rufus said as he pulled on the arrow bisecting his brain. That caused our dwarf to stumble drunkenly to the side. "I'm fine. I'm fine."

He was lurching toward an area where I'd *not* had a chance to check for traps. "Stop!"

"Don't worry. It's nothing a Clan Rudnik war mage can't walk off."

The next trap Rufus triggered must have been earth-based, because the floor came alive with two big chunks of stone rising around him… And then slammed together so incredibly fast that Rufus got smashed *flat.* We all got splattered by red droplets.

Azarin screamed. I winced.

The stone and Rufus sandwich sank into the floor, but there was no time to stand there in horror because the water was ankle deep and rising fast. The collapse was spreading. Other sections of the chamber were crumbling, allowing even more water to rush in faster. Rufus had suffered a terrible fate, but if we didn't get out of here right then, we'd be joining him shortly.

We got to the bottom of the stairs. I made sure everyone was accounted for and went in last. Trax was the only one left behind, but he could breathe underwater just fine and didn't need us, so we started climbing.

Everyone was still stunned by the loss of one of our own, but once we were a bit farther up the stairwell, the rushing water noise was muted enough we could hear each other better, but we still had to shout. The light leaking from the box made the enclosed space incredibly bright. Every little rusty pinhole in the box emitted an eye-searing beam of light. Even moving the box under my cloak didn't help, as the light went right through the fabric.

Azarin was staring, wide-eyed. "Rufus popped like a grape."

"Did anybody catch what he was shouting about?" I asked.

"Something about betrayal, I think," Rade answered. "Then that arrow got him! And the stones themselves… The poor bastard."

Sifuso threw up at the memory, and I'd seen him eat week-old dead mice.

"I bet it's that Latrocinium whore betraying us," Azarin said. "She's probably up there with Cutter Joran and an army of bandits right now, waiting to rob us."

"But why would the Latros betray us? We got this thing for them." I shook the box for emphasis.

"I don't know. I don't think like a criminal. But who else could it be? She's probably already murdered Danny, Bognar, and Morton."

Even if Azarin was right, the only way out was up. The water was still rising and the doorway to the chamber was half covered. "We might be walking into an ambush. Be ready to fight."

"Krachma will take lead." The lob thumped his mace against his big palm. "They make Krachma's dwarf flat. Krachma is angered by flat dwarf."

If enemies were waiting for us, we were in an awful position. The stairwell formed a fatal funnel with nowhere to hide. All they'd need to do was toss some spells down this narrow shaft or fill it with bullets and we were doomed.

Because Sifuso's fighting was so hot or cold, either vicious or cowardly, and it was hard to predict which lizard man we'd get, I passed the box off to him. "This is the only thing we have to bargain with. Get in the very back and protect it with your life."

"I will," the lacertian vowed.

Then I got behind Krachma and pulled my gun. "Lead the way, big guy."

A bit of climbing later, we got our answer as to who had betrayed us. Dathka Walker was waiting at the top of the stairs, but surprisingly it was as hostage, not hostage taker. She, along with Morton and Bognar, were on their knees, wrists bound. Using them for cover was the orc who'd tried to join our academy that morning—Gerzog was the name he'd given me—and at his side, looking awkward and ashamed, was young Danny.

26

"What the fuck, Danny!"

"Sorry, Mr. Carnavon. I didn't have no choice."

Furious, I leveled my pistol over Krachma's shoulder, but Danny ducked behind Big Bognar, whose plumpness made him a fine shield. I had no shot, but I was hiding behind someone even bigger than Bognar, who made an even better shield. "Go *Impervious*."

Krachma's skin turned grey—and based off experience, bulletproof—but that also rendered him completely immobile, which mostly blocked the narrow stairs. We were ten steps down. Rade was behind me, sword not yet drawn because a two-and-a-half-foot razor was a bit of a liability while surrounded by friends in a cramped space. Azarin was behind him, wand in one hand and pistol in the other, which was frankly worrisome, because she was such a bad shot with a gun, she was liable to nail one of us in the back instead of whoever she was aiming at.

"You're trapped, Outcasts. Send up your treasure or we'll start slitting throats." Gerzog yanked Dathka's hair back and placed a knife beneath her chin to prove his point, not realizing that of his three hostages, threatening her was by far the least likely way to persuade us.

The Latro assassin looked as furious as I'd ever seen anyone, and I'd been a miner in a realm noted for our tempers. "You're lucky you caught me by surprise, orc. If you kill me, the black band of Carcalla will hunt you to the ends of the realms. There'll be no place for you to hide. Cutter Joran will slice your cock off and force feed it to you! You're dead. Your whole family is dead!"

"You can run your suck, Latro, but you're nothing to be afraid of without your one high-level enchantment." Gerzog patted one of his pockets, which was probably where he stashed her shadow walking charm. "I'm not afraid of Carcalla. Your half-elf boss's reach ends at the edge of the Slumps. The Council rules everything above those, and the Tempus Metum runs the undercity below. Either of those, or a dozen other factions, would pay me a fortune for Korthican's beacon."

Considering how much light was coming from the box Sifuso was holding, even from way below us, it was pretty hard to deny that we'd found the thing. Crouched behind *Impervious* Krachma, I kept my pistol ready, but at this angle, only a bit of Gerzog's head was poking around Dathka. Danny was entirely behind Bognar. Nobody was hiding behind Morton, because gnomes were too small to be a good shield. Poor Morton's eyes were squeezed shut tight, and he was sniffling, like he was trying his best not to cry.

"You're not getting shit from us, Gerzog."

"Me landing twenty men upon this island suggests otherwise, Carnavon."

I didn't know if he was telling the truth or exaggerating to intimidate us, but Bognar snuck in a bit of a nod that warned me the orc wasn't lying.

"Those odds aren't so bad. We killed a lot more monsters than that today already."

"I saw the nasty purple pile you left behind, but you'll find us more capable than some noodle armed mutants, for I am Gerzog the Marauder, captain of the Tooth and Claw Mercenary Company."

I'd never heard of them, but Rade muttered, "Dammit..."

"Ah. At least one of you knows of us. You should, deadlander, seeing as how many of your kind we've slain in that sad realm. Explain to your friends why you should hand over your treasure and give up while you still can. You may confer amongst yourselves. Do so quickly before my patience runs out."

I looked to Rade, and he whispered back, "The Tooth and Claw are a foul bunch of scoundrels and backstabbing trash, but they can fight. The nobles of some of our distant, savage kingdoms sometimes hire outsiders to burn villages and put down peasant uprisings. The Tooth and Claw are notorious even among those."

"Any chance they're honorable enough to let us all go if we hand over the box?"

Rade shook his head in the negative. "They're scoundrels."

I went back to aiming over Krachma's shoulder. "You've got a reputation alright. It's not a very trustworthy one, though."

"Such is life. You'll have to take me at my word that all I require is the treasure. Surrender it and we'll leave you be."

"Don't you dare, Carnavon," Dathka snarled. "That belongs to Carcalla. Give them nothing. Fight like a man."

Gerzog smacked her upside the head. "Shut up, woman."

For once, I agreed with the evil mercenary orc. Now was really not the time for Latrocinium bravado, because unless Cutter Joran was about to pull up in a boat full of thugs, her threats were empty.

"We're both reasonable sorts, Mr. Gerzog. How about as a show of good faith, you let our friends go, and then we can talk it out?"

"Treasure first, or we slay you and take it off your bodies."

It never hurt to try a bluff. "You know you can't, or you already would have. You could fill this tunnel with fire, but you haven't yet, because you've surely heard how delicate the lamp is. The slightest bump or unnatural change in temperature, and it'll shatter into a thousand pieces. Then all that precious Permanence will fade into the ether."

Gerzog's red eyes squinted hard at me. Apparently, he hadn't heard that before—because I'd just made it up—but such was the nature of myth and legend. Chronomancy was a lost art, so who was going to correct me? I thought my line of trogshit sounded rather convincing.

"Where else you gonna go? Through us? I see you're short a Squalo and a gladiator dwarf."

"They didn't make it. Trax got hit by a curse on the way in, and Rufus stepped on another trap when he ran down to warn us about you." Since we were all speckled with dwarf blood, that probably sounded plausible. "But I've still got a lizard who'll bite your face off and a lob who's tough as a boulder. If you start to make it past this rock, we'll drown that fragile lamp in seawater and ruin it."

Gerzog had an evil grin. "The old if-we-can't-have-it-nobody-will ploy. Classic. It's unfortunate this is how we met, Carnavon, because I could use someone ruthless like you in the Tooth and Claw."

"Is this the part where you try to get chummy and bribe me? Because I've already got a job managing an academy. Speaking of which, what the hell are you doing with these pricks, Danny?"

"Yeah, you traitorous ratlet!" Azarin shouted. "We took you in and treated you kindly. And this is how you pay us back?"

Danny peeked around Bognar's shoulder. "You did give me a chance, so I really am sorry. But that adventurer cousin I told you about was in Gerzog's company. When they heard Rufus' singing, and he knew I was an Outcast too, they came looking. He found me last night and threatened if I didn't help him, he'd hurt my family."

Gerzog's piglike nostrils flared as he snorted. "Why do you lie? You are no victim. I didn't threaten your family. You sold your loyalty for a bag of Tetars and the promise of a fat share."

Danny sounded sheepish, "Well, yeah. Got me there. That too."

"You two-faced son of a bitch," Rade sneered. "We broke bread together."

"Moldy bread! I'm tired of being poor, Lord Tartaros. Not all of us get to be born fancy noblemen like you."

Poor stupid Danny didn't even grasp that Rade wasn't a real noble. He was at best a bastard with delusions of grandeur. Now I was really pissed off. "Rufus died because of you."

"That's not my fault! Gerzog told me nobody was supposed to get hurt, I swear. I feel real bad about Rufus, I do. But I'm not as talented as you guys. You saw how bad I did in the arena. I'm never going to make it as a wizard, but I can make a good living as a mercenary."

"You think Gerzog's ever going to trust someone who's shown he's a lying fucker who'll sellout his friends so easily? Once he's used you, he'll get rid of you, just to save himself the hassle."

Gerzog nodded as I said that. "Perceptive. The Tooth and Claw's got no room for turncoats... Aziz, kill the boy."

Danny turned to look behind him. "No, wait, I—"

A spectral hand formed around Danny's throat and choked off any more words. He fell, kicking and struggling. I could no longer see him behind Bognar, but could hear every excruciating second of him getting magically strangled to death.

We were going through a lot of students today.

Gerzog watched Danny's slow, painful demise, and once the thrashing stopped, he said, "I despise disloyalty."

"The dumbfuck should've seen that coming," Azarin said.

I was seething. I'd liked Danny. He'd betrayed us, so I likely would've killed him myself, but this had all been so sudden that his casual murder still offended me.

Gerzog turned his attention back toward us. "That death's your last warning. You've got until the count of ten to give up before I kill the fat one. Then another ten before the gnome dies. Then you get one final count before I cut this pretty deadlander's head off. If you're so heartless I run out of hostages, then I'll risk hurting the treasure, even if it gets broke, so long as I get to pry it from your dead fingers."

Dathka butted in again, only this time, instead of being commanding, she sounded desperate. "You kill me, you'll be missing out on more coin than you can imagine. Carcalla will pay a big ransom for my return. I'm worth far more to him than some old enchantment."

"Why would the Latrocinium's master give a special shit about the likes of you?"

"I'm his daughter."

Now, surely, she was the one doing the bluffing, as her snow-colored skin and pitch-black eyes marked her as being from the Plane of Death, and Carcalla was an elf, or half-elf, if what Gerzog said was true.

Except Gerzog didn't immediately scoff at her claim. "There's rumors Carcalla sired a herd of bastards 'cross all the realms."

"Check my ears if you don't believe me."

The orc used his knife to sweep her black hair out of the way, and sure enough, her ears were a little pointy. Not nearly as pronounced as on the elves I'd met, but more so than was natural for any human. I guess that made her a quarter-elf?

Gerzog let out a low growl. "If you speak true, then you're too valuable to waste. We'll keep you as insurance until the treasure is sold, then sell you to your supposed father. If it turns out you lie to me, I'll make you beg for death."

"Have mercy on me too," Morton cried. "I never wanted to be an adventurer!" Then he could no longer hold back the sobs of fear and began to rant hysterically, "My family has little to pay a ransom, but you can have it all. The Smorps run the animal auction yard in the great market. Do you want an exotic pet? We offer the finest from every realm. My mother wanted me to be a zookeeper same as my father and grandfather and great grandfather before had been, unto ten generations of Smorps, but I have allergies! I tested well, so I foolishly wanted to be a wizard, but I only wanted to learn some peaceful sort of magic to get a nice job someplace civilized. I never wished for this life of danger. *Please don't kill me!*"

Gerzog the Marauder clearly wasn't in the mood to hear Morton's life story. "I have reconsidered. Rather than the fat human, I'll kill this small noisy one first." He paused long enough to lift a pistol and dramatically cock the hammer, the sound of which caused our gnome to cringe. "One… Two… Three…"

There was still daylight coming from above, but the stairwell had suddenly gotten a lot darker. I glanced back to see that Sifuso and the lamp were gone. He must have retreated back into the flooding chamber. *Dammit, Sifuso.* I couldn't give up the treasure now even if I wanted to.

Gerzog continued his count, slow and methodical, like he was weighing every single word as he gradually moved the muzzle of his gun downward toward Morton's head. "Four… Five… Six…"

With my left hand, I swept one of the clay *Obscura* balls off my belt, and keeping that hand hidden behind my body, held it in such a way that Rade could see it, and hopefully understand my desperate plan.

"Seven… Eight…"

I concentrated on the clay long enough to activate the Black within, then dropped the ball. It erupted into a cloud of thick smoke. Something flew by my ear as Rade threw another *Obscura* up and out of the hole. It hit the sand behind Gerzog and popped.

Now everyone was blind.

Krachma released his *Impervious,* but I was already shoving past him, throwing a handful of Red-activated screws. I couldn't see a thing, but tried my best to get them over and past our captive friends, to scatter among the unseen Tooth and Claw crew.

A pistol barked. Sparks were visible briefly through the smoke. Morton yelped. Bognar let out a wail that suggested he'd been the one struck by the bullet. Then Gerzog roared as Dathka did something mean to him. From the little I knew about her, she'd likely bitten him or something. My rush up the stairs was interrupted by tripping over something small and fleshy. Morton squealed in protest as I stepped on him.

Then I was out of the hole. The big soft thing I ran into first had to be Bognar, who'd flopped over into the sand. I went over him and scrambled, blind, trying to get away from the entrance before the *Obscura* smoke cleared. I only knew Rade was right behind me because of the sound of a steel sword clearing a leather sheath.

Suddenly, I was out of the smoke, and face-to-face with a large fellow with an eye patch. I think we were both surprised. He saw me. I saw him. He raised a hatchet. I shot him through his good eye.

The mercenary's head snapped back and he toppled into two of his comrades I'd not even known were there, but from the surprise on their faces, they'd not been expecting us to come charging out of the hole like madmen either. They went for their weapons too late. I was already flinging some Red their way, and in my desperation, I'd grabbed a *lot* more than a pinch.

The *Shroud of Fire* ignited and fell across their faces, thick as a blanket. Clothes and hair ablaze, eyes melting, they went flailing away. I didn't even see the other mercenary who shot me.

The bullet struck me in the hip, and even though the Frunza charm activated to stop it, the impact still felt like someone had hit me with a hammer. It spun me around, and combined with my momentum, I crashed into the sand and went rolling.

I looked up to see a dwarf with a grin and a smoking rifle. Then Rade came out of the smoke and smoothly ran his blade straight through that dwarf's chest. The dwarf let out a wide-eyed *oof*, before Rade put one boot against his belly and kicked him off the sword. When the dwarf landed, flat and awkward on his back, a fountain of blood erupted from the hole in his heart.

The *Obscura* died off, leaving the two of us in plain sight of a whole bunch of armed and dangerous men, who were just now seeing two of their comrades fallen in spreading puddles of blood and two more screaming and burning. There were more mercenaries standing around the ruins of the lighthouse, and many more farther down the beach. Some had gotten stung by the *Screws of Chaos*, but most were unharmed. Before I could pop another *Obscura*, barrels and wands swung our way.

The big man named Hans was about to blast me with some spell, except his arm got punctured by a *Dagger of Air*. The knocked aside wand fired a purple bolt that melted a circle of sand into glass.

Rade and I had taken the slow way out of the hole. Azarin must have used an *Ascend*, because now she was falling slowly out of the sky, wand extended, as she sent invisible knives zipping through flesh.

Even with that, we were all about to get shot or cursed, but thankfully, Rade had been faster than me, and the smoke from his second *Obscura* blinded everyone once more. They still fired anyway. I felt a bullet whiz past my head. Then a glowing spectral hand grabbed hold of my collar, yanked me violently upright, and hurled my body against the unyielding stones of the lighthouse foundation.

Fuck, that hurt.

Apparently, Aziz's spell didn't require vision to be deadly, because the hand didn't vanish. It picked me up and slammed me down *again.* I tried to grab it, but my flesh and blood hand passed through the ghost hand. Despite being incorporeal, somehow it was strong as a Fire Elemental, and it hoisted me effortlessly once more.

There was a loud *thump* and Aziz bellowed in agony. Immediately the spectral hand vanished and I was dropped on my ass.

When the *Obscura* dissipated, Krachma was standing there with his mace, while Aziz was lying on his back, with one leg bent at a really awful angle and a jagged bone sticking out the side. You did *not* want to get clubbed by a lob. The mercenary wizard saw the bloody bone protruding through his pants and began screaming for help.

All the help he got was Rade covering him with biting spiders.

With no real cover, I threw down another smoke cloud, followed by more screws. There was a lot of noise and chaos as we fought in the dark. Gerzog shouted orders, but I couldn't make them out over the ringing in my ears. That spectral hand had clobbered me good.

When the last of our *Obscuras* cleared, I realized the mercenaries were retreating, and I had no idea why, because they still had the numeric advantage. We'd killed several of them, but those who could escape were doing so. Bognar was lying there, and Morton was huddled at the top of the stairs. Gerzog must have carried Dathka off with him.

"Why are they running?"

Trax's oblivious yet enthusiastic voice appeared in my mind.

"*They are fleeing from the sea monster.*"

"What? What sea monster?"

Rade looked up from driving his sword into Aziz's neck to put him out of his misery. "There's a sea monster now?"

"Apparently!"

"*I arrived and began biting these very rude people, when they suddenly became very frightened, declaring a sea monster to be present, so the green one in command ordered them to fall back to their boats.*" When Trax came around the side of a brick wall, he still had a severed arm clamped between his razor-sharp teeth. "*Wait. Could they have been talking about me? Am I the sea monster?*"

"You're *our* sea monster, buddy." I limped over and clapped Trax on the back, and it was a good thing I was wearing gloves, so I didn't cut my hand on his hide. "Good job."

"I'll take the high ground and keep an eye on the enemy." Azarin did a quick *Ascend* and landed on top of the largest rock pile.

Bognar was still on his side, pathetic and bound. "Uh, guys, I think I've been shot."

Rade went over and cut Bognar's hands free. "Indeed, you have. That looks exceedingly painful."

"It does hurt a whole lot."

Gerzog's blindly fired bullet had been meant for Morton, but he'd thrown himself down the stairs in the dark, and it found poor Bognar instead.

"How bad is it?"

"The bullet's stuck in his thigh. There's no exit wound. There's not that much blood, so the artery has not been severed." Rade took out a silk handkerchief that was so white and clean that he surely must have stolen it from someone more respectable than us, and pushed it against the hole. When Bognar cried out, Rade gave him some encouragement. "You have done well, my friend. Your bravery is a credit to the Slumps. Now hold this here to keep your blood inside, and later it will leave a fine scar to accompany the story."

Bognar gritted his teeth and kept pressure on his wound. "I'm sorry I let you down. Danny volunteered to watch that side of the island, but he didn't say nothing until they were already right on top of us."

I looked toward the body of our dead traitor, lying there blue-faced with his tongue sticking out and nearly bitten off, only a few feet from the wizard who'd killed him. "That wasn't your fault, Bognar. It's mine for being too trusting."

Azarin was atop the rocks, lying on her belly to not provide a tempting target. "Gerzog and his men are heading for their boats. Looks like they left more men there to guard them. I think they're going to regroup and all come back to wreck us."

"Does he have Dathka?"

"He's got her thrown over one shoulder. Unfortunately, she's kicking, which means she's still alive."

I looked around, seeing no sign of our lizard man. "Where's Sifuso and the lamp?"

Trax sent us a mental picture of our lizard man crawling across the ceiling of the flooding chamber and escaping through one of the newly formed holes in the roof. "*The lizard told me he was going to keep the treasure away from the bad men.*"

"That's actually a good idea. Hey, everybody, Sifuso didn't run on us. He's hiding the lamp from Gerzog. Lacertians can swim and burrow, and they're masters at concealment."

Azarin called down to us, "Too bad he's got the sense of direction of a brain-damaged griffon."

I lifted my glove and *Ascended* up next to her. As soon as I landed on the rock pile, I saw what she was talking about, as there was a growing bulge in the sand as Sifuso clawed his way to freedom… Right between Gerzog and his boats.

27

They were about a hundred and fifty yards away, so all I could do was watch helplessly as the mercenaries dragged Sifuso out of the ground and beat him mercilessly. The box holding Korthican's lamp must have gotten knocked open, because a brilliant beam shot upward, cutting a path through the overcast sky, so bright, it was surely visible in the city.

"They've got Sifuso," I told those who couldn't see what was happening.

"And our treasure," Azarin added, before she must have realized how heartless that sounded. "And Sifuso, of course."

"We've got to try to rescue him." I slid down from the rocks and hit the sand. "Quick, search these bodies and gather their weapons and any element. We'll have to make a push."

"Across open ground?" Rade asked incredulously. "Into a dozen guns and wands?"

"How many *Obscuras* do you have left?" I patted my own pouches to check.

"None. I used them all up keeping us alive this long."

"I've only got one." That wasn't nearly enough cover to get us across the beach without getting ripped apart. "Azarin, are they coming back?"

"No. They've got the lamp and they're wading out to their boats."

Of course they were. They'd only retreated because Gerzog was too smart to fight a Squalo in the dark. Now they had a valuable prisoner to ransom and the treasure they'd come here for had been delivered right into their hands. The Tooth and

Claw must not be a very caring bunch, because they hadn't even hesitated to abandon their wounded, so they didn't even have revenge to motivate them. There was no reason to waste any more effort trying to finish us off now.

Several gunshots rang out, and I flinched, because surely that must have signaled the end of unfortunate Sifuso.

Except Azarin exclaimed, "They're shooting our boats!"

Not only were they leaving, they were making sure we couldn't follow. They kept on reloading and firing, and the more holes they put in those planks, the harder it was going to be for us to repair.

The enemy was at too great a distance to be hit accurately with my bargemaster's handgun, but the dwarf Rade had run through with his sword had been armed with a rifle. Perhaps with it I could pick off a mercenary or two. I grabbed the long gun and patted down the corpse in search of more cartridges. I found three in his breast pocket. They were coated in blood, but hopefully, that hadn't had time to soak through the paper.

"*Ascend.*" I landed next to Azarin, went prone, and tried to figure out how to load the unfamiliar weapon. The design wasn't too different from the guns the Argents issued to our cadre's trappers, just of a shoddier make. The metal was pitted with corrosion, which disgusted me. No wonder he'd died so easily. Failing to do proper maintenance on your equipment showed a real lack of character.

I got the rifle loaded, cocked, and settled in behind it, bracing the wooden forearm against the ground for stability. Then I lined up the iron sights upon the upper chest of the nearest mercenary who was busy firing upon our boats.

"Hurry, or we're gonna have to swim home."

"I don't know how to swim." I pulled the trigger.

Crack.

The man was flung down by the impact. The shimmer left in the air told me he'd been wearing a charm to ward off bullets, but if his spine felt like my hip did from getting hit by this same weapon, he'd be aching from that for days. He got up and ran for the surf.

I broke open the action, fished out the smoking case, and shoved in the next. The dwarf's blood sizzled against the hot metal of the chamber.

The mercenaries were looking my way, and some were sure to shoot back. "Best get down, Azarin."

Impulsive as she might be, her father was some kind of warlord, so I didn't need to tell her twice that she didn't want to be where the enemy bullets were about to land. Azarin rolled over the edge and dropped.

I spotted Gerzog climbing into one of the boats; he was still holding Dathka. I didn't care for her at all, but if she really was Carcalla's daughter, my landlord surely wouldn't approve of me shooting through her to hit my target. I aimed, and waited for him to throw her down, and the instant Dathka was clear, I pulled the trigger.

From the flash, Gerzog was also wearing a protective charm, but the impact of the big rifle bullet still knocked him off-balance and sent him overboard. I really wish I'd been able to shoot that bastard with one of my experimental molten bullets instead, because I would've loved to watch him burn.

Bits of rock stung my face as a projectile hit just short of me. A magical bolt whooshed past overhead. Not knowing if my Frunza charm had time to recharge yet, I gave up my perch and slid down the rocks to escape. The other Outcasts were having to take cover as bricks exploded around them.

I reloaded as I ran to the side, looking for an angle on the beach. By the time I found one, the Tooth and Claw boats were already fully upon the waves. Half the men were rowing, while the other half kept shooting to keep our heads down. Thankfully, the waves made them even less accurate.

Seeing that the now soaking Gerzog had climbed back aboard, I shouldered the rifle and fired the last round at that retreating craft. There was a bit of consternation aboard as men got hit by splinters or fragments of lead, but that was all. And then they were off and rowing for the mainland.

Once it was unlikely the mercenaries would be able to hit me from so far away, I left cover and ran toward the dark lump on the sand that had to be Sifuso. When I got there, he was a mess. Scales had been broken off in clumps, revealing red flesh beneath. He'd been beaten and stabbed repeatedly, and by some miracle, he still breathed.

"Sifuso, can you hear me?"

"Barely, but I live." Then he let out a wheezy laugh. "Stuck me up here." He moved one weak claw to his chest, then touched his belly. "But lacertian heart are lower, here. Dumb orc thinks my body is dumb like his is."

I didn't know anything about lacertian biology, but even I could tell he was going to die if we didn't get him to a healer fast. "We're going to take you to the nuns of Saint Olga for a healing. You just rest."

"I was not coward. Know I did not run from this fight. I tried to hide the treasure. Did not… run… Just did not expect… them… here…"

It was surprising he cared what I thought of him as he faded out. "I know. You did good."

Except Sifuso had already passed out.

Trax padded up to me, chewing on a different arm. I could tell because the last one had been thick and covered in tattoos. This one was skinny and plain.

"*The lizard has drastically slowed his pulse. That is how his people bury their bodies and hibernate to survive the winters in cold realms. I suspect this state will help keep him from bleeding to death.*"

"Who're you eating now?"

"*You said to search the bodies for weapons. Danny had this.*" Trax held out the simple ice wand to me.

I took it. "That doesn't explain how Danny's arm ended up in your mouth."

"*The wand was in his hand. I was distracted.*" Trax spit out the severed arm. "*The traitor tastes of shame and failure anyway. What now?*"

Rade and Krachma were already checking our boats, but even from here, I could tell the damage was extensive. "While we fix those somehow, I need you to tail Gerzog to see where he lands. Stay out of sight. Then come back to give us a tow."

"*I shall do so. However, you may wish to expedite your repairs as much as possible.*" Trax took two big steps and dove smoothly into the waves. Within seconds, his back fin disappeared beneath the surface and he was out of sight.

"We're going to anyway, but why?"

Trax was fast on land, but he was a whole lot faster under water, and he was already so far away that the mind pictures I received weren't nearly as booming as usual. "*The monsters we fought earlier were nocturnal. They will likely receive reinforcements and return after the sun sets to reclaim their nest.*"

I looked toward where the afternoon sun was getting lower in the sky.

"Well… shit."

28

I sure wasn't going to get my deposit back on the rowboats.

The two we had arrived in had not only received a great many bullet holes, but one of the mercenaries had hit them with some kind of purple caustic spell that scorched and crumbled big parts throughout. However, the single rowboat brought by the previous group of less fortunate adventurers had only been shot a dozen or so times below the waterline. We set about cannibalizing our boats and used the wood and nails we salvaged for some hasty repairs. We didn't have any proper tools, but an axe that can chop people can also chop wood, and the steel butt cap of a bargemaster's pistol makes a decent hammer. Just make sure it's empty first.

With the sun going down, we'd loaded our wounded aboard, crowded in after them, and then set out upon the bay, only to immediately begin taking on water because our repairs weren't nearly as good as we'd thought they were. We used the pot Bognar had worn as a helmet to continually bail us out.

We could have put in more time and done more thorough repairs, but the big bulbous eyes that kept popping out of the water all along the beach—waiting for it to get dark so they could attack—had been an excellent motivator to get a move on.

It was very crowded in the boat—which had been shoddy before it'd been shot—to the point I was worried we would capsize. We'd lost two passengers and gained one, but that one was very small, so we managed to fit in the one boat, barely.

After a few minutes upon the water, I got so frustrated at the leak soaking my legs that I tried to use Danny's wand to plug it… the idea being that if that hole was frozen solid, no more water would come in. Except Danny's spell was one I'd not had the chance to practice much, and all I managed to do was turn the water that was already in the boat with us into an even colder slush.

Thankfully, the mutants didn't come after us. They scrambled up the beach, rushing to check on the safety of their eggs. The last thing I could make out before we got too far away was the monsters feasting on the corpses we'd left behind.

Sifuso remained unconscious, but Trax had probably been right about how lizardmen hearts worked, because he didn't appear to be getting any worse. Bognar, on the other hand, wasn't doing well at all. He was in a great deal of pain, and his skin had become paler than mine, and I'd come from a land without direct sunlight. If he got to Rade's complexion, he'd be dead soon afterward.

"I saw a church to the saint of fishermen not too far from the docks," I told everyone. "I don't know if they'll have a healer there, but it's Bognar's and Sifuso's best chance."

Azarin agreed. "Most healing magic is Life-based, but there's some water spells that heal too. Surely a saint of the sea will have someone who knows one of those. We'll carry them there fast as we can."

"That'll work, if they have healing at all and if we can afford to pay them," Rade said. "Olga is the saint of mercy, so her healers work cheaply compared to others, but even the Olgaites charge more than we can afford at the best of times. What will a sailor's saint charge to save these two?"

"It doesn't matter. We'll persuade them somehow." This was profoundly frustrating. We'd gone adventuring to earn our keep, and instead, we were going to end up in greater debt. But we'd already lost two students today—one to stupidity, and one to treachery—and I'd be damned if we were going to lose two more if I could help it.

We rowed as fast as we could toward the distant lights of the city. Tiny Morton was useless with an oar, so he was manning the bailing pot.

"This is all my fault. I waited for Ms. Walker, but I was unaware that I was being watched by those ruffians. As soon as she arrived, I told her our tale, but then we were set upon by surprise and taken prisoner."

"Too bad she didn't use her shadow magic to kill them all. It was nasty to fight against in the arena."

"She tried, but there were too many and it was too bright out. Gerzog struck her down, took her charms, then tied us up and gagged us and carried us aboard their craft. The entire time, they made cruel jokes about throwing me overboard, wondering aloud if gnomes float."

Krachma frowned. "Do you?"

"The answer is no. No, we do not."

More than anything else right then, I wanted Gerzog dead. That hate motivated me to row harder. "Did they say anything about where they'd go afterwards?"

Morton chucked another potful of water over the side. "Alas, no. All I can tell you is that the Tooth and Claw are a mean and degenerate lot, motivated entirely by greed, who rejoice in spite, not just against their victims, but to each other as well. Even during our short journey, I saw several of them get into fights with each other, and the only thing staying their hands from murder was the threats of their captain. From what I could discern, most were new hires from the city's lowest pits of scum, recently recruited by Gerzog's company."

That explained why only some of them had possessed magical defenses. Protective charms were expensive. Gerzog hadn't had any loyalty to his longer serving, more capable men either, because he'd abandoned wounded Aziz to his fate, and that mage obviously hadn't been some new recruit. I had bruises everywhere from getting slammed about by that spectral hand, and it was only Krachma's lucky leg break that saved my life. I assumed they hadn't been lying when Aziz claimed to be a rank two.

"Gerzog fled and didn't even bother trying to save his wounded." The rocking of boat was making me ill, but I was too cold to vomit, which was a bizarre and uncomfortable combination. At least talking helped me to focus my mind on something other than the discomfort. "He mentioned selling the lamp to the Council or the Tempus cult, but in a gang of cutthroats like that, surely he's got to tread carefully to not get robbed or betrayed first. We might be able to use that to our advantage somehow."

"You're thinking of going after the lamp again?" Rade was incredulous. "We were lucky to survive that fight. We'll be lucky to not sink and drown now."

"I'm mad too, but we're in no shape to take on an entire mercenary company," Azarin said.

You knew it was bad when the impulsive one was the voice of reason. "He can't get away with this."

"Just tell Carcalla what happened and let him send his goons after Gerzog. Carcalla's got an army."

She had a point. We'd done as Carcalla commanded. Surely our efforts would be satisfactory enough to avoid eviction. It wasn't our fault we'd gotten screwed over. We were student wizards, not adventurers. Maybe it was time to go home and lick our wounds. That would be the sensible thing to do. I followed Saint Persistence, so the idea of giving up galled me, but I needed to put the wellbeing of the Academy first. It might be the worst academy in the Core, but Gaul Haddar had left me in charge of it, and I couldn't let my temper get us all killed.

"Besides," Azarin continued. "If Dathka is who she claims to be, then Carcalla is going to move heaven and hell to get her back. Do you want to get in the way of that?"

"You're probably right."

"Of course I'm right. Kidnapping and ransoms are a normal part of doing business in Stormwolk. All the important families have been through it. I'm something of an expert."

"On doing the kidnapping, or being kidnapped?"

"Both," Azarin said proudly.

"*Hello.*" Trax's fin broke the surface besides us.

Morton saw the fin, screamed, "*Shark!*" and reflexively tried to hit it with his pot, which he promptly lost and dropped into the ocean.

"Relax. It's just Trax."

It was ironic that the presence of a sleek carnivorous killing machine would cause us all to breathe a sigh of relief, but such is the odd nature of friendship. A big grey hand rose from the water to hand the pot back. Embarrassed, Morton took it.

"*Would you like for me to assist you? You are very slow and bad at this.*"

Rade was already throwing the end of the rope overboard. "We're glad to see you, Mr. Bloodtrail."

The rope snapped taut, and Trax immediately began pulling us toward shore. "*I observed where the orc made landfall.*" He sent me a mind picture of an unfamiliar part of the bay where many large ships were docked. "*Should I go directly there?*"

"No. Take us to the place we launched from. There's a church near there. We need a healer before we need vengeance."

It was good and dark by the time Trax got us back to civilization. There were a couple of locals sitting on the end of the dock with fishing poles, only they got up and ran away when they saw us approaching. Probably to tell the fisherman I'd got the boats from that we'd lost his property. I didn't look forward to being yelled at. My hip hurt, I was covered in bruises, and my back and arms burned from the continual rowing. Lava was preferable to the ocean, and levitating barges were far superior to floating boats, and right then I'd have punched out anyone who dared disagree.

We tied up at the dock and wearily climbed up. It took a lot of effort to get hefty and delirious Bognar onto dry land, but Krachma and Trax were very strong.

A bunch of light charms were headed our way. That was a far larger reception than we deserved. The numbers made me alert and suspicious. I thought hard at Trax, *Jump back in the water and hide.*

"*A fine idea.*" Trax slipped off the edge of the dock and vanished into the dark water below.

Rade saw them coming and slowly moved one hand to his sword. "Why is there a mob waiting for us?"

Mob was a bit of an overstatement, but it was still a dozen toughs. I died inside when I saw it was Cutter Joran at the head of the approaching group.

"Good evening, Mr. Carnavon." He tipped his hat toward us. "Lady Garzade. Krachma the Killer. Mr. Prescott."

Rade frowned at the use of his birthname rather than the one he'd claimed for himself. "It's Tartaros."

"Sure. You're a nobleman the same way I'm the Lord High Emperor of Norto Molto and this is my royal guard." When Joran said that, his thugs laughed. "We're here to welcome you home, triumphant adventurers, for the whole city saw that great beam of light leap into the sky from somewhere upon the bay earlier. Hell, the real nobles probably even saw it way up in the Pallentine, and what else could that have been but a great and ancient treasure revealed? So where is it?"

"It got stolen."

"Oh?" Joran was suspicious, but didn't seem too surprised. "That's a development. By whom was it stolen?"

I was too weary to put up with Joran's threatening trogshit right now. "As you can see, we've got wounded. I'll tell you all about what happened out there, but please let my people carry these two to a healer first."

Joran scowled as he looked over our group. "Your headcount seems to be short a few."

"Some of us didn't make it."

He nodded, real slow. "Or you're a diversion, and they landed secretly elsewhere with the precious lamp."

"We're not thieves," I stated, flat and offended.

Rade coughed. "Well, some of us might have dabbled in such behaviors in the past, but that's not the case this time. As you can see, we were attacked."

"I shall not sob myself to sleep at night over the loss of any Outcasts, as there's too many high and mighty mages in the world as it is, to coddle the aspiring ones. However, my heart bleeds for every member of the Latrocinium... Where's Dathka?"

"She's been abducted by an orc named Gerzog."

I'd seen Joran aggressive and menacing before, but it had always been real contained. This was the first time I saw him become genuinely angry. His manner changed, nothing really perceptible, but the subtle shift was enough to make me in fear of my life.

"What did you say?"

"Gerzog the Marauder. Big fellow. Green. Tusks. A bit of a prick. I'm sure Carcalla will be getting the ransom demand soon. He's got the lamp too. The Tooth and Claw mercenary company jumped us after we fought our way through the monsters and defeated all the traps. They killed some of us, and these two are going to die if we don't get them help…" I gestured toward where Sifuso and Bognar were lying on the dock. "So *please* let them through."

"Where did he take her?"

Joran was one dangerous son of a bitch and he didn't care if my friends lived or died. Too bad for him, I did, and my Fogo temperament was showing through. "I'll tell you as soon as you let them pass, or let's fucking get this over with and it'll be more than these two needing a healer."

He surely thought about just killing me right there for my impudence, and it got real tense on that dock. I recognized two of the band with him as the higher-ranking mages he'd had with him the first time. With them fresh, and us in our current sorry and soggy condition, we wouldn't stand a chance.

Thankfully, even while angry, Joran remained sensible. "Fine. Let them through. Everyone but Carnavon. As spokesman for this band of rejects, me and him have got some business to discuss."

I looked toward Azarin. "Get them taken care of."

"I will," she promised.

Krachma picked up Big Bognar in his arms like a baby, while Rade and Azarin together struggled to lift Sifuso. Morton couldn't really do much to help, but he was quick to attach himself to that group rather than volunteer to stay with me.

Joran waved toward half his men. "Don't just stand there. Help carry their wounded… Then keep them company and make sure none of them run off until we get this mess sorted out. The rest of you remain with me." Then Joran raised his voice. "And as for you, Squalo. Don't forget I can understand your picture language. I already heard you, so I know you're out there skulking about in the waves. I assume you're the reason Carnavon knows where these thieves have taken my employee. You can come out now."

"*I do not think that is a good idea.*"

"Suit yourself." Joran walked across the dock, stopped right in front of me, and leaned in, uncomfortably close. "As for you, boy, best start talking, or I'll start slicing."

29

Late Eternanight, I found myself in the shadows of the Core City bay, sneaking up on the hideout of a mercenary band, accompanied by a crime lord's right hand, his assorted thugs, and a Squalo to steal back a priceless magical relic. And to think just a year ago I was in Fogo dreaming of becoming a rank-one wizard while trapping Fire Elementals for a living. Life is funny like that.

"Trax says he's sure this is the place," I whispered.

Joran and I were crouched in the dark behind a fence made of driftwood and wire. At the end of the road was a dimly lit warehouse. Even from two hundred yards away, it was obvious there were guards posted all over it. There was at least one on top of the flat roof, and more walking around outside.

"If you're lying..."

"Yeah, I'm dying. I know, painful dismemberment and flaying and whatnot, but I swear before all the saints we didn't take that lamp for ourselves."

"Yet the only person I trust to confirm your sad tale is conveniently missing, and possibly at the bottom of the bay."

"Dathka's likely in there too!"

He thumped me hard on the arm, warning me to keep quiet. I didn't know what Joran expected. It was hard to remain stealthy while someone keeps threatening and infuriating you, and it was doubtful anyone would've heard me over the crashing of the nearby surf anyway.

We watched for a bit longer. This neighborhood was surely busy during the day, but most of the laborers had gone home for the night. Lots of people still lived here, though, so there were witnesses about. We were on the beach, but everything past the sand was covered in buildings, and there were lit candles, lanterns, and light charms in some of those windows.

"Come on."

The two of us stayed low as we went back to where Joran's Latros were waiting. There were five of them huddled on the sand next to the grounded skeleton of an old fishing boat. All our light charms had been extinguished, but the moon was full enough we could still get about decently well. Seeing the moon so clearly had been a rare treat in Fogo. There was usually too much smoke, so I still marveled at the beauty of there being a big, round, shiny thing in the sky. It keeping me from tripping over anything in the dark tonight was a nice bonus.

"What's the deal, Cutter?" one of them asked.

"Assuming this hotland scrub isn't leading us into a trap, the mercs are holed up in the big warehouse at the back of the lane."

"I told you, I'm telling the truth. This is where Trax followed them. The mind picture he sent shows that place has its own little dock, and the boats Gerzog used are tied up there." Trax had even gotten close enough that he sent me a mental image of the bullet hole I'd put into one of the boats.

Joran looked toward the water where Trax lurked. "I could see that too. Fortunately for you, Squalos as a race aren't known for deceit. Their species produces no liars. They'll rip your guts out and eat them in front of you, but they're always honest about it."

Trax must have heard that, because he sent back, "*Thank you for this compliment.*"

"So we gonna go bleed these bastards or what?" That question came from the one Joran had previously identified as a rank-three mage. The rest nodded eagerly. The Latrocinium clearly didn't shy away from fights.

"Two problems, lads. I suspect there's a bunch of them in there. But worse, we're a long way from the Slumps. There's City Watch crawling all over this district. All these storehouses around us belong to trading companies, and the Council loves commerce above all else. We start a battle here, an army of blue coats will come running."

That was when I realized none of the Latrocinium were wearing their usual black armbands. They were proud to fly their colors in the Slumps, but in any of the more civilized parts of the city, that would just draw the wrath of the watch.

"I say we risk it anyway," said the rank three. "I could set the back ablaze, then as they run out the front, the rest of you gun them down."

"There'll be no risking arson with one of our own maybe inside," Joran responded.

One of the Latros was far more grizzled than the others, and you know what they say about someone who lives to old age in a young man's game… "I know this place. It belongs to one of the traders who on occasion employs this company of fools. I think he gives the mercs a place to sleep and gather recruits while they're in the Core between jobs. The Tooth and Claw haven't clashed with us before now, but we can't have some mercenary stroll through the gate, thinking he can throw his weight around in our territory. It sends the wrong message."

Joran nodded at that wisdom. "Gerzog has got too big for his britches, and he'll find the Latrocinium aren't some deadlands peasants to be pillaged."

"What if we wait until it's darkest, right before dawn, when most of them is deep asleep, go in real quiet like, and start strangling," suggested another. "Easy as stealing a baby."

I was aghast. "You guys steal babies?"

"Figure of speech," Joran responded. "Folks who work the sea are early risers. The longer we wait, the more likely we get identified. We're going now, quiet as we can, and we need Dathka, the lamp, and this upstart orc's life, in that order. Anybody fucks that up, I'll end you myself."

Joran putting the girl before the treasure told me there might be something to her claim of being Carcalla's daughter. "So is Dathka really your boss's kid?"

"That's stupid. Of course not," Joran snapped, and considering how collected he usually was, his denial had come out too fast, which told me it was likely true. "That's just a ruse she came up with in the moment to keep herself in one piece, and you'd best forget you ever heard such nonsense."

"Consider it forgotten... Now I'll wish you gentlemen good luck. Regardless of what you all decide to do, me and Trax are out."

"The hell you are," said the rank three. "The rest of our crew is watching your friends to make sure they don't run off. We're short-handed and got no time to send for help. A Squalo by himself is worth ten regular men in a fight."

"*That is flattering. However, that would only be possible if I have the element of surprise.*"

Joran laughed at that, which was a bit unnerving, as I was used to being the only one who could understand Trax clearly.

"We made a deal to clear out some ruins in exchange for the rent. Those ruins got cleared. All this trogshit afterwards? Not my academy's problem."

"I see it a bit different," Joran said. "It's very much a big fucking problem—for you—because our deal was for you to recover treasure. I've seen no treasure yet, but that great big light shooting into the sky told the world there was treasure there. Treasure which you likely stole for yourself."

"You know that's a lie."

He shrugged. "All that matters is that's what I'll tell Carcalla when I justify to him my killing of you and all your friends. It doesn't take a great leap of imagination to believe you found the lamp, then murdered Dathka before sending it off with one of your minions to sell."

If my dad had still been alive, he would have told me this was what I deserved for dealing with dishonest crooks. "That's a scummy move."

"Should I be corrected as to your innocence later, like, say, by finding the treasure clutched in the dirty hands of an orc... Oh well, live and learn. Well, you won't, seeing as how you'll already be dead—unless you pitch in and help fix your mistakes."

It pissed me off that I'd gone across realms merely to trade callous noblemen for petty gangsters. I'd vowed to become a wizard so I'd never be powerless again, but no matter where I went, I kept running into assholes coercing me to do things against my will. I dreamed of the day I'd achieved a high enough rank to blast all of these little tyrants straight to hell. That day was still a lot of effort and practice away, but right that minute, I was done being bullied.

"Fuck you, Joran. Kill me then and get it over with."

Two of the Latros promptly drew daggers, and they'd surely have gutted me and left my body in the sand behind this rotting sailboat, but Joran held up one hand to stop them. Then he flashed me an unnerving smile. His teeth were very white in the dark. "Ah, there's that notorious hotlander temper all your people are supposed to possess. Good to see you've got some of that fire in your belly, boy. Fine. I'll let you keep your dignity, by offering an addendum to the deal. You and your Squalo help us right now, today's failures are forgiven, and that's another month of rent considered paid in full."

I was a little surprised my defiance hadn't gotten me stabbed, but I was barge cadre, so haggling was in my blood. "Three months."

"Don't push your luck."

"Alright, how about one month if I help get back your girl, another month for the lamp, and a third if we kill Gerzog? Our previous agreement about splitting any loot evenly—other than the lamp which is all yours—remains in force."

"The balls on this one..." the old gangster muttered.

"Naw, it's good, Vilko. I appreciate the rare show of audacity in this city of lemmings." I didn't even know what a lemming was, but Joran held out one hand. "We've struck a deal, Carnavon, with these men and the saints as our witnesses."

"And Trax. He's got a real good memory." I spit on my palm and we shook on it. The former gladiator had a grip like a Red miner. "So, what's the plan?"

"Let's go see if your Squalo is as good at surprise as he claims."

30

You might think Squalos are scary, but you don't really grasp just how terrifying they can be until you watch one hunting. Most of the time, Trax just stands there, staring blankly with his beady black eyes, perfectly quiet and sort of physically awkward, not moving until he needed to. When he does move, there's always a swiftness to it that warns you there was a lot more where that came from. Watching Trax in a straight-up fight was impressive. But turn him lose to stalk unsuspecting prey in the dark… May the saints have mercy on the spirts of those he was about to slay. He'd been my most stalwart friend since I'd arrived in the Core, and I'd come to love Trax like a brother, except seeing him in action that night was rather unnerving, because unleashed, my fishy brother was *terrifying.*

"*I would not be so ruthless now, but these mercenaries were exceedingly rude earlier. They are also the direct cause of the death of our dwarf. Who I did not particularly care for, but he did not deserve to be so thoroughly squished.*"

What happened to Rufus was pretty brutal, I thought back.

"*There was not even enough left of him to be eaten. A shameful waste of perfectly good meat.*"

That sounded horrible, but I reminded myself that Squalos considered eating their dead a great honor. I'd already promised Trax he could eat me when I died, which, with the way things were going lately, might be sooner rather than later.

From the corner of the warehouse, I watched as Trax silently moved up behind another guard. For being so large, his movements were incredibly fluid. When the guard glanced behind him, Trax simply sank lower to the ground into the deeper shadows. The instant the guard looked away, Trax pounced. And by *pounced*, I mean launched three hundred pounds of carnivorous death upon him. The poor bastard didn't even make much sound, because Trax ate half his neck in one bite.

"*That is the last of the guards on the perimeter.*"

"Didn't anyone ever tell him it's not polite to talk with your mouth full," Joran whispered, and then chuckled at his own joke. Of course, the Latros had no idea what he was talking about, because they couldn't understand Squalo language.

Joran found all this murdering to be funny, but Trax was so brutally efficient, I was starting to feel pity for our enemy… Just a little.

"*Do not feel bad, Carnavon. I recognize this scent. This one was also on the island. He fired a gun at your female but missed.*"

Well, fuck him, then, I thought.

"*I do not think that action would be appropriate.*" Trax moved back to us. His snout was covered in blood. "*The exterior threats have been eliminated. The path is clear.*"

"It's time to demonstrate our devotion to Saint Murder. May Brotbeck enjoy tonight's offering." Joran drew his sword. "Let's go, boys."

Unlike Rade, I knew very little about swords and fighting with them. Our deadlander's enchanted blade was a long skinny thing, made for quick movements and thrusts. Joran's was more of a long meat cleaver, like an implement a farmer would use for butchering livestock rather than something a duelist would use in an arena, but Joran had a legendary record that put my meager one to shame, so I kept my ignorant critique to myself.

We headed straight for the nearest door. The plan was to strike fast, get what we'd come for, and get away before the watch was summoned. I was glad for this plan, as I wanted no quarrel with the Core City Watch. Sure, one of their inspectors tried to frame me for murder, but Adderlane had been corrupt and quite possibly insane. The other inspector I'd dealt with, Borg, was actually rather helpful and gave me useful advice. I'd hate to repay that kindness by getting caught working for the city's most notorious gang.

Having been a trapper, I knew how to move fast and quiet. The Latros were good at it too, probably having gained that knowledge through various acts of burglary and assassination. All of us sounded like clunking, clanging oafs in comparison to Trax, who glided along behind us like some apparition from the Plane of Death.

One of Joran's men tried the door, but of course it was locked. He produced a pouch of tools from inside his coat and went to work on the mechanism. Before I could count to twenty, there was a *click*, and we were in.

I won't lie. I was scared to death. Danger was an old friend of mine, but it had come in the form of fire and monsters. I'd never wanted to conduct midnight raids on a mercenary company. I'd killed men before, but only in self-defense. This was different. Except, by robbing us and leaving us to die, the Tooth and Claw had demonstrated themselves to be no different in morals than the elf pirate who'd destroyed my family's barge.

That comparison made me feel a bit better about what we were about to do.

The building was mostly one big interior space. A single light charm had been set to float above the center, which provided just enough light to navigate, but nothing more. There were boxes, barrels, and crates stacked everywhere. It reminded me of the inside of the Red warehouses in Fort Silver, only this was far larger. There was a balcony and second floor above the back of the big room. Up there were more lights, and I could make out a few voices talking. That would be where most of the mercs would be sleeping.

Joran took the lead. I'd say he was confident, but that wasn't quite the right word. It was more that he'd done this sort of dangerous thing so many times, he was simply unmoved by it all. Murderous violence came naturally to him. This was his element, just like Trax in the sea.

There were some bedrolls thrown down on an open spot on the warehouse floor. From the empty bottles lying around, the mercenaries had celebrated today's score with a lot of drinking. A few men were lying there passed out and snoring.

One of the Latros nodded toward them and ran his finger across his throat, but Joran shook his head in the negative. We'd leave those be. Killing them might make enough noise to alert the others above, and by the time these woke from their drunken stupor, we'd be gone. I was glad for that decision, because I couldn't stomach the idea of killing someone asleep in their bed. I wasn't squeamish about killing. That's just part of living. But everyone I'd killed so far had been face-to-face, and they'd had it coming.

The Latro wizard took a device from his belt. It was a small spool of wire attached to a copper box in the middle. He tied one end of the wire to the leg of a shelf, and wrapped the other around the handle of a chest, just high enough that if one of these men got up, they'd surely trip over it. He paused just long enough to whisper some activation command to the box, then left it there, armed and deadly.

Joran reached the stairs and started up. It was nearly impossible for his boots to not make a noise on the metal steps, but he kept his steps natural and unhurried. If someone heard him, they'd just assume one of their fellows from below had awakened and was coming to join them. He reached the top, looked around, then signaled for us to follow.

The top floor contained more storage, though it was all smaller and lighter goods piled onto shelves, which we stopped and hid behind. There were several doors leading to who knew what, and at the end of the balcony was where most of the Tooth and Claw were gathered around a Red-fueled heater. There were about fifteen in total. They sat around on boxes or lay on the floor, and from the looks of things, much like downstairs, they'd been celebrating. The ones who were still awake spoke with the slur of happy drunks. We were outnumbered, but we were in far better condition than our foes.

I didn't see Gerzog, but I spotted the strong one named Hans. One of his arms was in a sling from where Azarin sliced him with air daggers, and he had a brown bottle in the other hand. He was the only one standing, and that was to address the crowd.

"So then Aziz says to the monster, 'Sorry we tried to milk you, but we thought you was a *girl* minotaur!' Hah ha!" The mercs laughed, and Hans lifted his bottle high. "To lost comrades. You will be missed, but when Gerzog returns from selling our prizes, we shall gladly split up your share!"

"Staverton," Joran whispered at the Latro wizard. "Announce our presence."

"With pleasure, Cutter." He pulled out a wand and pointed it at the mercs. "*Concuss.*"

I'd not seen this spell before, but it must have been air-based. As all the small items in a ten-foot circle—dust, playing cards, coins, cups, bottles, hats, even a few loose knives—all got sucked into the center, held together and floating for the briefest moment as the drunken mercs stared at it, confused, before everything exploded outward in a shockwave of wind and deafening noise.

The members of the Tooth and Claw were sent flailing. The ones who'd been sitting were knocked over backwards. Glass shattered and shelves toppled. The men who'd been asleep were startled awake. One unlucky bastard caught one of the pocket knives with his thigh and started screaming.

"Could I pay you to teach me that one?"

"No," the wizard told me. "Learn your own spells."

Joran stepped out into the open and began walking toward the stunned mercenaries. "Where is Gerzog?"

Hans got up and stumbled, dizzy. "*What?*" Then he saw Joran approaching and reflexively whipped up a wand in his good hand. "*Eradicate!*"

A crackling purple bolt flew across the room to smack Joran square in the chest.

Of course, that potent-looking spell accomplished absolutely nothing. Joran just smiled and wagged one finger, like *oh, you shouldn't have done that.* And poor Hans just stood there stupidly, not grasping what had gone wrong with his spell, because Nulls were rare as vegetarian Squalos, until Joran lopped Han's wand arm right off.

They might have been hardened killers, but between the surprise of the spell and the sudden amputation, the Tooth and Claw recoiled in terror. Joran certainly knew how to make an entrance.

"I am Joran Vanderhelst, representative of Carcalla, master of the Latrocinium, and I have asked you a simple question. Where's Gerzog?"

Hans was staring at his stump in horror as it squirted. Then he looked back up at Joran, surprisingly defiant. "Go fuck yourself, you—"

Joran kicked Hans in the chest so hard, the big man went stumbling back. The window he crashed into, having just been cracked by the *Concuss*, broke around him, and Hans flipped end over end out into the night.

At the same time, one of the mercenaries downstairs must have risen and run into Staverton's tripwire trap, because there was a *boom,* and the entire building shook.

"Must I raise my voice? *Where is Gerzog the Marauder?*"

We were badly outnumbered, but the mercenaries didn't know that. The rest of us had come out from hiding, and if they'd not been cowed before, seeing us pointing weapons at them, with a blood-covered Squalo among us, took the fight right out of them.

"Gerzog left a couple hours ago," a mercenary shouted. "Please have mercy."

Joran gave that one a maniacal grin. "Do I look like the sort of man who gives a shit about the kindly whims of Saint Olga? The fat lady of mercy won't save you from me. Only honesty can save you now. Vilko?"

"Yeah, Cutter?" the old gangster responded.

"Who's the saint of honesty?"

"Not really sure. Honesty don't get much worship in the Slumps. Though Sarda's the Saint of Truth. I only know that cause that's who the magistrates make you swear to when you have to go to court."

"She'll do." Joran laid his sword up against one of the mercenary's necks. That man's flinch was enough for the blade to break skin. "You lot will swear by Saint Sarda and talk fast. For every lie you tell, I'll take a life. Every truth you give me, I'll spare one. Where's Dathka Walker?"

"Who?"

With the flick of his wrist, Joran cut that man's head clean off. Either that big cleaver was enchanted or that was the sharpest steel I'd ever seen. The rest of the mercenaries recoiled in terror. "The really pretty deadlander woman you took… *who works for me.*"

"Gerzog has her with him," one of them quickly supplied. He must have figured the sooner he satisfied Joran's demands, the greater his chance of survival. "Gerzog told us he got an offer for the treasure. He was gonna keep her around as insurance against you Latros 'til the deal was done, and afterwards, he'd probably sell her to the Tempus cult. Because they're at odds with Carcalla, they'd surely pay a bunch of Obols for one of his children."

Naming that dark bunch was enough to get the Latros to share an uneasy look. The Tempus Metum were fanatics who hid out in the undercity, plotting how to throw open the locked gate to the forbidden Realm of Time to destroy us all for reasons that only made sense in their demented mutant brains.

"Where?"

"Gerzog didn't say! That's the truth. That's all I know, swear to Sarda!"

Joran stepped toward him and lifted his sword menacingly.

"You said if we spoke true, you'd spare us!"

"I did say that." Joran lowered his sword. "Vilko, shoot this coward."

The old gangster didn't hesitate. All of a sudden, my ears were ringing, and when the grey smoke cleared, the Tooth and Claw was down another recruit.

One of the Latros returned, and I'd been so gripped by the show that I'd not even realized he'd ever left. "The other rooms are clear, Cutter. But lights are coming on in town. The locals have heard the noise."

That meant watchmen would be coming to investigate soon, and the Core City Watch was not to be trifled with.

"The rest of you idiots listen and listen good. You have offended Master Carcalla. Your company ceased to exist the second you crossed him, but unemployment is preferable to death. Be thankful I lack the time to kill you all. If any of you talk to the watch about what transpired here, I'll find out, then you and your entire family will die. Now fuck off."

31

We got out of the dock district fast as we could. This wasn't the Latro's territory, but the old man, Vilko, had done a lot of crime here in his youth, so he knew every back alley and side street to help us avoid witnesses and watchmen.

It was just me and the murderous Latros now. I didn't even have Trax to watch my back. Even with a city that had dozens of different species living in it, Squalos stood out. Being so noteworthy, we'd had no choice but to separate, so after thinking to him that we'd meet back at the Tube, he'd dove into the bay and swam off.

After half an hour of walking in what felt like circles, we ended up in an unfamiliar part of town full of industrial buildings. I was thoroughly lost, but Joran seemed to have a destination in mind.

As we made our way down a garbage strewn alley, I asked him, "What's our next step?"

"I'm still deciding that."

"I've been thinking and have an idea. Gaul Haddar tracked me down here in the Core because I was still wearing a charm that had been issued to me by my nobles. He'd enchanted that one for them."

"And so?"

"When I fought Dathka in the arena, she had a really potent enchantment on her that let her go in one shadow and come out another. That's got to be a high-level spell. Whoever made it for her should be able to sense its presence, just like Haddar did to me. If Gerzog's got that on him now, the wizard who made it should be able to find it."

"Good thinking. Except it was given to her as a gift recently, after the wizard who made it died. You mages get used to thinking there's an easy solution to everything. Snap your fingers, poof, magic does all the work."

"Don't pin that trogshit attitude on me, Cutter. I was an honest laborer my whole life."

"Whatever. We're going to have to do this the hard way. Shake some trees and see what falls out. What do you know about the Tempus Metum?"

I cringed at the thought of those freaks. "I fought some of them in the undercity once. The Council and every civilized kingdom has banned them because they're nuts." I didn't add aloud that I'd learned the elf pirate who killed some of my family was probably related to the Tempus cult somehow, because that was none of Joran's business. "Do you know how to find them?"

"Vaguely. When we talk, it's through intermediaries." Our conversation continued as Joran turned us down another narrow alley. Some of the little frog-faced people lived here, and hid in their trash piles as we passed by. "The Latrocinium will parley with the Tempus Metum when we have something they want, or they've got something Carcalla wants."

I was aghast. "You trade with those freaks? They're evil."

"Many say the same about us Latros, except our so-called *evil* has kept peace and order in a place forsaken by our betters."

To me, the Slumps were violent and lawless slums. "That's peace?"

"Relatively. The Slumps would be a cannibal wasteland like the undercity if it wasn't for us. Everyone with any sort of power has to deal with those we find unsavory to get by. Even the high and mighty Nexus Council in their castles in the sky are no different. We all do what we have to do."

"The Council wants to keep the Great Machine turning. The Latrocinium wants to turn a profit. But Tempus Metum wants to unleash the most dangerous force ever known so it can invade the Core and conquer all the realms just like it did to Time. These things aren't the same!"

Joran didn't seem to like me pointing out that obvious flaw in his worldview. "That's over my head. I leave the thinking to Carcalla. I'm just a simple gladiator."

That was a load of trogshit, and we both knew it.

The alley brought us to a narrow, twisty street, and Joran stopped there to give orders to his crew. "The heat's probably died off enough. We'll spilt up from here. Staverton, go to the market and see if the Tempus cult there is willing to meet. Vilkos, Rowley, and Lionel, hit up our sources around the waterfront and find out if anybody saw where Gerzog took Dathka. Obson, you go update the boys keeping an eye on the other Outcasts about what happened and tell them they're not in the clear yet."

His fixation on my friends was exasperating. "Leave my people be. You know we didn't do anything wrong."

"That's likely, but I'm not a man easily convinced. Which is why you're staying with me until you can look Carcalla in the eye and explain how you failed him so badly."

32

Just after sunrise, I was back in Carcalla's office, sitting in the same chair, waiting for the same dangerous crime boss, looking at the same magic window, only this time, it showed some idyllic farming village in a realm that looked warm and soft and covered in fruit trees. Since I was about to be confronted by an elf who'd likely be furious that I'd lost the treasure he'd sent me to collect and gotten someone who was likely his daughter kidnapped in the process, I really would've preferred to be in that lovely bit of countryside than here.

Joran was in the other chair, drinking a cup of tea. A few hours ago, I'd watched him mercilessly terrorize a mercenary company, and here he was now with a little porcelain cup and saucer, all polite manners and whatnot. For whatever reason, that made me dislike him even more.

"It's not my fault Dathka got grabbed. You're the one who sent her with us."

"Word of advice to you, Carnavon." Joran took a sip. "When the boss gets here, don't go tossing about blame. He hates it when men don't accept responsibility for their mistakes."

I was exhausted, but at least they kept it decently warm in here. My sopping wet cloak was hanging from a peg downstairs next to my dirty boots. I was in my bare feet upon the wooly carpet, which again, struck me as a marvelous invention. The comfort was making me sleepy, but I needed to be alert and quick-witted here, as my life was just as likely to end here as in the chamber with all of Korthican's traps.

Carcalla entered, still in his bed robe, and went to his desk. I remembered the proper protocol and stood, treating him like he was a noble.

"Sit down. I'll deal with you in a moment."

I did as I was told.

Joran put his now empty cup down on the little table between us. "There's been no sign of Gerzog yet. The Tempus intermediaries are claiming they know nothing about this. I told Staverton to secretly grab one off the street and torture him just in case."

"And?"

"He knew nothing."

"He knew nothing, or claimed to know nothing?"

"Staverton knows six spells and five of them are useful for torture. The cultist was truly in the dark."

"Damnable apocalypse worshippers are good at keeping their network contained. I'd say roll up more of them, but now's not the time to risk a war with the undercity. We're already up to our necks in nightbolgs they've chased upwards as it is, and who knows what other horrors they'll force up here and set loose to attack our people." It was actually heartening to hear that Carcalla gave a damn about the fate of the Under Slumpers, but then he had to go and add, "Massacres are terrible for business."

"What do you want me to do next?" Joran asked.

"Call up *everyone.* Every snitch, every source, every set of eyes. Promise them a good reward. Bribe our friends on the watch. Send someone to the Collegium and hire a scryer. Anyone who wants to keep secrets, make an example of them." Carcalla frustrated was even more menacing than Carcalla cold. "I want that orc found."

"It'll be done." Joran stood and began walking away.

"And Joran…"

He paused. "Yeah, boss?"

"You shouldn't have sent her on this."

The arena champion I'd watched strike fear into an entire mercenary band pretty much by himself got real nervous. It was in that moment I realized, even as deadly as Cutter Joran was, Carcalla could crush him. And I didn't mean by the power of his organization, but Carcalla, by himself, right that instant.

"I got no excuse, sir. At the time, I thought this run would be a simple test to ease her in. The likelihood of a real treasure still being there after all these years was so unlikely, I underestimated the threat presented by other interested parties. I recognize now I was mistaken."

"Indeed, you were… You may go."

Duly chastised, Joran bowed his head, then left.

Carcalla sat stiffly in his big leather chair. This time, he didn't offer me a drink of fancy dragon rum. His expression was really difficult to read, though I got the distinct impression I was lucky to still be alive. "Tell me exactly what transpired."

I did so, careful to leave nothing out, and to be as forthright as possible.

My story took long enough the window changed twice. First, a mist-shrouded bog populated by that strange race of frog creatures I'd seen a bunch of times around the Core, and then to a searing sea of churning lava, which wasn't Fogo, but was clearly upon the Elemental Plane of Fire. I hoped the timing of that somewhat familiar image was a sign of good fortune.

It was not.

"I am so very disappointed right now, Mr. Carnavon. If I'd thought it was likely the lamp was still there, I would have sent professionals to retrieve it, not you bungling imitators. When the burglary of a mansion in the Aventine found an old letter from Councilman Korthican which mentioned a secret door, I considered sending a proper expedition, but I thought to myself, with the island being picked over so many times over the centuries, what were the odds any treasure remained? In the end, I never bothered… Until the Outcasts came along, and I saw an opportunity to satisfy my curiosity with little effort or expense."

"After doing a bit of research on the place, I kind of figured that's what was happening."

"You're not as stupid as I thought, yet you still failed me."

"We did as asked. We got betrayed and ambushed. And your da—" I was so tired, I nearly screwed up and said *daughter*, which was likely the case, but the Latros were keeping up the fiction that she was not, so I would too. "Dathka wasn't put in danger by us. We lost a few students in the fight against those who took her."

"I am aware of these mitigating circumstances, but I'm still angry it happened at all." It must have been a cold sort of angry, because he didn't really look angry. More… ambivalent. Which probably made it worse. "Joran offered to dispose of you for me, but I told him to wait, because a deal is a deal, and someone is only as good as the promises he keeps."

That was a relief. "Thank you, Mr. Carcalla, sir."

He chuckled, and the cruel nature of that sound did actually turn out to be worse than the somehow hateful ambivalence. "Oh no, you misunderstand me. Today is Fireday. I originally gave you until the 23rd, Waterday, tomorrow, to bring me the treasure of Korthican's Warning or face a violent eviction. That deal remains in effect."

"What? Gerzog's got the treasure!" Carcalla had just dispatched all the resources of the Latrocinium to find him. What was I supposed to do that they couldn't? "How am I supposed to do that?"

"You likely can't. That doesn't concern me. I gave you until the end of Waterday, so that is what you shall have. Then the eviction will proceed. As for the previous months' past due rent, I can't have people thinking I've become soft by forgiving it, so I suppose we'll just have to collect those months from your hide." Behind Carcalla, a plume of fire rose into the smoke-blackened sky. "Good day to you, Mr. Carnavon."

33

When I reached the crossroads between the Slumps, I was sorely tempted to keep on walking to the Great Machine instead. It being Fireday, I could just give up and go back to my home realm. Not Fogo. That was second Fireday. This was fourth, so the gate would take me to a different kingdom somewhere else on the Elemental Plane of Fire, but it would be a lot more like what I was used to. Surely, they'd have barge cadres based there too. Some bargemaster would be in need of an experienced trapper. I could give up on this becoming a respected wizard nonsense and lead a simple life of honest labor out on the fiery wastes, as so many generations of Carnavons had done before me.

There'd be no more futile struggling to keep a masterless academy alive. No more risking life and limb in arenas just to earn a few coins. No more being strongarmed into absurd adventuring. No more thankless effort expended just because some bossy tyrant demanded it.

So tempted, I'd had to pause there at the crossroads to whisper a prayer to Saint Persistence, because even someone who wasn't by nature a quitter needs help at times. The bystanders gave me a curious look, so I made it a silent prayer.

My patron saint didn't care for whiners, so I kept it brief and simple: *I'm stuck and don't know what to do. If I run, I'm a coward. If I stay, Carcalla will make an example out of me. I know you're not big on handing out miracles, and that we should work hard and make it on our own, but if you could spare one of those rare miracles, that would be greatly appreciated. Amen.*

Looking out over the city, I took it all in. From the trash and graffiti all around me, to the opulence of the superior districts, and then up toward the palaces in the sky. Which I'd hoped to someday be able to call home.

I'd sworn to become a mighty wizard because I was tired of being helpless and pushed around. Fleeing to a different kingdom on the Elemental Plane of Fire would just put a different noble family's boot on my neck. My brothers and sisters and nieces and nephews who I'd sworn to help would remain in servitude to the Argents. The lost of Barge 519 would go unavenged. And what about my friends? We'd made a pact. The Outcasts were in this together. I couldn't just abandon them. Plus, there was the matter of the lovely Azarin, and I'd never met any girls on the Plane of Fire like her, that was for sure!

It turned out I hadn't needed a miracle to keep going. I had only needed focus.

"Thank you, Ketekunan. Back to work."

The artificial mountain that was the Great Machine was still there, beckoning me home, but I took the low road to the stinking Under Slump anyway.

The others weren't back at the Tube yet, so I had no idea about their status. Bognar and Sifuso might have died before they could get a healing for all I knew. Carcalla had his peculiar code of honor, so I was certain he'd tell his men not to harm my friends… until tomorrow's deadline at least.

As soon as I entered the cold, dreary, sideways space of the Tube, the ghosts began to wail. We'd been away for an entire day, so they'd probably gotten their hopes up that the living had finally abandoned the place.

"Sorry to disappoint you!" My shout echoed through the ruins. "I'm not giving up. I've got a job to do and an academy to build. If you don't like it, you can just move on to the deadlands already. It's been fifty years since you got squished! *Get over it!*"

I went out the hole in the wall of our water training room and went straight to the canal, crouching at the edge. "Hey, Trax. Are you here?"

His sleek grey head popped out of the water. "*Hello, Carnavon. Your yelling at the ghosts woke me from a pleasant nap.*"

I'd spent an entire day rowing, fighting, and the whole night running or creeping about. I was so tired, I could barely keep my eyes open. "You've got no idea how nice sleeping sounds right now."

"*I am happy you are not dead.*"

"Me too, buddy. However, I might be dying tomorrow if we don't figure out how to catch Gerzog fast." Having gotten pretty good at Squalo speech, I concentrated on remembering my conversation with Carcalla, and that was enough for Trax to get the gist of it. "As you can see, time is of the essence. You're a master hunter; any chance you can track Gerzog down?"

Trax stared at me with his beady black eyes for a long time as he thought it over. "*I do not think the orc was wounded during our battle, so I have no blood trail to track. I recall his scent, but we would need to be much closer for me to sense him.*"

"What about Dathka? She got slapped around on the island."

"*I would have to return to the shore, find their boat, and go from there.*"

We didn't have time for that, and that was assuming said particular boat was still where the mercs left it. The survivors had been as eager to avoid getting entangled with the watch as we had been. "She got scrapped up while fighting me in the arena the other night. Would that help?"

"*That would only enable me to track her back to here. However, being familiar with her scent, I can assure you that her body has not been chopped up and thrown into the city's canal system anywhere near here.*"

"Well, that narrows it down helpfully." A noise came from the front of the tower. The ghosts there began to shriek. "Hang on. Hopefully, that's the others getting back."

Except it wasn't my fellow Outcasts, but rather an old man in a long grey coat, waiting politely outside our recently ruined front door. He knocked again on the wall. "Hello? Is anyone home?" The grisly apparition of a smashed flat peasant floated by him, moaning piteously. "Anyone alive, at least?"

Right away, I recognized the kindly fellow who'd granted me my first rank. "Tester Pivorotto?"

He smiled when he saw me. "Ah, there you are, Ozwald Carnavon of Fogo. I was told I could find you here." As I got closer, he gave me a sympathetic grimace, before lying, "You're looking… well."

For how battered and dirty I was, with blood-stained bandages on my neck and arm, he was being far too kind. "Forgive my appearance. It's been a rough day. It's good to see you, sir, but what're you doing here?" I came out and glanced around my seedy neighborhood, which was populated with miscreants and desperate refugees from the worst realms, but thankfully, it was still early enough in the morning that most of the unemployed layabouts hadn't woken from their drunken stupors yet to embarrass me further. "The Under Slump isn't a place for respectable members of society."

"Heh, I've taken contracts in some of the foulest pits in the seven realms, lad. I'm no stranger to squalor. Besides, if you're worried about my safety…" He patted a wand tucked into his belt. "Testers are taught a thing or two about defending ourselves."

"What's that one do?"

"It liquifies bones. Turns them into a sort of calcified slurry. Have you ever seen what happens to a body once all its bones reach the consistency of jelly? It's most unpleasant."

"Huh… Nasty." I didn't know Pivorotto's rank, but that was a good reminder that it was far higher than mine. "Come in, Tester. I apologize for the state of the place. We had a bit of an incident with an out-of-control earth spirit. Please forgive the ghosts. They're insufferable."

"I can see that. I was a boy when Primopolus' magnificent tower fell over to crush part of the city. We all felt terrible for all the poor unfortunates caught in its path."

"Have a seat." I gestured at the finest of the stools Bognar had cobbled together out of scrap. You were supposed to offer your guests refreshments, but we were out of damned near everything. "Are you thirsty? We've got water. It's from the canal rather than a globe, but it's been strained and boiled."

"I'm fine. Thank you." Pivorotto grunted as he sat down. I wasn't sure how old he was, but if he'd been a kid when the tower had fallen, that had been over fifty years ago, so I guessed he was about sixty. "All that walking's hard on the knees. I've only been back in the Core for a couple of weeks. I suppose I got used to riding about on barges rather than marching everywhere. That said, I certainly don't miss the endless, relentless, merciless heat of your realm constantly trying to snuff out my will to live."

"I miss warmth." I had no idea what brought such an illustrious man here, but I wasn't about to ruin the opportunity. I pulled up a crate to sit on. "Is this about the Academy of Outcast's request for a tester?"

"In a roundabout way, yes. My organization gets rather cross with those who can't afford to pay us, but I must admit, when my fellow testers told me of your visit, I was intrigued. Of the legions I've given the test to, you stood out."

"Going from a zero to a one, entirely self-taught, can't be that unique."

"It was more the audacity of your attempted bribery, followed immediately by your tragic death."

"Oh yeah." I had to chuckle. "About that..."

"I know, you faked your death at the hand of a Fire Elemental in order to break your contract, then somehow the rumor was that you were alive, but were a criminal who'd tried to assassinate Dardick Argent. All of Fogo was talking about it."

"That was all a big misunderstanding. Me and the ambassador get along fine now." Which was a bit of an overstatement, as I'd not seen the man since he'd written up the papers declaring us to be an officially sanctioned academy, while simultaneously cursing me for inconveniencing him and threatening me to not do anything which might give Fogo an even worse reputation than we already had. "We got that all worked out."

"Good. Because later, the rumor in Fort Silver and among the barge cadres, was that not only was Oz Carnavon still alive and a free man in the Core, but now he was managing a magical academy for the brutal enforcer Gaul Haddar… While Haddar somehow went back to the Core and in the span of one day went up two ranks? The stories that came back through the gate were all very confusing."

"Haddar won a duel against a mad rank ten who was the real assassin. Then he wanted to go back to hunting pirates, but before doing so, he declared the formation of an academy, as was his right as a newly appointed master wizard, and merely delegated the management responsibilities to me in his absence. We all look forward to his return. It's all very standard really."

"Uh huh." Pivorotto looked around our haunted ruins, obviously too smart to buy in to my line of trogshit. "And where are the rest of your students?"

"They're… on a field trip. They should be back soon."

"And how many students do you have in need of testing services?"

"About a dozen. Well, it was. A couple of them left us and, sadly, two died… Yesterday."

Pivorotto winced. "That's unfortunate."

"And to be perfectly honest with you, two more of our students are at the healers being treated for their wounds. I'm still not sure how we're going to pay for that. It's been a hell of a week, sir."

"It sounds like Gaul Haddar's academy has gotten off to a rocky start."

"A bit. We do have potential, though."

"*Such potential* is what they always say during the funeral services of young mages after they tragically obliterate themselves. Do you have any instructors?"

"We're still working on that." Pivorotto had always struck me as a decent and honorable sort, so I wasn't going to waste his valuable time trying to slap a coat of paint on a turd and try to convince him it was a nugget of gold. "To be perfectly frank with you, sir, all we've got is an official proclamation that we're a school. We've got very little element to work with, no money, and this fine establishment you see around you, that we only got for free because nobody else wanted to be pestered endlessly by the restless dead. Except now we're beholden to the gang lord who rules this slum for letting us live and practice here. Our recent desertions and casualties are a result of us going on an adventure in pursuit of the rent. That's just the beginning of our problems, as this morning has presented me with a deadline for another seemingly insurmountable challenge, and I shall not bore you further with my tale of woe... We do still need a tester, though."

The old man seemed genuinely concerned for me. "This is quite the trial you've taken on here, Mr. Carnavon."

"It's never boring, I'll say that. But with rank comes prestige and opportunity. In the off chance we somehow figure out our current problems, nobody was going to want to join an academy if they can't rank up. The other testers showed me what your organization charges, and there's no way we can afford anything even sort of approximating that. I got the distinct impression we're beneath their contempt."

"Don't mind them." Pivorotto waved one hand dismissively. "When the Council made getting our approval mandatory for everyone's progression through the lower ranks, it was good for organized wizardry in general, and it was especially good for my guild's business, but some testers developed an elitist attitude because of it. I feel we should be servants, not masters. My purpose is to help the talented reach their potential. Or in your case, the untalented, but fixated."

I chose to take that as a compliment. "Thank you."

"Tester Ritter gave you the standard rate, which is what we can soak the proper academies of the Collegium for. They can afford it. But each tester is an independent contractor, so we have some leeway in how we choose to spend our time. As long as we kick back a percentage of our labor, our guild is satisfied. That's why I'm here."

"What do you have in mind?"

"Sometimes when we are contracted by poorer nobles to test their subjects for magical affinity, testers can agree to work for a pittance compared to our normal rates under an agreement that, should those ranked subjects grow in wealth or prestige, we will be compensated accordingly later. This provision is seldom taken advantage of, because most testers aren't the gambling sort."

"Are you?" I'd never heard of him frequenting the card tables around Fort Silver.

"Not really, no… but you could probably twist my arm into stopping by your academy periodically to test your people. No more than once or twice a year at most. It would be a day of my choosing, at my convenience. On my own schedule, of course, whenever I return home to the Core between my usual paying contracts."

I was stunned. "That's incredibly charitable of you." Then I grew suspicious, because from what I'd seen here, it was rare for anyone in the Core to ever do anything purely out of kindness. Practically everyone in this city always had an angle they were working. "What's the catch?"

"A wise question. But there isn't a catch that I can think of. To be fair, Mr. Carnavon, I've been doing this a *long* time. I've put away enough for a comfortable retirement. I've traveled to more kingdoms than I can remember, tested tens of thousands, and I've watched the light go out of their eyes when I shattered their dreams and told them they're destined to be mundane. It's uncommon to have anyone test as a zero and then come back and try again and make rank one later. And most of those received a great deal of help from a wizardly relative or parents wealthy enough to afford a tutor and an endless supply of element to play with. To pull it off through your own experimentation, with a single element, in an environment where practicing spells was forbidden, is a miracle."

And to think just this morning I'd been asking Saint Persistence for a miracle. Little had I realized, he'd already granted me one in my life. "From what I've seen from our other students, we're not as rare as you think. There's others who're willing to put in the work too."

"That's heartening. Are you a religious man, Mr. Carnavon?"

"I am, sir, yes."

"Are you familiar with Saint Sabriel?"

"I'm not, but there are a whole lot of them to keep track of."

"Indeed. The gods have appointed a saint for every virtue and condemned a notable fiend for every vice. One of my favorites is the Saint of Greater Purpose." He lifted a chain from around his neck and showed me a medallion that he wore next to his heart. It had a beautiful woman's face on it, and was obviously enchanted. "Sabriel's revered among the flotilla settlements of the mist lands where the Planes of Water and Air meet. That was my first assignment. I bring her up because the way the cadre folk are talking about you back in Fogo reminded me a bit of her story. She, too, was condemned to nothing, but thwarted destiny, made her own way, and went on to do great and important things."

"I like her already."

Pivorotto put the medallion away. "After I heard you were looking for me, I asked around about your academy and what you were doing down here. I was told about this gaggle of rejects, teaching each other spells they cobbled together on their own. The gossips of the Collegium have noticed, and they're eagerly awaiting your failure. But for me, what you're doing harkens back to the early history of magic, from before the Council organized everything. Back when there were no codified schools and we were taming wild magic from scratch. I suppose mostly I want to help because I'm curious to see how this works out."

"It'll either be brilliant or total shit. I can promise you that!"

He laughed. "Splendid. Then I'll draw up a basic contract. For now, I will consider my time a tithe to Sabriel. In the future, your academy can pay me what you can, when you can, and in the meantime, I'll stop by periodically to test your best and watch the show."

I couldn't believe this good fortune. Having a real official tester for our little academy would grant us more legitimacy. Word would spread that one could improve here *and* make it official. The number of recruits would grow, and with them, so would our combined knowledge of magic. The Academy of Outcasts would be on our way!

Now all we needed to do was survive tomorrow and we were set. I still had no idea how to do that, but as I learned in my short life, you mine the Red one swing of the pick at a time.

"You have no idea how much I appreciate this. We won't let you down."

"Once the contract is filed, other testers may stop by unannounced to audit my work for accuracy, but I doubt any of them will ever bother coming down to the Under Slump. I'm a bit odd in that I don't mind the smell. It's unfortunate the rest of your students are away—or recently deceased—as I've got a bit of free time this morning before my wife needs me to run errands."

"I could test again."

"I admire the spirit, but you've only been a rank one for a few months. Progressing that fast is unheard of unless you're some kind of prodigy."

"I only *tested* as a one a few months ago. Which was just confirming what I'd been working on for years before. I only knew four spells then, all Red-based. I've mastered more than double that now and added Clear and Black. I've played around with ten other spells in the meantime, but haven't gotten them down yet. I've practiced a lot, spent every spare Tetar on element, and put my spells to good use, producing effects on demand, even under pressure."

I wasn't even exaggerating either, because there's no pressure quite like *make this work right now or I'm gonna die.*

Pivorotto nodded along at my list of efforts. "This is why no one has ever accused a hotlander of being lazy."

We had bums just like everyone else; ours just had a tendency to get tossed overboard before they caused too much trouble for their cadre. "If the early ranks are based purely upon a measure of magical affinity, and I've doubled what I know from when last we met, then I'm confident I'm there."

"It's not a measure of labor, but of results. However, I suppose the test itself doesn't require much element to fuel it, so there's no harm in giving you a chance." He removed a white bracelet from his wrist, which I recalled he'd said was a material called ivory, carved from the tusks of a creature known as a doom whale, which came from the same plane of existence as Trax. "Don't be disappointed when you're found lacking."

"Disappointment hasn't stopped me yet." I took hold of the charm. "Ready."

There was no vocal component to the testing spell, and Pivorotto remained nonchalant. I think a tester's specialty was more about reading and interpreting the results more than any sort of difficulty in launching the spell itself. With their value being derived from the accuracy of their judgment, it was no wonder their guild kept their formula a secret.

There wasn't any way to deceive a tester as far as I knew, but just in case it helped, I tried to focus on the various enchantments I had stashed on me. That extra second of effort was likely pointless, but it gave me something to do other than be nervous while Pivorotto read my aura or whatever baffling thing it was that testers did.

Last time, the charm had turned ice cold. This time, it surprised me, as the ivory went hot. Not enough to burn a callused Fogo hand, but it probably would've caused someone from one of the lesser realms to flinch and let go.

"Well, I'll be a manticore's uncle..." Pivorotto gave me a big grin. "You continue to surprise me, Ozwald Carnavon, mage of the *second* rank."

That made me grin like an imbecile. "I knew it. I fucking knew it!"

"Maybe you're onto something down here, or perhaps it's the canal water. Well done. I don't have a log book handy, so I'll need to go and record this in the tester's hall immediately. I suppose I'll need to start a new book for the Outcast Academy anyway. Your entry in the Argent's book was already filled from listing off all your crimes!"

"Considering the nature of the students we attract, you'll want to buy a book with plenty of room to write."

34

It felt great to have my achievement recognized, but there was no time to celebrate. After Pivorotto left to file his papers, I called for Trax so we could get back to figuring out how to locate Gerzog the Marauder. Then I went to resupply and rearm from the supplies I'd left stashed here.

"*Congratulations on your promotion today.*"

"Thanks, Trax."

"*Condolences on Carcalla having you killed tomorrow.*"

"If they take it that far, they'll probably hunt you down too."

"*Unlikely. I doubt any of them can swim that well.*"

"We've still got a chance. All we need to do is track down Gerzog, Dathka, or the lamp before the Latrocinium can. If the Latros get them without our help, then we're useless and they'll still be mad at us. If Gerzog gets away with the treasure or Dathka dies, Carcalla will be furious, and we'll be convenient to blame."

"*The Latrocinium are the apex predators here. We are relative newcomers. I am a superb hunter in my own realm, but as you might have noticed, I sometimes struggle here.*"

I tried to decide if what Trax said was sarcasm, before it struck me that he was being serious. He actually thought I might not have seen that the gigantic, terrifying, aquatic carnivore who didn't at all understand the confusing customs of the land creatures stuck out *just a bit* in the big city.

"No… You?"

"*It is true. Things are simpler in the ocean. How can we find them before the predators do?*"

"I'm not sure yet." I went to the room that served as our kitchen and grabbed a chunk of crusty, dried out bread. I was starving. One nice thing about talking to Trax was that I could think at him while chewing. *Gerzog's a brute, but he struck me as a cunning one. He ripped off the Latros and the Latros' power is in the Slumps. He won't be in either of those districts.*

"*Why stay in the Core at all?*"

This is where potential buyers for the lamp will be. It was a good thing I'd gotten so much practice at Squalo thought language that I could send complicated ideas and Trax could follow along. *He ran off on a Fireday. There's nobody in my realm with the money or inclination to buy an object filled with Permanence that I know of.*

Then, as soon as I thought that, I realized there might be *one.*

The image burned into my memory was so strong, Trax saw it immediately. "*That is the pirate who attacked your family's barge?*"

It was. I still remembered him, standing there atop the legendary black barge we knew as the *Inferno*, haughty as could be, as they swooped in to steal everything we'd worked for, and when we wouldn't let them have it, they'd taken our lives instead.

The symbol he'd put on all his enchantments was *Aarhobad*, the elven name for their lost homeland in the Realm of Time, and Gaul Haddar reckoned this unknown pirate was at a shockingly high level of magical mastery, like a rank fifteen or higher, equivalent in power to a member of the Nexus Council. We didn't even know his name, let alone his motives, but he'd been stealing tons of Red for years. It made sense that he'd be interested in some of the rare and potent element from his home plane as well.

Except that was an absurd leap on my part. There was no evidence Gerzog even knew this pirate existed, let alone that he might be a potential customer for his treasure. No. It was far more likely that he'd try to sell Korthican's enchantment to someone here who was already known to him. Gerzog mentioned the Council or the Cult, as those were both obvious, as one would use the Permanence to maintain the Great Machine, while the other would try to break it. But there had to be others. A resource that scarce had to be in high demand for any wizard with enough skill to use it. There'd been an entire subclass of magic—chronomancy—based on that element once. There had to be hundreds of spells on the books, just waiting for a bit of Permanence to fuel them.

Permanence used to be so common, that Korthican used it make what was basically a gigantic light charm, and light charms were probably the single most common enchantment there was. They were so cheap and plentiful, even us poor folks took them for granted, yet here we were, fighting to the death over his, just because it wouldn't ever go out.

Still chewing my bread that was so stale it had likely been one of the reasons Danny betrayed us, I walked to the fire room. That was where I'd hidden the ammunition I'd been trying to enchant. While we puzzled out what to do, I could at least replace the cartridges in my belt loops that had been ruined by seawater. I didn't know how to find Gerzog yet, but when we did, I assumed he'd still be in need of a proper shooting.

I shoved aside the scorched log I'd been using for a target, and pulled out the box I'd hidden in a hole in the floor. Inside was supposed to be all my valuable components, but something was missing. "What the hell?"

"*What is wrong?*"

"One of my molten bullets is gone. I had one left that was loaded in a case, ready to go."

Trax padded over, put his nostrils next to the box, and sniffed. "*The female deadlander's scent is on this.*"

"That thieving bitch." I'd shown her what I'd been experimenting on, and when she'd returned to find us already gone, she must have come in here and stolen my work. She'd expressed interest in buying some of these from me, but why purchase what you can just steal and reverse-engineer yourself? "I've been robbed!"

"*That is most troubling. If she was present, I would bite her for this rudeness.*"

"I should've known. My dad always warned me to never consort with crooks."

"*When I was a pup, the bull who spawned me warned us to avoid entanglements with octars and valenos, because they are very dangerous. I believe this to be a similar lesson.*"

I knew Trax was trying to relate, sending me pictures of a tiny tentacled creature burrowing into a Squalo's skull to eat its brain, and another black and white creature who was built like a Squalo, only far bigger and stronger looking, but that really wasn't helpful right now. I was trying to find Dathka, so her stealing from me was a slap in the face. It was insult atop of injury! We'd been nothing but polite and professional the entire time since Cutter shoved her off on us, and this was how she paid back our hospitality?

"To hell with her. Gerzog can feed Dathka to the ratlets for all I care. She got her snobby ass kidnapped with my enchanted bullet on her, so she can..." I trailed off as I realized the implications implicit in my tirade. "She's got my enchanted item on her."

"*Correct. I believe that is why we are upset.*"

When Haddar had come through the gate, I'd been a few miles away in the Under Slump, and he'd still been able to track me down because I'd had one of his enchantments on my person. If she still had that single round in a cartridge loop or in a pocket, I should—theoretically at least—be able to do the same thing to her that Haddar had to me.

Because I'd been thinking hard, Trax caught most of that. "*So wizards can follow their own magic the way I can follow a trail of blood. Splendid. Where is she?*"

"I don't really know how that works yet. I'll have to figure that part out."

"*Excellent. Then we shall go to wherever she is and bite her for her thievery.*"

"No, Trax. We've got to rescue her from Gerzog."

"*We shall rescue her and* then *bite her.*"

I'd get Trax straightened out on that later, because right now, I needed to learn how to sense my own enchantments at long range, and I needed to do it fast.

35

The thing most non-wizards don't realize about working magic is how tiring it is. It's not tube-crawling, Red-mining levels of physical exhaustion; magic takes its toll out on your mind. Now I was both types of tired. I'd been going nonstop for a day and a night, so after another hour of intensely focusing on my warming bowl—trying to sense its presence at increasingly greater distances—I was worn right out.

I'm embarrassed to admit that while sitting in the entryway, struggling to keep my eyes open while Trax carried the bowl off ever farther, I'd fallen asleep.

I was awakened sometime later by someone gently prodding my leg with their shoe. I snorted myself alert and saw that it was Azarin standing over me.

"For a moment, I thought you were dead there." The concern was obvious in her voice.

"Never been better."

She was looking haggard, but I was glad to see she was still in one piece. "Why are you sleeping on the remains of an Earth Elemental?"

The dirt had been softer than the tower's bricks, but of the many things I had to catch her up on, that was the least important. I looked over to see that Trax was standing a few feet away. "Why didn't you wake me up?"

"*I thought that was a peculiar way to cast a spell, but I do not know how magic works.*"

Fair enough, and I badly needed the nap. I rubbed my face and asked, "How are Bognar and Sifuso?"

"Lucky to be alive. They're still at the church, resting. They'll both be fine, but my air dagger wand was the only thing we had the sea priest would accept to barter for a healing. That church is supposed to be for the saint of sailors, but it's more like saint greedy bastard, really."

"That's ridiculous." I'd looted that wand off a defeated Frunza Tarlev student fair and square, and given it to her as a gift. "What about the Latrocinium?"

"They were watching us like hawks, until a messenger arrived, then they just up and left. One of the scum had been aggressively flirtatious with me the entire time. After getting their mysterious message, he wished me good luck in a very snide manner, before saying he'd *see me soon*, which makes me think I might need to stab him sometime in the near future."

"You might be onto something there. Carcalla's sticking to our original deal and deadline. We've got until tomorrow to bring him the treasure or we're still getting evicted."

"That seedy pile of eagle shit! After all we've been through? Fuck! If eviction's back on the table, why're you lying on the floor?"

I popped up and dusted some dead earth monster dust off my back. "It's a long story. Are Rade and Krachma here? Because it'll be faster to explain it once."

I'd told the student council, and Morton—as he was the only regular student remaining alive and uninjured, so I might as well include him—exactly what happened after we parted ways. The good news was, we'd found ourselves a tester. The bad news was… everything else.

"So, our only hope to avoid eviction, and likely worse is that Carcalla's illegitimate daughter happens to be a rotten thief?" Azarin asked.

"If I can figure out how to track my own enchantments like Haddar does, then yes."

"If you can, then do we have to save her? We could just arrive conveniently moments after that orc murders that deadland's bastard." Azarin looked toward Rade. "No offense."

"None taken, my lady. I am a deadlander's bastard. As the denied son of a nobility, I've been called far worse many times. Only, my father's a baron. Dathka's father is a murderous tyrant who rules a criminal empire with an iron fist. It would probably be best for our sakes to deliver her back to him alive, if possible."

Azarin sighed at that irrefutable logic. "Fine."

The six of us were in the kitchen, tired, dirty, and eating whatever the rats had left behind. You'd think that ghosts would scare off vermin, but both kinds of pests got along splendidly.

"This is all a moot point if I can't figure out how to track magic. Do any of you know anything at all about sensing enchantments?"

My answer was a bunch of head shakes and *no's*.

Our table was an old wooden spool. We all sat on chairs of Bognar's dubious construction beneath my light charm, except for Morton, who sat upon a stack of old boxes in order to be tall enough to be at eye level with the rest of us.

"If the master of our academy was actually here for once, I'm sure he could teach you," Rade said. "But if we had a rank-ten killer handy, we wouldn't have been extorted into working for criminals to begin with. Thus, as usual, we must make do on our own. I've never given the matter much thought, but surely between us, we can reason out a solution."

Krachma grunted in agreement. Which, for him, was an impressive contribution to the conversation.

Magical elements are a strange type of matter. Most things you could touch with your hands, see with your eyes, or smell with your nose, but elements were felt in the mind. Having a connection at all made you a mage, and the stronger that connection, the higher you'd be ranked. That increased connection was how they were able to wring more magic out of the elements than we were able to. I could only assume that sensing their presence worked on a similar scale. I had an affinity for Red, so I could usually tell when it was near. The others, not so much.

Luckily, that bullet was drenched in Red.

"Before you guys got back, I was experimenting with my warming bowl. Trax would carry it to different rooms and see how far away he could get before I could no longer feel the Red I'd left on it. If I clear my mind of everything else and really focus—"

"You'll pass out and be found snoring on the ground?" Azarin snort-laughed.

"I don't snore." I wasn't going to live that one down for a while. "I could still sort of sense its presence from one end of the Tube to the other. That's well over a hundred yards. Haddar did miles. I'm assuming the range scales with ability. He was an eight at the time. I'm a rank two."

"Which, by the way, congratulations on that!" Azarin exclaimed.

"I couldn't have done it without you."

"True. I really am a brilliant instructor of air magic."

Rade interrupted the flattery, "Alas, my friends, even at that impressive distance, considering the size of this city, finding your magic bullet in the Core would still be like finding the proverbial needle in the haystack. If you divided the city into hundred-yard squares and began walking up and down every street right now, nonstop, you should have the whole city covered in about five years."

"Now that I'm refreshed," I said that like my nap had been a strategic move, "I can go back to practicing with the bowl. I think I've kind of got the hang of it. I should be able to extend that range a bit."

"Excellent. Then we might be able to cut the search down to two or three years. *Or*, if I may present an alternative plan, the gate will be open to Qara Levu tomorrow, and I hear the Elemental Plane of Water is lovely this time of year. Perhaps they are in need of a new magical academy as well?"

The rest of the students thought that over, and I couldn't say I blamed them.

"The official-looking piece of paper I got from Ambassador Argent declaring that Gaul Haddar formed this place is only good for the Core, so I'm committed. But the rest of you don't have to risk the wrath of Carcalla. I wouldn't blame you for running. Escape to the water realm, and I wish you well."

Krachma ponderously shook his big rocky head. "Krachma does not like water realm. Krachma finds it too *moist*." He said that with a lot of disgust.

"Krachma is wise," Azarin agreed. "I would imagine that humidity would be an issue, what with it being the Elemental Plane of Water and all. I'm not going anywhere."

Part of me hoped she was sticking around for me, while the other part really wanted her to be somewhere less dangerous. Except, if I'd learned one thing about Azarin, it was that it did no good to push her, because no matter what, she was going to do what she wanted anyway.

Even Trax had an opinion. "*Qara Levu is only five thousand fathoms above the outer barriers of the Squalo Empire. However, I have not yet completed my mission of observation and education about the land races. Thus, I choose to remain here. I will happily eat your enemies as long as I do so.*"

"Thanks, Trax. That means a lot to me."

Rade gave us a sad smile. "Once again, there's no need for a vote, because as usual, Azarin and Trax agree with Carnavon, and this time, I have even been forsaken by loyal Krachma. We stand and fight."

"Hold on. None of us are crazy enough to want to fight the Latrocinium. We made an agreement to do our best to operate a school. It wasn't a suicide pact to take on the biggest gang in the Core. If you want to go, Rade, go. None of us will think less of you."

Azarin nodded at that. "In fact, we might still follow you, because we're being chased!"

Rade held up a hand to stop us. "Let the record show, that when Rade Tartaros makes a pledge, it will be kept."

"*Is this one of those secretary things? Should I be remembering this?*"

Rade didn't even need to understand that mental bombardment to guess what Trax was asking. "It is a matter of honor, my Squalo friend. It is settled. I have been chased from one home. I shall not be banished from another by mere criminals. We shall see this through to the bitter end." He lifted his chunk of stale bread. "For Rufus!"

"Hear fucking hear," Azarin said.

Rade was quite possibly deluded, but it was a brave, moral, loyal type of crazy which really made me appreciate the guy. "For Rufus."

"I'm glad the rest of you are so enthusiastic, but please forgive me, Mr. Carnavon, I really don't want to die," Morton quavered. "I feel terrible abandoning the lofty goals of our organization, and I truly appreciate all that you have done for me. However, I cannot in good conscience be brutally murdered by gangsters. May I be excused?"

Truthfully, I'd forgotten the little guy was there. And frankly, he wasn't very good at magic, or at all useful in a fight, so it wasn't like we were losing any capability without him. I already felt awful over the other students we'd lost to treachery and carelessness, so there was no need to pile another pointless death atop my guilt.

"Of course, Morton. Do what you need to do."

Azarin patted him on the arm. Even that was enough to knock the poor little fellow about. "It's alright. We still like you."

"It takes courage for someone to recognize his limits." Rade tipped his hat toward Morton. "May the saints grant you a long and peaceful life, my friend."

Krachma just scowled at him, and I suspected the lob wanted to call him a coward, because from what I'd learned about lobs, they'd fight to the death over which one of them had to do chores, but thankfully, Krachma said nothing as Morton climbed down from his boxes and scurried out the door. Like everything else here, the door was sideways, but he was short enough he didn't even have to duck.

Azarin waited to make sure he was gone, before saying, "The poor little guy's got a timid soul. I think he'd last ten minutes in Stormwolk before something swooped down and ate him. I had a puppy that happened to once. Morton reminds me of poor Stink Eye. It was very sad."

"Tragic… I'll go practice on the bowl some more. The rest of you, I'd say go ask around about Gerzog, but who are we going to talk to that the Latrocinium hasn't already? I suppose try to figure out what's the best districts to hit, then we'll just go there and wander around hoping to get lucky enough to find our magic bullet."

"Wait!" Morton shouted from the hall, rushing back into the kitchen so fast, he practically slid through the doorway on his heels. "I have an idea, Mr. Carnavon!"

He seemed downright giddy with excitement. "Spit it out already, Morton."

"With the extremely limited nature of your magical senses, covering the city on foot would be a logistical impossibility, as Lord Tartaros has so astutely pointed out. But what if there was a *much faster* method of travel available?"

Morton's feverish glee was a bit worrisome. "What kind of travel do you have in mind?"

36

"You've got to be kidding me."

The Smorp family business was located in a section of the grand market I'd never been to before, across from the gate to the Elemental Plane of Life. The pens were at the far end of the market disk, probably to spare all the merchants and customers from the smell. Which was rather strong.

"This is no joke, Mr. Carnavon!" Morton was excitedly leading me and Azarin through the market, and it was almost as if he launched into a memorized sales pitch: "At Smorp Brothers Exotic Animal Emporium, we always have a fine selection of flying mounts from the various realms in stock. Such animals are a popular symbol of status among the wealthier citizens who live in the highest districts of the Core. Anyone can pay an enchanter to fashion for them a flying carpet or a set of magical wings to get around up there, but why not arrive at the party in a more memorable style, upon the back of a majestic flying beast?"

Azarin had an answer for that. "Because you don't have to feed the carpet or shovel its shit."

"But such common implements of transportation lack the gravitas my family's clients seek. Besides, if they can afford to live in a floating sky castle, they've got plenty of servants to take care of the animals for them… A flying carpet?" Morton snorted. "How pedestrian."

I'd grown up so poor that I hadn't even known carpet was a thing until I'd stepped foot in Carcalla's office this week. Now I was being told there was a kind that could fly? Would the wonders of this city ever cease?

"I grew up riding giant eagles, Morton. I know all about how to care for flying mounts."

"Of course, Lady Garzade, and depending upon which animals my brothers have on hand today, your help should prove invaluable. As you're well aware, but Mr. Carnavon has yet to experience, airborne creatures of such size tend to have a temperament which can best be described as *flighty.*" Morton laughed at his own pun, then grew serious. "I mean, he'll need you to steer, lest he die."

"What's he talking about?" I asked.

"You'll be the passenger and concentrate on finding the magic bullet while I control the beast. Otherwise, you're probably going to get bucked off."

The plan had been to skim over the city's rooftops so we could cover far more ground in less time. Getting tossed hadn't been mentioned during that. "This idea is starting to sound worse and worse."

"Don't worry, silly. I've got you." Azarin casually blew off my rightfully justified concerns. "I've broken plenty of eagles. You just need to let them know who's boss. If you don't, they'll scrape you off on a mountainside or climb high and then go into such a steep dive that you'll float right out of the saddle, and when they pull up, you keep going without them!"

"That rarely happens to our customers. All of Smorp Brothers flying mounts receive some obedience training in their home realms before we take delivery of them here in the Core. We can't have our richest customers plummeting to their doom now, can we? That's terrible for repeat business."

It was still Fireday, so the heat coming through the gate made the market pleasant to me for once, but even here in the shadow of the Great Machine, it seemed most of the thousands of Core dwellers nearby were huffing and sweating. As usual, the place was packed with people, and the noise of endless commerce was deafening. This section of the market was especially vibrant and colorful, as everything grew in the Realm of Life. We passed creatures of a dozen races buying strange fruits and vegetables and the pelts of animals I'd never seen before.

When we approached the big metal gates of animal emporium, there was a single watchmen posted there, armed with a big wooden staff that obviously had some powerful enchantments on it.

"Don't mind him. It's protocol for the watch to keep someone with a disintegration spell on hand ever since the unfortunate Great Wyvern Escape of '75."

"Ooh, you've got wyverns? Impressive."

"Apologies, Lady Garzade. We *had* wyverns. Hence the escape part." Morton waved at the watchmen. "Good day."

"Good day to you, Mr. Smorp. It's been a while."

"That it has." Morton proudly swung open the gate for us. "Welcome to Smorp Brothers."

There were pens, cages, and tanks of water everywhere. The noise was even more overwhelming in here than out in the market. Except instead of haggling, it was hooting, crowing, barking, and grunting. And the smell. Saints alive, *that smell.* The only animals I'd ever worked with were Trogs, and those slime-coated things were downright fragrant compared to the pungent odor that hit my nostrils in here. Fogo didn't really have much in the way of animals—at least the kind that weren't made of fire—so this was rather overwhelming.

"Welcome to Smorp Brothers. How may I assist you today?" A gnome in an apron approached us smiling helpfully, then he saw Morton, and his expression changed to surprise, then anger. "What're *you* doing here?"

"Hello, Herbert."

"Hello, abandoner. Because yes, that's what we call you now, Morton, after you selfishly *abandoned* us."

The two tiny creatures squared off, and both were so flustered, I thought we were going to get to watch a gnome fight.

"I didn't abandon you. I provided two weeks' notice!"

"You broke Mother's heart when you told her you were leaving to study wizardry. What kind of foolish career is *wizard* anyway?"

That was an ironic question to ask, while surrounded by animals that had been gathered from several different planes of existence and brought through a world-spanning portal powered by a rotating man-made mountain to a city filled with magical wonders.

"Wizardry is every bit as respectable a trade as zookeeping!"

"Preposterous!"

Having brothers myself, I knew it would take them a minute to get the arguing out of their system, so I went over to see what was in the nearest cages. Some were easy to identify, as I'd seen dogs, cats, and mice before. A few I could recognize from the *Encyclopedia Ettymus*, like the monkeys and turtles. But the rest were mysteries. I could reason out a few, as there was a creature that looked a lot like our volcano snails, except this one didn't have red flesh or a black iron shell. It was all grey and boring, so that must have been a regular snail. Only it was the same size as the dogs, which was odd, considering I'd been told regular snails were small... It got me to thinking, though... If there was an iron shell version that big, I could probably level a city block with the resulting grenade.

In the water tanks were various kinds of fish and crunchy things with hands like pliers and lots of extra legs. Another glass tank had a ball-shaped creature that appeared to be made out of several hundred eyes. It floated there, staring at me with most of them.

"Don't tap the glass," Morton and Herbert both snapped at me simultaneously the instant I raised my finger to tap the glass. Then they went back to their argument.

As I wandered past the smaller cages, I realized there were rows and rows of bigger enclosures behind them. The first one had brown furry things with antlers, the second had scaly beasts that looked like quadrupedal versions of Sifuso, though they were probably slightly dumber, and the third held a larger version of monkey, only these were bright yellow and had an extra set of arms. When one of those burped, fire came out.

Fascinating as all this was, we were running out of time, so I returned to Morton's side to see if I might be able to hurry them up.

"You never wanted to clean out the pegasus' stalls," Herbert shouted. "You always left that to me, and they poop so very much!"

"I told you, I've got a note from the doctor saying I'm allergic to horses. That includes pegasi, unicorns, and all of the magical mutant half breeds. Even centaurs."

"Centaurs are not animals, Morton. They are paying *customers.*"

"I'm aware! I can be allergic to customers too. And what's your excuse for always leaving the care and feeding of the blobs and gelatinous monsters to me?"

"You know I simply can't abide the boneless ones." Herbert shuddered. "They're so *squishy.*"

"Thus proving my point. My condition is medical, while yours is all in your head!"

"Gentlemen, please." I stepped between them. "Apologies, Mr. Smorp, but this is an emergency, and Morton told us your emporium might be able to help."

Herbert scowled up at me. From my sorry, dirty, bandaged state, it was clear that I wasn't a man of wealth. "Who are you? One of Morton's wizard friends?"

"Watch your tone, Herbert. That's Ozwald Carnavon of Fogo you're speaking to. As the acting manager of the academy while the master wizard is away, he is a very important man."

"You're not even in a real academy," Herbert sputtered. "It would be one thing if you'd abandoned the family to go to school in the Collegium. We pay those wizards for their services all the time, so having an inside gnome there would be good for business. But your academy is in the Slumps! Who in their right mind would pay for spells from an Under Slump dreg?"

"*How dare you?*"

Morton's response was so loud and high-pitched that some of the other sales gnomes and customers looked our way, and the dogs began to bark. "Look, I know there's some issues between you brothers—"

"All fifteen of us are very cross with Morton for what he's done," Herbert said.

"Fifteen? By Naanwalla, my congratulations to the virility of father Smorp, and respect to your sainted mother," Azarin said. "But we really do need to move past this family squabble quickly. Gnomes are renowned for their business sense, so surely you can put aside your brotherly animosity long enough to help a potential customer. Morton said you'd have some flying mounts to choose from."

"We're sold out of most of them."

"I promised them we always have several flying animals in stock. That is terrible inventory management," Morton declared. "How unprofessional."

Herbert looked even more offended by that, so he coldly announced, "*However*, we did just restock on a new creature this week."

"Wonderful. Let's see it."

Herbert looked Azarin over carefully, and since she wore the light and billowy clothing common to air-realmers, that suggested she might know how to ride. "Before we do, and I say this with all due respect, I must warn you this creature is particularly volatile, and you might not be able to handle it."

That was the wrong thing to say to someone from Stormwolk. "I'm a Haatari storm chaser. I'm young, but I've been riding eagles since before I could walk, and I've herded griffons too. Are you trying to insult my honor?"

"That's *Lady* Garzade you're talking to, idiot," Morton warned. "She comes from a very prominent family."

I didn't know if Azarin counted as nobility or not, as her people had odd customs. Then again, her father was a general of some kind, so surely that meant something.

"Oh! I meant no offense, my lady. Your air-realm heritage is highly respected here. Smorp Brothers gets all our eagles from the finest breeders in Stormwolk, but I'm afraid we're fresh out of them right now. In fact, we have no air-realm beasts at all."

"Shameful," Morton muttered as he shook his head.

"In our defense, the Taagma Varagon put in an unexpectedly large order this month. You would know that if you ever came to family dinner, Morton… Ahem. As I was saying, the only flying creatures we have were recently captured from one of the more savage parts of the Elemental Plane of Life, and they're barely trained at all. I don't think they're quite ready for sale yet."

"We're in a hurry. Show me what you've got."

"Very well. Right this way." Herbert led us toward the back. "Smorp Brothers backs up all our animals, but because this is the first of this species we've worked with, I must warn you that there will be no refund should these particular beasts go on a murderous rampage."

We passed more pens and cages full of strange animals before entering an even more fortified enclosure. The walls were concrete and there were magical wards placed over the gates.

"Oh, you found a use for the old wyvern den," Morton said. "That's nice."

"Indeed," Herbert agreed. "After the last incident, the Council decreed that no more species of the dragon family were to be imported to the Core, even the smallest among them. No drakes, no dragonets, nor hydras, and especially no wyverns."

There was a blunderbuss in a glass case, which from the dust accumulated on it, had not been used for quite some time. It had a sign next to it which read: *In case of escape attempt, break glass, point at wyvern, and pull trigger.* Imagining one of the diminutive Smorps trying to use that enchanted cannon made me smile.

"Recently, our buyer in the Elemental Plane of Life was touring the primordial jungles far to the south of Hutan Gunang and found these marvelous creatures. He told me the warriors of that distant kingdom tame and ride these things into battle."

This cage was huge and made of steel bars. The thing inside was massive and colorful, covered in feathers that were purple, blue, or green. Except this was not like any of the birds I'd seen so far. It was currently on all four legs, but they were very uneven legs, with the front two being long and having some giant folding structure around them, while the back two legs were much shorter and thick with muscle.

When the thing saw us coming, it lifted its long head on a really long neck, which just kept getting longer, and longer, until it was looking down from far above us with two piercing orange eyes. It had an extremely long beak that ended in a point sharp enough to spear a man all the way through his torso. Except it probably wouldn't need to, as its skull was so long, it could no doubt swallow one of us whole. The gnomes would easily fit in one bite.

Its neck and elongated head were awkwardly disproportionate for its body. Then it bobbed that dangerous-looking head to the side, in a curious fashion that wasn't too different from our neighbors' chickens, only a few thousand times bigger.

"It's a third the size of a dragon!" Azarin exclaimed. "What is this gorgeous creature?"

"The natives of their land call them kwetzels. Isn't she a beauty? They come in so many different patterns and colors, if we can ever get them properly trained enough to stop attacking people, I suspect it will become rather fashionable to own one here."

Azarin approached the bars, clearly transfixed by the terrible majesty of the thing. "It's hard to judge the wingspan with them folded up like that."

"Over a hundred feet, though she wouldn't hold still long enough for us to get the tape measure out." Herbert looked to Morton. "Then it got agitated and tried to eat our brother, Abner."

"Is he alright?" Morton asked, concerned.

"Nothing a healing potion couldn't fix, but if you'd been here—"

Azarin wasn't going to let the Smorps get distracted fighting again. "How fast can they go?"

"Allegedly, they are rather swift. And one of this size could carry up to four or five hundred pounds. Please don't put your limbs through the bars, miss. She has no teeth, but routinely bites very large fish in half."

Of course, Azarin stuck her hand through anyway and patted it on the neck. Rather than attack, it just stared down at her with those eerie orange eyes, then the feathers around her hand shivered, and it emitted a clicking noise.

"Oh, she's a sweetheart. What's her name?"

"According to the buyer, this is *Fairly Deadly.*"

"Yeah, but what's her… Oh, I get it." Azarin went back to scratching the terrifying monster's neck. It leaned in for her to get a better angle. "Nice to meet you, Fairly. I'm going to take you for a ride across the city. Yes, I am. Who's a good girl?"

Fairly Deadly answered with an ear-splitting *shriek.*

"That's right, you're the good girl." Azarin looked back at Herbert. "Does she come with a saddle and tack? Otherwise, I can make a rope rig, but a proper saddle would be better."

"Of course, we have one, my lady, and this saddle was fashioned by the finest craftsmen of its home kingdom." Herbert was getting excited as he sensed a big sale approaching. "And how will you be paying for her?"

Morton had to go and ruin his brother's good time. "We can't purchase this beast, Herbert. We simply need to borrow it for the afternoon."

"What? Preposterous. Do you have any idea how much it cost to get a kwetzel all the way to the Core?"

"I can only imagine. However, this is very important."

"You know it's against policy to let customers take giant monsters on test rides, Morton!"

"I'm not a customer. I'm your brother. And this is a matter of life or death! My death, in fact."

"Oh, now that becomes *my* problem?" Herbert shouted, and then the two brothers went at it again. Luckily, their noise didn't seem to agitate the creature.

I went over to Azarin. "You really think you can ride this thing?"

"Well, I've never seen one before, but in principle, it shouldn't be too different from a giant eagle."

She sounded confident, but she was always confident, and that was scary. "And you expect me to get on there with you, and go high up into the air, and fly around at an alarming rate of speed, on *that*?"

"Oh, don't worry. You've got your glove. Should she throw you off, just activate a *Descend* before you hit the ground. You'll be fine."

"What if it crashes?" And then I watched in horror as the kwetzel rotated her massive stabby head, on the far too flexible neck, to scratch a point on her back where the saddle would most likely rest. "Or it decides it's hungry and does that and plucks one of us off for a midflight snack?"

"She wouldn't do that. Would you, girl?" Fairly Deadly brought her giant head back around and mashed her face against the bars right next to Azarin. There was a bony crest atop her head, and it hit the bars with a *clang*. Azarin stroked the feathers on her face. "See, Carnavon? The people of every kingdom have a natural gift. Your people are fire resistant. Mine are good at riding giant birds. This is clearly a giant bird… lizard… thing, which should be close enough to count. But that does give me an idea… Hey, Smorps."

Herbert shushed his brother. "Yes, my lady?"

"Sorry to interrupt your family drama. I've got no money, but I do have a proposition. This is an incredible flying beast, sure to command top Obols, but you've admitted yourself she's not yet properly broken. I know perfectly well how much an experienced sky rider would charge someone like you to train an eagle, and I can safely assume that something unique like Fairly here, they would charge even more. Only, you must bear this expense to train her properly first, because you don't want Fairly killing your customers."

"That sort of scandal does cause people to talk," Herbert admitted.

"And leave terrible reviews," Morton agreed.

"And here I am, a Haatari storm chaser, who was taught by the great Mazdak Garzade himself, offering to you my services, to train her for *free*."

"Hmmm…" Gnomes were known to be consummate businessmen, and Herbert was intrigued. "I'm listening."

"I'll start immediately by taking her on a tour of the city. Doing so will demonstrate my skill to you. This outing will also serve as fine advertising. Surely when people look up to the sky and see this big, beautiful, unique girl, they'll ask *where can I purchase such a glorious creature for myself?* And I will shout down to them, go to Smorp Brothers."

"If we do this, be sure to tell them that our kwetzels come in many different vibrant colors to choose from," Herbert said.

Morton made a solemn plea to his brother to try and seal the deal. "I'm aware you feel betrayed by me pursuing my own goals, brother, but you also know I am a gnome of my word. Lady Azarin is what she represents herself to be. Her father is a noteworthy champion among the Haatari. If she says she can tame a kwetzel, then that is the truth. Allowing her access to this beast would help us both."

"Fairly Deadly being trained by a such a prestigious storm rider family could be another selling point," Herbert mused. He might be angry at his brother, but he still trusted Morton's judgment when it came to moving exotic pets. "Very well. You may take the kwetzel out for the afternoon, and we will see how it goes. I will, of course, have to place a charm upon the beast, which would render her unconscious should she rebel and try to escape. If that doesn't work and we have to put her down, Morton, you're on blunderbuss duty."

"A perfectly reasonable precaution. Can't have her flying around the Core unsupervised! I'll even throw in teaching Fairly how to carry an extra passenger." Azarin thumped me on the arm. "Me and Oz here together will still be under the weight limit."

"Wonderful!" Herbert was clearly overjoyed at this arrangement. "I look forward to working with you, Lady Garzade. I shall have my men prepare her to fly."

I suspected Fairly Deadly might have actually understood what Herbert said, as she lifted her massive beak and made a joyous scream.

37

I lived upon barges most of my life. Suspended by air magic, I suppose you could describe what our barges do as *flying*. Except it's more of a slow and steady, ponderous form of levitation.

This was not that kind of flying. It was not that *at all.*

"Shit fucking hell!" I held on to the ropes as hard as I could as the kwetzel dove. My guts lurched into my throat. Wind roared in my ears and whipped tears from my eyes. Half blind, the ground was a blur beneath us.

Azarin just giggled.

Then Fairly extended one giant wing a bit farther, and suddenly, the ground was on the *other* side of us. Everything shifted so fast, snot flew out of my nose. My body started to rise up out of the saddle, so I squeezed my thighs and did my best to hold on. Then the other wing moved, and everything flipped around the other way.

"Fuck!" My ass slammed back against the saddle. Then my stomach caught up with all the spinning and it took me everything in my power to not throw up on Fairly's feathered back. Though at this speed, if anything came out, it would probably just come back and hit me right in the face.

"What a splendid maneuver! She's got some good mobility for such a big girl. She's not quite as limber as an eagle, but she's got a tighter turn than a griffon, that's for sure."

We were going way too fast. We were much too high. This wasn't right. We shouldn't be up here. Through my involuntary tears, I could tell we were now even with the top of the Great Machine. The mechanical nature of the thing became more obvious this close, as there were metal walls studded with rivets, and through the gaps could be seen gigantic turning gears. It was the most complicated device mortals had ever built.

And we were going to run straight into it.

I couldn't help it. I screamed like a little girl.

"Do you mind? You're yelling right in my ear." Azarin did something with the ropes in front of her, and then we were tilting so far that down was now sideways. The cords secured to my harness snapped tight and kept me from sliding off. The people in the market were *very small* below us.

Collision averted, we were now veering away from the Great Machine. Which was fortunate, as now I noticed there were watchmen stationed in turrets around the top of it, surely prepared to destroy anything that threatened their precious structure. They watched us suspiciously as we passed by. Azarin waved at them.

"Good girl. When we get you home, I'm going to make sure you get lots of treats. What do kwetzels eat anyway? Herbert mentioned fish. Do you like fish?"

Fairly Dangerous screamed, and hers was far louder than mine.

"Fish it is, then."

We were gliding straight and flat away from the market. That part wasn't so horrific. It was the climbing, turning, and swooping that made me ill.

The initial leap into the air had been the worst part. While Herbert's men saddled the beast, and Azarin figured out the nature of the reins, Morton had thrown a safety harness on over my clothing. Then we'd climbed aboard, which by itself was rather frightening, as clambering up a big feathery thing that was big enough to smash you then eat your flattened corpse was no small feat in and of itself. But then came the crouch and jump, where Fairly demonstrated her muscled back legs weren't just for show. The leap had been so powerful, and the acceleration so fast, it must be something like how a bullet felt when being fired from a gun.

"I love this. Isn't this great?"

While she was having fun, I was so sick, I could barely talk. It was freezing, yet my body was covered in sweat. There was so much wind, we had to shout to be heard at all. "Yeah. It's great."

Fairly's wingspan was enormous. Each wing folded down really compact, and once extended, they seemed to go forever. Every flap was a violent snap that made my teeth clack. Luckily, Fairly was so efficient, she seldom needed to flap to maintain altitude.

"I've not flown in forever. Now this is living." At least Azarin was having a fine time. She was in her element. In fact, this was how her people found their magical element, chasing storms across the Plane of Air, on creatures not so different than this. "Not that I don't enjoy the snuggling, but could you loosen the death grip just a bit? You're going to break my ribs."

I forced myself to relax.

She took a deep breath. "Much more comfortable, thank you. Alrighty, let me work with her for a little bit, get familiar with her quirks, and then we'll get on with the mission."

We spent the next twenty minutes swooping around the market. True to her word, whenever anyone looked up, curious to see what the massive shadow flashing past was, Azarin would shout at them to go to Smorp Brothers. It was unlikely anyone heard her. If the Smorps decided to keep this up, they'd probably need to invest in a banner.

After a few minutes, my stomach calmed and I'd run out of water to lose in a cold sweat. The view from up here truly was breathtaking. The Core City went on a great distance. The sheer inconceivable majesty of the place was awe-inspiring.

I might have found the point where beauty overcame fear.

Then Fairly banked hard to the side to avoid a flock of ocean birds, the saddle creaked, ropes pulled tight, down was to the side, and I was back to being terrified.

Azarin got our ride leveled out again. "I think I've got the hang of this. The way she moves, I imagine Fairly's kind spend a lot of time circling, riding currents, and watching for prey. You can start doing your thing. Let's find this magic bullet."

That was easier said than done. The farthest I'd been able to sense my bowl was after I'd asked Trax to swim down the canal with it, which had been maybe two hundred and fifty or three hundred yards, tops. And that had taken all the concentration I could muster.

Considering that was farther than I could reliably strike even a big target like a Fire Elemental with a trapper's rifle, I would normally have taken pride in that accomplishment, but right now, my range was insufficient for our needs. We were higher off the ground than that, and it was hard to concentrate on sensing magic while getting tossed around and praying to not tumble to your death.

"We need to get lower."

"Like how low?"

"Closer the better." As soon as those words left my mouth, I regretted saying them.

Azarin had a gleeful laugh. "You hear that, Fairly? It's time to skim some rooftops. I want to be able to reach out and touch the shingles. Let's see how much control you've got. Try not to plow us snout-first into the ground."

Azarin put us into a dive. Fairly shrieked in delight. I swore, held on tight, and squeezed my eyes shut. Not out of cowardice! I needed to concentrate on my magic. At least, that was the excuse I gave myself.

Finding the warming bowl required clearing my head and bringing the formula to mind. Magic's done by feel, more art than science. When you get a spell to bind to an object, there's a certain moment of connection between caster and element. When you're invoking, you're activating the element, giving that energy a direction, and then letting it go. Sort of like how Azarin was using the reins to point Fairly in the right direction, and then the kwetzel took that suggestion and did what it wanted. When you're enchanting something, it's more like you're locking the element in with the power of your will, and that energy remains there, just waiting to release like a compressed spring. You can feel that built-up energy, sort of like Fairly's back legs as she'd gone into the crouch, and setting off the enchantment was just like her leap. It wanted to go off.

Having created that enchantment, I was connected to it. I just had to listen for the call of compressed energy.

When I opened my eyes, we were only about thirty feet off the ground and moving so fast, the buildings were passing by like streaks. People were screaming and running from us. I closed my eyes again.

"Maybe I should coax her just a teensy bit higher."

"Good idea!"

The flapping made me a bit more confident. Flapping meant climbing. I cleared my head and tried to relax. My grip must have loosened a bit, because Azarin asked, "You're not taking another nap again."

"No danger of that. I'm trying to concentrate."

"Fairly and I will carry on, but if you start snoring, I'm going to have her do a flip."

"Please don't. Pass over the districts around the bay first."

The reasoning for starting there was that once word got out to the various powerful factions around the city that there was a bit of Permanence on the loose, they'd all be looking for it. The wealthier districts would have more potential buyers, but they'd also have a lot more watch presence, and the Council automatically claimed the rights to any Permanence in the Core. Gerzog would surely prefer to sell it than have it confiscated.

With Carcalla looking for him, Gerzog wouldn't go anywhere near the Slumps. He'd kept Dathka as a bartering chip against the Latros, but why risk running into them at all? The Cult of Tempus was another potential buyer, but if Gerzog went down into the remains of the ancient civilization from before the building of the Great Machine, the cult would just take it from him. Their goal was to open Time and kill us all, so it was reasonable to assume they weren't exactly sane or honest in their dealings.

"Why there?"

"The watchmen would arrest him, the Latros would skin him alive, and the Cult would probably do whatever it was that insane mutants do to their victims. Gerzog can't leave the Core, because he has to stay close enough to be able to show off the goods and make a trade. He's likely in a district with enough people he won't stand out, so probably among the laborers and tradesmen."

"Wow. That's smart."

I took the compliment but didn't tell her I'd gotten all that from Rade, because he'd worked for less than honest merchants before and picked up a few things and the movement of stolen goods.

We went over the bay first. From up here, a hundred ships were in view, and farther out in the waves, Korthican's Warning and dozens of other islands. Out beyond that, the water went on and on. Since that ocean would eventually connect to the Elemental Plane of Water, it wasn't infinite, but it sure was close.

Azarin took us up the coast a bit, but not sensing anything from the docks and boats, we turned inland. We went over neighborhoods full of homes and shops, then over areas of industry where Fairly had to fly between billowing smokestacks, and the ashen air reminded me of home.

From there, we could see but one tiny edge of the city, where the buildings went from dense to sparse, and then it was rectangles of fields as far as the eye could see. Past that were forests, and beyond that mountains, real ones, even bigger than the artificial Great Machine. Keep going that direction, and we'd eventually reach the Elemental Plane of Earth. Up would take us toward the Air Realm. It was doubtful scum like Gerzog would be in the countryside or the city's upper areas, though.

There weren't very many maps of the world. Not that wise men hadn't figured it out over the last several thousand years, but rather because it was too hard to draw. The drawing in the *Encyclopedia Ettymus* had looked like a tangled mass of string. I'd seen others where it looked like a ball of yarn. Seven different cords, to be exact, all of them colliding, knotted together, and hopelessly entwined.

Everyone knew the Core was in the middle of the seven intertwined realms, heaven was above, hell was below, and the sun and moon and stars went around the outside. It was all very simple.

We turned back into the city, and I realized that even with this speedy method of searching, it was going to take a lot of luck. This place was just so damned *vast*. Expanding for forty-five hundred years, the city covered valleys and hills and crawled up mountainsides and was built into plateaus, all connected by roads and highways.

Then there were islands in the sky and bridges between them all. Amidst all that were all manner of conveyances, mundane and magical both. There were canals and rivers and lakes, with smaller craft travelling across all of them. There were millions of living beings down there, and time insufficient to fly past them all.

We flew back and forth for hours. It was a good thing today was Fireday, which was by far the warmest day of the week, because any other time, I likely would've frozen up here. Azarin was fine. She was used to this. All I could do was try and focus on the magic instead of the discomfort. Azarin had warned me we were running out of time, because Fairly was starting to get hungry and cranky. I really didn't want to see what she did when she was famished and had two delicious meaty snacks conveniently on her back.

Then suddenly…

"I got something!"

38

It had been the faintest sensation, but I'd been certain. That had been *my* spell craft.

I opened my eyes to find we were flying over an unfamiliar part of the city. It was tidy streets consisting of close-packed, white, four-to-six-story buildings. "Where are we?"

"I don't know. I've not been here either."

Glancing over my shoulder, the Great Machine was behind us, so we were on the opposite side of the market from the Slumps. Then I noticed at every corner, there was a church, and there was a particularly impressive, giant super church in the distance.

"I think this is the Cantor's District." I didn't know much about the place, except that it was to aspiring priests, nuns, and monks what the Collegium was to us wizards. "Why would Gerzog be here?"

"Maybe he's found religion and come to forsake his evil ways?" Azarin laughed at the idea. "Doubtful. Let's go shoot him."

The feeling was gone. "Turn back. The bullet's behind us somewhere."

"Hang on." When Azarin pulled on the rope, Fairly shook her massive head in protest. She really was getting tired and cranky. "I know, girl. We're almost done, then I'll take you home, and Herbert will give you all the fish you can eat."

The kwetzel relented and performed one of those rapid dropping spins. I suspected she did that just to damage my calm, but at least we were headed the right way.

I focused as hard as I could, fervently hoping I'd not imagined the sensation. Being a self-taught rank two, what the hell did I really know about tracking magic? But after a moment, I felt it again. "Veer left."

Azarin did, and as we went over a big wooded estate, the feeling grew stronger. And once we were past its walls, it tapered off. By the time I spoke, it'd vanished entirely. "That's it. The bullet's in there."

Azarin leaned down to pat the kwetzel's neck. "Thank you. I'm guessing we've probably flown over two hundred miles back and forth today. That would've taken a lot longer to walk! Good girl. If Herbert doesn't feed you extra fish, I'll feed you Herbert… Now what?"

"Drop me off and I'll go scout it out. Tell the others where I'm at, return Fairly, and then meet me back here. This district looks like it's filled with decent folk. Be discreet. Make Trax wear his disguise." That was just a shower curtain and a basket meant to pass as robes and a hat, but in a city with this odd a population, that actually helped a lot.

"Promise you won't do anything stupid without me."

I didn't know if she was worried about me getting hurt, or if she just didn't want to miss out on the revenge and payback. "I'll try to stay near that big estate, but if Gerzog moves, I'll have to follow him. I'll leave a message somehow if he does."

"You could always stab yourself and Trax can follow the smell."

"Yeah, but he chastises me whenever I get injured."

"He's a big softy." Azarin had slowed Fairly down so much that we were no longer gliding, and the kwetzel was forced to start flapping to keep us in the air. "I don't see a safe place to put this big girl down around here."

I'd been afraid of that, but there was a small field below us, and based off the grey lumps, it appeared to be where the locals had shoveled all their snow. I started unbuckling my harness. "Like you said. I've got an air glove."

"You're going to do it?" She was more excited than concerned, because this was the sort of ridiculous thing she'd do without thinking it through. "You mad man. Don't worry. You've been practicing. You're rank two now. Rank twos are practically indestructible!"

That was a load of trogshit, but her confidence helped. "I'll be fine."

"I'll get us lower."

Once I was free of the straps keeping me from falling off, I leaned in over her shoulder and kissed her on the cheek. "For luck."

"See you soon… I just hope you jumping off doesn't teach Fairly the wrong message, and whenever she gets tired, she starts spearing and removing passengers."

I climbed out of the saddle, and when I went from leather to feathers, it was a whole lot slicker than expected, and I ended up sliding and then tumbling off the side of the kwetzel.

Not only was this the farthest I'd ever tried to descend, rather than a smooth step off, I started out flipping wildly end over end. My cloak flew up and wrapped around my face so I couldn't see the ground. Azarin was about to watch me break every bone in my body.

Except I stayed calm, pulled the cloak from my eyes, extended my hand toward the ground—which was already closer than expected—and activated the spell.

"*Descend.*"

The Clear embedded in the glove came to life, and the air wrapped around me, not solid, but a whole lot firmer than normal. The spell slowed me down a lot, the wild spinning stopped enough that I was able to aim for the snow pile rather than the hard frozen ground, and I got my feet under me—then I hit.

It was still way too fast, and I ended up tumbling and rolling through the snow. I hit my already bruised hip and tweaked my left wrist.

On my back, I just lay there, looking up at Fairly Deadly hovering over me. Azarin leaned over her neck, and both of them looked concerned. Yes, my landing had been so poor, I'd even made the kwetzel worried.

Azarin shouted, and was so distant, I could barely hear her over the beating wings. I think she said, "Did you break anything?"

I forced myself to get up, waved in a manner that suggested it hadn't hurt at all, and began brushing myself off. I even had a few feathers stuck to my cloak from my tumble. Then I noticed a woman and her children standing on the sidewalk, so transfixed by the gigantic kwetzel, they hadn't even noticed me fall out of the sky.

"Smorp Brothers has got all sorts of flying mounts," Azarin yelled at them. "These even come in different colors!"

As Fairly Deadly flapped away, the little girl bounced excitedly and clapped her mittens together. "Mommy, may I have a pink one?"

39

I'd been worried that Gerzog might have gotten suspicious if he'd seen us fly by, thinking it was someone searching for him. That, or maybe the locals would get excited about a flying beast dropping off a wizard with a familiar description. As it turned out, I'd been paranoid for no reason, because as I walked through the Cantor District, several other flying mounts or magical conveyances passed by overhead.

When one big grey bird flew past with several passengers on its back, I noticed it was heading for a sky island that was suspended over the rear of the district, atop which had been built the biggest and fanciest church I'd ever seen. That building must have been as important as it looked, because it was attracting a lot of traffic from the city's loftier districts. Fairly Deadly wouldn't have been noteworthy in this crowd.

And crowded it was. The extra Fireday heat brought with it a warm breeze from the market. It was dinnertime, yet a great many people were out and about on the streets to get some fresh air away from their stuffy winter homes. Though this district was dedicated to the study of the gods and saints, the residents were as normal as everywhere else. Laborers, rowdies, families, and traders all came and went between a great many establishments. There were dozens of taverns and pubs. For whatever reason, I'd expected the religious district to be holier.

I made my way toward the estate. When I paused to concentrate, I sensed the magic bullet in the distance ahead. It was faint, but getting warmer.

There seemed to be a church on every street in this neighborhood, but as I walked, reading the signs, it turned out most of those buildings were actually schools sponsored by the worshippers of various saints. I'd assumed they were churches from the symbolic statues out front. This really was like the Collegium, only less ostentatious. There were still lots of magical effects at work, like moving picture illusions on some of the walls, and talking or singing advertisements, but it wasn't nearly as flashy as I'd seen previously.

The people were also a bit friendlier and less standoffish. I received a great many nods of greeting from total strangers. In the Collegium, those would've been sneers. In the Slumps, those nods of greeting would be followed by both parties checking their pockets to make sure the other hadn't robbed them.

The residents here were mostly human, amongst many others. Some I was familiar with, like dwarves and gnomes, and a few I'd seen only in passing before. There were gnome-sized lizard men who looked like miniature Sifusos. Then there were muscular orange people who looked like lobs—but their bodies weren't cursed with bits of rock—those must have been hobgoblins. There were a lot of those here. They must be very religious.

There were watchmen about on patrol, but not nearly as many in other districts. If I were to guess why, it was that a well-behaved people tended to police themselves. With the City Watch being the Council's eyes, and so few of them here, someone like Gerzog would be able to avoid them easily. There were a surprising number of orcs too, so he wouldn't stand out that much. I guess the orcish presence made sense, as the gods had lifted up several notable saints from that race. From what I understood, orcs also had an inordinate number of fiends appointed, to balance things out. Gerzog definitely seemed to fall more on the destined-for-hell side of things.

I reached a tall white wall. The magic bullet was somewhere on the other side. I followed the wall around to the front where there was an open gate with a big sign over it, declaring this was the Habitation of Phradumius. I didn't know who or what that was, but it was open to the public until sundown. People were coming and going through the gate, and from the robes and holy symbols, most were various kinds of clergy.

I watched the entrance for a while; the bullet remained inside. There really wasn't a good place for me to sit unnoticed. There were no beggars here, no nearby businesses I could pretend to be frequenting, and it was too cold for anyone to just be standing around. I'd told Azarin I'd try to meet her here, but if Gerzog had men stationed in any of the nearby buildings, they'd be sure to spot me loitering.

There were two guards posted at the gate, but they weren't watchmen. They were from some other militant group I'd not seen before, wearing long black coats with a silver dagger patch sewn on their sleeves, and big fur hats with the same symbol pinned to the front. Both wore a sword and a pistol on their belts. They seemed alert, but were cordial to the people entering.

"Those are Paladins of Kielgrad," someone said from behind me. I turned around to see a plump, grey-haired, rosy-cheeked halfling woman, carrying a bag of groceries. Halflings were taller than gnomes, near dwarf height, but not nearly as thick and musclebound. The only thing hairy on her was her head and her bare feet. I don't know how those weren't getting frostbite. "I saw you staring at them. It must be their turn to man the shrines today. Don't worry. They're fair lads, as they serve Saint Loyalty. Not at all like the Paladins of Zumlane. Those judgy bastards. They were here yesterday, all scowling and watching everybody all suspicious, like we're just itching to do some crime."

"Zumlane is the Saint of..."

"Justice."

"Got it. Are paladins like watchmen?"

"Oh, not at all, boy. The Watch answers to the Council." Then the tiny round grandma pointed skyward. "Paladins answer only to the gods. You must be new around here."

"That I am." And talking to a local gave me an excuse to keep watching the entrance in case Gerzog came out, so I was happy for the company. "I've only been in the Core for a few months, and this is my first time in this district. It's rather nice. That great big church suspended over there is pretty impressive."

"Oh, lad, that's *the* Cathedral. That's where all the priests gather to commune with their saints and manage the spiritual welfare of all the kingdoms. Do you know nothing?"

My people were devout, but it was a pragmatic sort of devout. Our saint was all about hard work, and we prayed to him to keep ourselves in one piece long enough to get that work done. Most barge cadres weren't big on the organized part of religion, priests of Ketekunan were few and far between, and our set of encyclopedias had been missing the volume detailing the history and organization of said church.

"I know a bit, just not how things are done around here. Like, what's this place here they're guarding?"

"You've never been to a holy site before? What kind of horrible backwards kingdom are you from?"

"Fogo." When I said that, she shrugged like she'd never heard of it. "The one with all the lava."

"Oh, that miserable fire realm. You poor thing. Well, come on, then." With her free hand, she grabbed mine and tugged me toward the gate. "I didn't know you were an escaped slave."

"Indentured servant." Breaking free would cause a scene, so I let her drag me along.

"Same difference. Such barbarity is illegal in the Core. In this city, all are equal, and upon holy ground, all are uplifted. The militant orders guard the shrines. Our tithes from the churches maintain them. The Council even donates magic to make them spiffy. I can't believe you've been in the city so long without paying your proper respects to the gods. That's bad luck, that is. You're just begging to get cursed with misfortune."

She was probably right, but if I ran into Gerzog and ended up shooting him in the face on holy ground, that would probably make the gods even more upset with me. "Thanks, but I've got an appointment I need to—"

"Nonsense." Halflings had surprisingly strong grips for such small people. "It only takes a minute to walk through the gardens and leave an offering."

The paladins were watching us now, so I was committed. "That sounds great."

"We got us a first-timer," she said as we reached the gate. "There you go, hotlander. Say hello to Saint Prudence for me. She's the best."

"I will. Thank you, ma'am." I nodded at the paladins as I walked through. "Good day to you, sirs."

They nodded politely back, logically assuming I was a bumpkin here to see the sights, rather than a wizard who'd been wronged, plotting revenge upon a thieving orc.

I entered a big courtyard, and suddenly, it was no longer winter. There was green grass, flowers, big trees, and even leafy bushes sculpted to resemble animals. I was still getting used to the idea of plant life, so that really was something. I'd never seen a real garden before.

Even better, it wasn't cold in here. Though the whole place was open to the grey sky, the temperature began to rise as soon as I stepped through the gate. It wasn't even a sharp change, like the shock of coming in from the cold into a room with a fireplace so hot that the change would make your ears prickle and your skin hurt, but rather, this was a gradual, gentle warming. It was still chilly in here by Fogo's burning standards, but it was downright pleasant compared to the altitude and wind chill I'd been suffering under all day.

Forget paying respects to the gods. I'd come back just for the magical weather.

There were meandering footpaths through the garden. People strolled down those or lounged on the grass, having pleasant conversations. There were birds flying around in here, probably glad to escape the winter outside. Some chirped and sang. The entire place had an aura of calm and contemplation about it. My home had been nothing at all like this, and it still managed to feel like home.

It didn't seem like something that would attract filth like Gerzog the Marauder, but I could still sense the bullet nearby, so I picked a path that went in that direction and set out.

I hoped to spot him and follow him to someplace that wasn't crawling with paladins. I didn't know much about their attitudes, but they'd been well armed, and surely wouldn't care for anyone disturbing the peace here.

There were statues scattered throughout the garden, standing on plinths. The statues were of various races and species, dressed in many different ways. Some wore next to nothing, while others were in suits of armor or big flowing robes. I was a little surprised when I saw one statue move and begin speaking like a real person, until I realized that was simply some manner of magical animation.

People would gather around a statue, then it'd come to life and begin telling them a story. When the stories were over, they would leave some small offering at the base: small coins, scraps of food, crafts, and even a dead mouse. That one had been left by one of the strange frog race at the foot of a statue of a lizardman, but it had been done so respectfully that surely it hadn't been meant as an insult.

I wondered if these statues were what those saints had really looked and sounded like before they'd been uplifted to immortality. There were thousands of saints, but this place only had dozens of statues, so I doubted mine would be represented. Which was unfortunate, as it would've been a treat to see an image of Ketekunan better than a wood carving stuck on a barge hull.

I rounded a corner, and there was a statue shorter than the others. It looked very similar to the halfling grandmother who'd shoved me in here, and when I checked, sure enough, the brass plaque at the base declared this to be Gwyneth, Saint of Prudence. No wonder this was her favorite; they could have been sisters.

Wait... Could I have been guided here by a saint, disguised as a mortal? There were stories about that sort of thing happening. Then I laughed at myself, because that was downright silly.

"I was told to say hello… Hello." The statue didn't come to life and regale me with tales, so I didn't really know what else to do. I knew prudence had something to do with having good judgment and discipline—which I could certainly use—and my saint wasn't around to ask for help, so she would have to do.

"While I'm here, I could use some help. I'm looking to put things right. I've got good folks counting on me, but I owe favors to evil men. I've made promises which I tried to keep, but I got betrayed by someone I thought to be a friend and wronged by a thieving orc. If I can't keep those promises, then decent people—who I'm responsible for—are going to suffer. The lucky ones will be homeless, and the rest of us will be dead. As is poor Rufus already, may he rest in peace." I had a dark thought that made me chuckle. "He sure could have used some prudence coming down those stairs! The poor guy… Forgive me, that was probably inappropriate."

I didn't know what to leave for an offering and began patting myself down. I had almost no money left, and the only other things of value on me were rounds of ammunition, element, or enchantments, and it wouldn't be *prudent* to give those up, especially while looking for a fight. Then I found something that might be appropriate.

"I hope this is acceptable," I told the statue as I placed a single blue and green kwetzel feather on the ground before it. The statue remained unanimated, but the saint seemed to have a happy expression on her rotund face. "Good. Then I shall carry on. Please, give my regards to Saint Persistence should you see him in the heavens."

After I'd wandered for a half an hour, I found myself in the very back corner of the Habitation. For whatever reason, this part was far less crowded than the rest. The bushes were overgrown. If they'd been carved into animals before, they were now animal-shaped blobs. Everywhere else, the grass was carefully cropped to an even length, while in this one part, it was wild and had patches of dirt where nothing grew. The trees drooped with moss. No birds sang here. And somehow, it even seemed just a bit colder.

I heard a familiar voice coming from the other side of the bushes.

It was Dathka Walker, and she was talking to somebody.

Crossing the grass, I crept up closer. Strangely enough, she didn't sound angry or defiant, nor was she begging for mercy. She didn't sound like a prisoner at all. Her tone was the same as when I'd been talking to Saint Prudence. Dathka was praying to a saint.

I snuck around the corner, one hand on my pistol, the other on my bag of Red, to find her all by herself, sitting at the foot of a statue, alone, unbound, and totally free, with her captor nowhere in sight.

"Well, some fucking rescue this is turning out to be!"

40

Dathka was clearly surprised by my sudden arrival. "Carnavon?"

"Where's Gerzog?"

"Obviously not here. I escaped him hours ago." She saw that I was ready to draw my weapons. "So you can relax."

"You relax." Was this some kind of trick? Had she escaped, or had he let her free? Was this a double cross? Or, since we'd already been double-crossed, a triple cross? I didn't know. This was exactly why I should never have consorted with crooks to begin with. "As of this morning, Carcalla's got the entire Latrocinium tearing the city apart looking for you. What the hell's going on?"

"I told you, I escaped." She remained seated but slowly lifted her hands to show me they were empty. She was wearing the same black clothing she'd been wearing on the island. Other than a split lip and some cuts and scratches, which were alarmingly red against her eerily white skin, she didn't appear to be too damaged. "The minute I could escape my bounds, I did."

"What're you doing here? Hiding?"

"No," she snapped, offended at the suggestion. "I'm no coward." Then she nodded toward the statue behind her. "I'm seeking inspiration."

"For what?"

"How to best kill Gerzog, slaughter all his men, and reclaim the treasure so I can present it to my father to regain his trust and respect."

It was then I noticed what name was on the plaque for this particular statue.

Brotbeck. Saint of Murder.

Well, shit... No wonder this section of the Habitation of Phradumius was so abandoned and unloved.

Brotbeck was represented as a thin, gangly man, with protruding eyes and a receding hairline. In his bony hands, he held the symbols of his office, a garrot and a knife. I was really glad this statue didn't come to life and tell us his story as, frankly, I didn't want to hear it. The illusionists who'd gifted their enchantments to this place had probably refrained from animating this unsavory one, because hearing the story behind his ascension would likely scare the children.

"He grant you any wisdom yet?"

"If the gods had granted me wisdom, I wouldn't still be here, sitting uselessly upon my ass now, would I?"

As fine of an ass as that may be, I trusted her about as much as an expanding lava bubble that was about to burst. "I don't even know how this guy rates sainthood. Murdering seems more life fiend behavior to me."

"Maybe the gods think some pricks just need killing... How'd you find me anyway?"

"You're a no good, dishonest, thief." I held out one hand. "Give me my enchanted bullet back."

She scowled, then touched her pockets until she found it and pulled it out. "I forgot I even had that on me." She tossed it over. "Here."

I caught it, then held the round of ammunition up to the light to inspect it. The wax paper case seemed intact, and the enchantment felt just as I'd left it. I hurried and stuck it through one of the empty loops on my belt.

"Gerzog seized both my pistols, so I've got nothing to shoot it out of anyway. The bastard stole all my charms too. I've got nothing left but my wits."

"And your oh so charming personality."

"Before you lip off too much, I do have this." Dathka had showed me her empty hands, but with the flick of a wrist, she dropped something from her sleeve into her palm. I think it was a shard of glass, with a handle of wrapped rag. "I broke an old mirror in the room I was tied up in and used this to cut myself free."

"Then why not run back to the Latros for help? I'd think flesh and blood murderers will be of more use to you than an absent immortal."

"The world is never absent murder, Carnavon." Dathka sighed as she decided to level with me. "I can't return as a failure. Ever since I arrived in the Core, I've been trying to earn my father's respect. He told Cutter Joran to teach me, to see if I was worthy of the family business. Watching over you Outcasts was a test to see how I could manage on my own. Instead, I got outmaneuvered by a mercenary and placed the Latrocinium's interests in danger. I've become a liability, and there is nothing that the great Carcalla hates more. If I come back crying for Latrocinium help, it marks me as weak. I must handle this without them, and return my captor's head, or my father will for sure send me back through the gate."

"I'm sorry you've got daddy issues, but if I don't bring back the treasure, we're still getting evicted."

"You know when that happens, he'll surely kill a couple of you at least, as an example to everyone else why debts must be promptly paid. That's his way."

"Your dad and his pet gladiator have made that abundantly clear. So where's Gerzog?"

She remained cagey on that topic. "I don't know where he is right now."

"But you know something. You know where he's going to be, don't you? You need to do this without Latro help? Well, the Outcasts sure as shit aren't Latros. You can look your father in the eye and tell him you did handle it on your own, by gathering forces who were already in his debt. He's out nothing. Problem solved. Let's go."

"Hmmm…" Dathka studied me, and must have decided I meant business, because she turned back at the statue and said, "I asked you for help, Brotbeck, and it seems you have answered my prayers in a rather direct fashion." She stood, then bent over to gently place her offering at the statue's base. "Praise Murder."

"Is that an ear?" It sure looked like a human ear, or at least most of one.

"It's from one of the men Gerzog left guarding me. When I said I cut myself free, I wasn't only talking about the ropes."

41

Dathka and I left the Habitation of Phradumius and started east.

"Once Gerzog finds out you've escaped, won't he change his plans?"

"Doubtful. He couldn't have known I could hear some of their conversations through the vents of the room I was held in. Gerzog's found a buyer and they're going to meet later to exchange the treasure for a chest full of coins. I intend to relieve him of both those things, as well as his miserable life."

"And you're going to do that with what? Your piece of glass?"

"I'll find a way."

"Yeah, I've already got a way. Slow down." When she kept walking, I grabbed her by the arm to stop her.

"Unhand me."

"No." I glared at her, because I'd had about enough of this snooty Latro thinking she was better than me. "Not until you listen." One of the black-coated Paladins of Kielgrad looked askance at me manhandling a woman, so I quickly let her go and lowered my voice. "Use your brain or I'm out. I'm not one of your idiot gang. You can go fight a band of mercenaries on your own, or you can go back and beg your fiend for someone else to come save you."

"Brotbeck is not a *fiend.*" I noticed she'd palmed her improvised weapon again, prepared to gut me right here in the street in front of hundreds of nice church-going folks. "Take that back."

It was funny she thought that was the most offensive thing I'd said. "Fine. But we do this the smart way. How many men will Gerzog have with him?"

"I don't know. More members of his company showed up at their hideout and left with him. So at least four or five. Then we might also need to contend with whoever his buyer is."

"Two of us against that? Bad odds. I've got friends coming to meet me here."

"There's no time to wait." Dathka looked toward the setting sun. "They're supposed to meet an hour after the gate's closing, and we still have a ways to walk."

I pointed toward where she had her glass shard hidden. "Then cut yourself."

"What's wrong with you?"

"So Trax can follow us. It doesn't need to be deep. Just enough to leave a drop or two every block will be enough for his nose. He's really good at that."

Dathka was aghast. "Why don't you cut yourself?"

"Because my father wasn't an angry gangster I need to impress." I'd gotten a couple cuts on the island, but they were dried out. "You want the Outcasts with us or not?"

She growled at me, but didn't hesitate too long. "Fine." She looked me right in the eyes as she held out her arm and sliced a small cut. She did her best to hide the fact it hurt.

I glanced back, but thankfully, the paladin hadn't noticed the bloodletting. I didn't know how the Saint of Loyalty felt about strange deadlander girls cutting themselves in the street, and didn't really care to find out.

"Satisfied, Carnavon? I'm not too proud to turn down the aid of one of the elite Squalo Hunter Killers before a battle."

I'd forgotten she believed that about Trax, and I wasn't about to correct her misconception while she was standing there with a bloody shard of glass in hand. "Now we can go."

We set a brisk pace through the Cantor's District. From all the singing coming from the various churches, now I understood how this place had gotten its name. My people sang on the barges, and even sang while we worked, but our songs were simple, honest, sometimes funny, often dirty, and always had a rhythm you could swing a pick to. The songs here were… uplifting. I wasn't used to reverence. These people were singing in such a way their saints might listen.

"Where are we going?"

"They're meeting on the lift platform that goes up to the Cathedral. I couldn't make out all the details or with who, but Gerzog was crowing about how they were going to get so many Obols, they'd never need to work again. They're probably selling it to some rich fool wizard, who'll hide it in his treasure room, where all that precious Permanence will go unused. Just another wealthy man's bauble, when instead it should be used for good."

The way she said the last part, I could tell she was genuinely angry about that. "*For good?* Why do you care? Carcalla would do the same thing."

"No, he wouldn't," she snapped.

"Trogshit. Don't get all high and mighty with me. Your dad's a crook. If things had gone according to plan, and we'd brought the lamp back to him, he'd be selling it to the highest bidder right now, same as Gerzog."

"You know nothing."

"How am I wrong? How are the Latrocinium who rob and murder and tax the Slumps going to use this bit of lost element *for good*? If Carcalla actually cared about doing good, he'd donate it to the Council so they could keep the Great Machine running that much longer."

She sneered at me and remained silent. It was probably good we dropped the subject, as I was angry and running on almost no sleep, so was likely to say something offensive enough that would cause her to run back to Daddy, demanding to have me scalped.

When Dathka mentioned the meeting was on a lift, I'd expected something like the lifts we'd used for carrying Red up to the barges. Ours were just big enough to hold two men and a cart, and were hoisted by pulleys, rope, and muscle. This thing was thirty paces across, enclosed with clear glass walls, and rose smoothly even with two dozen people and a couple wagons aboard. It must have used the same kind of levitation enchantment as a barge or air cart, but it kept on rising, so it was capable of reaching much higher altitudes than either of those.

The base of the Cathedral was probably four hundred yards above. Living beneath the Slump, I was no stranger to seeing the undersides of sky islands, but our slowly descending and perpetually-threatening-to-crush-us-all roof was ugly, jagged rock, crumbling basements, and leaky pipes. For this one, the magically suspended rock was polished smooth beneath, and painted with religious murals. It was rather impressive.

There was also a great curling roadway and stairs up to the Cathedral, but it seemed everyone coming from the Cantor's District preferred to wait for the magical lift. I couldn't fault them that decision. My legs burned just looking at all those stairs.

With hundreds of people in the lift plaza, it wouldn't be too hard for us to find a spot to sit and wait unseen to watch for Gerzog. We didn't even stand out with our hoods up, as most everyone who wasn't originally from some freezing realm was dressed for the weather.

There were several carts here selling food. I was so tired that I'd nearly forgotten how famished I was, but now that I could smell the cooking meat and spices, my stomach reminded me with a violent rumble.

"You hungry?" I asked Dathka.

"I've not eaten in two days. What do you think?"

"I'll take that as a yes."

"No. Gerzog took my coin purse," she muttered. She wasn't too proud to get help stalking a bunch of mercenaries, but apparently, asking for food was a line too far. I thought Dathka was a horrible person, who worked for even worse people, but I was also a gentleman, and it was the tradition of the cadre folk to never let someone go hungry if we could help it.

"I'll be right back."

I found a stall selling roasted chicken parts, except when I checked my pockets, I didn't have nearly enough. Food was pricy in this district. I couldn't afford the next one either, but at the end of the line were some of the little frog-faced creatures, who were cooking mysterious kinds of meat on skewers over a burn barrel. It dripped oil that caused the fire to pop and spit, and it smelled weird, but I was too hungry to be proud. They didn't speak the trade tongue, but by pointing and holding up fingers, we came to a deal that I could afford.

I returned to Dathka carrying two sticks full of some kind of cooked animal and held one out to her. "Here you go."

She eyed the meat suspiciously. "Do I look like I would eat that?"

"You look like you'd eat corpse flesh straight from the coffin." I took a bite from one. It was chewy. The flavor was… present. "It's not that bad."

"That's a brave man, eating something prepared by filthy Kurbogs."

I managed to swallow the greasy clump. "So that's what those frog fellows are called?"

"Kurbogs are a scavenger race, so you're likely eating ratlets they snared from the sewers."

"Naw, I know what ratlet meat looks like. I live with Trax, remember." I happily took another bite. "You want this or would you prefer to be self-righteous and starve?"

Dathka relented and took the stick from me. "If I die of dysentery, my ghost will haunt you."

I sat next to her. "We've got so many ghosts in the Tube, what's one more?"

We ate and watched the crowd. I didn't spot any watchmen. Occasionally, a paladin would pass through, wearing different colors and heraldry to mark their order. There were a lot of priests going up and down the lift, each roundtrip of which took about ten minutes. Carriages rolled through, both magical and pulled by animals. If Gerzog arrived in one of those, we'd have a problem, unless we got lucky and caught sight of his ugly green face through a window.

I decided to try and make conversation with the surly deadlander. "When I showed you that molten bullet spell—which you stole like a rotten thief—you mentioned having a bunch of people you intended to kill. Anybody in particular you feel like telling me about?"

"That's none of your business."

"Keep your secrets, then. I'm plotting a great and terrible revenge myself, against a real bastard of a pirate. He's an elf actually. I heard Carcalla's only half elf. How's that work?"

"How do you think it works?"

"Assuming elf parts match up to humans, the actual workings of the endeavor seem straightforward and aren't really in question. I mean, how does that kind of existence fit into the grand scheme of things? With the elves being near immortal string pullers in all the positions of authority, do they accept your dad? Or do they treat him like he seems to treat you?"

Oh, that drew her ire. "Go to hell, Carnavon."

"I grew up in Fogo, which by most accounts is pretty similar to Hell. Except we're still alive upon our lake of fire and not quite as damned for eternity."

"I lived on the literal doorstep of Hell. You know nothing of the place. Now be silent so I can end this orc and get my property back."

"Yeah, he took all your stuff. Does that include your shadow-walking charm? Because that's a potent spell. If he's learned to use it..."

"It's a higher-level enchantment. I doubt it."

I didn't care for how she dismissed my reasonable concern. "How'd you wind up with a charm that powerful anyway?"

She paused for way too long before replying, "It was a gift."

"Did your dad give it to you?"

"No. It doesn't matter who gave it to me, only that it's unlikely Gerzog's figured out how to use it already. Even with my affinity being shadow magic, it took me far more than a single day to make it work at all."

"Only morons underestimate their enemies, Dathka. If what Gerzog told me is true, and I've got no reason to doubt this part, he's a rank higher than me, and I beat you even when you had that charm. I wouldn't be so arrogant."

She gritted her teeth.

That attempt at conversation ended rather poorly. It made me thankful the Outcast's deadlander wasn't a stuck-up sour-puss. Though, to be fair, Dathka was a lot nicer to look at than Rade. It was unfortunate she had the personality of gurgler.

Time passed with no sign of the orc. The sun sank behind the mountains, but it didn't really matter because this district had more light charms hanging everywhere than the Collegium did. It was so bright, it might as well have been noon time, except the charms here were set to give off a warm, rosy glow. Combined with the echoing hymns, it gave the district a very peaceful feel… Which we would likely be ruining very soon.

With a belly full of mystery meat, it took everything in my power to not nod off to sleep. I actually might have for a bit, but I didn't know for how long, because Dathka elbowing me in the arm brought me right back.

Gerzog the Marauder had arrived.

42

Five mercenaries entered from the opposite side of the lift plaza. Knowing what I knew now about the Tooth and Claw mercenary company, seeing them dressed in priestly robes was amusing. They must have stolen their outfits from the same place, because they were all the same grey color, and bore the symbol of some saint I wasn't familiar with. The robes didn't fit right, especially on Gerzog, who was so big, his barely went over his shoulders and he couldn't close the front at all. Beneath that, he still wore the same rugged adventuring clothes as before. He carried a wooden box, which was the perfect size to hold Korthican's lamp. This container was sealed better than the old, rusted one we'd found it in, since we weren't all getting blinded by leaking light.

The other mercs were a goblin, another orc, and two humans, one of which was female. They were all armed, but whatever church they were impersonating must have been a militant one, because nobody batted an eye at the sword and gun belts. The woman had a lump under her robes like she was hiding a big backpack.

The two of us stayed seated and watched from beneath the shadows of our hoods.

"How do you want to play this?" Dathka asked.

"I haven't seen any paladins for a minute, but I don't think they're going to like us starting a fight here."

"Then they'll be extra cross once I plunge this into Gerzog's neck." She patted the spot where she'd hidden her shard.

I could appreciate the bloodthirsty enthusiasm, but my goal was to get the lamp without getting killed or arrested. "Easy. Let's wait and see what they do."

It was looking doubtful my friends would arrive in time. Gerzog had claimed to be a rank three, and who knew what the rest of them were capable of. I'd gotten my hopes up that we'd have help, but it was a long walk from the Under Slump.

The lift was on its way back down. The mercs headed for the spot where they'd be able to board for the next trip.

"We're going to have to follow them up." I stood, keeping my head averted in the off chance Gerzog glanced this direction. "You still bleeding?"

"I've picked at the scab just for you. Now I'll probably get an infection and need my arm amputated because of your bright idea, and it'll have been for nothing since your Squalo's not here."

As long as she was dripping enough for Trax to know where we'd gone, I was happy. "You'll be fine. Tell Brotbeck it's a sacrifice."

"I've promised Saint Murder Gerzog's blood, not mine."

"Let's not keep him waiting."

The lift came down, smooth and silent. It rode on greased rails along a central shaft that the road and stairs corkscrewed up and around. Thankfully, a carriage rolled up in front of us and we were able to walk directly behind it as it rolled toward the lift. The carriage was a magical one, its driver a simple wooden golem, and it had wheels that were powered by a Red-fueled engine. I could only tell the source of its energy because of my sensitivity to the element of my home realm.

The lift stopped. Glass doors opened on all four sides and the passengers debarked. The family who passed us seemed to be having a fine time. Once they were clear, the waiting people filed in. There were priests, merchants, and regular folks wearing what was probably their finest clothes, excited to visit the holiest site in the Core. Everyone politely left space for the carriage and some carts, and the golem was careful not to roll over anyone's toes.

Dathka began moving around the carriage to flank Gerzog, but I grabbed her wrist and shook my head *no*. There were children present, shoving and teasing each other, while their parents gently chided them to behave. She saw them, then gave me an angry scowl—at least she kept her head. Dathka was cold-blooded enough to go for it, but we couldn't risk a confrontation within the close quarters of the lift with all these innocent bystanders around.

My nerves were stretched thin. This felt like I was back on the lava wastes, chasing an Elemental to collect the Red from its heart. Only this time, I was by the center of religion for all the realms, while looking for the opportunity to do great harm to a scum-sucking orc. If I screwed this up, I'd be every bit as dead as if an Elemental had burned me to ash.

The doors slid closed. The lift started its slow and gentle climb.

Through one carriage window and out the other, I kept an eye on Gerzog and his crew. The only rider inside the carriage was an elderly priest in green robes, but he was napping, so no one noticed my spying.

The mercs seemed wary, but in good spirits. They were about to get rich. They certainly weren't expecting anyone to attack them here. That was probably why this was the place chosen for their trade. Who would be stupid enough to cause a ruckus in the shadow of the holiest place in the Core and risk offending every church?

Well, besides us, obviously.

The male human had a fresh bandage covering one side of his head. When I looked to Dathka, she nodded. "That's the one I slashed. He must have had a healing potion to be back on his feet so soon, missing an ear."

From how flat the bandage was lying, it hadn't been a good enough potion to grow it back. Of all the mercs, that one looked the surliest, and who could blame him?

Gerzog said something that made the others laugh. From the way the regular people reacted, the joke must have been unexpectedly crude for clergy.

The ride was surprisingly smooth. This levitation magic was far superior to what we had on our barges, and after being flung about by Fairly Deadly all afternoon, this ascent was rather nice in comparison. The illuminated city stretched below us, until we were passing through a hole in the rock. Rather than darkness, we were treated to carved and painted images which scrolled past, telling us the stories of the gods and creation.

We reached the top, and outside the glass was the biggest building I'd ever seen. It wasn't as large as the Great Machine, but it must have been second in the Core only to that construct in sheer impressive majesty. It was light and splendor as far as the eye could see.

Only the side of the lift facing the Cathedral opened, and everyone shuffled that direction… except for Gerzog and his crew, who remained waiting in the back.

The golem driver moved its arms to feign whipping some imaginary horses and the carriage we were using for concealment began rolling. It was either move with it or risk being spotted.

While the passengers were walking out the main door, a smaller, man-sized opening appeared in the glass over by Gerzog. A man in the same grey robes as the mercenaries was standing there, and he beckoned for them to follow him.

There was no way for us to go that way without getting spotted, so we had no choice but to get out with the crowd. Ahead of us was a wide avenue with huge pillars on each side leading to the Cathedral. By the time I turned back, the smaller opening was already closed and the mercs were gone.

"Come on. This way." I walked quickly through all the happy people around the side of the lift, and thankfully, Dathka followed. It took us a moment to get around it without making a scene, and there were several paladins around. I did my best to look like a regular visitor, marveling at all the fancy displays. Which was easy, as everything up here was covered in art and gold. It turned out the main church liked to decorate its home as lavishly as Carcalla had his, only these guys clearly had far more money than our landlord.

On the barge, I'd heard tales of the riches of heaven, but the priests who were still alive seemed to be doing pretty good for themselves too!

The side Gerzog exited was far less crowded. There were no worshipful masses here, but there was no sign of our target either.

We were overlooking the edge of the sky island, and the only way they could have gone was down the nearby entrance to the corkscrew road. Without any paladins nearby to make suspicious, we picked up the pace.

We kept going down and down, and when we didn't see Gerzog, I began to fear he'd not gone this way at all, and we'd lost him. Had we missed some side door? Had he already made the trade? The lift went past us going down, and I held my breath as I searched the other side of the glass. The mercs weren't aboard.

"We should have attacked when we had the chance," Dathka spat. "If he escapes because of your overabundance of caution, I'll—"

I put my finger to my lips and internally whispered a thanks the Latro shut up. Then I pointed toward where I could faintly hear someone talking below.

Using the side pillars for cover, we crept closer to get a better look. The space a quarter corkscrew below was well lit by suspended light charms. There were wide, flat platforms with benches and shade upon them, spaced every so often along the climb for people sturdy enough to use this route to rest their legs, take in the sights, pray, or contemplate life. This one had a bronze statue of some saint in the middle, and around it were assembled about a dozen people. They were all dressed in similar grey robes, but from the wary separation, these were obviously two different groups.

The new bunch all appeared to be legitimate priests of some sort, though most were fairly young, and looked like they'd be capable in a fight. The one in the middle was ancient compared to the rest. Despite that, I didn't think the staff he leaned on was for walking. Something warned me this older fellow had some serious magic on him. He had white hair and skin darker than Gaul Haddar's, so the pale scars left on his face by the claws of some monster long ago really stood out. He was the one doing the talking.

"If you've wasted my time, Gerzog, you'll be on your way back to the deadlands, only this time, it won't be to torment the peasants, it'll be as a ghost."

The priests were armed too, and though no weapons had been drawn, nervous hands rested on hilts and wands.

Gerzog still held the box. "You know me, Father Orlogo, I keep my word." He slowly opened the lid of the box, just the tiniest crack, just for a second, and even that was enough to scald the eyes of everyone present.

When I blinked away the purple blobs enough to see clearly again, the flash had caused some of the priests to pull their weapons, thinking it was some kind of trap, which caused the mercs to react in kind.

The old priest snapped, "Stand down, fools. Even the Tooth and Claw isn't foolhardy enough to shed blood on holy ground."

"I told you it was the real thing." Gerzog set the box on the ground and stepped back from it. "That was a peek. If I opened it all the way, the whole city would think sunrise came early."

"Then the Council would know it was here, and they'd send the watch to claim it, and neither of us would get what we want," Orlogo said. "Keep that closed. I'm convinced."

"You gonna break that thing open and take the Permanence, cleric?" the female merc asked. She had a thin, hideous face, and was bent like a hunchback beneath her borrowed robes. "Or are you gonna take this to your realm and hang this lamp atop your church like you's got your very own sun?"

"What the faithful of Saint Ulmorn do with our rightful property doesn't concern the likes of you, harpy."

Gerzog showed his tusks. "It's not yours yet."

"Then let's finish this transaction, so I never have to look upon your grotesque visage again." Orlogo snapped his fingers, and two of his men picked up a chest and brought it forward. They set it between the two groups, near the feet of the bronze saint, and opened it, revealing the most coins I'd ever seen.

The mercenaries looked real excited about that. I would be too if I were them. That was more than enough money to buy out the contracts for every member of my family and then some. That was "bribe your way into any academy you want" money.

I got real close to Dathka so I could whisper in her ear, "I've got one *Obscura* left. I can pop it, then we grab the lamp and run." I would've loved to go for that chest full of Obols too, but there was no way I could carry both.

"You take the lamp. I made a vow to take Gerzog's life."

Good for her, but my saint wasn't big on suicide. "Suit yourself. You'll have seven or eight seconds of cover."

I'd been so focused on treasure, and Dathka on revenge, that we'd not heard someone walking down the road, to spot us crouching suspiciously in the shadows behind a pillar. I turned around when this someone cleared his throat.

"Are you lost?" the black-clad paladin asked, rather loudly, as he illuminated us with a light charm strapped to his wrist. "Can I help you?"

A few things happened all at once.

Everyone looked our way.

Father Orlogo—probably being a man of some importance around here—began casually ordering the paladin to go away because this was none of his business.

Except Gerzog and his men saw me and Dathka, and the one who'd gotten de-eared by her earlier roared, "*You!*" and heedless of everything else, went for his pistol.

Which one of the priests who'd pulled his wand earlier clearly took as a threat, because he immediately started blasting.

It all went downhill from there!

43

The bullet meant for Dathka spanged off the pillar in front of us, as the merc who fired it was engulfed in a cloud of flesh-dissolving acid. The resulting screaming and flailing drowned out any attempt by the senior priest or Gerzog to restore order, because then everybody was moving, shooting, or slinging spells at each other.

Those two groups had trusted each other even less than I'd thought!

One of the priests grabbed hold of Father Orlogo and began pushing him toward safety. Another one went for the lamp, only to get zapped with some kind of electrical spell and was sent sliding across the ground, robes smoking.

The paladin ducked behind us. He was about my age, and from the lack of insignia on his coat compared to other paladins, was probably of very low rank. All this chaos seemed to have taken him by surprise. At first, I thought he was trying to warn me and Dathka of something, but then I realized he was speaking into one of his magical charms. "There's a disturbance by the statue of Saint Gratitude. The priests of Ulmorn are fighting each other." We couldn't hear the response from the charm, but after a pause, the paladin said, "I don't know why they're fighting. Just send help. There's a bunch of them."

Dathka started toward Gerzog, but the paladin grabbed hold of her cloak. "Don't go down there, miss. The followers of Saint Violence are a rowdy sect." He must have mistaken us for innocent pilgrims in need of protecting. Then his charm asked another question, and he said to it, "No, not by Saint Gertrude. *Gratitude*, on the rest platform by the—"

Dathka coldly kneed the poor fellow in the balls. He gasped and let go, allowing her to get back to her mission of revenge.

The magical communication had gone out either way, and the religious version of watchmen would surely bust heads as thoroughly as their non-religious counterparts. The box holding the lamp was still sitting there next to the statue, forgotten in the chaos. Now was my chance.

"Sorry, friend," I told the doubled over and wheezing paladin, then sprang up and ran for the treasure.

Most of the priests had taken cover on one side of the platform and the mercenaries on the other, except for the main orc himself, who was rushing his enemy.

Gerzog got hit by a spell, but it flashed and fizzled against one of his protective charms. He caught that priest by the collar and swung him so hard against the base of the statue that I could hear bones crack from across the platform. Orcs are *strong*. But from there, Gerzog didn't head for the lamp. He was fixated on his retirement coins.

Except, just as he grabbed the handles and hoisted up the chest, a concussive air spell struck him. Gerzog's mass and protective charms kept him from getting bowled over, but the magical wave of force smashed the chest open, spilling all the Obols.

"No!" Gerzog watched in horror as his money went rolling in every direction. "Kill these wretched p—"

I didn't know if he was about to say *priests* or *pests*, because that was when Dathka leapt onto his back and went to stabbing. She wrapped her legs around his waist, one arm around his neck, and the other arm became a blur of motion as she slammed the shard into his ribs over and over. Gerzog roared and spun around, Dathka clinging to him like one of the Smorp Brother's monkeys hanging from the bars of their cage, and her stabbing arm never stopped moving.

If he'd had any protective charms remaining after being hit by back-to-back spells, Dathka burned through them in the first few hits, and then blood went flying. It was savage.

Gerzog proved to be one tough orc. He threw himself back against the statue, and she was between him and it. Dathka hit hard and her grip loosened, which allowed Gerzog to reach over his shoulder, grab her by the hair, pull her over, and fling her against the ground. She hit on her back and bounced.

She was dazed and helpless as Gerzog lifted one big boot to stomp on her head flat, but then he stumbled off-balance—I'd thrown a *Shroud of Fire* in his face. Sadly, he was at the far end of my range, so his clothing and hair didn't ignite, but it was enough to make him flinch away.

I'd been going for the treasure, but diverted to save Dathka's life instead. Curse my quality honorable upbringing. I slid on my knees next to her, leveling my pistol at Gerzog's head.

Except that same priest with the air spells had the bad timing to hit the center of the platform with another concussion just as I pulled the trigger. It knocked me sideways over Dathka. Gerzog was sent lurching back. Instead of splitting his skull, my bullet barely grazed his cheek. Coins went flying.

Worst of all, that spell knocked over the box with the lamp. It toppled, and I barely had time to close my eyes and slap one hand over them.

When the lid popped open, it was so bright, it was like the sun had landed on the platform; like getting a regular light charm shoved into each eye. Everyone on the platform, merc, priest, assassin, or paladin, all got flash-blinded.

Except for me, because I'd already had a glove clamped across my face. I shoved my empty pistol back in the holster, and crawled toward the light, which I could still see the glow of through eyelid, leather, and the meat of my hand—no wonder Korthican's neighbors had complained—until I bumped into the box. I fumbled about, hit something that felt like metal or glass, shoved it back inside, and slammed the lid shut.

Thankfully, that ended the searing light. I didn't know what enchantments the mercs had put on this box to contain the brightness of this ridiculous thing, but I was glad they had.

Glancing around, through the flashing purple blobs that were consuming most of my vision, it looked like everyone else was even more disoriented than I was. Gerzog was obviously in pain, but sadly not dying, as he patted the many bleeding holes in his ribs, before finding what he was looking for. He stuck two fingers into a wound, and grimaced as he fished around, pulling out the broken piece of glass that had snapped off inside of him.

"*I'm gonna kill you!*"

It was sorely tempting to go over there and stab him while he was blind, or reload my gun and shoot him, but then I'd still be stuck here with a bunch of angry mercs and incoming paladins, and I'd rather not end up in prison for defacing a holy site. There was a whooshing noise as the glass lift went past. On the other side a whole bunch of pilgrims were staring at us, wondering what the hell was going on.

That gave me an idea. I stuck the box under one arm, and pulling Dathka's sleeve with the other, I dragged her upright. "Come on!"

Having been absolutely clobbered by Gerzog, she moaned in agony, but managed to stay on her feet, wobbling and blind, as I led her toward the central chute. It was probably a good thing she had no idea where I was taking her, because—being sane—she would have certainly refused.

The safety rail was about waist high, and Dathka stopped when she bumped into it. The passing lift was close enough we could reach out and touch the glass. "What's happening?"

"We're getting out of here."

As soon as the roof of the lift went by, I shoved Dathka over the rail. She screamed, but only for a second before landing with a *thump*. I vaulted over after her.

I hit the glass roof, and all was well… except it turned out the top glass was just there to keep the rain off the passengers, not to support the weight of two people suddenly landing on it.

Crack.

I looked down just in time to see the spreading fracture beneath my boots, before it all came apart around us. The floor shattered, and we tumbled into the interior of the lift.

44

I found myself lying face down on the wooden roof of a big wagon. Dathka was next to me on her side, and by all the saints, the lid to the lamp remained closed. When I went to sit up, there was a lot of tinkling and crunching, which was when I realized we were both covered in broken glass, and any sudden moves might result in getting cut.

Turned out, the lift's roof was made of a bunch of different smaller panes of glass, rather than one big magical one like each of the sides. And we'd only shattered one of those panes, rather than the entire thing, which would have dropped jagged shards onto all the innocent passengers.

As for them, from the noise they were making, most were confused or frightened, while a few cooler heads were urging the others not to panic. The merchant's wagon was tall enough that they hadn't even seen us lying atop it yet. There'd just been an extremely bright light coming up the chute, and then a moment later, some glass had broken.

We'd been lucky to hit the wagon. Between the tall body and big wheels, that extra ten feet of falling probably would've injured a lot more things than my pride.

"Don't move," I whispered to Dathka, who was still getting her vision back.

"I'm scared to. Did we fall through the lift?"

"Yeah."

The passengers hadn't spotted us yet, only because the merchant's wagon was really large and the roof was flared out to the sides, but as soon as we reached ground level, this lift would surely be swarming with investigating paladins. At minimum, they'd confiscate our treasure. At worst, they'd blame us for all the violence above and we'd be off to jail in chains. We needed to get out of here, and that wasn't going to happen through the front door.

There was a hole above us, and through it, I could see the corkscrew road passing by. "Do you trust me?"

"Not particularly," Dathka hissed.

"Then you can stay and get arrested. Otherwise, stand up real gently so we don't get cut, and then hold on."

She sighed. "Fine."

When we got up, the passengers spotted us and began shouting. I ignored them as best as I could as I shook the broken glass off my cloak. "Ouch." I got a few little cuts anyway. Trax would have no problem finding us now! With the box tucked tight under one arm, I lifted my air glove skyward. "Grab tight."

"This had better work," Dathka said as she wrapped her arms around me.

If it didn't, we'd find out really fast. "I've never tried to *Ascend* with this much weight before."

"Are you calling me fat?"

Rather than answer that, I concentrated on awakening the Clear embedded in my glove. When I felt the air solidify and wrap around my extended arm, I willed it to pull us upward. "*Ascend.*" I'm fairly certain that if I'd tried this on the ground, the spell would've barely lifted us at all. Except we were on a descending platform, so it was more like the spell held us in about the same place as the floor kept going down without us.

Dathka held on to me hard as she had Gerzog when she'd been trying to murder him. The broken pane passed us, and then we were dangling in the open shaft.

"Shit!" she exclaimed as she tried to squeeze the life out of me.

That was probably what I'd sounded like flying on a kwetzel. From the lights of the district, we were probably halfway to the ground, but thankfully, there was a patch of corkscrew road only twenty feet away and below us. This was going to be the tricky part.

"Hang on."

I focused on the road as my target and cut the spell. We began to drop. "*Descend!*"

My descent was rough even at the best of times, but with a box in one arm, and a shrieking deadlander hanging off me, it proved even clumsier. We went down at an angle, way too fast, bashing first against a pillar, then tumbled over the metal railing. We hit the road and went rolling.

The stupid box popped open again.

The beam of light illuminated the entire district. If the authorities hadn't known we were here before, they sure knew now!

"Why didn't Gerzog install a latch on this damned box?" Totally blind, I crawled toward where I thought I'd dropped it and fumbled about until I found it and slammed the lid shut.

The two of us lay there, waiting for our eyes to sort of clear.

"They're going to catch us," Dathka said. "We should get our stories straight."

"We're not caught yet." I stumbled back to my feet. "I've got to get this stupid thing to your dad or else."

"Why do you care so much about your fake wizard school?"

"It's not fake!" I shouted. "It's all we've got! And I'm not going to let some prick take what little bit of hope we have left away from us."

With the box in hand, I half-blindly groped about for the safety rail. I might as well keep moving until I could see fully. At least this felt like I was doing *something.*

Dathka swore at me, but from the noise, I could tell she'd followed.

A few seconds later, I was still seeing stars and spots, but I was making progress. "There were some tall buildings all along the lift plaza. If we find a good angle, I might be able to *Descend* us to the roof of one of those. If we're lucky, nobody will be looking up when we do."

"A moment ago, you almost broke our necks going a fraction of that distance."

"You got any better ideas?"

"I got an idea," Gerzog said as he stepped out from behind the pillar right below us and pointed something at my chest. "Hand over the lamp."

I didn't know if he had a wand or gun aimed at me, but whatever it was, it was sure to be deadly. But how had he gotten below us?

"You son of a bitch." Dathka was outraged. "You learned how to use my shadow charm."

"I did." Gerzog held something up, but it was still too blurry for me to tell what it was. "Whoever enchanted this is good. Really good."

"My mother gave that to me."

"That makes me using it to kill you an even sadder story." Gerzog turned his weapon toward Dathka.

I stepped in front of her just as he fired.

I could pretend I'd done that out of honor, but the truth was, Dathka had no charms left, while my Frunza Tarlev protective charm was still on my person. I could take a hit and live. She couldn't. And two versus one was better than me fighting Gerzog by myself.

The weapon turned out to be a gun, which I learned the hard way, by having the lead ball flatten into a pancake against my abdomen. The protective spell took most of the impact, but it was paper thin, and a whole lot of that energy managed to sneak through in the form of a nasty gut punch.

Dathka rushed past as I fell on my ass, launching herself at the much larger orc.

It was two versus one, except he was nearly three times her size and she was unarmed.

At least, I thought she was unarmed, until she revealed that she had a knife that she tried to bury in his chest. Then I realized that was *my knife*. The thieving skag must have taken it off me when she'd been hanging on to me for dear life.

Fat lot of good my knife did her, though, as Gerzog smashed the barrel of his empty pistol against her. Dathka went rolling away.

I yanked out one of Azarin's *Jolt* rods and threw it. Gerzog ducked as the sparking metal flew past his head. That gave me enough time to abandon the box, get up, and charge. I closed enough distance that this time, my *Shroud of Flame* set his grey robes ablaze.

Gerzog got burned good, yet he calmly shrugged out of the burning priest's clothing and tossed the flaming bundle at me. I swatted it out the air in a shower of sparks, not realizing he would be right behind it.

Orcs hit really hard.

That shot rocked my head back on my neck. His knuckles left a dent in my cheek. I reached up and slugged him right back, which he clearly hadn't expected, but hitting an orc's jaw is like punching wood. I think I hurt my hand more than I hurt him.

He dropped the pistol and yanked a short sword from his belt. I leapt back as the steel whistled through where I'd just been.

I responded with more Red. But when the *Shroud of Fire* cleared, Gerzog wasn't there.

Confused, I blinked for a few seconds, thinking my lamp-damaged eyes were playing a trick on me, then Gerzog came out of the shadows of the pillar fifteen feet behind me. I turned just in time to see him aiming a wand. I was in the open. He had me dead to rights.

"*Shred.*"

Out of pure instinct and desperation, I reached for the metal railing and willed the Clear embedded in my glove to activate. It was all the speed and violence of an *Ascend* but *sideways.*

I was pulled ten feet to the side in the blink of an eye just before glowing sawblades spun through my last location. My boots hit the ground, and by the time I slid to a stop against the railing, I'd pulled out a handful of screws and tossed them.

The *Screws of Chaos* ignited in midair. There was a shimmer around Gerzog as a few of sparked off of his protective charms.

He simply took a few steps back into the shadow of the pillar and vanished.

I spun around, but wherever he'd gone, it wasn't behind me. From the way he wasn't leaking blood from the many stab wounds Dathka had put in him above, he probably took a healing potion and was pausing to take another dose.

I used that opportunity to reload my pistol. I broke it open, fished out the spent paper, and went to pluck another from my belt. I'd practiced that move a lot and gotten to where it was rather smooth and fast, but I hesitated… and moved my hand to pick a different cartridge at the other end of the loops. I stuffed that one in, then snapped the action shut.

Dathka was down and looked to be in bad shape. He'd clubbed the snot out of her. I could hear the lift approaching, which meant the paladins from below were probably on their way up, and it was likely they could stop the thing at whatever level they wanted. I could also hear noise above us too, which meant more of them were on their way down to find the source of the incredible light burst. It was get out now or never.

"We've got to jump. You're going to have to hold on to me again."

Dathka had gotten to her feet. I didn't think it was possible for a deadlander to get any paler, but she'd managed to do so. "I can't. I think my arm's broken."

It took only a brief glance at the awkward angle of the bone beneath her sleeve to know that was true. I couldn't hold on to an awkward box and an injured woman and still control a *Descent*. I'd be sure to plant us all in the ground.

"It's alright. Get the lamp to Carcalla. I'll be fine," she said.

"Half a dozen priests just witnessed you attempt a murder on holy ground. You will *not* be fine." I looked around desperately but couldn't see any other options. "Hang on."

I ran over and scooped up the box, then took it to the rail and looked over the edge, the lift quickly approaching. "I sure hope these church guys will put this Permanence to good use."

"No, don't. I'm not worth it."

"Oh shut up." I didn't want to go through all this just to break the damned thing, so I picked up Gerzog's blackened priest robes, wrapped them around the box, and dropped it as gently as I could over the side.

"You fool!"

It weighed a lot less than Dathka and me, so it didn't break the pane of glass it landed on, but the *thump* was enough to cause the paladins inside to immediately stop the lift in place right below us. It would take them a minute to figure out what that noise had been.

I ran back to her. "You can stay here and be mad in jail, or we can go."

She was furious about losing the treasure, but she had the sense to not stick around and cry about it. "Let's go."

"We're going to try and float as far from here as possible. Just know I've never tried to hold this spell for that long." We went to the outside edge, and even in the dark, it looked like a *long* way down. "I'll aim for those rooftops, and I think we've got the angle to get there, but I don't know how good this is going to work."

Chest to chest, she wrapped her good arm around me, and I put mine around her waist and squished her tight—if Azarin saw us like this, somebody would be getting electrocuted, that was for sure—and then we went over the side.

I activated the *Descent* spell, and focused on those rooftops as best as I could. That's easier said than done when it feels like you're falling to your death, and the wind is howling in your ears, and your eyes are blinking away involuntary moisture, and a deadlander is screaming with her face shoved into your neck. It took everything I had to keep our feet under us, because at this speed, if we landed headfirst, we were going to die.

I'd been worried that someone below would see us, but that turned out to not be a problem, because one of the paladins must have opened the box. There was so much light shooting out of the lift shaft that nobody on the ground was going to be able to see a thing.

Problem was, neither was I.

I *think* we were still going the right direction.

I tried to remember everything Azarin had taught me about air magic, understanding the Clear, and the nuances of flying. Then the mental strain of keeping up the spell pushed all of that aside, and it was all I could do to keep the spell going. It was like suspending yourself from a bar and holding on as long as you can as your fingers burned more and more, and your muscles shook, until you just couldn't hold on anymore… only with my brain.

Except the spell broke before my concentration. We'd long wondered what the limits of this spell were. Welp… I found them.

My enchantment abruptly died. The Clear was all used up. We went from a haphazard, slightly slowed fall in a useful direction, to a total freefall at the mercy of gravity.

To my great surprise, that only lasted about two seconds before we crashed into someone's shingles.

45

We were lying there in the dark on someone's roof. Dathka was on top of me.

"That was kind of you to cushion my fall."

"You're welcome," I wheezed.

It took her a while to get up, on account of what had to be a terrible amount of pain from a cracked humerus. I wasn't doing so hot myself, but I was in far better shape than her.

I'd managed to get us to the right place. We were atop a six-story building overlooking the lift plaza. There were a bunch of light charms moving along the corkscrew road now as the authorities searched for the troublemakers, but we'd surely glided far enough to have dodged the paladins.

"We should probably keep moving."

"What's the point?" Dathka muttered. "We've lost the treasure. Father will be so disappointed."

Her bitter sadness made me thankful my own dad had been a good man. "He'll live. But you might not if we don't get you to a healer. At least we're in the best district to find one of those."

"No. The Latros have our own healer. I can suffer 'til then."

"So back to the Slumps it is. What about your vow to kill Gerzog?"

"Right now, my head's swimming, my arm's throbbing, and it's taking everything I have to not vomit from the agony. I'll get a healing and kill him tomorrow."

My saint would approve of such persistence. "That's the spirit!"

We set out across the rooftops. Luckily for us, the houses here were practically stacked on top of each other, and even the alleys were covered or narrow enough they were easy to jump across, so we'd be able to get far away from the Cathedral before we had to find a way to the ground level to cross a major street.

There were no light charms up here, so we had to navigate by the lights from far below. And the roof tops, though not very steep, were also rather icy. I was tired and hurting, so I had to be extra careful not to slip. With my glove used up until I could buy more Clear to enchant it again, if I fell off, I was going down the fast way. So we moved carefully from chimney to chimney, making our way westward toward the Slumps.

A massive shape rose from shadows of the next roof.

"Gerzog!"

I went for my pistol, but too late; the rush of wings whooshed behind me. Something crashed into my back, and I fell forward, slipping toward the edge. I clawed desperately for purchase on the snow-covered shingles, managed to stop my momentum, then caught a swift boot to the ribs for my troubles.

"Thought you saw the last of us, did ya?"

It was the female mercenary, and it turned out that her stolen priest's robes had been hiding *wings.* These weren't feathery, but were more like those of a bat. So that was what the old priest meant when he'd called her a harpy! And she must have carried the goblin merc with her, because that little bastard came around her legs and kicked me too.

That sent me careening over the edge.

I barely managed to catch hold of the gutter.

While I dangled there, six stories over the street, the goblin stopped directly over me, aimed a wand right between my eyes, and snarled, "We need this one alive, Captain?"

"I'm not sure yet," Gerzog growled.

Dathka cried out in pain as she got thrown down by Gerzog. "Let go of me, you beast!"

"I lost the lamp. I lost my money. I'm gonna salvage what I can by selling you. Not to Carcalla. Oh no. You don't get off that easy. I'm gonna sell you to whichever rival hates Carcalla the most, so they can carve you up slow and send him your pieces… Where are the others?"

"Caldwell and Torken got done in by the priests of Saint Violence," the winged woman reported. "Sorry, Gerzog."

"Then this is all that remains of my beloved Tooth and Claw."

"You brought that on yourself," I shouted. I held on as best as I could, and managed to get my boots against the bricks below to take a bit of weight off my hands. That made the gutter creak ominously as it threatened to tear itself off the wall, and the goblin shook the wand to warn me there'd be no funny business. "Your company's dead because they followed a greedy fool."

"No risk, no reward. I'll use what I'm paid for her to hire new recruits. We'll rebuild. There's always a war in some realm needing our kind. But will anyone pay a single Tetar for your rotten hide, Carnavon?"

"Your mom."

Gerzog snorted at that. "Kill him, Skelg."

"Gladly." The goblin began to announce some power word, but that got real difficult with a mouth that was suddenly covered in shadow spiders. "*Ack! Mrumph!*"

Skelg lurched back, spitting and clawing at his face.

I recognized that spell. "Rade! Over here!"

"Don't worry, my friend. Help has arrived."

I pulled myself up and back over the edge to see Rade Tartaros, sword in hand, striding across the rooftops from the direction we'd come from. A few feet behind him was Krachma, impatiently thumping his mace against his big rocky palm.

"Watch out. Gerzog's got the shadow-walking charm."

My warning came too late. These darkened rooftops were such a perfect place to use that enchantment, that Gerzog had already vanished, and taken Dathka with him.

The mercenary must have been done running, because he appeared between Rade and Krachma. It was only the incredible reflexes of our duelist that kept Rade from getting stabbed in the back. Gerzog swung, Rade dove forward, and rolled on his hands and shoulder, coming back up facing his foe.

"Clever trick, orc. But that spell's from my homeland. I can smell shadow magic a mile away."

Stuck between two capable foes, Gerzog just gave them both a savage grin. "Catch." And then he shoved the wounded Dathka toward the edge of the roof.

Krachma just watched her go, but Rade—who considered himself something of a gentleman—threw himself after her just as she went over. He caught her by the cloak, the sudden weight sliding him to the edge of the roof on his belly, where it took everything he had to hold on to her and not slide off.

Gerzog went at Krachma. The two giants collided, and though I couldn't tell in the dark, I imagined this would make our lob happy for once. I was forced to stop watching and roll out of the way as the goblin managed to scrape enough spiders off his face to activate his wand. It hissed and spit as a caustic hole was melted through someone's roof. Shingles crumbled and the wood beneath curled and scorched, but he'd missed me.

I set that little fucker on fire.

Skelg caught a snoot full of Red, and there was so much anger driving this *Shroud of Fire,* that his protective charm only held it off for a few seconds. Then the goblin was trying to run away from me across a slick roof with his hair on fire.

The woman hit me with an air-dagger spell. My Frunza charm flashed and sparked as the first ones bounced off, then I felt a flash of pain as hardened air sliced open my cheek. She'd been aiming for my eyes.

"That's my boyfriend, bitch!"

Azarin's *Jolt* hit one of the mercenary's bat wings and stuck there, crackling, sparking, and smoking. All the merc could do was twitch as the spell surged through her muscles.

I looked over my shoulder to see Azarin, Trax—and surprisingly enough—Morton, rushing from the other direction across the rooftops.

Seeing prey, Trax moved with incredible speed, covering the distance in seconds, to scoop up the still burning goblin, and before that poor fool had any idea what was happening, Trax was cramming him into his mouth and *chewing.*

"*Hello, Carnavon,*" Trax sent enthusiastically. "*Thank you for leaving such an obvious trail.*"

Arms and legs were hanging out and flopping about—and the noise! *The crunching!* I was glad the relative darkness spared us from the goriest details.

The goblin screamed at being eaten. The flying woman screamed at the sight and leapt straight into the air. Gerzog looked back from where he was battling Krachma, to see that he was now badly outnumbered, and no matter how tough he might have been, no one wanted to fight a Squalo. He stepped away from our lob and vanished into the shadows.

The harpy was flapping and gaining altitude, but Morton shouted, "Not so fast," as he brought up—not a wand—but a blunderbuss I'd last seen on the wall of the wyvern pens at Smorp Brothers that was nearly as long as he was tall.

BOOM!

The recoil knocked our gnome over backward, but a bunch of holes appeared in one wing. The mercenary shrieked as that wing collapsed, and she went spiraling down. She landed on her hands and knees, and immediately began to beg.

"Wait! Spare me. I can—"

Crunch.

Krachma, being deprived of an orc to fight, promptly bashed her over the head with his mace.

"I think that harpy was surrendering," Azarin said.

Krachma shrugged.

"I could use some help," Rade said, still lying on the slick roof, and his grip on Dathka's hood was the only thing keeping her from falling to her death.

"If you drop your sword, you could use both hands!" Dathka cried.

"I'm far fonder of this sword than I am of you. Krachma, would you kindly assist me?"

The lob bent way over the edge, and with seemingly no effort, hoisted Dathka up and dropped her onto the relative safety of the roof.

During all that, I was searching for any sign of Gerzog. I wasn't going to let him escape again. "Dathka, what's the range on your shadow-walking spell?"

"Twenty paces, line of sight. Ten second recharge."

Gerzog had been looking past Trax when he'd vanished. So I started running that way. As I passed Trax, I said, "Quit eating for a second and help me catch Gerzog."

"*I am happy to assist.*"

Blaaaarg. Trax promptly regurgitated the half-chewed goblin, which was, quite possibly, the single worst thing I'd ever seen and definitely the worst sound I'd ever heard. The goblin's body landed with a wet *splat.*

Azarin put one hand to her mouth. "Oh, that's unsettling." And then she ran after us. As she passed by Morton, she asked, "Are you injured?"

Our gnome was still struggling beneath the weight of the smoking blunderbuss. "I'm fine, Lady Garzade. Don't mind me. I shall be along in a moment."

We rushed across the roof. With gun in hand, I kept checking chimneys and clotheslines. I was assuming he'd want to keep the high ground, but he might have jumped off. "Trax, watch the ground on the left, Azarin watch the right."

I didn't need to worry about that, though, because no sooner had I given those orders, I spotted Gerzog lurking just ahead of us.

Then he was gone.

I assumed he'd keep trying to get away, then Azarin said, "Uh… guys?"

Trax and I turned around. Gerzog had stepped out of the shadows behind Azarin and grabbed her. He was now using her for cover with his sword lifted beneath her neck. "Take another step and she dies."

Trax froze in place. "*I believe the orc is telling the truth.*"

I raised my pistol. The hammer made a metallic *click* as I cocked it with my thumb.

"Easy there, boy." Gerzog crouched as much of his bulk behind Azarin's slim form as possible. "Here's how it's gonna work. You all stand down, while me and the lady go for a walk. Once I'm away, I'll let her go."

"*That part is not the truth.*"

"Yeah, I figured that, Trax… That's not going to happen, Gerzog."

"Then I can slit her throat and you can watch her bleed out."

"You try that and I'll blow your brains out." Unfortunately, it was too dark to see the sights atop my gun, or I would've risked taking the shot. I needed to be precise to hit the parts of him that were sticking out from around her, without hitting her, and that was real hard to do by feel. But if I pulled my light out of my pocket, he'd know what I was planning to do.

"Allow me to be of assistance," Morton said, as a ball of light popped into existence overhead. "I don't know any combative magic, but that may be of use to you."

I lined up the now starkly visible sights on Gerzog's ugly mug. "Thank you, Morton."

"Go for it. A single bullet would bounce off my charms. And I'll shadow-walk away before your Squalo can reach me. Then you can watch her twitch, helpless, gasping her last, knowing you failed. The deadlander's spell has already recharged. Try me, Carnavon."

As Gerzog and I stared each other down, Azarin asked, "Do I get a say in this matter?"

"Shut up," Gerzog snarled. "Hold still."

"That's a fine idea." Azarin flashed me a grin. "*Impervious.*"

As Azarin's skin went grey, I realized she hadn't been exaggerating earlier. That spell looked as solid as Krachma's. She really had been practicing her earth magic a lot.

I'd been practicing too, and in that instant, I focused on the enchanted cartridge loaded in my pistol.

Gerzog understood too late what was happening, and the edge of his blade dulled against skin that was temporarily as impenetrable as stone. Even the statue version of Azarin had a mischievous expression.

The merc looked up just in time to see the muzzle flash of my gun. A shimmering distortion appeared in the air as the bullet smacked harmlessly into the protective spell in front of his face.

"Fool!" And Gerzog vanished into the night.

Except when he stepped out of the shadows, twenty yards away, I spotted him thanks to the magic bullet still stuck to his face that was beginning to glow orange.

The lead continued heating up, burning through his remaining protections, and Gerzog roared his fury as it seared through his flesh. Skin blackened and split. Blood hissed into steam. He clawed desperately at his face, but the bullet had turned into molten spall, and the droplets rolled down his arms, burning to the bone as they went.

The defiant roars of Gerzog the Marauder turned to squeals of pain as his thrashing caused one of those drops to get in his eye. And trust me, having worked with fire most of my life, molten metal really doesn't give a shit how tough you are.

It took ten seconds for the shadow-walking charm to recharge. It took me a third of that to reload my gun. I was out of enchanted rounds, but that didn't matter, because with his protections being temporarily used up, my bullet plowed a hole right through his chest.

He took a few halting steps back, bumped into a chimney, and slowly sank down it until he was seated, confusion written all over his face. I'd gotten him in the heart.

I turned back to make sure Azarin was unhurt, and as the *Impervious* turned to dust around her, she exclaimed, "I told you all I was getting the hang of Krachma's spells!"

Krachma walked up next to her and poked her in the neck with one thick finger to make sure she wasn't lying. Seeing no wound on her, he nodded, satisfied. "Krachma is best teacher."

I turned back to Gerzog. I'll give the orc credit. Even mortally wounded, he still had the determination to reach into his vest to pull out what I assumed was another healing potion. He even managed to free the stopper with his teeth and began to drink it, before Dathka walked up and smacked the vial out of his hands.

I'd expected her to say something, to get in some last words of victory, but she must have been in too much pain to bother, because she just stabbed him in the neck and chest with my knife a couple dozen times. When she finally stopped, she was breathing hard from the exertion, and Gerzog was very much undoubtedly dead.

Only after she was certain he was done for, Dathka gloated, "I will warn my sisters to watch for the ghost of Gerzog the Marauder as you wander past Surnod Lin on your way to eternal torment, so my family may mock and spit on you one last time. Enjoy hell, you bastard."

"*That's nice. Can I eat him now?*"

"Sorry." I patted our loyal Squalo on the shoulder. "Loot first, *then* eat. You need to stop eating magical items, Trax. That can't be good for you. But loot fast, guys. Somebody surely heard that and called for the paladins."

Rade inspected the gnawed and gooey goblin, then gagged. "I'm not touching that one's pockets!"

Once we'd gathered up all the Tooth and Claw's magical items, element, and coins, the Outcasts fled the Cantor's district and ran for the Slumps.

46

Since the last couple of days had been a nearly nonstop sprint, I was so exhausted that I slept until late in the afternoon. I woke up halfway through Waterday, the sundown of which was the deadline that Carcalla imposed upon us. Rising early wouldn't have done me any good, as I'd done all I could. If the Latrocinium still wanted to evict us, and most likely kill me as an example of what they did to debtors, at least I'd go to my public execution well rested.

I woke up to find the Tube was so busy that the activity was even drowning out the wails of the ghosts. Big Bognar had returned from the healers, and in an attempt to repay Azarin for her bartering an expensive wand to save his life, he'd vowed to fix the place up. He was a terrible wizard, but he was a good carpenter. The constant hammering did give me a headache though.

It was also surprising to learn that while I'd been out, we'd attracted a few more new recruits, and unlike Gerzog and friends, these were legitimate students. Though Rade had told them to come back tomorrow so they wouldn't be in the crossfire should Carcalla throw us out tonight. Worst-case, they'd come back to find the Tube abandoned. Best-case, our numbers would grow.

If our landlord was merciful—however unlikely that might be—things were really looking up for the Academy of Outcasts. Word of our existence was spreading. We now had access to a tester, so our students had a real opportunity for official advancement. The mercenaries had lots of coin on them, probably scooped hurriedly off the floor after the priest of Saint Violence burst their money chest, and it was more than enough for us to live off of for a few months. As for the future beyond that, some of us were making a good bit of money from the arena, and Azarin and Morton now had a contract to train the flying animals at Smorp Brothers. All that would hopefully be enough to keep us stocked up on practice element.

If you do things different than everybody else but still win, they'll hail you as a genius. If you do things different than everybody else but you lose, then you're just an idiot.

I discovered that Sifuso had set up a strange little memorial shrine in the big training room. I don't know what odd saints the lizard people followed, but he'd constructed little dolls out of rags, clay, and sticks, and set them on the floor amid a bunch of candles and small animal bones. Oddly enough, the faces he'd carved bore an obvious resemblance to Rufus and Danny. I would never have guessed Sifuso was so artistic.

"What're you doing?" I asked him.

"This is the way of my people, to remember the fallen of the tribe."

"Rufus, I get. Respect to the great war mage of Clan Rudnik, may he rest in peace. But Danny was a no good, two-faced, rotten traitor, who sold us out the first chance he got. And you especially nearly got killed for it."

Sifuso licked his eyeball with his forked tongue as he thought that over. "Outcasts have formed a tribe. Not a good tribe. More like the leftovers and garbage none of the real tribes wanted. But that garbage became a tribe. Even real tribes have scum. Some scum is worse than others, but they were still part of the tribe. I did not say this is to honor them. It is to remember them. The elders of a tribe tell the stories of those who came before, so the hatchlings can learn from them, both good and bad."

That was surprisingly wise for the weird lizard. "I guess your shrine can stay, though we should probably do something nicer and more respectable, and less… creepy." I waved toward the pile of mouse skulls. "But what'll you do with those dolls if we get evicted?"

"Then the tribe is dead, there is no one to teach, and these can go in the canal with the rest of the trash."

It turned out lacertians weren't as big on sentimentality as I'd thought.

Just before sundown, the Latrocinium arrived, and the student council went out to meet them.

Last time, Cutter Joran had strolled up on foot with a handful of his gang. This time, the Latrocinium rolled up in intimidating style in a magically propelled carriage that was covered in steel plates and protective enchantments, accompanied by a small army of thugs.

Me, Azarin, Rade, Krachma, and Trax waited for them by our charred front door.

When the neighborhood saw the black and yellow banner draped over the side of that monstrous carriage, they all ran and hid. Curtains were pulled tight. Shutters were closed. Children were herded inside. Even the dogs were scared to bark and the chickens stopped clucking.

"That sure is an awful lot of them," Azarin said.

"Hmmm… Maybe I should have run for the realm of water after all," Rade mused.

"Too damp," Krachma grunted. "Krachma rather die."

"Excellent point, my friend."

There had to be a hundred thugs, all of them wearing a black band on their arm, and every last one was armed. I recognized a few familiar faces from our raid upon the Tooth and Claw's waterfront hideout. Those gave me respectful nods. That respect would not stop them from killing us all should their boss order it, of course. Still, it was nice to see.

The Latrocinium spread out around us as the carriage slowed and came to a stop only a few feet away. This thing had so much magic on it that I could practically smell the Red coming off its power source. Instead of a golem driver, the two insectoid beasts with sword hands which normally protected Carcalla's office rode on top. Radiating danger, they surveyed us with their blank stone eyes.

A metal door on the side creaked open and set of stairs was lowered.

Joran didn't bother with the steps. He just hopped out and swaggered over to greet us. "Good evening, Carnavon. Can't say I'm surprised to see you still here. Hotlanders are notoriously stubborn." Then he gave Azarin a little bow. "My lady. Proving Stormwolk to be as headstrong and heedless of danger as claimed." Then he smirked at Krachma and Rade. "You two ne'er-do-wells I thought would be smart enough to get out while the getting's good."

Rade waved one hand dismissively. "As a noble house in exile, I enjoy taking up lost causes."

"Krachma hates being wet."

Joran didn't know how to respond to that bit of out-of-context nonsense from our lob, so he turned his attention to Trax. The two dead-eyed killers thought greetings at each other. After a moment, Joran cracked a smile, nodded respectfully at Trax, then returned to the carriage.

What did he say? I thought.

"*May our parley remain placid, but should it end in violence, then he would be honored to kill and eat me. Which is a traditional Squalo greeting. I returned this greeting, then I implied that as a mighty Squalo, I would be able to devour him whole, while as a feeble human, he would be forced to cut me into steaks, cook my flesh until tender, then further render me into bite-sized chunks using utensils before he would be able to consume my flesh. This is humorous because human teeth are ineffectual, and your jaws are weak.*"

Wow. Spending time around all us sarcastic humans, and Trax was starting to get some attitude on him. "You sure told him what's up."

Joran thumped the side of the carriage. "All clear."

The next person to get out was Dathka Walker. She looked better than last night, but was still battered, bruised, and had one arm in a sling. The Latrocinium may have had their own healer, but he must have not been a really strong one. She remained stone-faced as she looked us over. You'd think that she'd feel some measure of gratitude for all the help we'd given her, enough to maybe even advocate for us to her father, but if so, she gave no indication.

Rade, of course, tried to be charming, as usual. "Ah, the dangerous lily of Surnod Lin is looking beautiful as ever. In case you forgot, when last we met, you were a bit more flustered, as I'd just saved you from falling to your certain doom."

"Are you trying to get yourself killed, Tartaros?" she asked.

"I was merely reminding you of our recent adventures..." Rade trailed off as he saw who else was getting out of the carriage. He'd not seen Carcalla before, but my description of the pointy ears and distinct facial scars had done the man justice enough that it was obvious who this was. Rade gulped. "Never mind."

Carcalla was dressed in a black suit. Once free of the confines of the carriage, he placed a black top hat on his bald head. He looked around the pathetic clearing that served as our yard, then snapped his fingers.

Promptly, several goblins ran around the side of the carriage and began unstrapping things from the back. Within seconds, they'd assembled three chairs and a table, and then they hurried out of the way. Carcalla and Dathka sat on their side of the table. Joran remained standing, wary behind his boss. There was only one chair on the Outcasts side. Carcalla gestured toward it. Being the Outcast's appointed spokesman and designated sacrifice, I sat down. The rest of the student council remained a polite distance behind me.

Another goblin brought out cups and a bottle, and began pouring wine for the three of us at the table. I was glad for that, because my nerves were making my mouth really dry.

"So, Mr. Carnavon, I've been thinking about our arrangement."

"As have I, your landlordship."

Carcalla gestured to where his gang was waiting just out of earshot of our conversation. "I had this show of force all ready to go. It's been a while since the denizens of the Under Slump have had a proper reminder of what happens to those who cross me. There would've been some gunfire and general butchery, then we'd burn your things and whip the survivors in the street. Such displays are necessary from time to time to keep order."

I took a sip of the wine, and thankfully, it was sweet, and not at all like his insane dragon death rum or whatever that had been. I didn't think I could bear the indignity of coughing myself to death in front of my friends. Getting shot, stabbed, beaten, or cursed to death was a proper respectable way to go. Dying because you can't handle your drink is just embarrassing.

"Except then my associate, Dathka, returned, with quite the tale. You're a persistent lad."

I looked to Dathka, but she was staring at her lap. It was noteworthy he called her an associate, rather than his daughter. Either he didn't want to admit it in public for her safety, or maybe when you're a gang lord, daughterhood had to be earned. It could go either way.

"I'm not sure what she told you, but we spared no effort to get back your treasure from the orc who stole it. We only lost it because—"

"Because you were stupid."

I was argumentative by nature, but didn't think debating that point would do me much good right now.

"Well, you and Dathka were both stupid. Though she was actually stupider, because she should've known better. You're an ignorant newcomer to this city. She should've realized how foolish it was to go off on her own after escaping, rather than swallow her pride and return to me so we could have struck with the full might of the Latrocinium. If she'd done that, then we'd be celebrating our treasure, rather than mourning its loss to the Nexus Council."

She kept her eyes averted as Carcalla said all that. I suspected somebody was getting sent back through the gate next Deathday.

"So the Council got the Permeance, then?"

Carcalla nodded. "Paladins of Kielgrad found it and turned it over, as is legal and just, for the greater needs of the Core… I'm sure a Councilman is cracking it apart as we speak to feed it into the Great Machine, as they have done with ten thousand other relics before it."

I nodded along, as if I was all broken up about that. Honestly, I'd rather see that most precious of all elements go to keeping the gates operating—and millions of people living—for a bit longer, than whatever petty thing Carcalla intended to do with it.

"Priests of Ulmorn, Saint of Violence, tried to claim the lamp was rightfully theirs, and that they needed it for some war they're fighting against some unholy horde of darkness in some subterranean realm somewhere… I neither know, nor care, about the details. All I know is that I was robbed of something I wanted."

"How much could you really want it, considering you didn't even know the lamp still existed a week ago," Azarin said helpfully.

Carcalla scowled at her. "Are you the one in the negotiating chair?"

"Nope."

"Then be silent… Joran, should this air-realmer interrupt us again, teach her that is inappropriate behavior."

"Sure thing, boss."

"Though, it would sadden me to see such a lovely face marred. The world has lost too much beauty as it is. If she talks again, just chop some of her fingers off or something."

I looked over my shoulder to make sure Azarin realized that wasn't an idle threat. She was biting her tongue. Her saint watched out for those who made rash decisions, but miracles only go so far.

"Apologies, Master Carcalla. All the Outcasts put in a lot of sweat and blood to try and get you what you asked for."

"Yet you still failed. And as we previously discussed, there is a cost for failure. The deadline is upon us. I cannot see the sun from here because of the slouching sky island in the way, but we can assume your time is almost up. Where is my treasure, Mr. Carnavon?"

I pointed at Dathka.

Carcalla looked at her, then back at me, then snorted. "Well played… But not what we agreed."

"Did Cutter Joran not tell you? He amended our deal."

Carcalla was difficult to read, but I could tell from the scowl that he'd not known about that. "What do you mean?"

"When we were searching for Gerzog, Joran and I came up with a new arrangement. He was acting as your representative. All past due rent forgiven as before in exchange for our help, and one month's rent paid for by the return of the treasure, another for killing Gerzog the Marauder, and a third month for the return of your da—" I caught myself barely in time. "Your associate, Dathka Walker. This was sworn to in front of some of your men, who I'm happy to pick out of this crowd."

Carcalla turned his malevolent gaze upon his subordinate. "Is this accurate?"

Joran was glaring at me, as it had been easy for him to make big promises before the treasure had gotten lost. "I don't recall that specifically."

"If I may call upon one of my associates, who you'll surely find to be an impeccable witness, he can testify that this is the truth."

Carcalla gestured for me to proceed.

"Trax. Would you kindly demonstrate your memory of that particular negotiation?"

When the Squalo padded forward, about fifty Latros readied their weapons, but Carcalla held up one hand to indicate it was fine. The crime boss appeared curious as Trax rummaged through the pouches of his bandolier and pulled out a crystal sphere.

The memory image which appeared above Trax's thought globe was clearly a Squalo-eye view of the world, with me, and Cutter, and the Latros all looking especially soft and edible. I was speaking, though to Trax's ear, I must have sounded a lot more high-pitched than I really was.

"*How about one month if I help get back your girl, another month for the lamp, and a third if we kill Gerzog?*"

Then Carcalla watched in silence as the image of Joran agreed to that, and we shook on it. When the memory winked out, Joran groaned, because he knew he'd fucked up.

"Thank you, Trax."

"*I am the best secretary ever.*"

"There you have it, sir. As the notable Joran Vanderhelst himself has declared, the Squalo race produces no liars."

The veteran gladiator gave me a look that let me know I would be on his bad side forever, but I'd won this one. "Sorry, boss. I must've misremembered. It's as Carnavon says."

Carcalla nodded slowly. "Such is the danger of delegation, but the Latrocinium keeps its promises. Continue."

"We couldn't recover the lamp, but the Outcasts saved Dathka's life and ended Gerzog's. We're paid up for the next two months... During which we'd be overjoyed to continue with our previous deal of paying you the agreed-upon rent or providing the services of one adventuring party to you every month."

Carcalla stared at me for a long time, weighing our value to him as treasure hunters, versus what it would be worth to slaughter us in public as an example. Then he gave me a predator's smile. "If wizardry doesn't work out for you, Mr. Carnavon, I'm told the Council can always use more lawyers in the Pallentine."

I didn't know if that was a compliment or not, so I just nodded politely.

"Very well. Your academy has bought itself a bit more time. Spend it wisely."

Everyone on the student council breathed a sigh of relief at that, except for Trax, who was still playing with his memory sphere. Apparently, he had recorded some exciting images of fish, and watching them swim by was far more interesting to him than our negotiations.

"Thank you, sir."

"Luckily for you, Outcasts, there's no shortage of dangerous sites scattered across the realms I'm curious to have explored. We'll be in touch about the details of your next expedition."

"Wonderful." I said that with forced enthusiasm. "I look forward to finding you some replacement treasure, even more valuable than Korthican's lamp. Having seen the size of the chest the priests of Violence offered for one antique enchantment, I see now why some people like adventuring."

Carcalla swirled the wine about in his glass. "You really don't understand, do you? You think I want relics with Permanence in them for the money? I have money. It can buy *almost* everything."

Now I was genuinely confused. "Then what do you want these relics for?"

Carcalla pointed up. "For that."

I craned my neck back, not understanding. The only thing above us was the rotten underbelly of the Slump, slowly, inevitably crushing us. "What?"

"My kingdom is in two parts. One of which sinks a few more inches every year. Hundreds of thousands live beneath that threatening shadow, and forsaken by the law, they pay me for protection. I can hold back the monsters and chaos, but I can't protect them from the insatiable pull of gravity. What power kept those mighty islands aloft for thousands of years? What power, once deprived, has condemned so many of the great works of this city to rot?"

My mouth fell open in surprise. "You want Permanence so you can put the Slump back where it belongs."

"I fear lifting an entire district is beyond anyone now. Even the mighty Council couldn't do that today, but for what they would spend to keep the Great Machine turning for a few more days, I should be able to thwart time enough to anchor the Slump in place for centuries."

So that was what Dathka meant when she'd claimed Carcalla would use that rarest of all elements for good. "I had no idea."

"Few do. Perhaps this knowledge will make our arrangement seem less like dangerous slavery, and more like a beneficial service. You wish to make this fallen tower your home? Then help me save it."

I honestly didn't know what to say to that. Carcalla was still a rotten, murdering, thieving crook, but he was at least trying to keep the poor folks he preyed upon from getting smooshed.

"I told you so," Dathka muttered.

"Yeah, you did. Sorry I didn't believe you."

"Touching," Carcalla said. "Unfortunately, Dathka, your presence in this city has needlessly complicated my business. I still don't know what I should do with you."

On that topic, I kept my big mouth shut.

"I'm not going back to Surnod Lin. You know what I must do."

"Being gifted a single powerful charm doesn't make you a real mage. You've made a significant vow to personally deliver specific souls to Saint Murder, but you lack the skill to reach those, and even if you could, you lack the power to even scratch them. I asked Joran to train you in our ways, but you don't listen. You need to learn some humility. You're too impulsive and impatient."

"It's easy to urge patience when you're a half-elf who'll probably live to be three hundred. I don't have the luxury of waiting for everyone I've vowed to murder to die of old age like you can."

"Oh, I'm sure you'll worry me to death long before that, sullen girl." Carcalla clearly didn't want to have this family spat in public, and I didn't want anything to do with it at all, but sadly, he turned his attention back to me, and there was a worrisome gleam in his fake eye. "You have convinced me of the earnestness of your endeavor, Mr. Carnavon. I will proclaim for all to hear that the Academy of Outcasts isn't a scam. You have here a genuine school, which—though flawed—has noble intentions. Thus, in our newfound spirit of partnership, the Latrocinium will be sending you some rank ones to receive training."

"What… *Her?*"

"Among others. I've found a few associates with untapped potential."

Dathka looked at her father in disbelief, and then at me, disgusted. "Ew. You want me to train with the Under Slump dregs? You can't be serious!"

Cutter Joran chuckled at her indignity. I turned back to see that my people were aghast.

"My decision is made. I shall be sponsoring some students to attend the Academy of Outcasts," our landlord declared that part loud enough that all the Latros and witnesses could hear him. A few, not knowing any better, cheered at that news.

Ten minutes ago we'd been expecting them to kill some of us and chase the rest off. I didn't know if this was better, or worse.

"Since my blessing will add to your prestige, I will of course expect a significant discount on their tuition, Mr. Carnavon."

47

A week later, I got summoned to the market.

The new year's festivities were still in full swing. The illusion of a giant 4582 floated around the Great Machine, with the numbers changing form based upon which gate they were currently moving over. From here, the four digits appeared to be on fire.

I stopped at the gate of the Fogo Embassy and identified myself to the enforcers stationed outside. "Ozwald Carnavon of the Academy of Outcasts, presenting myself as requested by Ambassador Dardick Argento."

"Oh, it's this fucking guy again," said one of them.

He looked kind of familiar. "Are you all still sore about me setting the embassy's roof on fire? I answer to Gaul Haddar. Take it up with him. Just tell Dardick that I'm here like he asked."

The enforcers still didn't like me, but they'd been expecting me, so grudgingly opened the door. "Right this way, your illustrious wizardship."

Naturally, the nobility of my homeland were still rather sore about my skipping out on my contract. By myself, I wasn't that important, but that sort of behavior set a bad example which might cause the rest of the cadre folk to get unruly, thinking they might have options other than working themselves to death for the rest of their lives. So the grumpy greeting was to be expected.

However, I wasn't too worried about being back in Argento territory. Gaul Haddar was Baron Argento's most powerful and valuable wizard, so when he'd proclaimed he was opening a school and leaving me in charge of it in his absence, nobody—not even the baron's own son—was going to give me any trouble.

Unless... Gaul Haddar had finally caught up with those pirates he'd been chasing, and the elf killed him, and with nobody left to protect me, the Argents would finally be able to get rid of a nuisance who'd made them look bad.

Sadly, I thought of that possibility just as the gate closed behind me. Oh well. I was committed now. If they tried anything, my last act of defiance would be to feed Dardick an activated snail grenade.

But it turned out this wasn't an elaborate ruse after all, as Ambassador Dardick Argent was sitting in his black lava rock courtyard, reading letters. He just shook his head, bemused, when he saw me. "If it isn't Oz Carnavon, crawler, trapper, and rank-one wizard. How's the magical academy business?"

"The Outcast Academy is doing well, thanks for asking. Our numbers are growing steadily, we've got a tester, a marvelous facility, the blessing of our local... nobility, and our own adventuring company." My people were sparse on the protocol nonsense, even our aristocracy, so I simply pulled out a chair and sat down across from him. "And I'm a rank *two* now."

"Fancy." Dardick shooed away his guards. "I thought for sure by now you'd have humiliated yourself and died poorly."

"Surprisingly, not yet." Even though Dardick once had me tortured, I really didn't think he was a bad sort. His main concern was looking after his family's interests in the Core, and by all accounts, he was a much more reasonable man than his cruel father. "So why'd you send for me?"

"This." Dardick handed over an envelope. The wax seal bore the mark of Gaul Haddar. "It's for you. It just came through the gate in a diplomatic pouch today."

That made no sense. "Today's not Fireday."

"No. It appears your master wizard's pursuit of the pirates who've troubled us so much has taken him to other realms. Go on. Open it. My mage says it's got so many spells upon it to make sure only the right person reads it, that if I were to try, it would melt my face off."

That certainly sounded like something Gaul Haddar would do.

Not knowing how the traps worked, I took my time, making sure the letter got a good look at me first, then I made sure to speak clearly. "I am Ozwald Carnavon, and I take possession of this." When I broke the seal, tiny glowing scorpions formed and ran across my hands. I flinched so violently that I nearly dropped it. They clung to me, stingers poised to strike. They must have decided I was who I claimed to be, because they shimmered and dissipated into nothingness.

"I know Haddar founded your little school and saved you from the consequences of your oath-breaking, but frankly, that man terrifies me." Dardick took a sip of his tea. "Good luck."

"Thanks." I pulled out the letter, unfolded it, and began to read.

To Oz Carnavon,

I have little time. I trust that you have managed my academy well. If you have brought shame to my name, I will be most displeased.

I write this because I have no one else I can trust in the Core. The threat I investigate is much greater than mere piracy. The theft of Red is merely the beginning. His reach spans all the realms and many kingdoms. I do not know his motives, but his plot threatens the Nexus itself.

The elf who destroyed Barge 519 is named Kayul Sakiel.

He was trained in the Core and achieved the tenth rank there fifty years ago. Learn all you can about him for me. Tread carefully. Trust no one. Neither Council nor watch. He has sunk his hooks into the nobility and the clergy. His forces are secret but legion. His magical power is far greater than mine.

I will return when I can.

– Gaul Haddar of Ashen Harran, wizard of the tenth rank.

The second my eyes passed the signature, the letter burst into flames.

"Fuck!" I dropped it as fast as I could, and still managed to burn my fingertips.

The paper disintegrated into unreadable ash before it even hit the floor. It was a good thing I had a sharp memory.

Dardick watched the last of the note burn itself into oblivion with one raised eyebrow, before asking, "So… how's Haddar?"

There was a pitcher of water on the table, which I stuck my reddened fingers in to quench the pain. "He's fine. He said you'd better be taking good care of the academy he sponsored or else."

"Ah yes, of course he'd say that…" Dardick tilted his head, trying to decide if I was lying or not. "But to show how magnanimous my family is, I think I'll send your school some complimentary Red."

That would be useful. I was going to need all the help I could get, because I now had the name of the elf who'd killed my family.

Kayul Sakiel.

Haddar had taken the time to underline the word *far* several times when he'd said Sakiel's magical power was far greater than his. Last year, Haddar told me he'd estimated this pirate to be a rank fifteen or higher, which would make him one of the most dangerous wizards in all the realms. I was barely a rank two.

I had a lot of work to do.

I was so distracted by my thoughts of revenge, that I'd not even realized I'd turned my back on the ambassador of my noble house and begun walking away.

"Carnavon?"

I snapped out of it. "Yeah?"

"Congratulations on the promotion."

The Story Will Continue In
Academy of Outcasts
Book 3

SIGN UP FOR LARRY'S NEWSLETTER

https://monsterhunternation.com/signup-for-the-newsletter/

We won't sell your info or spam you with too many posts. This is almost exclusively for book-related things!